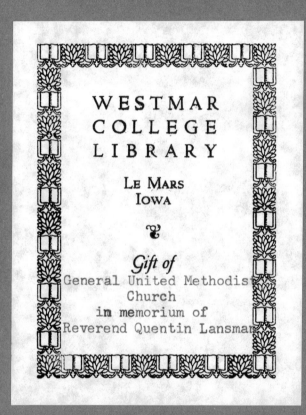

HEAR AMERICA SINGING

BY
WILLIAM ATTAWAY

ILLUSTRATED BY
CAROLYN CATHER

INTRODUCTION BY
HARRY BELAFONTE

THE
LION
PRESS

PUBLISHERS, NEW YORK

To Fran

CONTENTS

INTRODUCTION

IT IS THE YOUTH of the land who in the past couple of decades have given new and vibrant life to both the folk song and the folk singer. The traditional instrument of the folk musician, the guitar, is as necessary to the youngster of today as was the ukulele to his father. Folk singing is no longer a spectator sport—it is an essential part of growing up.

With all this passion for folk music, past and present, it is astonishing how many of our youth understand all the *how,* but none of the *why,* of folklore. Just what is folk music? How does it differ from other musical forms? When and why did it come about? And finally, what is to be learned from it?

Folk music is just exactly what it claims to be—the music of the people; not of individuals, but all the people. Originally, the term "folk" was applied only to the peasants and farmers of the Old World, who had never learned to read or write. The evolution of democracy slowly expanded the meaning of the word until it came to stand for all proud and common people. And it is our folk songs, the living record of all our hopes and dreams and aspirations, our foolishness and our mistakes, and even our deepest fears, that have traveled down the generations from one singer to another, and spread across the world with our wandering minstrels.

Those who perform folk music have long since deserted the definitions of the medium put out by scholars who like to fit things neatly into pigeonholes. Much that was once called primitive, or tribal, music, many tunes written by popular composers, some "art songs" from the concert stage, and most ditties sung in the city streets have passed into the realm of folk songs. The only requirement was that the song express an emotional truth which the common man could embrace as his own.

The folk tradition is as old as time and as current as now. America has always been singing, charging, borrowing, creating its folk self. We began with the chants of the Indians, for many long eons the only Americans. Then came European adventurers and explorers—trappers and traders singing in Spanish and French as they sought their fortunes in the wilderness. Pilgrims and Puritans followed, singing hymns as they built settlements. The songs and the singers never stopped coming and over the centuries all the different ethnic groups from the major continents of the world brought their songs to the melting pot of the New World.

The dominant tradition in all this singing history came from the British Isles and from Africa. The cultural "wedding" of these two strains produced a music of such vitality that it has moved the world.

White performers from the early 1800s until the 1920s made fortunes caricaturing Negro plantation humor. They donned black grease paint and called themselves minstrels. Negroes, in order to work on the stage, had to also become minstrel men. Many of the songs from these shows, which began as an attempt to ridicule, survived because of the talent of Negro performers such as Bert Williams.

Spirituals brought African harmonic patterns together with the King James Version of the Holy Bible. The result was a body of religious folk music that will last throughout time.

The type of folk song we know as the blues started somewhere in that part of the South known as "The Black Belt" and spread fast and far. It has become the musical trademark of America, and has influenced just about all the popular music of our time.

The blues have been described in many colorful ways. It has been likened to the "wail of a lonely man whose heart is down"—it has been called the music of "false and lost loves," "singin' to keep from cryin'." W. C. Handy, creator of "The Saint Louis Blues," once described the blues as "a state of mind."

Somewhere about 1910, the blues hit Tin Pan Alley. Immediately, sensing the economic possibilities, the music machine began to grind out one imitation after another of this folk form. The result was a watering down of the blues to make it palatable in smart supper clubs and proper for records and radio. Ordinarily, this would have been enough to destroy a folk form, but the blues was too tough to die. As a matter of fact, it began to spawn other folk forms: Gospel shouting, modern folk ballads built around industry and the city streets, jazz in all its forms, and that strident newcomer, rock 'n roll.

One of the children of blues and rhythm, jazz, quickly evolved into a full-fledged folk art in its own right. Coming up through ragtime and Dixieland, jazz became America's top art export. New Orleans jazz men such as King Oliver and Louis Armstrong became names known both at home and abroad. There are probably more variations of the jazz form than any other type of music. The most important variation was called "Bop" by its originators, a few decades ago. Charlie Parker, the sax man who epitomized Bop, gained great fame, but died in his middle thirties. His influence on jazz, however, is as strong as it ever was. Today, almost any piece of tape containing a riff by Charlie Parker automatically becomes a collector's item.

However, the 1940s and the 1950s were the Golden Age for collectors of folk music. There were both major and minor figures involved in making America folk conscious. The recording companies were raiding the folk libraries of collectors fresh from the field, and more than a few radio channels devoted themselves exclusively to jazz and folk singers. The Lomaxes, John and Allan, pioneered the taping of the folk music of all America, north and south, in the fields and factories, in the work camps and on the chain gangs, and wherever people sang their own songs. The Library of Congress expanded its archives, and it is now the single greatest source for American researchers in the field of folk arts.

Cities such as New York and San Francisco have become a mecca for hundreds of young people with guitars and songs to sing. Their fathers, a short generation ago, had filled the concert halls to hear the "hootenannies," which featured blues singers, guitar slickers, gospel shouters, boogie-woogie piano masters, ballad and country-western singers, and groups whose folk harmony had rocketed them to the top of the best-seller list. But now, the sons regard all of this as rather "square." They have new heroes. The below-voting-age population knows that one is of the past generation who doesn't appreciate the genius of folk "composer" Bob Dylan.

The latest child of blues and rhythm, rock 'n roll, is still too young to be fully assessed. Many of the early rock 'n roll haters, who saw in this simplified form with its nonsense lyrics and heavy backbeat, a threat to all culture are now having second thoughts. Although it began as dance music, rock 'n roll has developed its own artists and musicians. The talented "Beatles" did more than any other group to create high standards for the performers in this medium. As a consequence, the discotheques are usually crowded with people of all ages doing the frug, watusi, mashed potato, monkey and pachango.

All the folk arts are essentially performing arts. It is a field concerned with people. From beginning to end, the history of our songs is the saga of America. Here are all tales of the great, the near great, and the ordinary man; all the men who lived and died during the past six hundred years, who through their laughter, toil and tears made America the great nation where a man can still shout for peace and freedom. In a sense, this music is their story.

Harry Belafonte

O' *wondrous sunlit morning*
I was dreaming in the sky
And I seemed to see a vision
Of this nation by and by
There were shining cities rising
Across an endless plain
The laughter of happy children
Came driving like the rain
And I looked upon a people
All standing free·and strong
Their hearts were singing—singing
And my heart filled with song . . .

CHAPTER ONE

IN
THE
BEGINNING

THERE WAS THE WORD

SOME OF OUR greatest folk poets were backwoods preachers. They often began their sermons: "In the beginning, there was the Word!" In every literal sense this statement has meaning—even with a small "w" the spoken word has been crucial in the creation of man's culture. It was for many centuries the only means of communication between men. The invention of writing was a great advance in civilization, but it is surprising how many important societies were able to get along without it. The Incas built a magnificent civilization that encompassed most of what is now Peru and extended into the neighboring countries of South America, and all of this without a written language.

When the world was much younger, the tribes of men had to have some way of passing along from generation to generation what they had experienced and learned collectively as a people. The spoken word simply could not take care of this need. There were too many combinations of sounds for the minds of men to retain and repeat down through the ages. Even the professional storytellers could not remember them all in proper sequence.

Something was needed to help him recall.

So it came about that musical sounds were added to the words to create the *chant*.

24

As all of this happened before the time of written history, we cannot know exactly when the chant was developed or how rapidly the practice spread. It probably developed in many parts of the world at about the same time. Now men found they could retain the history of their people by repeating words and phrases to these musical sounds.

They added drums to mark the rhythmical beats or time units, and between each time unit they chanted an indefinite number of words. Here were the first two elements of music: *rhythm* and *melody*. There is a third element called *harmony,* a blending of tones, which was unknown to primitive peoples.

THE FIRST AMERICAN

THE AMERICAN INDIAN, long before the first European set foot on these shores, had developed the chant to its highest form. The variety and complexity of their rhythmic patterns have not been surpassed. Despite tribal differences and languages, the music of the American Indian can be recognized by the simple melody line sung in a falsetto voice, broken by unexpected pulses of liquid sound.

Every Indian chant was related to some aspect of survival in the wilderness. Most chants were ceremonial, passed along from generation to generation by the medicine men. The Cheyenne were noted for their skill in the chase and their deadly aim with the bow and arrow. After a successful buffalo hunt they would chant the praise of the young warriors and their weapons:

> *Bearer of the Sacred Bow,*
> *Bearer of the Sacred Bow,*
> *You should carry a bow of elm,*
> *You should carry a bow of elm!*

The Dakotas (or Sioux), the most numerous of any Indian tribe in the United States, were fierce warriors in the defense of their western hunting grounds. This translation of a war chant has the majesty of an anthem:

25

Comrades, kinsmen,
Now have ye spoken thus,
The earth is mine,
'Tis my domain.
'Tis said, and now anew I exert me!

The coming of the European brought many changes to Indian life and tradition, and it brought war of a kind unknown to tribal people. The Indian had always fought for survival or for honor, but against the white man he fought for survival on this continent.

This was more than war between peoples, it was a war between cultures. The Indians had no idea of personal ownership of land, to them the tribe was everything and owned everything. The white men brought with them the philosophy of private ownership; they thought their treaties made with individuals should be binding on the tribes for all time.

Our history books make much of the bad faith shown by white settlers and the innocence of Indians, who did not understand that they were selling their ancestral homes forever. But it is doubtful that anything could have done more than delay the conflict between the red and the white man. European culture by its very nature was bound to destroy the hunting ground of the Indian.

Against the superior weapons of the endless tide of white men flowing from Europe, the Indians fought valiantly but in vain. The Coyote warrior, separated from his fellows after the losing battle, had only the Great Spirit of the Sky to comfort him:

O great expanse of the blue sky,
See me roaming here
Again on the war-path, lonely;
I trust in you, protect me!

American history has finally come to understand the valor of the fierce Indian. The great skill, strategy and endurance of their leaders is now a valued part of Americana.

Perhaps the most famous of all is the Apache warchief, Geronimo. In a medicine-song, he sang of his own final flight through the sky to the place of the Great Spirit:

O, ha le
O, ha le!
Through the air
I fly upon a cloud
Towards the sky, far, far, far,
O, ha le
O, ha le!
There to find the holy place,
Ah, now the change comes o'er me!
O, ha le
O, ha le!

The primitive music of the American Indian, with its high, quavering tones and sudden pulses, imitated the many voices of nature. There was the ripple of the happy waters in his children's lullabies; the cry of the eagle and the sound of the hunting wolf in his war songs; the sigh of wind and the rustle of leaves in his laments and death dirges; the wistful calls of water-birds in his love songs; and in his appeal to the Great Spirit, there was always majesty.

A strong strain of Indian approach to music underlies all our New World folk singing. We are the musical heirs of a people who lived close to nature and heard and understood the many voices of the wilderness.

27

CHAPTER TWO

THEY CAME
TO
THIS LAND

THE DRAGON SHIPS

THE HEART OF AMERICA is a big heart, warm and strong, full of patterns and colors like one of grandma's quilts. The immigrants from the misty isles of the North Sea and the Steppes of Russia, from across Europe down to shores washed by Mediterranean waters, from the Far and Near East, and from Black Africa were all absorbed into this patchwork heart. They brought with them their lore and culture, and the third element of music—*harmony*.

The first Europeans to see the New World and leave a record of their coming were searching for adventure. It must have been a strange dawn when the horned Vikings sighted these shores.

Imagine yourself an Indian peering from the shelter of the forest. You stare, terrified but fascinated, at this unbelievable sight. From a dragon shell, which looks like a monster riding the waves, springs a blond giant. He wears the hide of an animal; great goat horns seem to jut from his brow. To you, he is half man, half beast—perhaps a god!

The purpose of the Viking leaders, Eric the Red and Lief Ericsson, was plain as they pointed their naked swords at this new continent.

There were professional minstrels to sing the Norse *skalds,* the ancient songs of the Vikings, but among the oarsmen, there were warriors who had been farmers and herdsmen. They sang the simple folk songs of home.

This melody from the district of Gudbrandsdal is a typical Norwegian folk song of lost love:

I laid me down to rest, and the hour it was late,
I knew not of pain or aching sorrow;
Then word came to me from my sweetheart so dear
To hasten to her ere the morrow.

No one have I ever loved so dearly.
No one have I ever loved so dearly.

Then quickly I sped to her lofty bow'r
Where oft 'twas my wont to be faring;
A group of fair maidens surrounded my love,
Her form for the cold grave preparing.

I fled from the room to the meadow green,
The bells in the church 'tow'r were tolling;
But nothing I heard, naught but anguish did I know,
My heart's grief was far passed consoling.

The Norseman left little behind him to mark his stay. He beached his vessel just long enough to discover there was nothing here to plunder, and he departed. To the watching Indians, the landing soon must have faded into a dream. The only thing that seemed to make it real was a footprint in the sand and the echo of a song.

THEY SOUGHT FOR GOLD

THE BLACK-BEARDED SPANIARD followed a vision of gold to the New World. He left behind legends and in many cases his bleached bones.

In the log book of a Spanish ship is the beginning of written history for the New World. The log is signed by an Italian, a sea captain whose name is known to all Americans—Christopher Columbus. It was in 1492, as we all know, that this Italian was financed in his impossible voyage by the Queen of Spain. A beautiful legend tells us that his voyage was made possible when Queen Isabella sold her jewels.

Three centuries of explorers and plunderers followed Columbus. To the Indians of South and North America these Spanish soldiers were cruel gods in shining armor. They were mounted on strange, four-legged beasts, called horses. In fact, the first primitive people to see the Spanish Conquistadores thought the horse and rider were one animal.

Although the Spanish enslaved and tortured the Indians in Mexico, Peru and North America, from California through Florida, they were the first Europeans to colonize the New World. The adventurers who led them, Balboa, Cortés, Ponce de León and Coronado, were or became titled lords. Their followers were often simple folk, peasants for the most part. These people sang the folk songs that influence our musical heritage today. All over the Southwest we still hear the medieval Spanish airs.

Cruelty and sentimentality seem to go hand in hand in the heart of the Spaniard. The same man who could kill and torture by day, at night could sing this sensitive bolero:

UNTO A POOR BLIND LOVER

Unto a poor blind lover
I show'd compassion, I show'd compassion.
I show'd compassion
Unto a poor blind lover.
Might I not soothe his sorrow
In such a fashion, in such a fashion.

The Spanish did not see love as a happy state; it was an opportunity to suffer exquisitely. This folk song from Old Castile expresses this idea:

If 'tis sorrow so to love thee
Swift I welcome pain to prove me.
I will suffer anguish burning.
Come then, rend me, blessed yearning.

One New World song solidly based in old Spanish folk tradition is "Cielito Lindo." It is now so associated with the Rio Grande area that it has to be considered Spanish–American.

34

CIELITO LINDO

By the Sierra Morena I wait, Cielito Lindo,
As twilight dies,
Searching the dark for the starlight,
 Cielito Lindo,
Of your bright eyes.

Ay, Ay, Ay, Ay!
Whispering of you,
My heart will sing the joy you bring;
 Cielito Lindo,
I love you.

TRAPPERS AND TRADERS

THE FRENCHMAN CAME TO TRADE. But the Frenchman's heart was light; he laughed as he loaded his ships. He learned from the Indian the art of living in the forest, to trap and to hunt. His job was to supply the furs for all Europe.

Furs were more than protection against the cold, they were the mark of rank and power. The kings of Western Europe had long since used ermine as the symbol of royalty.

Early in the sixteenth century Jacques Cartier sailed up the St. Lawrence River to open the interior to trappers. Champlain founded the settlement of Quebec, and it became the city that presided over France's fur traffic for more than a century. Radisson extended the fur trade from the Northern Great Lakes to Hudson Bay, and France and England fought a series of bloody wars for the control of North America and the fur trade.

But the Frenchman who paddled the canoes, and traded with the Indians for the beaver and fox pelts, laughed a lot—even as he died. He sang the folk songs of home.

The song "Alouette" was originally sung by farm women while plucking fowl. It was also perfectly fitted to the beat of the canoe paddle.

> *Alouette,*
> *Gentille alouette,*
> *Alouette,*
> *Je t'y pleumerai.*

This translates, of course, into:

> *Skylark,*
> *Pretty skylark,*
> *Skylark,*
> *I shall pluck you now.*

Russell Ames, in the *Story of American Folk Song,* tells us that in the Cajun or "Evangeline" country, a region of Canada near Nova Scotia, the ancient Norman ballads are still sung today. He gives an example of a humorous treatment of what must have been a tragic marriage:

THE LITTLE HUSBAND
(Le Petit Mari)

> *My father he found me a little husband,*
> *Oh, Lord, what a man, what a tiny man.*

36

I lost him down in the sack of straw,
I lit my candle to go looking for him.
The sack of straw it caught on fire.
And then I found him all burnt up.
I laid him out on a little saucer.
The cat came and took him for a mouse.
"Oh cat, oh cat, leave my husband be."

THERE WAS NO WAY BACK

THE BRITISH TRADITION became the solid base of European influence in the New World, with other Western cultures blended into it. Later we shall discuss the powerful tide of non-European influence on the New World.

The English came first to Roanoke Island, just off what is now North Carolina. Sir Walter Raleigh tried nobly but failed to found a permanent colony there. Then, in 1607, the British founded Jamestown on a swampy island in the James River. It proved to be the first permanent English settlement.

These resolute settlers had one thing in common—to make a success of the settlement or die. There was, they finally realized, no way back to England.

37

The ballads these people sang were centuries old. They usually told tragic stories. One of the most famous is this ancient version of "Barbara Allen":

In scarlet town, where I was born,
There was a fair maid dwellin',
Made every youth cry Well-a-way!
Her name was Barbara Allen.

All in the merry month of May
When green buds they were swellin'
Young Jemmy Grove on his death-bed lay,
For love of Barbara Allen.

And the song continues through many verses to its inevitable conclusion—death for all concerned:

As she was walkin o'er the fields,
She heard the dead-bell knellin';
And every jow the dead-bell gave
Cried "Woe to Barbara Allen."

"O mother, mother, make my bed,
O make it saft and narrow:
My love has died for me today,
I'll die for him tomorrow."

"Farewell," she said, "ye virgins all,
And shun the fault I fell in;
Henceforth take warning by the fall
Of cruel Barbara Allen."

They also must have sung the classical ballad, the tragedy of "Lord Randall," who has to tell his mother that he has been poisoned by his sweetheart. The fate of the hunting hawks and dogs who ate the scraps from his sweetheart's table gives us an indication of what is to happen:

38

"And what became of them,
*   Lord Randall, my son?*
And what became of them,
*   my handsome young man?"*
"They stretched out and died.
*   Mother, make my bed soon,*
For I'm wearied wi' hunting
*   and fain would lie down."*

These first English settlers almost failed in their attempt to remain on the coast of Virginia. Starvation during the third winter almost wiped them out. Captain John Smith, who legend says was saved from being killed by unfriendly Indians by Pocahontas, pulled them through the awful winter. He bought corn from the Indians and would not give any of it to the gentlemen who thought they were too fine to work. Many of the first families of Virginia spring from those same gentlemen who became dirt farmers overnight.

THEY KEPT ON COMING

THE STREAM OF IMMIGRANTS that were to make up the colonies never stopped coming—and perhaps never will.

In the folk songs of America are echoes of all the world's great cultures, sometimes combined. In the process they become uniquely American.

The Dutch, who founded New Amsterdam, and bought Manhattan Island with a handful of trinkets, knelt to sing a prayer of thanks to God for their safe arrival. It remains the national hymn for our celebration of the Thanksgiving holiday:

THANKSGIVING PRAYER

We gather together
*   to ask the Lord's blessings*
He chastens and hastens
*   His will to make known*

The wicked oppressing
 now cease to be distressing
Sing praises to His name
 for He forgets not His own.

The Swedes made another remarkable purchase. For a bottle of whiskey and a few strings of glass beads, they bought from the Indians both sides of the Delaware River. They built Fort Christina, and quickly made the surrounding countryside as much like old Sweden as possible. In their new orchards they sang:

 The apple trees grow in the orchard fair,
 The orchard fair, the orchard fair,
 The angels are guarding the blossoms there,
 In Summertime, in summertime.

The Germans came to Pennsylvania, and today you can tell their farms by the neatness of the big red barns and well-tended fields. They brought asparagus, carrots and the cucumber to the region, and the song, "Must I Then" ("Muss I Denn").

Must I then, must I then,
Go afar from the town,
Far from the town,
While you, my love, remain?

When I come, when I come,
When I come back home,
Come back home,
I will haste to you again . . .

Although the Italians could claim Columbus, the discoverer of the New World, and the namesake of the continent, Amerigo Vespucci, no great wave of immigrants from Italy immediately followed. A handful of Venetian glassmakers in Jamestown, a hundred Northern Italian farmers in Delaware, a smattering of Turin weavers in Georgia and a few thousand others scattered along the Atlantic Coast were enough to add the flavor of Southern Europe, though.

This Barcarolle, "Santa Lucia," comes to us from old Naples:

Santa Lucia,
Santa Lucia.
Who then will sail with me,
In my bark o'er the sea.

Many religious groups followed the example of the Puritans and Pilgrims and fled to freedom in a new land. The Scottish Highlanders came to North Carolina because they were denied the right to play the bagpipes by the English King. Other Scots settled with the Irish in central Pennsylvania and became known as the Scotch–Irish. Quakers, Baptists, Mennonites, Amish, Huguenots and scores of others found tolerance here for themselves and their songs.

One group of Americans, the Negroes, came against their will. They arrived as early as 1619 at Jamestown. More than forty years later slavery was introduced, and Africans were brought over to work the Virginia tobacco plantations.

This song by an American Negro writer suggests that the harm done to the mind of the captive African might have been worse than that done to his body.

Strange lands, strange things,
New Gods, new kings,
Old home done fade away,
Dark night, darker day.

CHAPTER THREE

EARLY
COLONIAL
TIMES

THEY SOUGHT FREEDOM

THE NAME PILGRIM is given to one who for religious reasons travels far to a holy place. It was in 1620 on a clear, cold November day that 102 brave English Pilgrims, fleeing from religious persecution, sighted these shores. Their ship, called the *Mayflower* because it had a sweet smell from years in the wine trade, had been blown off course; unable to locate Virginia, they stepped ashore on Plymouth Rock.

With the soldier Captain Miles Standish as a leader, their settlement prospered. The following autumn they were able to hold a feast to give thanks to God for His blessings. This was the first Thanksgiving Day.

Although a deeply religious folk who knew mostly sacred songs, these verses from a ballad sung during their third year in the New World show us they knew how to laugh at themselves:

> *The place where we live is a wilderness wood,*
> *Where grass is much wanting that's fruitful and good . . .*
> *Our mountains and hills and valleys below*
> *Being commonly covered with ice and with snow;*
> *And when the northwester with violence blows,*
> *Then every man pulls his cap over his nose;*
> *But if any's so hardy and will it withstand,*
> *He forfeits a finger, a foot, or a hand.*

When the spring opens we take the hoe,
And make the ground ready to plant and to sow;
Our corn being planted and seed being sown,
The worms destroy much before it is grown;
And when it is growing, some spoil there is made
By birds and by squirrels that pluck up the blade;
E'en when it is grown to full corn in the ear
It is often destroyed by raccoons and deer.

The Puritans, a short time later, arrived in Massachusetts Bay, carrying their Bibles and a royal charter. Although these two groups, the Pilgrims and the Puritans, had dreamed of a life in the New World free from religious persecution, they became intolerant of those who did not share their beliefs. The death penalty was inflicted for a variety of offenses, not only for murder, but for idolatry, blasphemy and witchcraft. Their intolerance reached backward to the old country, and for two centuries they worked on Christmas Day to dramatize their break with the Church of England.

Soon, every waking moment was haunted by fear of the wrath of a vengeful God. To that feared Deity they sang the Psalm known as "Old Hundred":

All people that on the earth do dwell,
Sing to the Lord with cheerful voice,
Him serve with fear, His praise forth tell,
Come ye before Him, and rejoice.

THE YANKEES

IN SPITE OF THEIR DIFFERENCES, all the settlers of the Atlantic coast, from Virginia through Connecticut and Maine, became known as Yankees. And Yankees of New England were forbidden frivolity by their religious beliefs, even banning the playing of the fiddle—calling it "the devil's own instrument!" In fact, the dominant mood of New England is perfectly summed up by the text around the first letter of the alphabet in the "New England Primer":

A is for Adam.
In Adam's fall,
We sinned all.

We have more understanding of the strictness of the New Englander when we consider the harshness of his environment. The first colonists, and their descendants for almost two hundred years, had to do everything for themselves. They built their own cabins out of logs, ground corn by hand, made moccasins and shoes from the hides of wild animals and very often wove the material for their own clothing or wore buckskins. They ate from homemade pewter or wooden dishes, washed them with soap made from ashes and fats; and after a workday that stretched from sunup until after dark, saw themselves to bed by the light of freshly dipped candles. In short, their never-ending battle to survive took the kind of stern discipline that gave them a bleak view of the spiritual world.

All Yankees were not as severe as the Pilgrims and the Puritans. The Methodist Church, which had taken root in areas along the coast, wisely gave their followers some emotional release by allowing the words of popular ballads to be altered to make them acceptable as hymns.

Lines such as: "Saw ye my true love?" easily became "Saw ye my Savior?"

The Methodists especially liked the melody of this well-known folk song:

Go tell Aunt Dinah,
Go tell Aunt Dinah,
Go tell Aunt Dinah,
The old grey goose is dead.

The one that she's been savin',
The one that she's been savin',
The one that she's been savin',
To make a feather bed.

50

With brand new words praising God, it appears as song No. 187 in the "Methodist Hymnal."

The Episcopal Church, the established Church of England, flourished in the middle colonies. They reversed the Methodist practice, and created popular ballads from church hymns. In church they sang:

Oh when shall I see Jesus
And reign with Him above
And drink from the flowing fountain
Drink everlasting love.
And to glory I will go,
And to glory I will go,
Will go, will go,
And to glory I will go.

However, when people came together for a social after a church meeting, this same song became:

I'd rather live a beggar
While here on earth I stay,
Than to possess the riches
Of all Americay
And to begging I will go,
And to begging I will go,
Will go, will go,
And to begging I will go.

Despite moments of freedom and lightness among New England settlers, the general spirit of colonial America was one of restraint and denial. In fact, it was not until the early eighteenth century that a musical instrument, other than a pitch pipe, was allowed at a New England church service.

This strictness was especially difficult for the young people of the community.

51

PLAY PARTIES

THE YANKEE TEEN-AGERS reasoned that their elders could not object to their playing children's games. So, they made up singing and dancing games, like those played by young children, and beat out time by clapping their hands. These games became known as play parties.

The play-party idea spread like wildfire, and soon became an important recreation in all the colonies. It enabled the hard-working farmers to escape the harsh realities of everyday life by a return to childhood's happy abandon.

One play-party song which has survived until now is this bit of untitled poetry:

> *There she stands, a lovely creature,*
> *Who she is, I do not know;*
> *You can catch her for her beauty,*
> *Make her answer, yes or no.*

Many of the dances were done in a circle with each couple changing partners and progressing completely around to their original place.

> *Lost my partner, what'll I do?*
> *Lost my partner, what'll I do?*
> *Lost my partner, what'll I do?*
> *Skip to my loo, my darling.*

I'll get another one, prettier'n you,
I'll get another one, prettier'n you,
I'll get another one, prettier'n you,
Skip to my loo, my darling.

There were literally thousands of play-party songs created in the colonies up through the eighteenth century.

From Pennsylvania:

I brought her water in my glove,
I sent a letter to my love.

From New York:

A tisket, a tasket,
A green and yellow basket.
I sent a letter to my love,
And on the way I dropped it.

From Florida:

Rise, sugar, rise
Take your finger from your eyes,
Look to the east, look to the west,
Look to the one you love the best.

From North Carolina:

> *Hog drivers, hog drivers, hog drivers we air,*
> *A-courtin' yer darter so sweet and fair;*
> *And kin we git lodgin' here, o here—*
> *And kin we git lodgin' here?*

From Connecticut:

> *O Charley he's a fine young man,*
> *O Charley he's a dandy,*
> *He loves to hug and kiss the girls,*
> *And feed them sugar candy.*

Along the entire eastern seaboard:

> *The higher up the cherry tree,*
> *The sweeter grow the cherries,*
> *The more you hug and kiss a girl,*
> *The sooner she will marry.*

The Negro influence on Southern play-party songs gave them added color and imagination. "A Moste Strange Weddinge of the Ffrogge and the

Mouse," an old English ballad, was made into a charming dance song satirizing the manners of country gentlemen:

> *Mr. Frog he went a-courtin', unh-hunh,*
> *Mr. Frog he went a-courtin', unh-hunh,*
> *Mr. Frog he went a-courtin' an' he did ride,*
> *Sword and pistol by his side, unh-hunh.*

The song relates how Mr. Frog won the hand of Miss Mouse, and describes the various animals who came as wedding guests:

> *First to come was Mr. Snake,*
> *Slid right over the weddin' cake.*
> *Next to come was Mr. Bug,*
> *Drank hard cider from a jug.*
> *Next to come was Mr. Mole,*
> *Fell right into a gopher hole.*
> *Next to come was a brindle cow,*
> *Couldn't dance 'cause she didn't know how.*

The song ends with an invitation to all:

> *There's bread and cheese upon the shelf,*
> *If you want any, just help yourself.*

Another Negro dance song told of the raccoon's vain plea to one better situated:

> Possom in the 'simmon tree,
> Raccoon on the ground,
> Say the raccoon to the possom,
> "Won't you throw some 'simmons down?"

And still another gave this example of poetic justice:

> Sheep and the goat went huckleberry huntin',
> Say the goat to the sheep,
>   "Won't you gimme a little mutton?"
> Then the goat fell down and skint his shin,
> Oh, measie-mighty, how the sheep did grin.

"Cindy" was the heroine of a thousand adventures and verses. A few of the best known are:

> I wish I was an apple,
> A-hangin' in a tree,
> And ev'ry time my sweetheart passed,
> She'd take a bite of me.
> She told me that she loved me,
> She called me sugar plum,
> She throwed her arms around me,
> I thought my time had come.
>
> Get along home, Cindy, Cindy;
> Get along home, Cindy, Cindy;
> Get along home, Cindy, Cindy;
> I'll marry you sometime.
>
> She took me to the parlor,
> She cooled me with her fan,
> She swore I was the purtiest thing
> In the shape of a mortal man,

Cindy got religion,
She had it once before;
But when she heard my old banjo,
She was the first one on the floor.
Cindy went to the preachin',
She swung around and around;
She got so full of glory,
She knocked the preacher down.

One aspect of all folk music is its ability to change with the times, and even from singer to singer. Many songs that we now think of as either ballads or lullabies began with the sound of hand-clapping at some colonial play party.

THEY RESHAPED THE BALLADS

THE GERMANS IN PENNSYLVANIA, although intensely religious, engaged in singing games even on Sunday. Others, such as the Dutch of New York, the hardy Swedes of Delaware, the French Catholic, who were building their villages in Louisiana, and their Huguenot countrymen in South Carolina, the Spanish who were fighting to survive in Florida, and the African concentrated in the South, were all busy advancing the folk music of America.

Certainly, any list of contributors to our folk heritage must include Jews, Russians, Italians, Poles and practically every other European ethnic group. Although thinly scattered throughout the early colonies, they were to America what salt is to soup. The first musical soup would have been tasteless without that sprinkling of salt.

Naturally American folk singing soon reflected an American spirit. All the settlements were faced with the same challenge in the New World. The immigrants had to learn to act for themselves, depend on their own resources and create methods to cope with their problems. The challenge of conquering the wilderness could only be answered by those capable of becoming independent.

Everywhere, the European ballads began to be reshaped to express the growing sense of democracy in the New World. Lord Randall lost his title and became Johnny Randall, Willie or Billy Boy, and his story became quite local.

> *Where have you been all the day,*
>   *Billy Boy, Billy Boy?*
> *Where have you been all the day,*
>   *charmin' Billy?*
> *I have been all the day*
>   *courtin' of a lady gay,*
> *But she's a young thing,*
>   *and cannot leave her mother.*
>
> *Is she fit to be a wife,*
>   *Billy Boy, Billy Boy?*
> *Is she fit to be a wife,*
>   *charmin' Billy?*
> *She's as fit to be a wife*
>   *as a fork fits to a knife,*
> *But she's a young thing,*
>   *and cannot leave her mother.*
>
> *Can she bake a cherry pie,*
>   *Billy Boy, Billy Boy?*
> *Can she bake a cherry pie,*
>   *charmin' Billy?*
> *She can bake a cherry pie,*
>   *quick as a cat can wink its eye,*
> *But she's a young thing,*
>   *and cannot leave her mother.*

An American sense of justice gave Barbara Allen a kinder ending, and she was no longer the cruel vixen of the English version:

> *Sweet William was buried in one graveyard,*
> *Barbara Allen in another;*
> *A rose grew on Sweet William's grave,*
> *And a briar on Barbara Allen's.*

They grew and they grew to the steeple,
And there they grew no higher;
And there they tied in a true-lover knot,
The rose clung 'round the briar.

"Pop Goes the Weasel" was originally British slang meaning that something was headed for the pawnshop. By the time the New Englanders had settled the best locations east of the Appalachian ridges, the song had become fully American and referred to the ability of the weasel to appear and disappear right before your eyes.

All around the mulberry bush,
The farmer chased the weasel,
And that's the way the money goes,
Pop goes the weasel.

A penny for a spool of thread,
A penny for a needle,
And that's the way the money goes,
Pop goes the weasel.

Feudal Europe had many ballads in which the symbol of a farmyard fowl was used to express resentment against the nobility. Young girls were turned into white swans to escape their pursuers, and ducks and geese that laid golden eggs and had silver feathers were stolen by peasant boys. The Negro, who had always used animals in his folk tales, symbolized himself as the indestructible gray goose, stronger and more enduring than his white master:

Well, las' Monday mornin'
Lawd, Lawd, Lawd,
Well, las' Monday mornin'
Lawd, Lawd, Lawd.

Some of the lead lines describing the events of that fateful Monday are:

My daddy went a-huntin',
Huntin' for the gray goose,
An' he took along his Zulu,
Well, up to his shoulder,
And the gun wen' boo-loo,
Down he come a-fallin',
He was six weeks a-fallin',
He was six weeks a-pickin',
He was six weeks a-cookin',
An, the fork couldn' stick him,
An, the hogs couldn' eat him,
So they taken him to the sawmill,
An' he broke the saws' teeth out,
An' the last time I seed her,

She was flyin' 'cross the ocean,
Had a long string o' goslins,
An' they all went "Quonk, quonk."

"The Hangman's Tree" was sung in one form or another in all Europe. This Americanized version was popular in the East:

"Slack your rope, hangman,
O slack it for a while;
I think I see my father coming,
Riding many a mile.
O father have you brought me gold?
Or have you paid my fee?
Or have you come to see me hanging
On the gallows tree?"
"I have not brought you gold;
I have not paid your fee;
But I have come to see you hanging
On the gallows tree."

In the deep South hanging was not always done within the law. Here is one of the ballads that tells the sad story of injustice:

Winter has gone and the leaves turn green,
Winter has gone and the leaves turn green,
Your innocent face
I wish I had never seen.

The bow was bent and the rope was strung,
The bow was bent and the rope was strung,
An innocent man
You have all hung.

So come O my love and see me die,
So come O my love and see me die,
Lift up your innocent face
See me dance in the sky.

AND THE RIDDLE SONG

THIS RIDDLE SONG came a long way across the ocean from England to the Southern mountains. It took on the humbleness of the simple country folk who used it as a courting song.

I gave my love a cherry that had no stone,
I gave my love a chicken that had no bone,
I told my love a story that had no end,
I gave my love a baby with no cry-en.

How can there be a cherry that has no stone,
How can there be a chicken that has no bone,
How can there be a story that has no end,
How can there be a baby with no cry-en?

A cherry when it's blooming, it has no stone,
A chicken when it's pipping, it has no bone,
The story that I love you, it has no end,
A baby when it's sleeping, there's no cry-en.

THE LYRIC SONG

GENERALLY, THE SETTLERS in early America had to make their own entertainment. Except in those settlements where it was strictly forbidden, music and song played an important part in colonial family life. The English lyric song was as popular then as it is now. However, the music that had formerly been composed for the mandolin and the lute was changed to fit the emotions of pioneers and their families. This lyric song always brought tears to the eyes of hard-bitten farmers:

Black, black, black is the color
*   of my true love's hair,*
Her lips are like some rosy fair,
The prettiest face and the neatest hands,
I love the ground whereon she stands.

I love my love and well she knows
I love the grass whereon she goes,
If she on earth no more I see
My life will quickly fade away.

I go to Troublesome to mourn and weep
But satisfied I ne'er could sleep.
I'll write to you in a few little lines,
I'll suffer death ten thousand times.

So fare you well, my own true love,
The time has passed and I wish you well;
But still I hope the time will come
When you and I will be as one.

Black, black, black, is the color
*   of my true love's hair,*
Her lips are like some rosy fair,
The prettiest face and the neatest hands,
I love the ground whereon she stands.

And this fragment of a lyric song has been woven into many American folk melodies:

O look at the little turtle dove,
A-skippin' from vine to vine;
He's mourning for his own true love,
Just as I mourn for mine.

THE LULLABY

WHILE THE MEN worked hard all day, the women had a thousand tasks around the house. Part of their work was to put the children to sleep. This Indian lullaby was sung in practically every home:

Rock-a-bye baby, in the tree top,
When the wind blows, the cradle will rock,
When the bough breaks, the cradle will fall,
And down will come baby, cradle and all.

Although Jewish families were thinly scattered among the colonists, they had a strong and vibrant culture that influenced all. This lullaby sung by Jewish mothers quickly became popular in non-Jewish homes:

To my little one's cradle in the night,
Comes a new little goat snowy white;
The goat will trot to the market,
While mother her watch will keep,
To bring you back raisins and almonds;
Sleep, my little one, sleep.

A Pennsylvania Dutch mother, as she rocked the cradle with one hand and churned butter with the other, would croon, "Schlof, Bubela" ("sleep Little One"):

Sleep, little one, sleep,
Your daddy guards the sheep,
Your mother tends the little lamb,
In the sweet green meadow land,
Sleep, little one, sleep.

It is believed that the Negro mother in Virginia adapted some part of an English ballad to create this fanciful go-to-sleep song:

Hushaby,
Don't you cry,
Go to sleepy, little baby.
When you wake,
You shall have
All the pretty little horses—
Blacks and bays,
Dapples and grays,
Coach and six-a little horses.
Hushaby,
Don't you cry,
Go to sleepy, little baby.

CHAPTER FOUR

WE
WERE
ALWAYS
GROWING

THE BACK COUNTRY

BEFORE THE END of the colonial period, when the English still controlled the Atlantic Coast, the most adventurous settlers had started to explore the back country. The dangerous frontier that these people faced was on the eastern fringes of the Alleghenies, and stretched down through the Shenandoah Valley in Virginia into the Piedmont area of the Carolinas.

THE WAGONERS

THE WAGONERS WHO drove the pack trails through the Appalachian back country sang, as they went their lonely and dangerous way, of loves more imagined than real:

OLD SMOKY

On top of old smoky
All covered in snow,
I lost my true lover
By courtin' too slow.

For meetin' is a pleasure
And partin' is a grief
And a false hearted lover
Is worse than a thief.

A thief, he'll but rob you
And take all you have,
But a false hearted lover
Will drive you to your grave.

Your grave will decay you
And turn you to dust,
Not one gal in fifty
That a poor boy can trust.

"Old Smoky" was originally known as the "Wagoner's Lad," and contained these details of the hard life of the drivers:

It's raining, it's hailing,
The moon gives no light,
Your horses can't travel
This dark lonesome night.

Go put up your horses,
Feed them some hay,
Come sit down here beside me,
As long as you stay.

And to this kind offer the driver is made to answer:

My horses ain't hungry
Won't eat your hay,
So farewell, my darling,
I'll feed on my way.

OLD DAN'L

DANIEL BOONE, who was born near Philadelphia, was mainly responsible for the settlement of Kentucky. With six other men, he set out to cross the Allegheny Mountains and to explore the wilderness to the west. Except for

Old Dan'l and his brother the entire party was killed by hostile Indians. But this did not stop other settlers from following the path he blazed through the Cumberland Gap.

CUMBERLAND GAP

Lay down, boys, and take a little nap,
Lay down, boys, and take a little nap,
Lay down, boys, and take a little nap,
Fourteen miles to the Cumberland Gap.

The first white man in Cumberland Gap,
Was Doctor Walker, an English chap.

Daniel Boone on Pinnacle Rock,
He killed Indians with an old flintlock.

Cumberland Gap is a noted place,
Three kinds of water to wash your face.

Cumberland Gap with its cliff and rocks,
Home of the panther, bear, and fox.

Me and my wife and my wife's gran'pap,
All raise Cain in Cumberland Gap.

FIDDLIN' AND STOMPIN'

BACK COUNTRY PEOPLE from North to South were not bound by those strict rules of conduct enforced along the coast. They were true pioneers, breaking away from the customs of England, becoming purely American in outlook. They won their land by "tomahawk claim," by force from the Indians. They hunted and fished for their food and they raised their children to believe they were the equal of any man.

For amusement they held barbecues, where deer and oxen were roasted whole; they had houseraising parties for newlyweds, with dancing and celebrating for several days and nights; and there were shooting matches, wrestling bouts and other contests of strength. They sang their folk songs to the music of the fiddle and the dulcimer.

One of the best fiddlers' tunes ever played at a backwoods party was "Sourwood Mountain . . ."

Chickens a-crowin' on Sourwood Mountain
Hey ding-a-dong-diddle-i-day
So many pretty girls I can't count 'em.
Hey ding-a-ding-a-dong-diddle-i-day

My true love is a blue-eyed daisy
She won't come and I'm too lazy.

Big dog bark and little one bite you
Big girl court and little one spite you.

One of these days before very long
I'll get my girl and I'll be gone.

SQUARES AND REELS

EVERY COUNTRY FIDDLER had to know the dances of his particular region. There was one tune, however, that fitted most of the square dances and reels of the entire back country; and men in homespun hunting shirts and deerskin leggings would set the floors to rocking when they heard:

TURKEY IN THE STRAW

As I was a-gwine on down the road,
With a tired team and a heavy load,
I cracked my whip and the leader sprung,
I says day-day to the wagon tongue.

Turkey in the straw, haw, haw, haw,
Turkey in the hay, hay, hay, hay,

Roll 'em up and twist 'em up
    a high tuck-a-haw,
And hit 'em up a tune called
    Turkey in the Straw.

Oh, I went out to milk, an I didn't know how
I milked a goat instead of a cow
A monkey sitting on a pile of straw
A-winking his eye at his mother-in-law.

Well, I met Mister Catfish comin' down the stream;
Says Mister Catfish, "What do you mean?"
I caught Mister Catfish by the snout
And I turned that catfish wrong side out.

Then I come to the river and I couldn't get across
So I paid five dollars for a blind horse,
Well, he wouldn't go ahead and he wouldn't stand still,
So he went up and down like an old saw mill.

As I came down a new cut road,
I met Mister Bullfrog a-courtin' Miss Toad,
And every time Miss Toad would sing,
The old Bullfrog cut a pigeon wing.

THE OLD BANJO

WHEN SOUTHERN TENNESSEE mountain folk held a hoedown, the musicians would literally make a banjo talk. With fiddles and harmonicas in the background, the banjo was free to speak about the good taste of the roasted groundhog:

GROUND HOG

Old Joe Digger, Sam and Dave,
Old Joe Digger, Sam and Dave,

74

Went a-hog huntin' as hard as they could stave.
Ground hog! Ground hog!

Whet up your axe and whistle up your dog,
Whet up your axe and whistle up your dog,
We're off to the woods to hunt ground hog,
Ground hog! Ground hog!

He's in here, boys, the holes wore slick,
Run her, Sam, with your forked stick.
Stand back, boys, and let's be wise
I think I see his beady eyes.

Up jumped Sam with a ten foot pole,
To roust that ground hog out of his hole.

Work, boys, work, just as hard as you can tear,
The meat'll do to eat, and the hide'll do to wear.

Here he come all in a whirl,
He's the biggest ground hog in this world.

Here comes Sal with a snigger and a grin,
Ground hog grease all over her chin.

Come here, ma, make Sam quit,
He's eating all the hog and I can't get a bit.

Watch him, boys, he's 'bout to fall,
He's et 'till his pants won't button at all.

WITH A GRIN

THE FOLK BALLAD was often used to commemorate an event, chronicle some exciting happening or even to relate the story of a disaster or accident. According to the Lomaxes, leading authorities in the folksong field, "Springfield Mountain" is the actual account of the death of Timothy Myrick, a young man who in 1761 was bitten by a "pizen sarpent."

SPRINGFIELD MOUNTAIN

On Springfield Mountain there did dwell,
With a ri-ting-a-tim, ring a-tid-en-nah-den-ay,
On Springfield Mountain there did dwell,
    Tim-a-row!
On Springfield Mountain there did dwell
A lovely youth whom I knew well,
With a ri-ting-a-tim, ring-a-tid-en-nah-den-ay.

This lovely youth one day did go
Down to the meadow for to mow.

He mowed a while and then did feel
A pizenous sarpint bite his heel.

He turned around and with a blow
He laid that pesky sarpint low.

They carried him to his Sally dear,
Which made her feel so very queer.

"O Johnny dear, why did you go
Down in your father's field to mow?"

"Why, Sally dear, I suppose you knowed
When the grass gits ripe it must be mowed!"

Now Sally had two ruby lips,
With which the pizen she did sip.

Dear Sally had a hollow tooth,
And so the pizen killed them both.

So Johnny died, gave up the ghost,
And off to heaven he did post.

Come all young girls and shed one tear
For this young man that died right here.

Come all young men, and warning take,
And don't get bit by a rattle-snake.

Springfield Mountain has now become a hundred other mountains located all over America, especially in the Far West, as versions of this song spread. Perhaps its popularity is due to an American need to grin at even the most serious of subjects.

JUST PLAIN FOOLISHNESS

THE BACKWOODS GREW the kind of man whose sense of humor often verged on the ridiculous. Rather, it was the laughter of a half-wild spirit; of a man who sought release from utter loneliness in periods of absolute nonsense.

Like a playful child, the frontiersman enjoyed sticking out his tongue at even the most sacred things.

I WAS BORN ABOUT TEN THOUSAND YEARS AGO

I was born about ten thousand years ago,
There ain't nothin' in this world that I don't know;
I saw Peter, Paul and Moses playin' ring around the roses
And I'll whip the guy that says it isn't so.

I saw Satan when he looked the garden o'er;
I saw Adam and Eve driven from the door;
And from behind the bushes peepin', I saw the apple they were eatin'
And I swear I was the guy what et the core.

I taught Sampson how to use his mighty hands;
I first showed Columbus this happy land;
And for Pharaoh's little kids I built all the pyramids
And to Sahara carried all the sands.

I taught Solomon his little ABC's;
I was the first man to eat limburger cheese;
And while floatin' down the bay with Methusalah one day
I saw his whiskers floatin' in the breeze.

I was there when Alexander crossed the sea,
And I always cheered him on to victory—
And when King Darius died, I was fighting by his side,
So he gave his cha-ri-ot to me.

I was present at the battle of the Nile;
And did the bullets fly, well I should smile:
And when Pharaoh hit the King with a cutlass on the wing,
I was lying at the bottom of the pile.

I saw Nero fiddling when he burnt up Rome;
I told him it looked like his future home;
When he had the nerve to swear, I dragged him from his chair
And broke a Pilsner bottle on his dome.

Queen Elizabeth she fell in love with me;
We were married in Milwaukee secretly,
But I got tired and shook her and went off with General Hooker,
A-fightin' skeeters down in Tennessee . . .

JUST PLAIN LIARS

AND OF COURSE there was always the tall, tall tale. This song, included in the collection of folk songs compiled by Richard Chase, was the favorite of no less a person than George Washington:

THE DARBY RAM

As I went down to Darby Town
'twas on a market day,
and there I saw the biggest ram
that ever was fed on hay—
that ever was fed on hay!
And there I saw the biggest ram
that ever was fed on hay!

And if you think this is not so,
for maybe you'll think I lie—
Oh you go down to Darby Town
and you'll see the same as I—
and you'll see the same as I.
Oh you go down to Darby Town
and you'll see the same as I.

This ram he had four feet, sir,
on four feet he did stand,
and every track he made, sir,
it covered an acre of land—
it covered an acre of land.
And every track he made, sir,
it covered an acre of land.

And one of this ram's teeth, sir,
was hollow as a horn,
and when they took its measure, sir,
it held a bushel of corn.

ALWAYS "GREENSLEEVES"

THE FOLK SONG, as a rule, is always in the process of change. But every rule has its exceptions. This was the one folk song that survived all the centuries, practically untouched. It had come down from Elizabethan England to present-day America without being rewritten.

Although its subject matter was romantic love, it remained a favorite of both Pilgrims and Puritans. The frontiersmen also learned this song, as nearly as they could, in its original form. It was simply too beautiful to change.

GREENSLEEVES

Alas my love you will do me wrong
If you cast me off so discourteously
And I have loved you so very long
And delighting in your winning company.

Greensleeves you were all my joy
And you know Greensleeves you were my delight
Greensleeves you're my heart of gold
No one else but my dear Lady Greensleeves.

I have been ready and at your hand
For to grant whatever your heart would crave
And I have waged both my life and land
Your dear love and your good will to hold and have.

Well I will pray to our God on high
So that thou my constancy mayest see
And that yet once more before I die
Thou so surely wilt vouch safe to love me.

Greensleeves now farewell adieu adieu
For to God I pray Him to prosper thee
For I am still thy one lover true
Come to me once again and do love me.

BROADSIDE BALLADS

EARLY IN THE SEVENTEENTH CENTURY, colonial America discovered a type of song which had long been popular in the British Isles. These were called broadside ballads, probably because they were originally printed on broad sheets of paper and sold in the streets. There was no music, just a text, usually bad poetry dealing with some recent event. The buyer was then expected to sing the text to the tune of some well-known folk melody.

The most popular American Broadside came from England and related the hanging of the notorious pirate, Captain William Kidd, in 1701. As the song was adopted here, the name became changed to Robert.

CAPTAIN KIDD

Oh! my name was Robert Kidd, as I sailed, as I sailed,
Oh my name was Robert Kidd, as I sailed;
My name was Robert Kidd, God's laws I did forbid,
And most wickedly I did, as I sailed.

Oh! my parents taught me well, as I sailed, as I sailed,
Oh, my parents taught me well, as I sailed,
My parents taught me well, to shun the gates of hell,
But against them I rebelled, as I sailed, as I sailed,
But against them I rebelled, as I sailed.

I murdered William Moore, as I sailed, as I sailed,
I murdered William Moore, as I sailed,
I murdered William Moore and left him in his gore,
Not many leagues from shore, as I sailed, as I sailed,
Not many leagues from shore, as I sailed.

I steered from sound to sound, as I sailed, as I sailed
I steered from sound to sound, as I sailed,
I steered from sound to sound, and many ships I found,
And most of them I burned, as I sailed, as I sailed,
And most of them I burned, as I sailed.

I'd ninety bars of gold, as I sailed, as I sailed,
I'd ninety bars of gold, as I sailed,
I'd ninety bars of gold, and dollars manifold,
With riches uncontrolled, as I sailed, as I sailed,
With riches uncontrolled, as I sailed.

To Newgate I am cast, and must die, and must die,
To Newgate I am cast, and must die,
To Newgate I am cast, with sad and heavy heart,
To receive my just desert, I must die, I must die,
To receive my just desert, I must die.

Take warning now by me, for I must die, I must die,
Take warning now by me, for I must die,
Take warning now by me, and shun bad company,
Lest you come to hell with me, for I must die, I must die,
Lest you come to hell with me, for I must die.

There were hundreds of broadsides written of the sensational "Captain Kidd" variety. Russell Ames gives this example of one of the earliest which describes a bloody French and Indian attack on the little Dutch outpost of Schenectady:

They threw the Infants in the Fire,
The Men they did not spare;
But killed All which they could find
Tho' Aged or tho' Fair.

The broadside ends with an account of the swift revenge of the colonists:

Our soldiers fell upon their Reare,
And killed twenty-five
Our Young Men were so much enrag'd
They took scarce One alive.

The broadside ballads were the work of men who in modern times would have worked in the song factories of Tinpan Alley. Churchmen of the day preached against this type of song sheet, calling it an outrage against good taste and decency, and "bad news put to borrowed tunes."

However, many of the outstanding men of the day loved this type of song. Benjamin Franklin, one of our greatest Americans, composed broadside ballads when he was only nine years old. One was entitled "The Lighthouse Tragedy," another, "Blackbeard, the Pirate."

CHAPTER FIVE

STARS
AND
STRIPES

REVOLUTIONARY TEA

THIS NATION IS the child of a bloody revolution against the pride of kings and the might of professional soldiers. The thirteen colonies felt some loyalty toward the mother country but their loyalty was rewarded with tyranny. They were taxed solely for the benefit of England. Especially resented were the Sugar, Stamp, and Tea Acts, laws which took from the colonies even their small profits on luxuries.

This led to the most remembered tea party in all history. A group of patriotic Americans, as a gesture of protest, raided the ships of the East India Company and on the night of December 16, 1773, dumped their cargoes of tea into Boston Harbor.

Wary of naming names, the people of Boston sang a song whose meaning was clear.

REVOLUTIONARY TEA

There was an old lady lived over the sea,
And she was an island queen.
Her daughter lived off in a new country
With an ocean of water between.
The old lady's pockets were filled with gold,
But never contented was she.
So she called on her daughter to pay her a tax,
Of three pence a pound on the tea,
Of three pence a pound on the tea.

"Now mother, dear mother," the daughter replied,
"I shan't do the thing that you ax;
I'm willing to pay a fair price for the tea,
But never the threepenny tax."
"You shall," quoth the mother, and reddened with rage,
"For you're my own daughter, you see.
And sure 'tis quite proper the daughter should pay
Her mother a tax on the tea,
Her mother a tax on the tea."

And so the old lady her servant called up,
And packed off a budget of tea,
And eager for three pence a pound, she put in
Enough for a large family.
She ordered her servant to bring home the tax
Declaring her child should obey,
Or old as she was and a woman most grown,
She'd half whip her life away,
She'd half whip her life away.

The tea was conveyed to the daughter's door,
All down by the ocean side.
But the bouncing girl poured out every pound,
In the dark and boiling tide.
And then she called out to the Island Queen,
"Oh mother, dear mother," quoth she.

"Your tea you may have when 'tis steeped enough,
But never a tax from me,
But never a tax from me."

The first man to die in the war for independence was a Negro, Crispus Attucks. He died in the famed Boston Massacre, when the unarmed populace was fired upon while attempting to oust the British soldiers. The Boston Massacre became the torch that inflamed the colonies, and led inevitably to Concord Bridge, where the embattled farmers finally "fired the shot heard 'round the world."

The Revolutionary War song, which has become as much a part of our folklore as the "Give me liberty or give me death" speech of Patrick Henry, was composed by William Billings. It was the marching song of the Revolution.

CHESTER

Let tyrants shake their iron rod;
And slav'ry clank her galling chains,
We'll fear them not; we trust in God,
New England's God ever reigns.

The foe comes on with haughty stride,
Our troops advance with martial noise,
Their vet'rans flee, before our youth
And Gen'rals yield to beardless boys.

These were the stirring words that gave the rude farmers, who made up the Continental Army, a sense of national purpose. This poet of the Revolution must also have had a profound influence on the framers of the Declaration of Independence.

And as the young women watched their men shoulder their muskets and march away, they sang an American version of the Irish tune "Shule Aroon." They called it "Johnny Has Gone For a Soldier."

Sad I sit on Butternut Hill,
Who could blame me, cry my fill?

90

And ev'ry tear would turn a mill—
Johnny has gone for a soldier.

Me O my, I loved him so,
Broke my heart to see him go,
And only time will heal my woe—
Johnny has gone for a soldier.

I'd sell my clock, I'd sell my reel,
Likewise I'd sell my spinning wheel
To buy my love a sword of steel—
Johnny has gone for a soldier.

George Washington, the Commander-in-chief of the Continental Army, gathered recruits around the new flag designed by Betsy Ross. It had thirteen stars and thirteen stripes—one for each of the thirteen colonies that became the United States of America. And the new country had a new song called "Yankee Doodle."

It is ironic that this song was first used by the British with lyrics that mocked the ragged Continental Army. As a matter of fact, the term "Yankee doodle" was British slang for "a New England ragamuffin." But the colonists adopted this song and created a new set of lyrics to make it their own.

YANKEE DOODLE

Father'n I went down to camp
Along with Captain Gooding
And there we saw the men and boys
As thick as hasty pudding.

Yankee Doodle keep it up
Yankee Doodle Dandy
Mind the music and the step
And with the girls be handy.

There was Captain Washington
Upon a slapping stallion
A-giving orders to his men
There must have been a million.

Then I saw a swamping gun
As large as logs of maple
Upon a very little cart
A load for father's cattle.

Ev'ry time they shot it off
It took a horn of powder
And made a noise like father's gun
Only a nation louder.

There I saw a wooden keg
With heads made out of leather
They knocked upon it with some sticks
To call the folks together.

Then they'd fife away like fun
And play on cornstalk fiddles
And some had ribbons red as blood
All bound around their middles.

Troopers too would gallop up
And shoot right in our faces
It scared me almost half to death
To see them run such races.

I can't tell you all I saw
They kept up such a smother
I took my hat off, made a bow
And scampered home to mother.

There is another verse to "Yankee Doodle" known to all American children. Strange to say, this particular verse was not sung by our Continental Army; it was a derisive song used against the British Oliver Cromwell by his enemies:

Yankee Doodle came to town
A-riding on a pony
Stuck a feather in his cap
And called it macaroni.

It is worth noting that the American Army did not quickly forget how the British had laughed at them. And when General Cornwallis surrendered to General Washington at Yorktown in 1781, the song played by the American band was still "Yankee Doodle."

After the war the people sang a song with lyrics by Joseph Hopkinson adapted to the tune of "The President's March." It expressed what was in their hearts.

HAIL COLUMBIA

Hail Columbia, happy land
Hail ye heroes, heav'n-born band
Who fought and bled in freedom's cause
Who fought and bled in freedom's cause.
And when the storm of war was gone
Enjoyed the peace your valor won
Let independence be your boast
Ever mindful what it cost
Ever grateful for the prize
Let its altar reach the skies.

Firm, united let us stand
Rallying round our liberty
As a band of brothers joined
Peace and safety we shall find.

THE WAR OF 1812

THE WAR WAS a result of fear and misunderstanding. The British did not trust the United States because we were expanding rapidly in all directions. The United States declared war on Great Britain because the British had been impressing American ships and not respecting America's neutrality rights in the war that England was waging at that time against France. That the British were fighting another war made it easier for the young nation to declare war, for England had most of her military forces involved with the French.

The United States Army was poorly trained and lost most of their battles; but at sea the Americans were more adept. The U.S. ship *Constitution* defeated the British frigate *Guerrière* in the icy waters off Newfoundland. A broadside ballad immediately appeared to praise the victory.

THE CONSTITUTION AND THE GUERRIÈRE

I often have been told
That the British seamen bold
Could whip the tars of France
So neat and handy O!
But they never found their match
Till the Yankees did them catch,
O the Yankee tars for fighting
Are the dandy O!

The Guerrière, a frigate bold,
On the foaming ocean rolled
Commanded by Dacres
The grandee O,
With the choicest British crew
That a rammer ever drew:
They could whip the Frenchmen
Two to one quite handy O!

The first broadside we poured
Brought their mizzen by the board
Which doused the royal ensign
Very handy O;
Then proud Dacres he did sigh
And to his officers did cry,
"I did not think these Yankees
Were so handy O!"

In the popularity of this song which celebrates the first real United States victory of the war, there is a humorous point, which at the time was overlooked—the music and lyrics (with very slight changes) were borrowed from "A Good Old Glass of Brandy, O," a favorite drinking song of the enemy.

The foot soldiers of the war, unlike the men of all other wars, never created for themselves a marching song that caught on. With lyric changes they made do with the popular songs from the Revolution. Finally, Samuel Woodworth, who was famous for writing "The Old Oaken Bucket," wrote a marching song, "Hunters of Kentucky," to the tune of "Yankee Doodle." Unfortunately, the war had ended before the song became popular.

HUNTERS OF KENTUCKY

We are a hardy, free-born race,
Each man to fear a stranger;
Whate'er the game we join in chase,
Despising time and danger;
And if a daring for annoys,
Whate'er his strength and forces,
We'll show him that Kentucky boys
Are alligator horses.
Oh! Kentucky, the hunters of Kentucky,
Oh! Kentucky, the hunters of Kentucky.

The War of 1812 ended on Christmas Eve, 1814, just as futilely as it began. Andrew Jackson's final victory over the British at New Orleans was fought six days after the peace treaty had been signed.

HIS SOUL GOES MARCHING ON

THE CIVIL WAR produced many great men, of whom the greatest was, without doubt, Abraham Lincoln. A roll call of heroes, from both North and South, would be endless—hardly a family in America is without at least one. The war also produced many great songs, beginning with "The Battle Hymn of the Republic":

Mine eyes have seen the glory
of the coming of the Lord;
He is trampling out the vintage
where the grapes of wrath are stored;
He hath loosed the fateful lightning
of His terrible swift sword,
His truth is marching on.

Glory, Glory Hallelujah,
Glory, Glory Hallelujah,
Glory, Glory Hallelujah,
His truth is marching on.

I have seen Him in the watch fires
of a hundred circling camps;
They have builded Him an altar
in the evening dews and damps;
I can read His righteous sentence
by the dim and flaring lamps,
His day is marching on.

I have read a fiery gospel
writ in burnished rows of steel:
"As ye deal with My contemners,
so with you My Grace shall deal;
Let the Hero, born of woman,
crush the serpent with his heel,
Since God is marching on."

He has sounded forth the trumpet
　　that shall never call retreat;
He is sifting out the hearts of men
　　before His Judgment Seat;
Oh! be swift, my soul, to answer Him,
　　be jubilant, my feet!
Our God is marching on.

In the beauty of the lilies
　　Christ was born across the sea,
With a glory in his bosom
　　that transfigures you and me;
As He died to make men holy,
　　let us die to make men free,
While God is marching on.

This first inspired battle hymn was written by a woman, Julia Ward Howe. It was sung to the tune of "John Brown's Body." In 1862 it appeared in *The Atlantic Monthly,* and Mrs. Howe was paid the magnificent sum of five dollars for her literary efforts.

The song "John Brown's Body" was not originally about the fierce Abolitionist. Research has shown that the John Brown mentioned in the first version was Sergeant John Brown of Boston. But the popularity of the song was based on its identification with the John Brown who was hung for trying to free the slaves by declaring a personal war on the United States. John Brown's body was removed from the gallows in Charleston, Virginia, on December 2, 1859, and two short years later, thousands of Union soldiers were chanting a new marching song:

John Brown's body lies a-mouldering in the grave,
John Brown's body lies a-mouldering in the grave,
John Brown's body lies a-mouldering in the grave,
But his soul goes marching on.

Glory, glory, hallelujah,
Glory, glory, hallelujah,
Glory, glory, hallelujah,
His soul goes marching on.

He's gone to be a soldier in the Army of the Lord,
His soul goes marching on.

John Brown's knapsack is strapped upon his back,
His soul goes marching on.

John Brown died that the slaves might be free,
But his soul goes marching on.

The stars above in Heaven now are looking kindly down,
On the grave of old John Brown.

The first Negro troops joined the Union Army early in 1862. They were the men of the First Arkansas Regiment. Before the War Between the States had run its bloody course, the North was using many Negro troops.

They marched to the song of the First Arkansas Regiment:

Oh, we're the bully soldiers of the "First of Arkansas,"
We are fighting for the Union, we are fighting for the law,
We can hit a Rebel further than a white man ever saw,
As we go marching on.

Glory, glory hallelujah,
Glory, glory hallelujah,
Glory, glory hallelujah,
As we go marching on.

See, there above the center, where the flag is waving bright,
We are going out of slavery; we're bound for freedom's light
We mean to show Jeff Davis how the Africans can fight,
As we go marching on!

"The Battle Cry of Freedom" rallied the Northerners around the flag and aided enlistment:

We are marching to the field, boys,
We're going to the fight,
> *Shouting the battle cry of freedom,*
And we bear the glorious stars
For the Union and the right,
> *Shouting the battle cry of freedom.*

The Southerners countered with their own "Battle Cry of Freedom":

We are marching to the field, boys,
We're going to the fight,
> *Shouting the battle cry of freedom.*
And we bear the Heavenly cross,
For our cause is in the right,
> *Shouting the battle cry of freedom.*

The great marching song for the Confederate soldiers was, of course, "Dixie's Land":

I wish I was in the land of cotton,
Old times there are not forgotten,
Look a-way, look a-way, look a-way
Look a-way Dixie Land.

In Dixie Land where I was born in,
Early on one frosty mornin'
Look a-way, look a-way,
Look a-way Dixie Land.

Then I wish I was in Dixie,
Hooray, hooray,
In Dixie Land I'll take my stand
To live and die in Dixie
Away, away
Away down South in Dixie.

The Union soldiers sang their own versions of "Dixie":

Then I wish I was in Dixie,
Hooray, hooray,
In Dixie Land I'll take my stand,
To flog Jeff Davis and his band,
Away, away
Away down South in Dixie.

The great song of the Confederacy was probably this appeal for Maryland to secede from the Union. The lyric was sung to the tune of "Tannebaum," and though Maryland stayed with the Union, the song became an inspiration to the South.

MARYLAND, MY MARYLAND

The despot's heel is on thy shore,
Maryland, my Maryland!
His torch is at thy temple door,
Maryland, my Maryland!
Avenge the patriotic gore
That flecked the streets of Baltimore,
And be the battle queen of yore,
Maryland, my Maryland!

The War Between the States came at a time in American history when sentiment was more openly expressed than it is today. Songs appealed to the emotions, and it was quite common for people to cry when listening to a sad tune. The Civil War had more than its share of "tear-jerkers." Here is one which became very popular in the North:

BROTHER GREEN

Oh, brother Green, do come to me,
For I am shot and bleeding,
And I must die, no more to see,
My wife and my dear children.

My little babes, I love them well,
Oh could I once more see them,
That I might give a long farewell
And meet them all in Heaven.

Many songs were written about Abe Lincoln, but none was great enough to survive the years. The great poems written by Walt Whitman, "O Captain! My Captain!" and "When Lilacs Last in the Dooryard Bloom'd" were never successfully put to music.

Here is a brief example of the kind of doggerel sung in honor of the Commander-in-chief:

Old Abe Lincoln came out of the wilderness,
Out of the wilderness, out of the wilderness.
Old Abe Lincoln came out of the wilderness,
Many long years ago.

We all know "When Johnny Comes Marching Home" as a song of many wars. Few people realize that it was created to express the country's hope for an end to the Civil War.

When Johnny comes marching home again,
Hurrah, hurrah!
We'll give him a hearty welcome then,
Hurrah, hurrah!
The men will cheer, the boys will shout,
The ladies, they will all turn out,
And we'll all feel gay when Johnny comes marching home.

The old church bell will peal with joy,
Hurrah, hurrah!
To welcome home our darling boy,
Hurrah, hurrah!
The village lads and lassies say,
With roses they will strew the way,
And we'll all feel gay when Johnny comes marching home.

Get ready for the Jubilee,
Hurrah, hurrah!
We'll give the hero three times three,
Hurrah, hurrah!
The laurel wreath is ready now
To place upon his loyal brow,
And we'll all feel gay when Johnny comes marching home.

The war came to an end, and the victorious Northerners, in the words of Abraham Lincoln, set out to "bind the Nation's wounds." Lincoln himself became a casualty of the war, assassinated by a second-rate actor, John

Wilkes Booth. This had been a war to split families down the middle, to separate brother from brother. The song that follows shows the grief for one family when "one came home, one stayed behind."

TWO BROTHERS

Two brothers on their way,
Two brothers on their way,
Two brothers on their way,
One wore blue and one wore gray,
One wore blue and one wore gray;
As they marched along their way,
A fife and drum began to play,
There on a beautiful morning.

One was gentle, one was kind,
One was gentle, one was kind,
One came home, one stayed behind;
A cannon ball don't pay no mind,
A cannon ball don't pay no mind,
Though you're gentle or you're kind,
It don't think of the folks behind,
There on a beautiful morning.

Two girls waitin' by the railroad track,
Two girls waitin' by the railroad track,
For their darlin's to come back;
One wore blue and one wore black,
One wore blue and one wore black,
Waitin' by the railroad track,
For their darlin's to come back,
There on a beautiful morning.

WARS AND RUMORS OF WARS

THE WAR BETWEEN THE STATES marked the last clash of armies on the United States mainland. Since that time we have fought two World Wars and several conflicts called "police actions." The actions against Spain, the Philippines, and Mexico were all more rumors than wars.

Wars fought for no good reason seldom produce songs of merit. In Havana Harbor, February 15, 1898, 260 sailors and officers lost their lives when America's greatest battleship, *Maine*, exploded in a white, hot sheet of flame. Although it was doubtful that the Spanish had anything to do with the tragedy, the United States declared war. Admiral Dewey went into action against the Spanish fleet in Manila Bay and literally blew them all to pieces.

As Teddy Roosevelt and his troops sailed toward their destination on San Juan Hill, in Cuba, they had two popular songs to sing. The first came from a green paradise in the Pacific, Hawaii. It was written by the last of the Hawaiian queens, Liliuokalani, who even as an old woman was as exotic as the orchids in her hair. The title of the song, "Aloha Oe," is both a greeting and a farewell, hello and goodbye.

ALOHA OE

Aloha Oe
Farewell to thee,
Thou charming one who dwells among the bowers
One fond embrace,
Before I now depart,
Until we meet again.

The second most popular war song of this period was "There'll Be A Hot Time In The Old Town Tonight," written in 1896 by professional composers. It, of course, has more to do with carousing than soldiering.

As the Gay Nineties drew to a close, Americans were singing some popular songs, which have become almost folk songs by adoption: "When You Were Sweet Sixteen," "The Rosary," and others. Popular songs like these were sung during the little war with the Philippines. As the American foot soldier fought mosquitoes, dysentery and disillusionment while ending the Philippine rebellion, he sang this humorous ditty:

FILIPINO HOMBRE

There once was a Filipino hombre,
Who ate rice, pescado y legumbre;
His trousers were wide, and his shirt hung outside,
And this, I may say, was costumbre!

We lost much prestige as a nation by engaging in the action against Mexico, in which she lost over half her territory to the United States. Still, this war did not change our respect for the Mexican leader, Benito Juarez, a pure-blooded Indian. He has entered into our own folk legends; and always, we link his name with our own great liberator, Abe Lincoln. Our relationship with Mexico deteriorated further during the pursuit of Pancho Villa back and forth across the border in the early part of this century.

The Mexican conflicts produced a number of song parodies, none of which had sufficient merit to survive. In the following stanzas the volunteers who brought Mexico to her knees confessed their real reasons for fighting:

WE'RE THE BOYS FOR MEXICO

The Mexicans are doomed to fall,
God has in wrath forsook 'em
And all their goods and chattels call
On us to go and hook 'em.

We're the boys for Mexico
Sing Yankee Doodle Dandy,
Gold and silver images
Plentiful and handy.

THE DOUGHBOY

MANY OF THE SONGS of World War I came from Tin Pan Alley; from the commercial machine at its best. Moved by a true sense of patriotism, George M. Cohan went to work for the benefit of American morale. After trying in vain to pass the Army physical examination, he used his talent to write a call to battle. Its chorus will always be remembered:

OVER THERE

Over there, over there,
Send the word, send the word, over there,
That the Yanks are coming, the Yanks are coming,
The drums rum-tumming everywhere.
So prepare, say a pray'r,
Send the word, send the word to beware,
We'll be over, we're coming over,
And we won't come back till it's over over there.

The song-writing team George and Williams wrote a nostalgic piece that was sung both here and abroad:

IT'S A LONG, LONG WAY TO TIPPERARY

It's a long way to Tipperary
It's a long way to go;
It's a long way to Tipperary,
To the sweetest girl I know!
Goodbye Piccadilly,
Farewell, Leicester Square,
It's a long, long way to Tipperary,
But my heart's right there!

Probably Tin Pan Alley will never again achieve the heights of 1914. Among hundreds of great hit songs, we will always remember "K-K-K-Katy,"

"Ja-Da, Ja-Da, Jing, Jing, Jing," "Pack Up Your Troubles in Your Old Kit Bag and Smile, Smile, Smile," "Till We Meet Again" and "There's A Long, Long Trail A-winding."

However, the doughboys were not entirely dependent on manufactured tunes. Many of their best marching songs evolved in the true folk tradition. Every man, at some time or another, has heard this song or one of its parodies:

MADEMOISELLE FROM ARMENTIERES

Mademoiselle from Armentieres, parlay-vous
Mademoiselle from Armentieres, parlay-vous
Mademoiselle from Armentieres,
She hadn't been kissed in forty years,
Hinky dinky parlay-vous

She might have been old for all we knew,
When Napoleon flopped at Waterloo.

The medical corps they held the line,
With pinky pills and iodine.

The officers get all the steak,
And all we get is the bellyache.

The general got the croix-de-guerre,
And the son-of-a-gun was never there.

'Twas a heck of a war as we recall,
But still it was better than none at all.

And as always, in a hundred songs the buck private lamented his fate. This is one of the best known:

YOU'RE IN THE ARMY NOW

You're in the Army now,
You're not behind a plow;
You'll never get rich
    by digging a ditch,
You're in the Army now.

THE GI's

BY WORLD WAR II the official Marine Corps song, and perhaps the most celebrated of all service songs, came into its own. This song dates back to 1805 when the Marine Corps flag bore the inscription "To the Shores of Tripoli." It has been changed through the years, and reached its present form in 1942:

THE MARINES' HYMN

From the Halls of Montezuma
To the shores of Tripoli
We fight our country's battles
In the air, on land and sea.
First to fight for right and freedom
And to keep our honor clean
We are proud to claim the title
Of United States Marine.

In World War II the Army, for the first time, tried to create marching songs. When soldiers were inducted, they were handed song-sheets hot from the presses. But soldiers are notoriously stubborn about what they will, or will not, sing. The "GI" threw away the prepared stuff and fell back on popular favorites: this, for instance, dating from the Civil War:

110

I'VE BEEN WORKING ON THE RAILROAD

I've been working on the railroad
All the live long day
I've been working on the railroad
To pass the time away.

Don't you hear the whistle blowin'
Rise up so early in the morn
Don't you hear the captain shouting
Dinah blow your horn.

Dinah, won't you blow,
Dinah, won't you blow
Dinah won't you blow your horn?
Dinah won't you blow your horn?

Someone's in the kitchen with Dinah
Someone's in the kitchen I know-o-o-o
Someone's in the kitchen with Dinah
Strummin' on the old ban-jo
Fee fie fiddle-ee-i-o
Fee fie fiddle-i-o-o-o-o
Fee fie fiddle-ee-i-o
Strummin' on the old banjo.

The Negro drill sergeants introduced call and response as they shouted commands mixed with bitter truth:

> *You had a good home and you left*
> *You're right*
> *Jody was there when you left*
> *You're right*
> *Jody got your gal and gone*
> *You're right*
> *And left you here singing this song*
> *You're right*
> *Sound off*
> *One, two*
> *Sound off*
> *One, two*
> *One, two, three, four*
> *One, two*
> *. . . . . . three, four*

The dominant mood of the citizen-soldier is always complete disgust with the military machine, and a longing for home. This was the GI's adaptation of a popular song:

GEE, BUT I WANT TO GO HOME

> *The coffee that they give us,*
> *They say is might fine,*
> *It's good for cuts and bruises*
> *And it tastes like iodine.*
>
> *I don't want no more of army life,*
> *Gee, but I want to go*
> *Gee, but I want to go home.*
>
> *The biscuits that they give us,*
> *They say are mighty fine,*
> *One fell off a table,*
> *And killed a pal of mine.*

112

The clothes that they give us,
They say are good for France,
Both me and my buddy
Can fit into the pants.

The men in the ranks took great delight in deriding their officers:

There's a troopship that's leaving Bombay,
There's a troopship that's leaving today,
We're down in the scuppers eating cold suppers,
While the Wacs and the officers play.

So bless 'em all, bless 'em all,
The long and the short and the tall,
There's no icecream and cookies, for flat-footed rookies,
So cheer up, my boys, bless 'em all.

Their refreshing irreverance produced this parody used as a marching song:

Be kind to your web-footed friends,
For a duck may be somebody's mother.
Be kind to your friends in the swamp,
Where the weather is cold and damp . . .

Now you may think that this is the end – –
Well, it is

The GI sang many ballads while in the field, including "Roger Young," **"Lili Marlene,"** and the tunes composed by Private Cecil Gant. But generally, the World War II foot-soldier was not as sentimental as his predecessors. Perhaps, that was because the soldiers were younger.

TODAY AND TOMORROW'S
SOLDIER

THE TEENAGE SOLDIERS of Korea and Viet Nam possess a sophistication unknown in earlier conflicts. They do not gripe about the simple discomforts that usually bother soldiers. Their beefs are concerned with philosophy of war, itself—its effectiveness as an instrument of national policy. Of course, the young are very serious behind their laughter, but we must take into account the fact that our modern youngsters are better educated than past generations. Also, the objectives of wars are no longer simply to win. Now, we speak of "balance of power," "containment" and other concepts that have taken the place of victory. It is difficult to sing of these things.

Songs such as the "Ballad of the Green Berets" have not proved themselves the choices of the men in the field—even if they have hit the top of the recording charts at home. The man in Viet Nam is more likely to listen to rock n' roll on his radio than to gather for a "sing" in the rec. hall. He hums the songs of the latest movie musical, and is now more likely to see the big stars in person than when at home.

It is possible that superior electronic communications will in the future make it possible for the soldier to carry the cultural homefront with him wherever he goes; and except for a few parodies of pop songs, he will have no need to create.

CHAPTER SIX

OCEANS, LAKES, RIVERS AND STREAMS

GOODBYE TO THE BIG SEA

AMERICA WAS FIRST settled along its Eastern seaboard because that is where the sailing ships from Europe landed. The first colonists had raised their settlements on fair harbors, if such were available; not only to keep a sentimental eye on the big sea that connected them with the homeland, but because they depended on supplies brought from the old countries. As they became more self-sufficient, they moved farther and farther inland.

But before they said goodbye to the sea, their *chantys,* working songs of the sailors, had become an exciting part of our musical background. These songs were created to help the sailors work together on jobs which no single man could do alone. The chantyman, or lead singer, would execute the verse, and on the chorus, the crew would all sing and pull together.

The men who sailed the great square-rigged ships of the Black Ball Line sang this song as they hoisted the mainsail; over the years *main* was shortened to *man:*

BLOW THE MAN DOWN

Come all ye young fellows that follow the sea,
To my yeo, ho! blow the man down.
And pray pay attention and listen to me.
Oh, give me some time to blow the man down!

'Tis when a Black Baller's preparin' for sea,
To my yeo, ho! blow the man down.
You'd split your sides laughing at the sights you see.
Oh, give me some time to blow the man down!

'Tis when a Black Baller is clear of the land,
To my yeo, ho! blow the man down.
Our boatswain then gives us the word of command.
Oh, give me some time to blow the man down!

'Tis when a Black Baller comes down to her dock,
To my yeo, ho! blow the man down.
The lads and the lasses to the pierhead do flock.
Oh, give me some time to blow the man down.

Although the chanty was originally from Great Britain, it has been made into hauntingly beautiful ballads by Americans. This song began its life in the long hours between watches and spread all across America. Its title, "Shenandoah," is explained differently in every locality. In Virginia, where there is a river of the same name, people say that it comes from an Indian word meaning "daughter of the stars." Out West it is said that Shenandoah was an Indian chief whose daughter fell in love with a white trapper. From the reference to the "wide Missouri," the song probably grew out of a story told by a passing frontiersman.

Oh, Shenandoah, I long to see you,
A-way, you rolling river!
Oh, Shenandoah, I long to see you,
A-way, we're bound a-way,
'Cross the wide Missouri!

Oh, Shenandoah, I love your daughter,
  A-way, you rolling river!
For her I'd cross the rolling water,
  A-way, we're bound a-way,
    'Cross the wide Missouri!

Farewell, my love, I'm bound to leave you,
  A-way, you rolling river!
Oh, Shenandoah, I'll not deceive you,
  A-way, we're bound a-way,
    'Cross the wide Missouri!

CLIPPER SHIPS

EARLY IN OUR HISTORY American shipbuilders all along the Atlantic coast began to turn out a vessel unlike any other in the history of the world. These vessels were slim, low and rakish squareriggers, designed to outsail and out-maneuver anything else on the sea. They were like gigantic canoes, topped with more canvas than was safe to carry. They were known as *clipper ships*.

In these ships American sailors captured the trade of the world, and for a hundred years they outsped all their foreign rivals on all the oceans and seas. The men who launched the clippers were moved by the beauty of their creations; they named them with love: *Wild Pigeon, Syren, Sea Serpent, Witch of the Waves, Shooting Star, White Squall, Staghound.*

This beautiful capstan chanty was used by the crew as they turned the windlass that raised the anchor:

SANTY ANNO

We're sailing down the river from Liverpool,
Heave away, Santy Anno!
Around Cape Horn to Frisco Bay,
All on the plains of Mexico.

120

She's a fast clipper ship and a bully good crew,
Heave away, Santy Anno!
A down-east Yankee for her captain, too.
All on the plains of Mexico.

There's plenty of gold, so I've been told,
Heave away, Santy Anno!
There's plenty of gold so I've been told,
'Way out in Califor-ni-o.

Back in the days of Forty-Nine,
Heave away, Santy Anno!
Those were the days of the good old times,
All on the plains of Mexico.

Santy Anno was a good old man,
Heave away, Santy Anno!
Till he got into war with your Uncle Sam,
All on the plains of Mexico.

The clippers had their long day as the greyhounds of the sea; but that day had to end. Progress, in the form of the steamship, did what nothing under sail could have done—it drove them out of existence.

THE ERIE CANAL

AS THE COUNTRY expanded to the West, it became apparent that a canal would be needed to link Albany and Buffalo, the port at the head of the Great Lakes. That meant people could go from the Hudson River all the way to the lake ports in the Middle West and never set foot on dry land.

People laughed at the Erie Canal, that narrow, man-made ditch, in a song that related the story of an impossible storm;

THE E-RI-E

We were forty miles from Albany,
Forget it, I never shall,
What a terrible storm we had one night
On the E-RI-E Canal.

O the E-RI-E was a-risin'
And the gin was a-gittin' low,
And I scarcely think we'll git a drink
Till we get to Buffa-lo-o-o,
Till we get to Buffalo.

Two days out from Syracuse
The vessel struck a shoal
And we like to all be'en foundered
On a chunk o'Lackawanna coal.

We hollered to the captain
On the towpath, treadin' dirt
He jumped on board and stopped the leak
With his old red flannel shirt.

The cook she was a kind old soul,
She had a ragged dress,
We heisted her upon a pole
As a signal of distress.

The winds begin to whistle
And the waves begin to roll
And we had to reef our royals
On the raging Canawl.

When we got to Syracuse,
The off-mule he was dead,
The nigh mule got blind staggers
And we cracked him on the head.

The captain, he got married,
The cook, she went to jail,
And I'm the only son-of-a-gun
That's left to tell the tale.

THAR SHE BLOWS

THE YANKEES SENT whaling ships into the North Sea, and it was often three years before the sailors would again see their homes. Small boats, carrying oarsmen and a harpooner, did the actual pursuing and killing of the ocean's largest creatures. The men at the oars would sing:

And when this whale we did harpoon
He gave one splash with his tail
And he upset the boat, we lost five of our crew,
Neither did we catch that whale, my boys,
Neither did we catch that whale.

FLATBOATS AND RAFTS

CARGO WAS OFTEN floated down the rivers and streams on flatboats and rafts. The crews carried long poles to push away from the banks and clear the sandbars. They sang as they planted the poles in the river bottom and literally walked the boat on its way.

PUSH BOAT

Working on a push boat
For fifty cents a day;
Buy my girl a brand-new dress
And throw the rest away.

Pushing might hard, boys,
Sandbar's in the way;
Working like a son-of-a-gun
For mighty scanty pay

124

THE GREAT LAKES

THE LAKE SAILORS were mostly former salt-water men, and they brought to the fresh-water ships all the old chantys. Lyrics were altered to fit the new location:

RED IRON ORE

Come all ye bold sailors that follow the Lakes
On an iron ore vessel your living to make.
I shipped in Chicago, bid adeiu to the shore,
Bound away to Escanaba for red iron ore

Derry down, derry down, derry down.

PADDLEWHEELERS

ALONG THE MISSISSIPPI RIVER, one of the crew would throw a line overboard to measure the depth of the water. The muddy river bottom was constantly changing its shape, and the boats were in danger of getting stuck on a mud bank or sand spit. The man detailed to this important job used a length of twine with a lead weight tied to one end. He determined the river's depth by the markings placed at intervals along the twine. Markings and twine soon became *Mark Twain*.

The *lead man* made a song out of his job as he "sounded" the bottom and called back his findings to the river pilot in the wheelhouse:

MARK TWAIN

Mark Twain, Mark Twain . . .
One quarter off the starboard.

I like to work
For the Lee Line Trade
Walk and talk
Wit' the chambermaid.

Mark Twain, Mark Twain . . .
Three quarters off the starboard side.

I got a gal
Way back home
Comb her hair
Wit' a codfish bone.

The chantys that have survived through countless years of struggle to master all the oceans, seas and inland waterways of the world, have lasted far beyond their use as work songs. Somehow, the long, lonely times under the starry skies of unknown waters have brought out the natural poetry in the heart of the sailor. His earliest songs are still current, and tunes such as "Haul Away, Joe," "What Shall We Do With A Drunken Sailor," and "Fifteen Men On A Dead Man's Chest," to name some of the saltiest, and "Song of the Fishes," "The Lowlands, Low," "The Golden Vanity," and, of course, "Shenandoah," to name some of the most lyrical, are still sung on steamships and in modern navies.

CHAPTER SEVEN

MOVING
WEST

HOMESTEADERS

EVEN DURING THE CIVIL WAR, the government encouraged westward expansion. One hundred and sixty acres could be claimed, *free* by any citizen intending to homestead.

There is a song from Greer County in Oklahoma which expresses the general feelings of those who took advantage of the government's offer.

GREER COUNTY

Tom Hight is my name; an old bachelor I am;
You'll find me out West in the country of fame;
You'll find me out West on an elegant plain
And starving to death on my government claim.

Hurrah for Greer County, the land of the free,
The land of the bedbug, grasshopper, and flea!
I'll sing of its praises and tell of its fame,
While starving to death on my government claim.

130

Often these homesteaders built out of damp clay, or sod:

My house is built of natural sod;
Its walls are erected according to hod;
Its roof has no pitch but is level and plain;
I am always getting wet if it happens to rain.

HOSTILE INDIANS

DESPITE HARDSHIPS, the settlement of the West was an explosion of people, and it still continues today. One great danger of frontier travel, or settlement, was the presence of hostile Indians.

These verses detailing an attack on a wagon train come from a ballad popular at the time.

SIOUX INDIANS

We heard of Sioux Indians out on the plains,
A-killing poor drivers and burning their trains,
A-killing poor drivers with arrows and bow.
When you're captured by Indians, no mercy they show.

They made a bold dash and came near to our train,
And the arrows fell round us like hail and like rain;
But with our large rifles we fed them hot lead,
Till many a brave warrior around us lay dead.

We hitched up our horses and started our train,
Three more bloody battles while crossing the plains;
And in our last battle three of our boys fell,
And we left them to rest there in the green, shady dell.

The Indians of the Great Western Plains fought well, but the destruction of the buffalo, on which they depended for food, was their downfall.

BUFFALO HUNTERS AND SKINNERS

MILLIONS OF BUFFALO were destroyed; their bodies literally dotted the plains. Buffalo Bill played a part in this slaughter of the American bison, but he at least killed to feed the railroad crews; some, including a number of noblemen from Europe, killed just for sport.

The skinners sold the hides in the East, where they were made into coats and rugs. Years later, the bleached bones were gathered up for fertilizer. And now, except for a few government-protected herds, the buffalo is gone.

BUFFALO SKINNERS

Come, all you jolly buffalo skinners, and listen to my song,
And do not go outrageous, for the length it won't be long.
'Twas all in the spring of 'eighty-three, I happened in Jacksboro;
There I met with a fellow called Ira Crago by name.

It's "How do you do, young fellow, and how would you like to go
And spend one summer pleasantly among the buffalo?
If you will stay one summer through, then return to Jacksboro,
I'll pay all transportation from the range of the buffalo."

It's now our pleasures are over, our troubles have begun;
But with many six and buffalo guns, we thought our troubles fun.
Our lives they were in danger, but this we did all know,
For the Indians watched to scalp us, while skinning the buffalo.

It's now we're 'cross the Wichita, and homeward we are bound;
And in this God-forsaken country, I'll never more be found.
We'll go back to our wives and sweethearts, to tell others not to go
To that God-forsaken country among the buffalo.

THE FORTY-NINERS

WHEN GOLD WAS DISCOVERED in the California hills, the news rocked America. People set out for the gold fields in every conceivable contraption—covered wagons, carriages, horses, and even a hearse or two. The wealthy went by sea, which meant a long trip around Cape Horn to the West coast.

Rarely in history have so many diverse people set out for the same objective. Some, of course, struck it rich, but the majority suffered the long trip and found no gold. Many died along the way. Still, they were a rollicking, good-natured group. Even in the midst of the worst deprivation and misery, their songs attempted to be ridiculously funny.

The sweetheart of the forty-niners was always "Betsy":

SWEET BETSY FROM PIKE

Oh, don't you remember sweet Betsy from Pike,
Who crossed the big mountains with her lover Ike,
With two yoke of oxen, a large yaller dog,
A tall Shanghai rooster and one spotted hog?

One evening quite early they camped on the Platte,
"I was near by the road on a green shady flat,
Where Betsy, sore-footed, lay down to repose—
With wonder Ike gazed on that Pike County rose.

The Shanghai ran off, and their cattle all died;
That morning the last piece of bacon was fried;
Poor Ike was discouraged and Betsy got mad,
The dog drooped his tail and looked wondrously sad.

They soon reached the desert where Betsy gave out,
And down in the sand she lay rolling about;
While Ike, half distracted, looked on with surprise,
Saying, "Betsy, get up, you'll get sand in your eyes."

There were very few women in the mining camps. Perhaps, that is why in their songs the forty-niners kept away from love. "Clementine" was not exactly the girl of anyone's dreams.

OH MY DARLING CLEMENTINE

In a cavern, in a canon,
Excavating for a mine,
Dwelt a miner, forty-niner,
And his daughter Clementine.

Oh my darling, oh my darling,
Oh my darling Clementine,
You are lost and gone forever,
Dreadful sorry, Clementine.

Light she was, and like a fairy,
And her shoes were number nine,
Herring boxes, without topses,
Sandals were for Clementine.

Drove she ducklings to the water,
Ev'ry morning just at nine,
Hit her foot against a splinter
Fell into the foaming brine.

Ruby lips above the water,
Blowing bubbles soft and fine,
Alas, for me! I was no swimmer,
So I lost my Clementine.

The Gold Rush did not make everybody wealthy, but it did help to give us a coast-to-coast nation. And now, the far-western cities were developed enough to make the building of a transcontinental railroad a necessity.

STEEL TRACKS AND
IRON HORSES

THE WESTERN RAILROADS were built by Negroes, Chinese, Slavs and other ethnic groups in America. However, the railroad songs peculiar to the East and West are predominantly Irish. The great potato famine in Ireland had driven thousands of the sons of Erin to America. A majority ended up as laborers in the West.

The most popular railroad song of the day was:

PADDY WORKS ON THE ERIE

In eighteen hundred and forty-one,
I put me cord'roy breeches on,
I put me cord'roy breeches on
To work upon the railway.

In eighteen hundred and forty-two
I left the ould world for the new,
Bad cess to the luck that brought me through
To work upon the railroad.

The song plainly shows that "Paddy" found no bed of roses at his new job:

Our boss's name, it was Tom King,
He kept a store to rob the men,
A Yankee clerk with ink and pen,
To cheat Pat on the railroad.

It's "Pat do this" and "Pat do that,"
Without a stocking or cravat,
And nothing but an old straw hat
While Pat works on the railroad.

TIMBER

THE RAILROADS OPENED the country to the lumberjack, who called himself
a "shanty boy" because he lived in a temporary shanty in the woods. It has
been said that these men in a hundred years have cut a three-thousand mile
stretch of timber from Maine to the state of Washington.

They sang of their work and the disasters that happened on the job.

THE JAM ON GERRY'S ROCK

Come all you jolly fellows, wherever you may be,
I hope you'll pay attention and listen to me,
It's all about some shanty boys, so manly and so
   brave,
'Twas on the jam on Gerry's Rock they met their
   watery grave.

The song relates how six of the boys and the young foreman, Monroe,
volunteered to break the jam. Then tragedy:

They had not rolled off many logs before the
   boss did say,
"I would you all be on your guard, for the jam
   will soon give way."
He had no more than spoke these words when

136

the jam did break and go,
And carried away those six brave youths with
their foreman, young Monroe.

There is the familiar sentimental ending dating back to the old English folk ballad:

Come all of you brave young shanty-boys,
I'd have you call and see
Two green graves by the riverside where grows
the hemlock tree;
The shanty-boys cut off the wood where lay
those lovers low—
(Spoken:) 'Tis handsome Clara Clark and her true love,
brave Monroe.

The railroad era began in earnest just after the construction of the canals. And as early as the 1850s Yankee country along the Eastern seaboard was a network of rails; 8,000 miles of rails crisscrossed our land. One of the most performed songs in the theaters was:

DRILL, YE TARRIERS, DRILL

Well, every morning at seven o'clock,
There were twenty tarriers working at the rock,
And the boss comes around and he says "Keep still!
And come down heavy on the cast iron drill."

And drill, ye tarriers, drill!
And drill, ye tarriers, drill!
For it's work all day for the sugar in your tay,
Down behind the railray,
And drill, ye tarriers, drill.
And blast, and fire.

The desire of every boy in these times was to be an engineer in command of one of the great locomotives named after one of the Greek gods.

137

There was always a brass plate with Apollo, Mercury or some other glamorous inscription. And every boy had heard about the most famous engineer of them all, Casey Jones. Casey started working for the railroad at the age of fifteen, at eighteen he was firing the cabs. By the time he was twenty-six he was in command of a locomotive. Here is his tragic tale:

CASEY JONES

Now listen all you rounders, I want you to hear
The true story of a brave engineer.
Casey Jones was the rounder's name
On a six-eight wheeler, he won his fame.
The caller called Casey a half past four,
Kissed his wife goodbye at the door
Mounted the cabin with his orders in hand
Took his farewell trip to the promised land.

Casey must have had the power of prophecy, for he read all the signs correctly:

He looked at his watch and his watch was slow,
He looked at the water and the water was low,
He turned to his fireman and then he said,
"We're gonna reach Frisco but we'll all be dead!"

Just after he pulled up at Reno Hill the crash occurred:

The switchman knew by the engine's moan
That the man at the throttle was Casey Jones.
He pulled up within two miles of the place,
And Number Four was staring him in the face.

The actual accident happened at Vaughn, Mississippi. Sim Webb, his Negro fireman, warned Casey to jump, before saving his own life. But in the way of ballads, times, places and events are flexible; some songs place the scene out west, others in the east. And most versions give Casey the

138

credit for warning his fireman. But in any case, Casey lived up to the traditions of a captain. He died with his overland "ship."

> *Now the fireman jumped, but Casey stayed on,*
> *He was a brave engineer, but he's dead and gone!*

The legends of the early railroads closely paralleled those of ships at sea. There were ghost trains, hard-driving, relentless engineers, and now and again, romance flowered at either end of the long run.

Perhaps our greatest work legend is built around a black railroad laborer. In his fight against a machine he becomes an almost sacred symbol of man's courage in the face of impossible odds:

BALLAD OF JOHN HENRY

> *When John Henry was jest a little baby*
> *A-sittin' on his mama's knee,*
> *He picked up a hammer, a little piece of steel,*
> *Said, "hammer's gonna be the death of me, Lawd, Lawd,*
> *Hammer's gonna be the death of me."*

> *Well, the Captain says to John Henry,*
> *Gonna bring me a steam drill 'round*
> *Gonna take that steam drill out on the job,*
> *Gonna whop that steel on down, Lawd, Lawd,*
> *Gonna whop that steel on down.*

> *John Henry told his Captain,*
> *"Well, a man aint nothin' but a man,*
> *An' before I'll let your steam drill beat me down,*
> *I'll die with my hammer in my hand, Lawd, Lawd,*
> *I'll die with my hammer in my hand."*

> *Now the Captain said to John Henry,*
> *"What is that storm I hear."*
> *John Henry said, 'Captain, that ain't no storm,*
> *That's just my hammer in the air, Lawd, Lawd,*
> *Just my hammer in the air."*

Now the man who invented the steam drill,
Thought he was mighty fine,
But John Henry drove his fifteen holes,
While the steam drill made only nine, Lawd, Lawd,
The steam drill made only nine.

Then John Henry told his Captain,
"Looka yonder what I see – –
Your drill's done broke and the hole done choke,
An' you can't drive steel like me, Lawd, Lawd,
You can't drive steel like me."

John Henry was hammerin' on the mountain,
And his hammer was striking fire,
He drove so hard 'till he broke his poor heart,
And he laid down his hammer and he died, Lawd, Lawd,
He laid down his hammer and he died.

Well, they took his body to the White House,
And they buried him in the sand;
And every locomotive come a roarin' by
Says, "There lies a steel drivin' man, Lawd, Lawd,
There lies a steel drivin' man."

The drama of the railroads still touches us all today. In this age of air and space travel every boy still looks under the Christmas tree for his train set. Just as long as that remains true, we will continue to sing of the great days of the railroads, which carried not only passengers but folk music all over the land.

CHAPTER EIGHT

COWHANDS
AND
DOGIES

THE CHISHOLM TRAIL

ONLY TWO YEARS after the Civil War the first trail herds were being driven from Texas to meet the railroad spur at Abilene, Kansas. The routes followed by the cattle drives were to become famous. They had to pass through Indian country, over high mountains and across rivers bordering desert sands.

The most famous of all these trails came to be known as "The Chisholm Trail." It had been named after Jesse Chisholm, half-Scot, half-Indian, the man who blazed it.

THE OLD CHISHOLM TRAIL

Come along, boys, and listen to my tale,
I'll tell you of my troubles on the old Chisholm trail.

Coma ti yi youpy, youpy yea, youpy yea,
Coma ti yi youpy, youpy yea.

I started up the trail October twenty-third,
I started up the trail with the 2-U herd.

144

Oh, a ten-dollar hoss and a forty-dollar saddle,
And I'm goin' to punchin' Texas cattle.

I woke up one morning on the old Chisholm trail,
Rope in my hand and a cow by the tail.

The song goes on to describe every experience that a cowhand could possibly have along the trail; and then we get the details of his everyday life:

No chaps, no slicker, and it's pouring down rain,
And I swear, by God, I'll never night-herd again.

And finally the delivery of the herd at the railhead:

We rounded 'em up and put 'em on the cars,
And that was the last of the old Two Bars.

THE RANGE COULD BE FRIENDLY

THE COWHAND, or cow puncher, as he came to be called, was like the sailor, sentimental about his life. This is a song for the evening campfire:

HOME ON THE RANGE

O give me a home, where the buffalo roam,
Where the deer and the antelope play,
Where seldom is heard a discouraging word,
And the skies are not cloudy all day.

Home, home on the range
Where the deer and the antelope play,
Where seldom is heard a discouraging word,
And the skies are not cloudy all day.

AND NOT SO FRIENDLY

THE PRAIRIE COULD be unfriendly, too. For a sad campfire one might hear:

BURY ME NOT ON THE LONE PRAIRIE

"O bury me not on the lone prairie,"
These words came low and mournfully
From the pallid lips of a youth who lay
On his dying bed at the close of day.

"O bury me not on the lone prairie,
Where the wild coyote will howl o'er me.
In a narrow grave just six by three,
O bury me not on the lone prairie.

And saddest of all:

Yes, we buried him there on the lone prairie,
Where the owl all night hoots mournfully,
And the blizzard beats and the wind blows free
O'er his lonely grave in the lone prairie.

SONGS OF THE SADDLE

THE COWHAND DID what all drovers do to forget long hours ahead in the saddle—he sang in the wind, rain and dust. While passing through freezing mountain passes, or traversing the burning sands that had never known rain, he kept time by idly swinging his rope, one leg over the pommel of his saddle.

GIT ALONG LITTLE DOGIES

As I was walking one morning for pleasure
I spied a cow-puncher come ridin' along;

His hat was throwed back and his spurs were a-jinglin',
As he approached me a-singing this song:

Whoop-ee ti yi yo, git along little dogies,
It's your misfortune and none of my own;
Whoop-ee ti yi yo, git along little dogies,
For you know Wyoming will be your new home.

Early in the springtime we'll round up the dogies,
Slap on their brands and bob off their tails;
Round up our horses, load up the chuck wagon,
Then throw those dogies up on the trail.

Oh, you'll be soup for Uncle Sam's Injuns;
"It's beef, heap beef," I hear them cry.
Git along, git along, git along, little dogies,
You're going to be beef steers by and by.

At night the tired cowhand might be selected to guard the resting, but nervous herd. He would droop in the saddle and let his horse walk quietly, so he wouldn't "spook" the longhorns. When they stirred, or became restless, he would sing to calm them down:

NIGHT HERDING SONG

Oh, slow up, dogies, quit moving around,
You have wandered and trampled all over the ground;
Oh, graze along, dogies, and feed kinda slow,
And don't forever be on the go.
Move slow, little dogies, move slow.
Hi-o, hi-o, hi-o.

Oh, say, little dogies, when you goin' to lay down,
And give up this siftin' and roving around?
My horse is leg-weary and I'm awful tired,
But if you get away, I am sure to be fired;
Lay down, little dogies, lay down.
Hi-o, hi-o, hi-o.

147

Oh, lay still, dogies, since you have laid down,
Stretch away out on the big open ground;
Snore loud, little dogies, and drown out the wild sound
That'll go away when the day rolls around,
Lay still, little dogies, lay still.
Hi-o, hi-o, hi-o.

FOUR-LEGGED OUTLAW

A COW PONY was one of the *remuda*, or string of horses, on a cattle drive. The cowhand would need a fresh mount, sometimes two or three times a day. These were really wild mustangs, caught and broken to the saddle; and ready to revert to the wild state at a moment's notice.

The cowhand became deeply attached to individual mounts, especially those with spirit. He composed songs to celebrate the unbreakable broncos.

THE STRAWBERRY ROAN

I was hanging 'round town just a-spending my time,
Nothing else to spend, not even a dime,
When a feller steps up and he says, "I suppose
You're a bronc-bustin' man by the looks of your clothes."
"You guessed me right, and a good one," I claim.
"Do you happen to have any bad ones to tame?"
He says, "I've got one and a bad one to buck;
At throwin' bronc riders he's had lots of luck."

Well, its Oh, that strawberry roan,
Oh, that strawberry roan!
He says, "This old pony ain't never been rode,
And the boy that gets on him is sure to get throwed."
Oh, that strawberry roan!

I gets all excited and I ask what he pays
To ride this old goat for a couple of days.
He offers a ten spot. I says, "I'm your man,
For the bronc never lived that I couldn't fan;
No, the bronc never lived, nor he never drew breath

148

That I couldn't ride 'till he starved plum to death."
He says, "Get your saddle, I'll give you a chance."
We got in the buckboard and rode to the ranch.

Well, down in the horse corral standing alone
Was that old cavayo, old strawberry roan.
His legs were spavined, and he had pigeon toes,
Little pig eyes and a big Roman nose,
Little pin ears that were crimped at the tip,
With a big 44 branded 'cross his left hip;
He's ewe-necked and old, with a long lower jaw,
You can see with one eye he's a reg'lar outlaw.

Well, I put on my spurs and I coils up my twine,
I piled my loop on him, – – I'm sure feeling fine.
I piled my loop on him and well I knew then,
If I rode this old pony, I'd sure earn my ten.
I put the blinds on him, – – it sure was a fight, – –
Next comes my saddle, I screws her down tight;
I gets in his middle and opens the blind,
I'm right in his middle to see him unwind.

He went up towards the east and came down towards the west;
To stay in his middle I'm doin' my best.
He's about the worst bucker I've seen on the range:
He can turn on a nickel and give you some change,
He turns his old belly right up to the sun,
He sure is one sun-fishin' son of a gun!
I'll tell you, no foolin', this pony can step,
But I'm still in his middle and building a rep.

I loses my stirrup and also my hat,
I starts pulling leather, I'm blind as a bat;
With a big forward jump, he goes up on high,
Leaves me sittin' on nothing way up in the sky.
I turns over twice, and I comes back to earth,
I lights in a-cussin' the day of his birth.
I know there is ponies I'm unable to ride;
Some are still livin, they haven't all died.

149

THE SHOOT-OUT

WHEN THE DRIVE was over, and the cattle delivered, it was time for the cowhands to let off steam. They had spent months on the lonely trail, and their pay was burning holes in their pockets. They would sometimes explode with wild, animal joy and squander their wages in a single night. The cow towns hired marshals to keep order, but they could not always control the situation. And the combination of half-drunk Texas boys and guns often led to shooting.

There were rules to be followed in a gunfight. The men involved must face each other with holstered weapons. Then it became a matter of who could draw and shoot fastest.

Many songs were sung about the winners in these matches. And ballads such as "Gunfight at the O.K. Corral" and "The Desperado" take pride in those quick on the trigger:

> *He's a killer and a hater!*
> *He's the great annihilator!*
> *He's a terror of the boundless prairie.*

The most widely sung ballad in the cattle country was written about a cowboy who lost a gunfight:

THE COWBOY'S LAMENT

> *As I walked out in the streets of Laredo,*
> *As I walked out in Laredo one day,*
> *I spied a young cowboy all wrapped in white linen,*
> *Wrapped in white linen as cold as the clay.*
>
> *"I see by your outfit that you are a cowboy,"*
> *These words he did say as I boldly walked by;*
> *"Come set down beside me and hear my sad story,*
> *I'm shot in the breast and I know I must die.*

"It was once in the saddle I used to go dashing,
Once in the saddle I used to go gay;
First down to Rosie's and then to the card-house;
Got shot in the breast and I'm dying today.

"Get sixteen gamblers to carry my coffin,
Let six jolly cowboys come sing me a song,
Take me to the graveyard and lay the sod o'er me,
For I'm a young cowboy and know I've done wrong.

"Oh, beat the drum slowly and play the fife lowly,
Play the dead march as you carry me along;
Put bunches of roses all over my coffin,
Roses to deaden the clods as they fall."

OUTLAWS

LIKE HIS COUSIN, the English highwayman, the Western outlaw was the subject of much poetry and song. However, the western desperado, unlike his English counterpart, did not have to possess a heart of gold hidden under a rough exterior; he could be an unredeemed scoundrel and still become a treasured legend in his own time.

"The Wild Montana Boy," despite some verses according him a higher motive, obviously loved to destroy:

At the age of sixteen Jack left his happy home,
For the sunny shores of Texas he was inclined to roam.
He robbed the rich and as for the poor, their farms he did destroy.
He was a terror to old Texas, this wild Montana boy.

Old Sam Bass was all bad; and he and his companions thought nothing of shooting Rangers:

Sam had four companions, four bold and daring lads,
They were Richardson, Jackson, Joe Collins, and Old Dad;
Four more bold and daring cowboys the rangers never knew;
They whipped the Texas Rangers and ran the boys in blue.

However, the bad men like Jesse James, Billy the Kid, and Quantrell were always cast as "good" bad men. Their stories were changed to fit the Robin Hood pattern. Jesse James, for instance:

Jesse James was a boy that downed many a man,
He held up the Danville train,
He robbed from the rich and he gave to the poor,
He'd a hand and a heart and a brain.

The man who killed Jesse will never be forgiven by the ballad-makers:

Poor Jesse left a wife to mourn all her life
His children three were brave
But the dirty little coward that shot Mr. Howard,
Has laid poor Jesse in his grave.

Billy the Kid was practically crowned:

Fair Mexican maidens play guitars and sing
A song about Billy, their boy bandit king,
How ere his young manhood had reached its sad end
He'd a notch on his pistol for twenty-one men.

Quantrell, who used the Civil War as an excuse to raid, loot and burn, is here exonerated:

Charlie Quantrell-o, Charlie Quantrell-o-o-o,
Bold, gay, and daring stood old Charlie Quantrell-o.
What he taken from the rich, like tops and like best,
He always did divide it with the widow in distress.

HEART OF THE WEST

THE WEST HAS always been at its best when it is most sentimental. Here is a song of the modern West which has the status of a folk ballad. It is every bit as fine as "Home on the Range," which was sung over a hundred years ago . . .

RED RIVER VALLEY

From this valley they say you are going,
We will miss your bright eyes and sweet smile;
For they say you are taking the sunshine
That has brightened our pathways awhile.

Come and sit by my side, if you love me,
Do not hasten to bid me adieu,
Just remember the Red River Valley
And the girl who has loved you so true.

CHAPTER NINE

OF
AFRICAN
DESCENT

A LITTLE WHITE FLOWER

SOME HISTORIANS ARE inclined to blame slavery on the "villain tobacco," claiming that a demand for cheap labor in the tobacco fields of early Virginia made the enslaving of both white and black men profitable.

This is certainly valid, but the great slave trade could never have been built solely around the delicate tobacco plant. It took a hardier plant, one that could be left to the care of resentful, and often rebellious, fingers to make slavery a paying proposition. Cotton.

The black slave who worked the cotton fields under the whip of the overseer dreamed of just one thing: freedom. In every song, in all his humor and folk tales, he expressed his rebellion against the white master, the white society and the little white flower that ruled everything.

Negro song became a secret language telling two stories, one for the ear of the master, the other expressing his real feelings. For example, it was impossible for one man to pick a bale of cotton in a single day. This song expresses the slaves' sarcasm:

158

JUMP DOWN, SPIN AROUND

You got to jump down, spin around
 Pick a bale of cotton,
You got to jump down, spin around
 Pick a bale a day.

There was a skeeter
 Lit on my head,
Blinked his eye,
 An' I killed him dead.

And when the overseer was not paying much attention:

Won't jump down, spin around
 Pick a bale of cotton,
Won't jump down, spin around
 Pick a bale a day.

DISGUISED AS HUMOR

THERE WERE MANY ways of expressing resentment, of wishing bad luck on the old master. Some of these songs even made white people smile.

THE BLUE-TAIL FLY

When I was young, I used to wait
Upon old Master and pass his plate
And fetch the bottle when he got dry,
And brush away The Blue-Tail Fly.

Jimmie Crack Corn, and I don't care,
Jimmie Crack Corn and I don't care,
Jimmie Crack Corn and I don't care,
My Master's gone away.

We went riding one afternoon,
I followed with a hickory broom,
The pony being very shy,
Got bitten by a blue-tail fly.

The pony he did rear and pitch,
He threw old Master in a ditch;
The jury asked the reason why,
The verdict was the blue-tail fly.

So we laid old Master down to rest,
And on a stone this last request:
"Beneath the earth I'm forced to lie,
A victim of the blue-tail fly."

The Jordan River stood for the Mississippi or the Missouri, or whatever river stood between the slaves and the "campground" of freedom.

DEEP RIVER

Deep river,
My home is over Jordan, Lord,
Deep river,
I want to cross over into campground.

BOUND FOR THE PROMISED LAND

On Jordan's stormy banks I stand
And cast a wishful eye,
To Canaan's fair and happy land
Where my possessions lie.

I am bound for the promised land,
I'm bound for the promised land;
O who will come and go with me,
I am bound for the promised land.

"Moses" was the code name for Harriet Tubman, a Negro woman who led many slaves to the free North. When the slaves sang this song, they felt that deliverance was close at hand:

GO DOWN MOSES

When Israel was in Egypt's land
Let my people go
Oppressed so hard they could not stand
Let my people go

Go down, Moses, way down in Egypt land
Tell ol' Pharaoh, let my people go.

When Harriet Tubman led her people into the chilly river waters to throw the dogs of the pursuers off their scent, she made them sing:

WADE IN THE WATER

Jordan's water is chilly and cold,
God's going to trouble the water,
It chills the body but lifts the soul,
God's going to trouble the water.

Wade in the water,
Wade in the water, children.
Wade in the water.

They could tell each other to steal away to a secret meeting, or announce an attempt to escape, and the overseer would be none the wiser:

STEAL AWAY TO JESUS

Steal away, steal away,
Steal away to Jesus!
Steal away, steal away home,
I ain't got long to stay here.

My Lord, He calls me,
He calls me by the thunder,
The trumpet sounds within-a my soul,
I ain't got long to stay here.

Southern whites, sympathetic to the Negro's desire for freedom, formed what was called "the underground railroad." Slaves were smuggled at night from one way station to another. Freedom meant the North, and the slaves were told to follow the star pointed out by the Big Dipper, or "Drinking Gourd."

FOLLOW THE DRINKING GOURD

When the sun come back,
When the first quail call,
Then the time is come—
Follow the drinkin' gourd.
Follow the drinkin' gourd,
Follow the drinkin' gourd;
For the ol' man say,
"Follow the drinkin' gourd."

Sometimes, when a slave had taken more than he could stand, and seemed about to throw his life away by striking back, he could be counseled through song, to hold on, have patience and remember the biblical examples of fortitude.

KEEP YOUR HAND ON THE PLOW

Mary wore three links of chain,
Every link was Jesus name.
Keep your hand on the plow,
Hold on.

Hold on,
Hold on,
Keep your hand on the plow,
Hold on.

Got my hands on the gospel plow,
Wouldn't take nothin' for my journey now,
Keep your hands on the plow,
Hold on.

There is a spiritual that expresses the sadness and despair that a slave felt in his soul:

SOMETIMES I FEEL LIKE
A MOTHERLESS CHILD

Sometimes I feel like a motherless child,
Sometimes I feel like a motherless child,
Sometimes I feel like a motherless child,
A long ways from home, a long ways from home,
O—Lawdy, a long ways from home.

Sometimes I feel like I'm almost gone,
Sometimes I feel like I'm almost gone,
Sometimes I feel like I'm almost gone,
And a long ways from home, a long ways from home,
O—Lawdy, a long ways from home.

163

The Emancipation Proclamation freed the Negroes from slavery, and they created a host of songs to celebrate that great event. One of the best of these not only rejoices in freedom but grieves for the many thousands who died to achieve it:

MANY THOUSAND GONE

No more auction block for me,
No more, no more;
No more auction block for me,
Many thousand gone.

No more peck of corn for me.

No more driver's lash for me.

No more pint of salt for me.

No more hundred lash for me.

No more mistress call for me.

SINGING THE BLUES

THE "BLUES" MEANS black tears, a man in his music voicing all the trials that beset "the troubled in mind." Only when one has been beaten down by life and doesn't have the will to struggle back up, is too old to cry and too young to die, is unsure of land, love, luck and money, and is depressed about everything else is it time to sing the blues.

It started in the deep South sometime before the turn of the century. Some researchers trace the blues through the spirituals—citing such lines as: "Nobody knows the troubles I seen," "Sometimes I feel like a motherless child," "Lookout brother how you walk the cross, foot might slip and your soul get lost," and many others in the same vein. Others see in the blues the call-and-response pattern in vocalizing brought here by the first Negroes from Africa. These are both valid lines of descent.

Certainly, we can trace an actual blues pattern in many of the shouts and chants of the black field hand. These songs are tragic and sad and use what we now recognize as blues chords:

Lawd, Lawd, I been scratchin' at the ground,
Jesus, King Jesus, rise up once mo';
Lawd, Lawd, hear the bossman shoutin',
"Let me hear the ringin' of your hoe."

The Lomaxes collected this work song of the men who use an axe or a pick. The sun on the flashing tools are like a rainbow:

I got a rainbow, tied all around my shoulder,
Ain't gonna rain, ain't gonna rain.
Ev'ry mail day, I gets a letter,
"My son come home, son, come home."
I done walk till, walks till my feets gone to rollin',
Jes' like a wheel, jes' like a wheel.

The men on the chain gangs sang as they worked in the ditches, fields and turpentine camps:

Was early in the mornin', well uh,
When I rise up.
The sun was on his roller, the sun was on his roller,
When I rise up.

And then they worked to the rhythm of songs that were, more often than not, pure wish-fulfillment:

Take this hammer, carry it to the captain,
Take this hammer, carry it to the captain,
Take this hammer, carry it to the captain,
Tell him I'm gone, tell him I'm gone.

If he ask you, was I runnin'?
Tell him I was flyin', tell him I was flyin'.

If he ask you, was I laughin'?
Tell him I was cryin', tell him I was cryin'.

165

I don't want no, cornbread and molasses,
It hurt my pride, it hurt my pride.

Always we have to recognize the great genius of the work song, the man we knew as *"Leadbelly":*

Bring me a little water, Sylvie,
Bring me a little water, now,
Bring me a little water, Sylvie,
Ev'ry li'l' once in awhile.

The genuine blues can be 8, 10, 12 or even 16 bars, but that is today. A purist still insists the only true blues is the standard twelve-bar formula, and that must consist of exactly three four-bar units. However, all blues is rich in imagery and capable of endless variation within a quite rigid form. Also, as is true of all folk expression, there has been so much borrowing back and forth from singer to singer that it is difficult to attribute authorship of specific lines to any one person.

As everyone knows, the blues are never boring, however repetitive in form. Billie Holiday, who sang a lot of deep blues in her day, is reported to have likened it to a flood that "keeps coming on 'till you drown."

The first country blues, it is believed, came from the Mississippi delta country. The songs dealt with real things and had a stark, simple quality. Alan Lomax collected this bitter comment from the old blues. It explains much of the too loud laughter that comes from poor southern shacks:

You don't know, you don't know my mind;
Naw, you don't know, you don't know my mind;
When you see me laughin', I'm laughin' to keep from cryin'.

The blues is not an abstract; it is always near and personal. You can talk to it like an old companion.

Good mornin', blues—blues how do you do?
Said good mornin', blues—blues how do you do?
Said, "I'm doin' all right, and I come to worry you."

The blues dealt much with what has been called the "poor man's recreation," love:

> *I'd rather drink muddy water, sleep out in a hollow log,*
> *Said, I'd rather drink muddy water, sleep out in a hollow log,*
> *I'll be your man, baby, but I will not be your dog.*

Bumble-bee Slim, a popular blues singer in the thirties, dredged this blues up from his earliest remembrances of the Mississippi:

RISING RIVER BLUES

> *If the river keeps on rising, soon it will overflow,*
> *If the river keeps on rising, soon it will overflow,*
> *Now, if it keeps on a-running, I believe I'll have to go.*

> *Storm keeps on raging, rain keeps on falling down,*
> *Storm keeps on raging, rain keeps on falling down,*
> *Yeah, I'm gonna get meself a rowboat, and ride from town to town.*

There are blues lines and phrases that have been used and reused until they have become standard. Here is a verse that will be used one way or another as long as there is the blues:

> *Woke up this mornin', blues was all 'round my bed,*
> *Said, I woke up this mornin', blues was all 'round my bed,*
> *I didn't have nobody, to ease my weary head.*

William C. Handy had a lot to do with the acceptance of the blues by the general public. His "Memphis Blues," "Beale Street Blues," and popular "St. Louis Blues" all contain well-known lines from earlier folk songs, but he showed genius in organizing and presenting the unwritten music of his people. It is interesting to note that this most successful of the old blues men wrote his greatest hit, "St. Louis Blues," before World War I and was unable to get it published by any of the sheet-music houses. Handy had to enter the publishing business, himself, in order to publish his song.

167

ST. LOUIS BLUES

I got the St. Louis Blues, just as blue as I can be,
I got the St. Louis Blues, just as blue as I can be,
My man's got a heart, like a rock cast in the sea.

After the First World War blues had left the country and gone to the city. But it was all known as "race" music—music performed exclusively in and for the Negro communities. In the Negro slums from Memphis to New York, from Chicago to Kansas City and down to New Orleans, and in scores of other cities, the black blues men were honored artists.

Big Bill Broonzy, from Mississippi through Arkansas to Chicago, created many of the classic blues phrases used to this day. The chorus of his "Black, Brown and White" blues is his comment on the world of his day:

Now, if you're white, you're right
And if you're brown, stick around,
But if you're black, O brother,
Get back, get back, get back.

Leadbelly, the king of all the twelve-string guitar players, earned his freedom from a life sentence in a Louisiana penitentiary with this recorded appeal to the Governor:

I left my wife wringing her hands an' cryin'
Governor O.K. Allen, save this man of mine.

Had you, Gov. O.K. Allen, like you got me,
I'd wake up in the morning, an set you free . . .

Ma Rainey died in the late thirties, the undisputed queen of the blues. She came out of the minstrel shows and went on to write and perform one of the greatest blues hits:

SEE SEE RIDER

See see rider, see what you have done,
Lawd, Lawd, Lawd, made me love you, now your gal has come,
You made me love you, now your gal has come.

Bessie Smith, the protegée of Ma Rainey, lived completely the blues life. She, like most of her contemporaries, learned her art in the honkytonks and saloons. Her greatest song was composed by Jimmie Cox, a blues singer about whom little is known. But the song spoke for all the musicians who came up the hard way. Ironically, Bessie Smith, who died in Mississippi after a roadside accident because the available ambulance was for the exclusive use of white people, became well-known twenty-five years later. Then the playwright Edward Albee brought "The Death of Bessie Smith" to Broadway.

NOBODY KNOWS YOU WHEN YOU'RE DOWN AND OUT

Nobody knows you when you're down and out
In your pocket not one penny, and your friends, you haven't any,
But if you ever get on your feet again, then you'll meet you long lost friends.
It's mighty strange, without a doubt, nobody knows you when you're down
*   and out.*

Many great blues singers were women, which is not surprising because of their second-class status in a male-dominated world. And to be both a woman and a Negro in white America gave them a lot of blues material. Clara Smith, Chippie Hill, Trixie Smith, Lil Green, June Richmond—these are just a few of the names that come to mind. But there was a time when every saloon in the black ghettos of America had its piano and its blues singer.

Much of the music we call blues is not really blues at all. Tin Pan Alley has created a host of pop songs that have a blues flavor. Imitations have been written, such as "Wabash Blues" and "Birth of the Blues"; but the down-to-earth realism and folk poetry of authentic blues cannot be successfully faked.

Many of the blues rhymes are, in fact, worthy to stand all by themselves as poetry:

> *Lawd, wrap your arms around me, so that devil cannot hound me.*
>
> *I knows my baby, he's boun' to love me some,*
> *He throws his arms aroun' me like a circle 'roun' the sun.*
> *Well, I'm gonna buy me a little railroad all my own,*
> *Ain't gonna let nobody ride but the chocolate-to-the-bone.*

A listing of great names and credits in the blues field has little value here, because the blues have to be listened to. Whether instrumental or vocal it is what the individual artist does in performance that makes the blues come alive. Some of the boogie-woogie piano virtuosos—Pinetop Smith, Pete Johnson, Meade Lux Lewis—might be unknown were it not for the fact that their individual styles of playing are still alive on recordings.

The blues can never die. Its lasting importance goes far beyond its own rather rigid boundaries. It is the basis for all jazz, Negro gospel music, rock 'n' roll and, indeed, all the current popular and dance music created in America.

CHAPTER TEN

IN
OUR
DAY

THE CIVIL RIGHTS
REVOLUTION

THE GREAT DRIVE of Negroes for equality in America reached its height one hundred years after the signing of the Emancipation Proclamation. It is still in progress. It is characterized, thus far, by a philosophy of nonviolence. That, and the direct action of taking to the streets for peaceful protest, have achieved significant legal gains in the field of human rights.

The drive for civil rights has been led by young people. In the South they have staged boycotts, freedom rides, marches, sit-ins, wade-ins and even pray-ins, hoping to end segregation. In the North they have demonstrated, protested, marched and picketed against the discrimination practiced in housing and employment.

Although nonviolent protests are being abandoned by some Negroes, disillusioned by the failure of government to enforce the existing civil rights' laws, the peaceful civil-rights marching song has spread around the world wherever men practice peaceful protest.

174

WE SHALL OVERCOME

We shall overcome, we shall overcome,
We shall overcome, someday . . .
O deep in my heart, I do believe,
We shall overcome someday.

The young freedom marchers have shown great courage and patience when they have been faced with clubs and savage dogs. Their ability to maintain a sense of humor, even in the face of terror, is expressed in this song:

DOG, DOG

My dog a-love-a your dog,
And your dog a-love-a my dog.
Then why can't we
Sit under the apple tree?

My little doggie was playin' one day
Down in the meadow by a bundle of hay,
An' another little doggie came along,
He said, "Let's get together and eat this bone."

The moral of this song is obvious on the surface; but as one young civil-rights worker remarked: "It could also be saying that men don't have the sense of dogs."

THE ROOTS OF URBAN PROTEST

IN THE IMMEDIATE PAST the problems of war and peace, the great Depression following 1929, the drives to unionize the basic industries of the nation all contributed to the growth of urban protest songs. The singers of the civil-rights revolution raise their voices in a great tradition.

The labor unions sang of a martyred union organizer:

JOE HILL

I dreamed I saw Joe Hill last night
Alive as you and me
"Why Joe, you're ten years dead," I said.
"I never died," said he.

There were other songs that had use, but very little merit otherwise. "There Once Was a Union Maid," and "UAW-CIO" have never become part of our oral tradition.

When the Great Depression closed the factories and mills, men walked the streets singing:

I'm goin' down this road feelin' bad,
And I ain't goin' to be treated this a-way.

A researcher, Bruno Nettl, found this example of a complaint, which is sung to the tune of the "Crawdad Song":

Pittsburgh is a great old town, Pittsburgh;
Pittsburgh is a great old town, Pittsburgh;
Pittsburgh is a great old town,
Solid steel from McKeesport down.
Pittsburgh is a great old town, Pittsburgh.

Negroes played a part in all urban protest. During the Depression this was a popular blues-type song created by Washboard Sam:

> *I'm goin' down, I'm goin' down*
> *To the CCC,*
> *I know that the WPA*
> *Can't do a thing for me.*

FOLK ROCK

BOB DYLAN IS a part of what's happening now. He is one of a small, but influential group of young musicians who have tried to bridge the gap between folk music and rock 'n' roll. He is something new—a composer and performer in the folk manner who has created his own oral tradition among the youth of the world.

The influence of Dylan on the music that stands at the top of the selling charts is absolute: the hit songs of the day about war, death, teen-age revolt and poverty.

His message to parents was contained in these lines from "Times They are Achangin' ":

> *Your sons and your daughters are beyond your command,*
> *Your old road is rapidly agin',*
> *Please get out off the new one if you can't lend your hand,*
> *For the Times they are achangin'.*

The most important anti-war song of the new generation is Dylan's "Blowin' In the Wind," in which he asks the question:

> *How many roads must a man walk down*
> *Before you call him a man?*

And again about cannon balls:

Yes, 'n how many times must the cannon balls fly
before they're forever banned?

His answer to these questions is beautiful, but does not tell us a great deal:

The answer, my friend, is
blowin' in the wind . . .

It is undeniable that Bob Dylan reflected the attitude of some of the youth of America. He must be listened to and understood, if fathers and mothers want to understand the feelings of young adults.

ROCK 'N' ROLL

THE BEGINNINGS OF the music we call "rock 'n' roll" are in the deep South. It is in the blues chords of men like Muddy Waters, Big Bill Broonzy, Cow Cow Davenport, Kokomo Arnold and the other great blues men. The hard driving beat they developed became known as "rhythm and blues"— and for many long years it was heard only in Negro communities.

It is difficult to pinpoint the exact start of an era in music, but Ray Charles, a blind Negro singer, seems to be the most likely candidate. He first opened the door of the mass market for the new music when he wedded rhythm and blues and country music and added a flavor of gospel shouting. A smooth performer, who knew how to wring every drop of emotion from an audience, he seemed to satisfy an entire nation of divergent tastes.

Charles, blinded at the age of six by an illness, heard his blues in the South, and ten years later he had formed his first trio. His first big hit, "Hallelujah," opened night clubs and recording companies to all the gospel shouters and rock-pop artists.

In the fall of 1956 came the first of the white rock 'n' rollers, Elvis Presley, with "Hound Dog": "You ain't nothin' but a hound dog, crockin' all the time. . . ." "Elvis, the pelvis" they called him. He was immediately hated by the older generation and immediately loved by the younger generation.

Chubby Checker and his twist was the biggest sound when the music of the 60's began. Everywhere, one could hear:

> *Com'on now, baby . . . Let's do the twist,*
> *You know, it goes like this.*

And the teen-agers had a dance of their own—one that had not been handed down.

In 1964 the Beatles arrived with what has become known as the "Mersey sound." Rock 'n' roll was in. They performed and sang their own tunes: "I Want to Hold Your Hand," "She Loves You," "A Hard Day's Night," "Love Me Do."

179

The individual lyrics hardly matter. Nothing is deader than last year's rock 'n' roll hit. The lasting and important thing is the "sound" (the drive, beat, the thing that identifies the group).

Then came a young man named Berry Gordy, the head of Detroit's *Motown Records,* soared to the top with the Motown sound. This is a purely Negro sound replete with hand clapping and "yeah, yeah, yeah's" from the chorus. The Supremes, three girls who made it big, come from the Motown mill.

The California sound featured something described as "surfing music." The rock-pop singers from other parts of the country also had to find labels to identify their sound and make it profitable.

There were many reasons for the rise of rock 'n' roll to a position of undisputed supremacy in American music. First of all, we must take into account that this is dance music.

Before World War II the big jazz bands, Ellington, Basie, and a score of others, imitators and rivals, played the music that inspired all forms of the lindy hop. But after the war a new wave of young Negro musicians introduced a complex modern jazz which they called "bebop," or just plain "bop." It was definitely not created as an accompaniment to dance. It was music to be listened to, and jazz ascended to a concert level.

Rock 'n' roll was the revolt of the young—the return to the big beat, the simplicity of eight-bar measures repeated again and again. They took the blues, country and western, and the driving rhythm of the guitar and put them all into the hands of amateurs. And they had their dance music.

The commercial aspect cannot be ignored in evaluating the persistence of the new music. The earning power of the teen-ager has risen to the point where he is now able to spend ten billion dollars yearly in the consumer market, more than enough to keep his choice of music at the top of the charts.

Since its crude beginnings "rock-pop," as it has come to be known, has gone in many directions. The Beatles, ancient in their middle twenties, are experimenting with the possibilities of sound-making of themselves a hundred Beatles by means of tapes recorded on top of one another. Their record "Sgt. Peppers Lonely Hearts Club Band" took six months to record.

New groups and individuals moved swiftly into the vacuum left by the departure of the Beatles from the top of the lists: The Animals, the Monkees, James Brown, The Impressions, The Rolling Stones, and so on and on.

But as always in the land of rock, the individual song, lyric or even group is not the real thing. It is the whole sound that is important. And altogether the sound is youth.

BIBLIOGRAPHY

Russell Ames, *The Story of American Folk Song,* Grosset and Dunlap,
New York, 1955.

Granville Bantock, *One Hundred Folksongs of All Nations,*
Oliver Ditson Co., Philadelphia, 1911.

B. A. Botkin, *A Treasury of American Folklore,* Crown Publishers, Inc.,
New York, 1944.

————, *A Treasury of Mississippi River Folklore,* Crown Publishers, Inc.,
New York, 1955.

Oscar Brand, *Singing Holidays,* Alfred A. Knopf, New York, 1957.

Leon H. Canfield and Howard B. Wilder, *The Making of Modern America,*
Houghton Mifflin Co., Boston, 1950.

Guy and Candie Carawan, *We Shall Overcome,* Oak Publications,
New York, 1963.

Norman Cazden, *The Abelard Folk Song Book,* Abelard-Schuman,
New York, 1958.

H. A. Chambers, *The Treasury of Negro Spirituals,* Blandford Press,
London, 1959.

Richard Chase, *American Folk Tales and Songs,* Signet Key Books,
New York, 1956.

Charles Chilton, *The Book of the West,* The Bobbs Merrill Co., Inc.,
Indianapolis, 1962.

Natalie Curtis, *The Indians' Book,* Harper and Brothers, New York, 1907.

Richard A. Dwyer and Richard E. Lingenfelter, *Songs of The Gold Rush,* University of California Press, 1964.

Louis C. Elson, *Folk Songs of Many Nations,* The John Church Co., Philadelphia, 1905.

James J. Fuld, *The Book of World-Famous Music,* (Classical, Popular, and Folk), Crown Publishers, Inc., New York, 1966.

Indians of the Americas, National Geographic Society, Washington.

George Pullen Jackson, *Another Sheaf of White Spirituals,* University of Florida Press, 1952.

— — — —, *Spiritual Folk Songs of Early America,* Dover Publications, Inc., New York.

George Stuyvesant Jackson, *Early Songs of Uncle Sam,* Bruce Humphries, Inc., Boston, 1933.

J. Rosamond Johnson, *Negro Spirituals,* Edward B. Marks Music Corp., New York, 1940.

James Weldon Johnson, *The Book of American Negro Spirituals,* The Viking Press, New York, 1925.

— — — —, *The Second Book of Negro Spirituals,* The Viking Press, New York, 1926.

Johanna Johnston, *Together In America,* Dodd, Mead and Co., 1965.

Charles O'Brien Kennedy, *A Treasury of American Ballads,* The McBride Co., New York, 1954.

Sylvia and John Kolb, *A Treasury of Folk Songs,* Bantam Books, New York, 1948.

Beatrice Landeck, *Songs to Grow On,* William Sloane Associates, Inc., and Edward B. Marks Music Corp., New York, 1950.

Alan Lomax, *The Penguin Book of American Folk Songs,* Penguin Books, Baltimore, 1964.

John A. and Alan Lomax, *American Ballads and Folk Songs,*
The Macmillan Co., New York, 1934.

— — — —, *Best Loved American Folk Songs,* Grosset and Dunlap, New York, 1947.

— — — —, *Cowboy and Other Frontier Ballads,* The Macmillan Co., New York, 1938.

— — — —, *Folk Song U.S.A.,* Duell, Sloan and Pearce, New York, 1947.

Josephine McGill, *Folk Songs of the Kentucky Mountains,*
Boosey and Co., New York, 1917.

Ethel and Chauncey O. Moore, *Ballads and Folk Songs of the Southwest,*
University of Oklahoma Press, Norman, 1964.

Bruno Nettl, *An Introduction to Folk Music in the United States,*
Wayne State University Press, Detroit, 1962.

Theodore Raph, *The Songs We Sang,* A. S. Barnes and Co., New York, 1964.

The Ritchie Family of Viper, Kentucky, *A Garland of Mountain Song.*

Frank Shay, *American Sea Songs and Chanteys,* W. W. Norton and Co.,
New York, 1948.

Irwin Silber, *Songs of the Civil War,* Bonanza Books, New York, 1960.

— — — —, *This Singing Land,* Amsco Music Publishing Co., New York, 1965.

Irving Werstein, *The Many Faces of the Civil War,* Julian Messner, Inc.,
New York, 1961.

ABOUT THE AUTHOR

WILLIAM ATTAWAY is uniquely qualified to write a book about American folk music. After graduating from the University of Illinois, Mr. Attaway roamed the United States, from the Creole country in Louisiana to the logging camps in Washington. A native of Chicago, and later of New York City and the "new" San Francisco, Bill Attaway has managed to balance hectic metropolitan living with herding sheep on a lonely mountainside. Since he came from a musical family, his ear has always been ready to catch the wide variety of folk songs from all across the country.

As the composer of more than five hundred songs and the arranger for Harry Belafonte's most famous ones, Mr. Attaway has an enviable reputation as a professional in the field of folk music. Some of his most popular songs are "Cordelia Brown," "Judy Drownded," "Sloop John B." ("Nassau Bound") and "Mary Ann." He is the author of a charming, lively collection of folk music for children — *Calypso Song Book* (McGraw-Hill, 1957). Mr. Attaway now lives in Barbados with his wife, children and assorted pets.

WITHIN ASH AND STARDUST

CHANI LYNN FEENER

Swoon READS

SWOON READS

NEW YORK

A Swoon Reads Book

An imprint of Feiwel and Friends and Macmillan Publishing Group, LLC
120 Broadway, New York, NY 10271

Our books may be purchased in bulk for promotional, educational, or business use. Please
contact your local bookseller or the Macmillan Corporate and Premium Sales Department
at (800) 221-7945 ext. 5442 or by email at MacmillanSpecialMarkets@macmillan.com.

Library of Congress Control Number: 2018955799
ISBN 978-1-250-12379-4 (hardcover) / ISBN 978-1-250-12380-0 (ebook)

Book design by Liz Dresner

First edition, 2019

10 9 8 7 6 5 4 3 2 1

swoonreads.com

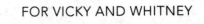
FOR VICKY AND WHITNEY

CHAPTER 1

"Delaney?"

Warm fingers brushed lightly against her elbow, and she pulled her gaze away from the unconscious Zane. When she did, she instantly felt guilty for not having paid better attention to the man at her side.

Ruckus was a mess, his brown hair, typically styled back, was mussed so that strands fell in front of his tired eyes. The yellow of his irises—rimmed in a dark forest green—was usually a bright, sunshiny color, but now was dull, like unpolished gold. His shoulders were hunched, and he was still in the tattered and dust-covered uniform he'd been forced to wear for the past few weeks.

The dirty uniform *Trystan* had forced him to wear.

Delaney took a deliberate step away from the bed, moving into Ruckus's arms when he lifted them to receive her. She'd been so distracted, she hadn't considered what he must be going through.

"I'm sorry," she mumbled against his chest, tightening her hold on him as she did. "About Pettus."

"We found the bodies half-buried in snow before we found you," Ruckus said, dropping his chin down on the top of her head. "Every time we uncovered another, I feared . . ."

"I'm fine."

They hadn't really had the chance to talk, not privately. Last night she'd been too worried over the Zane, and seeming to sense that, Ruckus had respectfully remained silent at her side. But it was morning now, proof in the beams of sunlight spilling in through the room's single window. It was deceptive, that sun, making the landscape outside seem more like a winter wonderland than the frozen death trap it could so quickly become.

Less than forty-eight hours ago, Delaney had almost died out there.

Trystan had as well. And he'd yet to wake up.

Her eyes shifted back toward him, watching the barely perceptible rise and fall of his chest.

"Did he—" Ruckus tentatively began, but she knew where he was going with his question, and stopped him with a swift shake of her head.

"No. Pettus died saving me from Olena. Trystan didn't touch him." She lifted a hand to cup the side of his face. "How are you doing?"

He hesitated, then glanced at the door. "Can we walk for a bit? I need to get moving. Standing still so long . . ."

Right, she hadn't thought of that. Being an Ander—a Vakar commander—meant he was used to constantly being in charge, always in motion, assuring things ran smoothly. Even when they'd been on Earth, he'd had a need to fill his days with activities.

She took his hand, linking their fingers, but couldn't get herself to move farther away from Trystan.

Seeing her hesitation, Ruckus sighed.

"I owe him my life," she tried explaining. "I would never have made it out there without him."

"You don't owe him anything." Ruckus glanced the Zane's way, his expression unreadable. "Even if you did, there's nothing you can do here but wait."

"I know." It still didn't mean she could ignore the tiny voice in her head telling her not to go. Right now they were safe, but experience on Xenith had taught her that could change quickly, and she wasn't willing to leave Trystan alone, just in case.

Ruckus, realizing that she wasn't going to be moved, shook his head in clear frustration. "Tell me about what happened."

"Pettus took a zee for me, and then he snapped Olena's neck. In that order. He was pretty badass, actually." Her voice caught at the end and she swallowed, refusing to break down right now. She and Pettus had been friends, but not like he and Ruckus had been.

Ruckus didn't seem to notice her slip anyway. His eyes were glazed over and he was staring straight ahead, clearly seeing something that wasn't really there. "I'm going to miss him."

"Me too." She pulled Ruckus closer, resting her head on his shoulder. Outside the door, she could see one of the two king's guardsmen who'd been stationed there.

Not to keep her and Ruckus in, they'd been quick to reassure, but just as a precaution should they need assistance. Under any other circumstances, Delaney probably would have found that funny. Now, though, with the words Sworn Sanzie had told her last night still ringing in her ears, laughter was the last thing she was capable of.

According to the Sworn, Trystan had ordered that if anything should happen to him, Delaney be put in charge. She'd been a bit skeptical at first, eyeing any of the Kints who came within ten feet of her or Ruckus. But not a single one of them had stepped out of line. In fact, they'd done exactly what Sanzie had said they would, following her orders whenever she'd given them.

Though, considering she'd only asked for a hot cup of squa, and to stay at Trystan's bedside, that wasn't really saying much.

"I'll have to mourn for him later," Ruckus said quietly, pulling her from her thoughts. "I didn't get a chance to last night."

Delaney pulled back enough to see his face. "Is there a traditional way to do that?"

He nodded. "During the war, losing friends was common. We developed a way to honor them, and their sacrifice. Pettus deserves that. He deserved a lot of things he'll never get now, but this I can give him."

"I'd like to be there, when you do"—she circled her free hand in the air—"whatever it is you're going to do."

"Of course." He smiled down at her sadly. "He would have wanted you there."

"Hey." She placed her free hand on his waist. "We're going to get Gibus back. I'm not going to let you lose another friend."

He started at that, began to shake his head, but suddenly one of the machines next to Trystan's bed started beeping loudly.

Before Delaney could even process what was happening, the door burst open and the doctor rushed in. Forced to step aside to give the older man room, she watched as he began typing away at the machine, checking the Zane in between each press of a button.

"What's going on?" Even after all the doctor's assurances that he'd be fine, part of her still feared the worse, and seeing all the flashing lights suddenly flickering across the monitors wasn't helping.

As if in response, Trystan groaned on the bed, all eyes darting to him, watching as he slowly blinked. He winced at the harsh overhead lighting, shifting.

"Zane." The doctor abandoned the machines, holding his palms out to Trystan. "You should remain lying down. Let me run some tests before you risk overexerting yourself."

Trystan ignored the suggestion, grumbling something as he sat up. While Delaney couldn't make out what he was saying, it was clear he was irritated. He was already in the process of yanking wires off his arms and chest, flinging the bits away from him in frustration. When he went to swing a leg over the side of the bed, the doctor waved his hands and tried desperately to get him to settle back down.

"Please, you've only just woken after being in a coma for over twenty-four hours. Zane, you must rest!" The doctor set pleading eyes on Delaney, inadvertently drawing Trystan's attention her way as well.

The strangled sound he emitted was so shocking, her spine actually stiffened. He was out of the bed, standing close enough that their chests practically touched, faster than she could blink.

She heard someone shift behind her, knew without having to look that it was Ruckus about to step forward and stop this. She lifted a hand to ward him off before he could. As terrifying as the hulking mass of alien in front of her was, it was obvious by the slightly glazed look in his cornflower-blue and crimson-rimmed eyes that he wasn't one hundred percent aware of what he was doing yet.

Trystan didn't seem to notice anyone else anyway, lifting his hands to delve into her hair. He was gentle, sliding his palms back to cradle the base of her skull and tip her head up. His gaze roamed over her face, probably noting the dark circles under her eyes and the cracks in her bottom lip that still hadn't completely healed. He looked five times worse than she did, but she didn't bother pointing that out.

"You're all right." His words were breathy, and she reached up to touch his wrists, comforting him even as she eased his hands away.

"Let's sit down." She guided him back toward the bed, urging him onto it.

He allowed it, perching on the edge, but was clearly ready to spring up again at any moment. When she went to pull back, his hands tightened on hers, and his grip didn't ease until she'd seated herself next to him.

"The doctor is going to make sure you're okay," she told him, motioning with her chin for the doctor to round the bed. "You were asleep for a long time. Do you remember—"

"You almost froze to death," he interrupted.

"Actually, thanks to you, she avoided that. You're the one who came dangerously close to dying." Sanzie appeared in the doorway, the relief on her face palpable. She'd been gone the past couple of hours, checking Inkwell's security precautions to make sure the Rex hadn't messed with anything vital during his stay.

Trystan went to rise, a dangerous glint entering his eyes as he let out a low growl. He paused when Delaney tugged him back, but he didn't try to sit up again.

Sanzie blinked, surprised by his reaction. She turned to Delaney questioningly.

"I think he's still waking up," she said. Then she addressed Trystan in a softer tone: "We're safe right now; calm down. I'm going to need you to focus on getting back to yourself, okay?"

He cocked his head and stared at her like she'd just said something cryptic. "You need me?"

"Yes." Not what she meant, but sure. "There's a situation, and I can't solve it without you. So take a breath and give yourself a moment to recollect, because I refuse to believe someone as hardheaded as you would allow brain damage to occur after spending just one night out in—"

"It was very cold," he cut her off quietly, but the look in his eyes had intensified.

She sighed. "True. How are you now? Cold, still? I could have them bring you some squa?"

The corner of his mouth tipped up, and he gave a slight shake of his head. "I just need another moment."

Delaney curled her fingers at the doctor, who'd only made it halfway around the bed before Trystan's outburst had stopped him. Once he was close, she stood, moving away a few steps to allow him easier access to the Zane.

"Let the doctor check you out," she told him, crossing her arms even as Trystan scowled when the older man reached to take his arm.

They made it silently through a good three minutes before Sanzie let out a sharp breath, drawing their attention her way.

"There's a ship approaching the West Gate," she informed them.

"We still have time." Delaney frowned. "The Rex gave Trystan until tonight."

"Maybe he grew impatient?" Ruckus suggested. He was watching her with an odd look in his eyes, but she didn't have time to decipher it.

"Check it out"—she nodded toward Sanzie, stopping her just as she was about to follow the order—"*carefully.*"

"Of course, Lissa." Sanzie bowed her head and disappeared into the hallway.

"He wouldn't bother coming on his own," Trystan said over the doctor's shoulder. "It's another, no doubt. Possibly a high-standing officer. He must have been waiting on Olena to call in, confirm the deed was done."

"You mean that Delaney was dead," Ruckus growled, and the Zane glared at him.

"Obviously."

"Well . . ." She did not have time for the two of them to go at each other's throats. "I'm alive, and Olena is the one who's dead, so we've got a serious problem."

"I'm failing to find fault with her death," Trystan said, though it was clear he was merely being flip, and didn't mean it. He wasn't stupid. While it meant she was out of their way and could no longer do harm, having a dead Lissa on their hands complicated matters in other ways.

"He's clear." The doctor pulled back and addressed Delaney. "But he needs to stay hydrated, and I wouldn't recommend any sudden movements for at least the next twenty-four hours."

"I am sitting right here," Trystan stated, glancing between the two of them. "Do not speak of me as if I am not."

"Apologies, Zane." He bowed to Trystan and fled the room without another word.

Delaney rolled her eyes, but before she could point out how rude the Zane had just been, Ruckus beat her to the punch.

"Clearly someone is feeling better," he drawled, shaking his head disapprovingly.

Sanzie came running around the corner, slightly out of breath. "We have a problem."

"Tell me something I don't know." Delaney rubbed at her temple, trying to stave off an oncoming headache.

"It's Rue Rantan," Sanzie said. "He's landed and he's already entering the manor. I have Tellers stalling, but he's demanded to see the Zane, in his study, within the next ten minutes."

"Or?" Ruckus asked, ignoring the Sworn's glare.

Delaney glanced between the two of them. She still didn't know anything about their shared past, other than the fact that there apparently was one. Seeing how annoyed Sanzie got anytime Ruckus spoke to her was puzzling.

"He's threatened to go to the Rex and inform him there's been a complication," Sanzie told them.

"So we stop him before he gets the chance."

"No." Trystan ground his teeth as he stood, giving away he wasn't feeling as well as his facial expression might have suggested. "As much as I'd like to put a zee through his brain, the Rue's disappearance would only cause us more issues. He's one of my father's most trusted advisers. We'll need to keep him alive and, ideally, under the assumption all is well here. Having him report back to the Rex in the positive will buy us more time."

"For?" Ruckus didn't sound convinced.

"Whatever our next move is."

"Can you do it?" Delaney asked, continuing once Trystan was looking at her. "You'll have to convince him that everything worked out. That Olena isn't a Popsicle out in the snow right now, and that you haven't sworn vengeance on dear ol' Dad."

He flashed her a grin, the same one that always sent a shiver of dread down her spine. "You aren't the only good actor here, Lissa. I've been managing my father's men since childhood."

"You'll need an explanation," Ruckus joined in, "a reason why the Rex hasn't heard from either you or Olena."

"I can handle this, Ander." Trystan ran his fingers down the soft material of his shirt and scowled. "But not in this. Medical wear will certainly give us away. Sworn," he said, addressing Sanzie, "go ensure the Rue stays put. Don't let him leave the study, for any reason. I'm going to change and get there as quickly as possible.

"You two"—he turned to Delaney and Ruckus—"stay here. It's imperative he and the Tellers that he no doubt brought with him don't see you."

"What if they do a sweep?" The Rex was the suspicious sort, Delaney knew. It was very possible he'd ordered his men to look through the manor, find visual proof of Olena.

Trystan paused, thought it over, and then said, "I have an idea. But you aren't going to like it."

"I CAN'T BELIEVE I'm letting you talk me into this," Ruckus said at her side as they descended the stone stairwell. "This could be a ploy, Delaney."

She couldn't blame him for thinking it; hell, only three days ago, she probably would have assumed the same. Now? Things were different. She wasn't ready to pick apart just *how* different, but they were.

"Do you have any better ideas?" she asked. "I'm all ears if you do."

"Sure," he said. "You and I get on a ship and get out of here."

"And leave Vakar to its fate? Gibus?" She reached out and linked their fingers as they came to the bottom and turned down the hall. "You wouldn't be able to live with yourself, and you know it."

Delaney certainly wouldn't be able to. Another change. After seeing firsthand what the Rex was capable of, after everything he'd done to her personally, and to the people she cared about, how could she in good conscience walk away? Wasn't going to happen. Especially when he'd made it so abundantly clear that Earth was on the line, more so than any of them had imagined.

They came to the end of the hall, where the last row of cells was. To his credit, Ruckus didn't hesitate in the doorway, though she felt his fingers tighten around hers as they approached the cell he'd spent the past few weeks in.

A Teller, who'd been introduced as Ezran, was leading them, and he was already tapping away at a clear control panel on the wall. The second the door swung open, he sent Delaney an apologetic look.

"Don't worry about it," she told him, even though he hadn't said anything out loud.

This was Trystan's plan: Place them in cells in case the Rex's men came looking. They'd expect to find Ruckus down here still—because why would the Zane let him out?—but Delaney . . . She was an added complication.

Shocker.

The cell next to the one Ruckus was to enter opened, and she took a deep breath. Apparently, there was a program that enabled the cells to appear empty from the outside, even if there was an occupant. He'd still be able to see her from within his own cell, through the connecting wall. It was new technology, created by the Zane on a whim in case safe houses—like the one she'd hidden inside in Vakar that time the bombs had gone off—were compromised. He didn't believe his father knew about it yet.

They had to hope that was the case, or she'd be an easy target, already jailed and everything. The only comfort was the fact that she still wore the fritz bracelet she'd taken from Sanzie the day before.

"Last chance to change your mind," Ruckus said as they stood before their cells.

"Trystan won't leave us in here," she assured him. "He needs us. And we need him."

It looked like he still wanted to argue that fact, but instead he pulled her close and pressed his lips to hers.

The spark in the center of her chest was immediate, and she sighed against him, linking her arms around his neck to keep him near when he would have moved away. She didn't care about Ezran standing less than ten feet from them, no doubt watching.

Still, the kiss didn't last long, and eventually she had to release him and step back.

"I've wanted to do that since I saw you standing outside that cave," he told her, a sad half smile playing at his slightly puffed lips.

Before she could say anything in response, he stepped away and entered his old cell. He watched as she got into motion, moving into the one next to his, then twirled a finger at Ezran, signaling he should close them up.

The Teller hesitated, briefly glancing Delaney's way. It wasn't until she smiled encouragingly that he followed the command, hitting the button on the wall panel that would seal them in, with no way out until someone hit it again.

Delaney exhaled a shaky breath, ignoring the tiny inkling of doubt that pooled in her gut. Sanzie had told her she was in charge while Trystan was out of commission, but he was back now. What did that mean for her?

What if, after handling Rue Rantan, Trystan decided he wanted to try dealing with the rest on his own? She didn't think he'd leave her locked in here, but she couldn't say the same about Ruckus. And there was no way she was going to allow him to stay in a cell. Not again.

She glanced over at the Ander, saw that he was watching her closely, probably following all her thoughts just by reading her expression. He knew her that well. It was why, when she'd agreed to Trystan's plan, he'd only put up a minimal struggle even though he hated the idea.

Ruckus was right—this was a risk—and the only reason he was willingly going along with it was because he trusted her. And she was doing it because she trusted Trystan.

She just hoped her trust wasn't misplaced.

CHAPTER 2

Trystan tried not to wince as he adjusted the buttons on his shirt, held his spine straight and his shoulders back, despite the lingering ache there. He really needed information about what had happened during the time he'd been unconscious, but it would have to wait. Right now they were all in danger if he couldn't pull this off.

Not that he doubted his abilities to do so. What he'd said to Delaney back there had been accurate: He'd been manipulating his father's horde for years.

He took one glance in the mirror while changing and had to quickly look away. His hair was in disarray, his skin sallow, and it was painfully obvious he needed a long, hot shower. Still, he could work with that.

Before he left his rooms, he noticed the "gift" from their Unveiling on the side of his dresser. The gold knife was small but sharp, the handle molded into a detailed depiction of a blaxa creature—similar-looking to an Earth lizard. It'd been the only item from the ceremony Trystan hadn't taken with him, and someone must have delivered it during his absence.

For no real reason at all, he took the small weapon with him, tucking it into his boot and out of sight. He could feel the press of metal against the side of his leg while he moved, making his way toward where the Rue waited.

A row of Tellers he didn't recognize lined the hallway outside his study. He didn't bother sparing them a glance, though it irked him that they were here. Of course his father would never send the Rue alone, and Trystan had expected him to bring along reinforcements, but . . . Silently, he counted at least a dozen, grinding his teeth in irritation as he did.

Trystan's men, those loyal to him, were stationed around the castle, with orders that should any of these Tellers branch off, they were to follow at a safe distance. Trying to stop them would be the same as admitting there was something to hide. Hopefully, if it came to that, Delaney and the Ander would already be safely confined in the dungeons.

Trystan paused outside the study doors, letting himself linger on the thought of the two of them down there. Together. Alone. Usually, he'd turn from that line of thinking. Given his current situation, however, an added level of anger was just what he needed.

He shoved the doors open with enough force that they clattered inward against the walls. He was already walking through as his eyes sought out the Rue, and it turned out he hadn't needed to bother imagining Delaney in Ruckus's arms after all. Seeing the smug look on Rantan's face was more than enough to get his blood boiling.

Because this was a show, and he had to cover the fact that his body felt like a lead weight trying to pull him down to the floor, he walked right up to the Rue and did the one thing he'd always wanted to do. He grabbed him by the throat and hoisted him up off the ground.

Rantan's eyes bugged out of his head, and he struggled, clawing at Trystan's wrists. The tips of his military-issue boots—laughable, considering he'd never once served in the army—scraped against the navy-blue carpet.

It would be so easy not to stop, to squeeze until he crushed the Rue's windpipe. But, despite the way he currently felt, he had more control over himself than that.

Unfortunately.

With one final clench of his fingers, he tossed the Rue against the wall, watching with a sick sense of pleasure as his skull cracked back against the white stone. His body crumpled to the floor, though it wasn't long before he attempted getting to his feet.

Trystan casually moved over to one of the chairs positioned at the side of the study, barely paying attention as the Rue tried again and again to regain his footing, only to fall back down in a heap.

Rantan was trying too hard, moving too quickly, knowledge Trystan now had firsthand experience with.

Even though it'd been less than an hour ago, it was hard to recall much of waking up. He'd done it, had seen the doctor and the wires hooked up to his body, and he'd panicked. His only thought had been of Delaney, and not even coherently. The most he'd been able to manage was her name, over and over again.

That moment he'd seen her standing there, whole, alive, that was the best second of his entire life. He didn't want to dwell on that. Especially not here, in front of his father's puppet. He focused instead on the fact that he was alive as well, that they'd both made it out of that cave to see another day.

That his father was the reason they had been there at all.

That this man currently crawling around on all fours was in league with him.

Trystan's gaze darkened, and then, amazingly enough, the Rue's survival instincts must have finally kicked in, for he stilled, the fear in his eyes apparent.

"I'm not sure if you've noticed, Rantan"—even Trystan was surprised by how casual his voice sounded—"but I'm in a mood today. You see," he said as he uncurled his hand on one of the armrests, tapped his fingers against the smooth white leather, "I lost something really important to me."

There was tension from the doorway, where he'd spotted two Tellers loyal to his father, but he wasn't worried about them. Sanzie was there as well, and he trusted her to keep his back safe.

"I wonder . . ." Trystan leaned forward, not much, certainly not enough to matter, what with the Rue all the way across the room, but still he flinched. "Do you know about that? Hmm? Do you know what my father has taken from me, Rantan?"

"I . . ."

Trystan clucked his tongue and sat back. "That's not a good response, certainly not one appropriate for your Zane."

Mention of his title had the opposite of his desired effect. Suddenly Rantan seemed to recall himself, and whose orders had brought him here. He pushed back onto his knees, though he didn't try to stand again. His glare was haughty, though it didn't do a decent job of masking his lingering fear.

"I've come under the order and protection of Rex Hortan," he said, his voice only wavering slightly at the end. "I am to report back that—"

"My betrothed is dead?" Trystan cut him off, and the other man blanched. "So you're admitting you came in here knowing what I'd lost? Knowing who was responsible?" He tsked. "I knew you were a fool, Rantan, but this is another level entirely."

"The Rex—"

"Isn't here," Trystan stated. "Which is a shame, though I imagine that was on purpose. You see, unlike you, my father doesn't have a death wish."

The Rue pulled back. "Threatening the Rex is treason!"

"So is threatening the Zane."

"I never—"

"Didn't you?"

Every time Trystan interrupted, the Rue's cheeks grew a little pinker. For a man who loved the sound of his own voice, not having an audience was probably excruciating. And humiliating. Trystan didn't care which he felt more, so long as he felt them both.

"You threaten me every time you're in my presence, Rantan," Trystan continued. "Every time you come around, breathing my air, huffing about my father. Telling me how badly you want to run off and inform him about my behavior. I've had enough. And not just of your veiled threats. Of you entirely."

"These guards are under strict orders to protect me," the Rue said, lifting his chin toward where the Tellers still stood sentry by the doors. "And they're bearing witness right now. Making note of everything you say to me, Zane. Kill me, and—"

"Kill you?" Trystan chuckled darkly. "Oh no, you misunderstand. I'm not going to murder you, Rantan. If I were, I wouldn't have dropped you like the pile of trash you are. At least"—he lifted a single shoulder in a bored half shrug—"not before I'd wrung the last breath out of you."

The Rue was clearly confused, on edge, and he waited, but when it became apparent Trystan wasn't going to say anything else, he frowned.

"Where is Lissa Olena? I've been ordered to return with visual confirmation that both you and she are well."

"*Well* is a fickle term," Trystan pointed out. "Do I look *well* to you, Rue?"

He stuck his chin in the air and huffed out, "You do not."

"Take my word for it: Olena doesn't look much better."

"Where is she, Zane?"

"Alive," he bit out, "but injured. My father grossly underestimated Delaney, and vastly overestimated Olena. She may have killed my Lissa, but Olena didn't make it out unscathed. I'll have you brought to her, if you insist, though I should mention she's currently undergoing surgery, and any interruption could result in her untimely demise."

Trystan had already ordered a surgical room set up, just in case. There was even a team of doctors within it, making as much noise as possible, so that it would be believable that an intense surgery was being done should anyone happen by the sealed doors.

"Actually"—he stood with a flourish—"now that I'm thinking about it, you're right: You *should* see her."

Rantan eyed him suspiciously, and for a moment Trystan feared he was about to call his bluff.

"My men should already be searching the castle," the Rue ended up saying. "They'll know if there's a medical team working. If this is a poorly veiled lie, they'll find out, Zane."

"With any luck," Trystan said, and retook his seat, "they'll be as incompetent as you and open the door themselves."

"The Rex wants Lissa Olena alive."

"So I gathered."

The Rue ran his gaze over Trystan, not bothering to cover his distaste now that he'd been told his life wasn't in danger. "You look this bad over one human? She was a means to an end. Now that she's gone—"

"My father has nothing with which to control me," Trystan declared. He stood a second time, adjusting his jacket in a clear show that he was done with this conversation. "Tell him he can expect me when I'm good and ready."

"You've been ordered to return with me," the Rue said. "Tonight."

"And I'm defying that order." He angled his head at Sanzie. "My Sworn will stay with you until your men return, confirming what I've told you about Olena. There are things I need to clear up here, before I even consider going to Carnage, least of which is ensuring *his Lissa* is in well enough condition to travel."

"We aren't finished here, Zane," Rantan called when he gripped the door handle, but Trystan merely grunted.

"Let my father know not to worry; I haven't forgotten where my loyalties lie." He turned and caught the Rue's gaze one last time. "I'll see him soon. Just not tonight."

Not wanting to give the other man even a second to argue further, Trystan yanked the door open.

Just as a Teller on the outside was moving to knock. The Teller stumbled a bit on his feet, straightening and composing himself as quickly as possible. Without sparing Trystan so much as a glance, he lifted his gaze to the Rue.

"There's a problem in the dungeons," he stated.

Trystan could practically feel the gloating look Rantan aimed at his back. He shared a brief knowing exchange with Sanzie and let out a heavy sigh. "Damn."

He swung at the unsuspecting Teller, rendering him unconscious with a single punch. Before the Rue could activate the fritz on his wrist, Trystan had his open and aimed at the center of his chest.

"I blame the Ander," he said to Sanzie with a shake of his head. Whatever had happened to tip them off, surely it hadn't been Delaney's fault.

Then he fired his weapon.

"I HATE THAT we're back here." Ruckus drew Delaney's attention from the doorway, where she'd been staring for the past ten minutes. He didn't like the way she was worrying her bottom lip, or how she stiffened every time a noise echoed down the stone hall.

Didn't like the thought that her reactions had less to do with fear of them getting caught, and more to do with worry for the Zane.

Not for the first time, he found himself wondering what had

happened between the two of them this past month. The words were on the tip of his tongue before he thought better of asking and contained himself, and his misplaced jealousies. In reality, it didn't matter. Whatever had taken place between her and Trystan, whatever he'd said or done to earn her trust, it was set.

The only thing Ruckus could control—and therefore the only thing he should be focusing on—was where he and Delaney went from here. Which, if he had his way, would be off this planet and back to Earth.

A thread of guilt wormed its way through his gut, and he tried to quell it. Yes, this was his planet, and he didn't want to see it destroyed by the greedy Kint. But he also didn't want to see Delaney hurt by it, and staying. . . . No good could come of that.

Already she was changed. He saw it in the way she stood, noted it in the way she glanced at Sanzie and Trystan. At all the Kint Tellers they'd passed since yesterday morning when they'd found her half frozen in the snow. The cilla suit had kept her alive, but there'd still been damage. She'd hardly noticed, too caught up in her fear for the Zane to see how stiffly she moved, how often she shivered.

"We won't be in these cells for long," she said then, misinterpreting his statement.

"No . . ." He waited for her to finally turn away from the door and look at him. "I meant *here*. You and me, so close to each other and yet . . ."

"How are your hands?" she asked after a moment.

He glanced down at them absently. He'd damaged them banging on the electric wall of this very cell when the Rex had ordered for Delaney to be taken away. They'd healed enough over the past few days that he could hold her hand with his own, but there were still raw patches along his fingers and the bases of his palms.

The initial pain had been nothing at the time, easily ignored. It was the panic that had overridden him, debilitated him. The thought that she was going to be killed, and that there was nothing he could do about it.

That he was trapped. Useless.

That he'd failed her.

"It should have been me," he whispered, needing to look away as soon as he spoke. "Instead it was the Zane. He was there for you when I couldn't be."

"Ruckus." She moved closer to the wall that separated their cells.

"Don't get me wrong," he went on, "I'm grateful that he was. He's the reason you're here, after all. But that doesn't change the fact that I wish it'd been me. What if it happens again? What if next time he's just as unable to help you as I am? What then, Delaney?"

"Then I figure out a way to help myself," she said confidently.

"What if you can't?" Now that they were on the subject, there was no point in backtracking. "This, what you're suggesting we attempt to do, is dangerous. In all likelihood, the kind of danger we can't get away from."

She inspected him. "You're angry with me."

"No." He shook his head, then closed his eyes and took a breath. "Yes. In a way I guess I am."

"Because I want to do this?"

"Because you're so willing to put yourself at risk," he clarified. "Delaney, Olena was *going* to kill you. I thought for sure when they dragged you from this room that it was going to be the last time I ever saw you."

They'd never bothered hiding things from each other before, so he let some of the inward fear shine through in his eyes. Let her see how terrified he actually was, hoping that she'd understand where he was coming from. What he was actually trying to say. He knew getting her to change her mind at this point was out of the question—she was too stubborn. But convincing her not to take any unnecessary risks? That he could do.

"I never want to feel that way again," he told her. "Please, don't make me."

The corner of her mouth tipped up reassuringly, and in that one move, he knew she'd picked up on his underlying meaning.

"I won't be stupid if you won't be stupid," she promised.

He grunted, unable to hold back his own smile. "That'll have to do."

"Can I help you?" Ezran called, a bit louder than necessary, from where he stood in the entryway. It was a signal for them to be quiet. Apparently the Zane's paranoia was going to work in their favor; the Rex had men searching the castle.

Ezran stepped into the room a second later. At his back were three other Tellers dressed in Kint blues, silvers, and whites. With his head held high, he led them toward Ruckus's cell, swinging out an arm when he was close enough, as if presenting him.

"The Ander," he said as the other three took Ruckus in. "Did the Rex give instructions on what was to be done with him from here?"

"No," one of them, a tall boy at least three years younger than Ruckus, informed Ezran. "Only that we should check to make sure he was still in place. We've been ordered to leave him here and let Lissa Olena decide what's to be done next."

At the sound of her name, Ruckus's jaw involuntarily clenched. For a split second he saw red before he was able to get ahold of himself. Being short-tempered had been a flaw of his since birth. It was one of the major reasons his father had insisted he join the army at such a young age. Then, the hope had been to teach him control. It'd done that, and then some.

In less time than it took the others to blink, he'd successfully schooled his features back into a blank mask. There was no point in showing fear here, or bothering to attempt conversation. They'd seen him; now they'd leave.

Only, they didn't.

The one standing closest to Delaney's cell frowned and stepped toward it.

Ruckus shifted on his feet, which was the wrong thing to do because the others took notice, despite how small the move had been. It was stupid to be twitchy—he'd been trained to be better than that—but it'd been less than two days since he'd gotten her back, and the thought of losing her again made him lose his cool.

"What is it?" one of the other Tellers asked the one now moving even closer to Delaney's cell.

"I thought I heard voices before we came in," he explained, eyeing Ruckus suspiciously.

Ezran glanced between them and snorted. "He talks to himself sometimes. He's been down here awhile. As you can clearly see, there's no one else here."

"Then why is the barrier up?" the Teller asked. When he didn't receive an immediate response, he added, "The *electrical* one? None of the other unused cells are activated. Why is this one?"

Because the shielding technology was built into the same electrical force field that kept prisoners in. Ruckus inwardly cursed. They should have activated the other cells, to be safe. It was such a minor mistake, and something he should have caught himself.

"It's an empty cell," Ezran said, instead of answering. "You can see that for yourselves, right now."

Delaney, who'd been standing as still as a ghost, merely took the weight off one ankle to rest it on the other then. But it was enough.

The Teller who'd been staring at the cell so closely sucked in a breath and activated his fritz. He aimed it at Ezran and growled, "Open it up."

"Excuse me?" Whoever had trained Ezran, Ruckus was impressed.

"I heard something. Almost like there's someone in there," the Teller said.

"Someone invisible?" the younger-looking one asked, not bothering to cover the smirk spreading across his face.

"I'm telling you, there's someone in there," he insisted.

"It's empty," the other argued, but when all that earned him was a glare, he waved Ezran on. "Just open it up so we can be done with this already."

"It won't open," Ezran gave it one last attempt. "That's why it's activated. We've been having problems with—"

"Forget about it." The quiet Teller who hadn't spoken up to this point walked over to the wall panel and hit the control pad before Ruckus could think of a way to stop him. A soft beep sounded, and then the pale blue screen that acted as both the cell door and front wall panel flickered and disappeared.

Leaving an exposed Delaney.

"Damn." Delaney lifted her arm and fired off her already activated fritz. She'd hit two of them between the eyes before they could react.

The third, Ezran took out with an elbow to the side, and then a twist of an arm around his neck. When the body dropped, the Teller's eyes widened and he stared down at it, clearly shocked by what he'd just done.

"Get me out of here," Ruckus ordered Ezran, another twist of desperate anger filling him up.

Delaney stepped from her cell and placed her hands on her hips, staring down at the dead Tellers. "Trystan is going to be *so* pissed."

CHAPTER 3

Delaney circled Rue Rantan for the fifth time. After taking out the Tellers downstairs, she and Ruckus had waited a few minutes before heading back up. Ezran had come with them and was now guarding the door, looking a little sick to his stomach.

She supposed that made sense, considering he'd just helped kill fellow soldiers. Though he was loyal to Trystan and had been told what to expect, there was a difference between imagining something and actually acting on it. Her gaze swept over to where the Zane perched against the edge of a large desk.

"Was this really necessary?" Ruckus asked, sweeping a hand through his dark hair as he glowered down at the Rue's unmoving body.

"I seem to recall," Trystan said, "your suggestion was that we do this in the first place."

"Yeah," he snapped, "and you corrected that logic by pointing out we needed him alive."

"This is only the second conversation you two have had today, and I'm already tempted to split you up like misbehaving children." Delaney sighed, rubbing at her temples.

Trystan gave her a dark, warning look, which she ignored.

Ruckus's expression wasn't any better.

So she'd bruised some egos? Seemed like the least of their worries at the moment, and it wasn't like either of them were being much help, constantly at each other's throats. Trying not to acknowledge one over the other, she circled the Rue's body one last time and then came to a stop between them.

"What do we do now?" she asked. "We can't exactly leave the Rex hanging."

"You mentioned my father gave me until tonight?" Trystan didn't seem happy about this prospect. "I could go now. I'd make it there in time. It'll be easy enough to explain that my anger got the best of me, and the Rue was the unfortunate recipient."

"And when you arrive without Olena?" Ruckus crossed his arms.

Trystan thought it over, then shrugged. "I'll have to come up with something on the way."

"Nope." Delaney shook her head. "That's out. Next idea?"

He frowned. "Delaney—"

"Great," she interrupted, "I do have one. Thanks for calling on me, Trystan. Ruckus and I already talked about getting to the Basilissa. She needs to know what happened to her daughter, that she no longer has to follow the Rex. With any luck, she'll help us stop him, and more immediately, come up with a way to rescue Gibus."

Delaney had been thinking more on it throughout the day. It still made the most sense. So far, the only people who knew Olena was dead were in this building, and all loyal to Trystan and her. So long as they kept it that way, they should be able to get back to Vakar in time to inform the Basilissa and get her to turn on the Rex.

"And how do you suggest we explain the circumstances surrounding Olena's death, hmm?" Trystan questioned, clearly not on board.

That could get tricky. Pettus had only been doing what he needed to in order to protect Delaney, but would Tilda see it that way?

"It's a risk we're going to have to take," she said. "We need Vakar's help, and the only way to get it is by convincing Tilda. Being their Lissa doesn't mean anything if their Basilissa isn't with us."

"She could denounce you," Ruckus told her. "Once she discovers you had a hand in her daughter's murder. That you were there."

Delaney blinked at him. "Are you siding with Trystan all of a sudden? Because I thought we'd already agreed on this. This makes the most sense." When neither of them reacted, she straightened to her full height—which was wholly unimpressive in their company—and stated, "Either help me figure out how to make this work, or get out of my way."

Neither one of them seemed very pleased by her edict, but they both sighed and clearly started thinking of solutions.

Trystan was the first to speak. "Traveling through Vakar right now is too risky. At least in any Kint ship. Too easily spotted, and once my father gets word where we are, and that Delaney survived, we'll have an even bigger problem on our hands."

"So we convince your father you have a legitimate reason for going," she said. "Make it so when you do show up at the palace in Vakar, and he undoubtedly gets word, you're exactly where he expected you to be anyway."

He cocked his head at her. "It isn't a terrible idea. However, I'm also not comfortable leaving Inkwell unprotected."

"You don't think anything is going to happen to Dom or the others, do you?" The citizens of Inkwell lived in town far enough from the palace grounds that Delaney hadn't visited yet, but she knew Dominan's house was close.

"It would be rash for my father to attack his own people, but we also don't know how the Basilissa will react once this news is delivered. I'd rather leave behind a way for civilians to safely flee if need be, and my personal ship is the fastest in the kingdom. What about the Ander's?"

"We can call Fawna and see how fast she can get here." Delaney motioned to Sanzie, who stepped forward and handed over a clear device, called a shing, which worked similarly to a cell phone or a computer. She held it out to Ruckus.

Ruckus shared a brief look with the Sworn over Delaney's shoulder, but before Delaney could question it, he took the shing, tapping away at the screen and moving off to the corner of the room. It began to emit a low beeping sound, and a second later his voice could be heard giving orders.

"You've got blood on your shirt," Trystan said quietly, and Delaney glanced down at the tiny red splatters dotting her chest.

"Yeah?" She flicked the folded fabric around her neck. "Well, your collar is crooked."

She couldn't hold back the laughter when he immediately reached to check.

"We're in luck," Ruckus said, walking back over to them. "Fawna was already close by. She'll be here in under an hour."

"Which doesn't leave us much time to plan," Sanzie pointed out as she took back her device. "We can't all make it into Vakar, and the Rex is still a problem. If he doesn't hear from someone soon, he'll grow even more suspicious."

"She's right." Trystan settled more comfortably against the desk, stretching out his legs and crossing them at the ankles.

He'd changed into his traditional outfit, long blue sleeves on a high-collared shirt that zipped up the front. White pants tucked into black boots, and there wasn't a single crease anywhere to be seen, like he'd taken the time to iron everything just before putting it on.

Delaney would have rolled her eyes at how impeccable he needed everything to be, especially at a time like this, but there were more important things to deal with than his weird quirks. "Is there someone here who he trusts?"

Trystan gave her a look, and she grunted.

Right. The Rex didn't trust anyone, not even his own son. Though, all things considered, that was sort of understandable.

"Who would he listen to the most, then?"

"Me," Trystan said, and she was already shaking her head when Ruckus came up with another suggestion.

"What if you video conference him? Give him a reason why you're refusing to return tonight, come up with some excuse to head to Vakar instead."

"You were attempting to manipulate the Rue into believing you were rebelling due to mourning," Sanzie recalled, turning to the Zane. "Perhaps you can use the same line of logic on the Rex?"

Trystan paused, thought it over, and ultimately discarded the idea. "He'd know Delaney's death would affect me; I did a poor job shielding that fact from him when I got back from Kilma, but the life of a human wouldn't be enough to warrant my disobedience in his eyes. If I push too hard, he'll only send more Tellers to retrieve me."

"What about Olena?" Delaney shrugged when they all looked at her. "It's not like we can leave her out there in the snow forever, and Tilda deserves the chance to say good-bye to her daughter in person."

"I could tell my father I'm delivering your body to her; he'll agree to that," Trystan surmised, "so long as I explain that it's an attempt to keep our peace treaty intact. You are her Uprisen heir, after all, and now he thinks you're dead."

"So you tell the Rex you're bringing Delaney's body to Tilda, but in reality, we'll be bringing her Olena's." Ruckus hummed to himself in thought. "We might also be able to persuade the Basilissa not to take Olena's death out on us by doing this. She'd be grateful for the return of her daughter."

"How do you explain to your dad where Olena will be during all of this?" Delaney asked. "Are we sticking with the injured-while-murdering-me story?"

"It seems to be the best angle we have," Trystan agreed. "Besides, more of a reason for me to go to Vakar. The Basilissa should be told of Olena's injuries in person. That's what I'll tell my father. It'll be impossible for him to find fault in that."

"All right, that's something then." Delaney wanted to ask the Zane if he was sure about talking to the Rex, but knew better than to do so in front of an audience. "What about when we get to the Vakar palace? I assume there are still a ton of Kint Tellers guarding the place. With this plan, you might be expected, but not us."

"It's impossible to know how many of them are loyal to my father, and how many will side with me," Trystan told them. "I'm not sure who was left there. I'd need a list of names before I could even begin to guess how much support we'd have."

"I've got friends," Ruckus said confidently. "Ones who can get us through the palace unseen."

The Zane tilted his head. "Are you referring to the ones who helped sneak you in the first time?"

Bringing up his failed rescue attempt probably wasn't a good idea. For a second there, they'd actually been having a civilized conversation. Now the Ander's eyes flashed with anger and he took a pointed step forward.

Delaney placed a palm on his chest, stilling him.

He took a deep breath. "You never found the people who helped get me into the palace."

"No," Trystan admitted. "I didn't. But I can't promise they haven't been discovered since. Obviously, there's a lot my father has kept from me. Hell, for all we know, this is yet another elaborate trap."

"That can't be true." That would suggest the Rex had wanted them to kill Olena, and Delaney highly doubted that. She'd seen the way he'd looked at the old Lissa, like she was the goose that laid the golden egg. He'd needed her alive. He would not be pleased to find out she no longer was.

"Olena was too important to him," Ruckus said, practically reading her mind. "He confessed that was the plan all along: to use her to gain control of Vakar."

"He told me that as well." Trystan sighed. "He only pretended to accept Delaney as a change of plan. He wanted to create unease among the people, manipulate them into believing having Olena on the throne was still better than allowing a human to take it." He held her gaze. "It wouldn't have worked in the long run."

"Comforting," Delaney drawled. "What do you know about the rest of his plan? Anything?"

It was a bit uncomfortable to realize that she hoped he didn't, even though that would leave them in the dark on what to expect next. The thought that he could be involved with his dad's scheming bothered her.

"I know he wants Earth," Trystan said.

"We all know that," Ruckus put in. "How about you give us a how? What does he intend to do with Vakar?"

"Going off what I'd been told, he wants to merge them. But he never intended to leave political control in Vakar hands. He would run things himself, from the sidelines."

"Using you as a figurehead." Surprisingly, Ruckus's words didn't sound mocking.

"I would have aided him in getting what he wanted," Trystan admitted, "yes. But only to an extent. I'd hoped that I could persuade him to alter his goals. To allow Earth to continue on as is, rather than taking complete control."

"But you don't know details?" Ruckus read between the lines. "He didn't confide in you."

Trystan's jaw clenched. "He did not."

"Tilda might know more," Delaney said. Either way, it wasn't like they were going to find out more here. "How long before your father loses his patience again and sends someone else?"

"For all we know, he already has." Trystan straightened from the desk, adjusting his shirt, and then toed Rantan's body with a grunt. "It's unclear how soon after his arrival he was supposed to call in. I should get to a com device soon, get this conference call over with before we're really out of time."

"There's still the matter of how we plan on stopping the Rex at all," Ruckus pointed out. "Say Tilda agrees to help us, turns against him. . . . Then what?"

"We'll start by taking the Vakar palace back," Trystan said. "Then Tilda can get word out to her people that she's no longer under my father's thumb."

"You mean your thumb?"

"Your people far outnumber Tilda's," Delaney reminded, drawing attention her way before they could start arguing again. "If she announces she's no longer going to do what he says, the Rex will declare war—you know, that thing we've gone through all of this to avoid?"

"We'll just have to hope she knows more about my father's plans and can help us before it comes to that." Trystan smoothed a hand over his hair, a nervous tick of his that gave him away.

"*Hope* isn't really a lot to go on right now." She didn't like feeling so many steps behind. "We need to find a way to get your father off that throne. Take away his crown, and we take away his army at the same time."

"I know that." Trystan sighed again. "But I don't know how yet, Delaney. We need more information, and right now Tilda is the only person I can think of who might have some. Who knows what my father's told her since taking Olena hostage?"

"You should call him." Ruckus motioned toward Rantan. "We've lost the luxury of time to figure things out further."

Trystan looked like he was going to argue, probably just because the Ander was the one telling him what to do, but he ended up gritting his teeth instead. "You two wait here, in case we're wrong and Rantan wasn't the only one already sent our way."

Sanzie went with him, leaving Delaney and Ruckus alone in the office. With Rantan's body.

"This is fun." Delaney scowled down at the Rue's lifeless form and then went to the desk, turning so she didn't have to look at him anymore.

"As long as Trystan can convince the Rex to let him make the trip to Vakar, it should be okay," Ruckus said, trying to reassure her. He was obviously able to tell she was still feeling antsy over this partial plan of theirs.

"And Tilda?" she asked. "How do we convince her not to shoot Trystan the second she realizes it's Olena in that body bag and not me?"

"She's smart. She knows that'll ensure war."

"She'll be standing over her daughter's corpse. I don't think she'll be thinking clearly enough to consider killing the Zane—who had a hand in Olena's death—a bad idea."

"We'll figure it out."

"Aren't you the one who used to tell me to always be prepared for everything?" she shot over her shoulder. If Trystan got hurt carrying out this plan, it'd partially be her fault for suggesting it in the first place.

Ruckus licked his lips and then moved closer, resting a hand on the narrow of her back. Leaning in, he brushed his knuckles against her wrist, where she had both palms flat against the desk.

"We'll have to take a stealthier route, past the East Mountains, in order to avoid detection on our way to Vakar," he told her. "That's plenty of time for us to convince the Zane not to stand anywhere near the Basilissa when we reveal that Olena's dead. He'll see the logic in being cautious."

She shivered before she could help herself, her mind already going back to the other day and the traumatic experience she'd had. The cave Trystan had gotten them into had saved their lives, but she could still recall the frozen feeling, the burning and the numbness that had followed.

All those times she'd been pretending to be Olena, coming so close to death in the forms of bombs and zees, and yet, it was the hypothermia that really stuck with her. That particular fear had sunk in its claws, deeply enough she could feel it wiggling in the back of her mind at even the mere idea of having to travel near or around another mountain.

"Hey." Concern thickened his voice, and Ruckus angled his body so that she was propped comfortingly against his warmth. The hand already on her back began rubbing soothing circles on her spine, while his other reached out to steady her hip. "We're in the midst of our spring season. Winter's already passed for Vakar."

Delaney dropped her head against his shoulder and let out a humorless chuckle. "How'd you know that's what I was panicking about?"

"Lucky guess." He shrugged, but when she glanced up and caught him staring down at her, he added, "I know you, Delaney." His brow furrowed, an almost bemused look passing over his features, and when he spoke again, his voice was no more than a whisper.

"Have you forgotten that?" he asked. "Have you forgotten us?"

"What?" She twisted in his hold and took his head between her hands. "Of course not."

He didn't appear convinced.

"Of course not," she repeated, sending the words through their fittings this time. Speaking telepathically had always seemed more intimate to her. During their time on Earth, the two of them had spoken that way often, even when alone.

And she realized with a start that they hadn't done so once since he'd found her in that cave.

"I'm sorry," she said. "For being so distracted."

"No." He shook his head. "No, I'm the one being ridiculous. It's just . . ." He trailed off, and before she could press him on it, he chuckled. "Never mind. It's me being insecure."

"Insecure?"

"Poor choice of words." He smiled and tucked a strand of hair behind her ear.

She didn't believe him.

CHAPTER 4

Trystan tried not to twitch at his father's perusal, knew that the other man's gaze kept coming back to the splotches beneath his son's eyes and the single strand of blond hair that refused to stay in place. Trystan did his best to act like he didn't care about these obvious flaws, keeping his shoulders stiff and his expression blank.

He had no idea if the Rex was buying it.

"I'm not sure telling Tilda in person that her daughter was injured is wise." His father tapped his fingers against the surface of his desk. "We've gained her loyalty by ensuring Olena wouldn't be harmed, after all."

"She deserves to know the truth," Trystan repeated, for what might have been the tenth time since the call had started over fifteen minutes ago. "And Delaney—"

"Right," he cut him off, "the newly deceased Miss Grace. That's what this is really about, isn't it?"

"She was Tilda's heir."

"She was human." The Rex paused, then canted his head. "Where is Rue Rantan?"

Trystan held his gaze unflinchingly, not bothering to answer. It was fairly obvious, seeing as how there was only one reason Rantan would miss an opportunity to make the Zane look bad in front of the Rex.

His father sighed, but it was impossible to tell if it was out of annoyance at having lost a valued member of his council, or just at his son in general.

"If you didn't want him dead," Trystan finally said, "then you shouldn't have sent him."

"I had hoped you'd have better control of your actions," the Rex replied. "But, yes, of course your misplaced feelings for the human getting the best of you was a possibility I'd considered."

Trystan stopped the disgust from showing on his face just in time. He'd hated the Rue, who'd been all but a waste of space since he'd first joined the council. But the man had been loyal to the Rex, if nothing else. Seeing how little his father appreciated that fact made his insides twist.

"I don't want Lissa Olena anywhere near Vakar without me present," his father said. "It's too risky, especially now that Delaney is dead. It'll put Tilda on edge, perhaps even give her foolish notions of rebellion."

"She's still in critical condition in any case," Trystan told him. "I'd hoped to leave Olena here, so she could continue getting medical attention. I'll allow her to conference call with her mother once I make it to Vakar, so that the Basilissa has proof her daughter is all right. I think it best we keep all of this to ourselves as well."

The Rex lifted a brow, a silent indication for him to go on.

"I'll tell Tilda I'm arriving with information, and show her Delaney's body once I'm there. If we inform her of her Uprisen heir's death without me present, I fear she might have the same rebellious reaction you hope to avoid."

Making sure his father didn't tell Tilda anything ahead of time also meant they'd have a better chance of controlling the story.

"All right," the Rex said, waving a hand. "Take Miss Grace's body to Tilda as a show of good faith, and tell her about Olena's injuries. But I want a full update, and to be notified as soon as Lissa Olena is out of surgery. Is that understood?"

"Of course, Father." Trystan bowed his head, keeping his gaze low to avoid eye contact.

"You have until tomorrow night to get to Carnage," the Rex continued. "If you aren't back by then, I'll be forced to send more men to retrieve you. Like a child."

"Once I've completed my business with Tilda, I'll board a ship immediately." The very thought of going back to that place made him want to vomit all over the sleek marble floor. But at least he'd know beforehand that Delaney was safe.

So long as they could convince Tilda not to do anything rash.

DELANEY ADJUSTED THE zipper on her coat, then tugged at the ends of her gloves to make sure they were secure. She fidgeted, doing pretty much anything and everything she could think of to distract herself from the awkwardness of her current situation.

At her left, Trystan stood statue still, eyes trained straight ahead on the slowly closing ship doors. He hadn't spoken since the call with his father, other than to mention that he'd bought himself until tomorrow night, as planned. Whether or not the Rex was actually going to let him get away with that was still to be seen, but what choice did they have but to try?

On her right, Ruckus had his arms crossed over his chest, and was glaring. He wasn't doing it at anything in particular, which was why it was so obvious that his angered look was really meant for the Zane.

Shocker.

Fawna had arrived with Ruckus's ship less than twenty minutes ago, and they'd had to wait to check airspace to make sure she hadn't been followed before boarding.

Delaney had yet to even see the pilot, though Ruckus had met with her already in order to ensure everything was going as planned and they were safe. Apparently, Fawna had been hiding close by ever since they'd been captured in the Vakar palace. She was so good at staying hidden, she'd trailed the Kint ships all the way from there to Inkwell without once being detected.

Finally the doors clicked into place, and sealed with a low hissing sound.

"Lissa." Sanzie turned to her, angling her body between the awkward little group and the doorway. "Would you like to get a refreshment from—"

"An entire galaxy of *yes!*" She was halfway to the Sworn, eager to get away from the uncomfortable situation, when she had a thought. Coming to an abrupt stop, she inhaled deeply, and then spun around to address the guys. "Don't kill each other, okay? In fact, let's just make that a general rule from here on out, so that I don't have to worry about it happening later on down the line."

Trystan's expression suddenly matched Ruckus's. "You can't be serious."

She held his gaze. "Deadly so."

"If you recall, we've already had this discussion, Lissa."

At the mention of their original deal to keep the Ander safe, her eyes narrowed. They'd made that agreement before Trystan's father had thrown a wrench in everything. He couldn't seriously think their previous understanding still applied, could he?

"What are you complaining about?" Ruckus asked him tersely, saving Delaney from having to come up with a response. "I have more reason to want you dead than the other way around."

"That is far from true, and you know it." Trystan turned and shared a cryptic look with Ruckus over his shoulder. For a split second it actually seemed like the two of them were on the same page about something.

It freaked Delaney out too much to want to stick around and decipher what exactly that was, so instead she took a pointed step back. "Guys."

"Yes, all right." Trystan grunted. "But I still don't like it."

"Join the club." Ruckus pushed past him, bumping his shoulder pointedly against the Zane's to jostle him.

"Nope." Delaney signaled to Sanzie to proceed, giving the other two her back. "Not staying for this."

When the Sworn had led her halfway down the hall and she still didn't hear the sounds of zee fire or punches being thrown, some of the tension in her shoulders eased.

"They fight like children," Sanzie said as she broke the quiet, irritated. "It is a disgrace to their stations."

Delaney blinked at the Sworn as they took another corner, for a moment unsure how to respond. "Haven't they always been like that?"

Even as she asked, she knew that wasn't the case. They'd always disliked each other, sure; that'd been apparent when she'd been pretending to be Olena. But there'd still been a level of feigned respect between them, if only to keep up appearances.

"Wux is still an Ander, and therefore he must follow the Zane's commands," Sanzie told her. When Delaney laughed, Sanzie sent her a confused sideways glance.

"Ruckus was Trystan's prisoner for weeks," she reminded Sanzie, finding it a bit strange she even had to. "There's no way he's going to do what he says now that he's free. And he shouldn't be expected to, all things considered."

"He's not Vakar royalty; therefore, he must fall in line when in the presence of the Zane."

"I'm thinking the dynamics from before no longer apply," Delaney stated. "Does this have anything to do with you and Ruckus, about your past?"

Delaney still didn't have any of the details, only that the two of them had once served together in the Vakar army until Sanzie had gotten into an accident. The Sworn had been abandoned by her squad and, weirdly, rescued by the Zane. She'd worked for him ever since. That left a lot of questions up in the air, but Delaney hadn't had the time to press for answers.

"How close were you two, anyway?" It dawned on her that Sanzie had been leading the way since they'd left the hangar. And that this was Ruckus's ship. "How do you know where you're going?"

"These particular crafts are all built the same." She shrugged.

Delaney halted, suddenly not finding any humor in this. "I've been on both Vakar and Kint ships before, Sanzie. I know that's not true."

"Different models," she insisted, but it was obvious Delaney didn't believe her. "All right, yes, I've been on this vessel. I used to know Fawna, too. It was a long time ago; this should be the way to the kitchen area, though."

Sanzie started forward, leaving Delaney no choice but to follow after.

"Eventually you're going to have to tell me the whole story," she said at the Sworn's back, noticing the way her spine stiffened at her comment. She tried to ignore the quick flash of jealousy and suspicion that rushed through her. With the future as up in the air as it was, the past shouldn't matter to her.

"There's not much to tell," Sanzie assured her. "When I worked for Vakar, we sometimes went on missions together. The Ander's ship is one of the fastest and most secure on the planet. Not all of them can successfully operate within, and outside of, Xenith's atmosphere."

This was the same craft that Fawna had used to travel to Earth, and they were currently flying on the planet the same way an airplane would. Delaney didn't know much about rocket science, but she was aware a fighter jet couldn't do the same things a rocket could.

"Here we are, Lissa." Sanzie stepped through an opening in the wall and entered the tiny kitchen area on the ship. She motioned toward a large black box-shaped device tucked into the corner that had always reminded Delaney of a vending machine. "Shall I make you some squa?"

They were still in Inkwell, and it was chilly on the ship despite the fact that Fawna had turned the heat on as soon as she'd docked next to the palace. Up until that point, she'd apparently kept all heating systems off to avoid being detected by Kint.

"Funny story . . ." Delaney moved into the room and over to the device, sending a smile over her shoulder to ease the bite of her words. "I've actually been on this ship before, too."

There was a smaller rectangle in the center of the device, about the same size as a laptop screen. Until Delaney pressed her finger to it, it was black, but then it lit up a pale yellow. Words she didn't know began to appear, separated by an outline of tiny circles. She'd memorized what most of them would give her while on her trip back to Earth, though she didn't recall ever having tried squa here.

Before she could overanalyze, she tapped one of the buttons near the bottom—the drink she'd been obsessed with herself—and watched as a row of white lights lit up around the outside of the entire device.

A small compartment slid open around her knees, exposing a panel of glass, and a whizzing sound filled the silence. A second later a cup was pushed forward, a light pink liquid sloshing around, close to spilling over the rim. It was almost exactly like a coffee machine back on Earth, and the first time she'd tried it, Delaney had expected scalding, stale liquid to meet her tongue.

Instead it had tasted like rich, hot strawberry milk and roasted cashews.

"What would you like?" Delaney asked as she reached down to remove her cup. She set it on the counter at the right, and then turned back expectantly.

"I'm fine, Lissa."

She thought about pushing, then decided against it. The screen had a small arrow at the bottom right, and she tapped it so that the items offered would change. Then she selected the one she knew Ruckus would prefer, and waited for that cup to fill.

"What did you guys end up doing with the bodies?" Olena wasn't the only one they'd brought with them. She tried not to picture the way Pettus had looked, lying in her arms on the ground. His skin had already begun turning an ashy gray, and he'd been cool to the touch in a matter of moments. There'd been a lot of blood, but Delaney couldn't remember now if she'd gotten any on herself.

"They're in the lower deck," Sanzie told her tentatively, "and out of sight for now. Once we've presented the Basilissa with her daughter, I assume the Ander will have your friend cremated."

"So you don't bury the dead?"

"We do not." She'd taken up a soldier's stance as soon as they'd gotten to the device, her arms crossed behind her back, her feet squared. It was the flash of interest in her eyes that ruined the stiff appearance now. "I read somewhere that it's something your people do, though. You put them underground?"

"Does that seem strange to you?"

"I guess I just don't understand," she admitted. "Is there a reason?"

"Different ones for different cultures." The machine made the same sounds, indicating her order was done, and she removed the cup she'd gotten for Ruckus. "We have many cultures on my planet. You guys just have the two here, right?"

"We have Kint and we have Vakar," Sanzie confirmed.

"What about belief systems?" When the other girl frowned, Delaney elaborated. "Religions?" More confusion. "Why do you cremate your dead?"

"Bodies take up space."

"Ruckus mentioned there was a ceremony," she said. "A way to honor the dead?"

"Yes," she nodded, "we have that."

Delaney wanted to ask more, but the drink in her hand was at risk of getting cold. "I need you to do something for me."

"Anything, Lissa."

Her quick agreement made Delaney feel slightly guilty about what she was going to ask next. Not enough not to do it, though. Part of her wanted to note the Sworn's reaction, try to see if she could figure out how deeply this dislike she had for the Ander went.

"Bring this to Ruckus, please." She held up the cup, lifting a brow when Sanzie merely stared at it. "Come on." She shook the cup, careful not to spill its contents. "I'm not trying to make you friends. You can tell him it's from me, even."

"Perhaps—"

"We're on the Ander's ship, Sanzie." It was easy enough to figure out what she'd been about to say. "I'm perfectly safe here. I'll be fine alone."

"And the Zane?"

"Oh," Delaney rolled her eyes, laying it on thick, "there's no way those two are still in the same room together. You get this to Ruckus, I'll make sure the Zane doesn't die of thirst."

It was probably the least funny thing she could have said, and they both sobered instantly. But it wasn't long before the sad look in Sanzie's eyes morphed into something knowing. Almost as if the Sworn were thinking about how messed up Delaney had been when they'd brought Trystan's body back. How she hadn't been able to leave his side . . .

"He saved my life," she said, by way of explanation. "I owed him. It doesn't change anything."

"Of course, Lissa." Sanzie took the cup still being held aloft and then nodded her chin at the device. "Seventh icon, three rows down. That's the symbol for squa, in case you weren't aware."

Delaney nodded, sort of wondering how this had turned on her so quickly.

"If there's nothing else, Lissa?" Sanzie waited for Delaney to shake her head, and then the Sworn took a deep breath and openly scowled. "Then I guess I'll be taking this to the Ander now."

DELANEY AMBLED DOWN the corridors, not really knowing where she might find the Zane. They had some time before they'd enter Vakar territory, which meant she could afford to search for him.

Deciding to be productive while she did, Delaney began to think of all the ways to deliver the news of Olena's death. There was no good way to tell someone their child was dead, even one as awful as Olena had been, and she dreaded having to do so almost as much as she did having to go back to the palace at all.

While she hadn't had to worry about Kints as much there, at least in the sense that during her initial stay Vakar had still been under its own rule, she hadn't exactly been safe. Actually, she'd been safer in Inkwell, with Trystan, than anywhere else so far.

Delaney turned the corner and paused. Somehow, she'd managed to find him just by wandering aimlessly.

The door to one of the supply rooms was open, giving her the perfect view of the Zane as his finger slid across a shing screen. He had an assortment of items set out on one of the shelves before him, and kept pausing to physically check them, picking an item up, setting it back down, only to repeat the process on another.

It sort of looked like he was doing inventory, which was a little funny, considering that was the type of job someone should be doing for him. He seemed pretty focused, movements easy and confident. The same way he handled everything.

There was no logical reason for her to be nervous, and yet . . . The last time they'd been alone had been in the cave, and not only did she not want to think about that, she also didn't want to talk about it.

She took a step back the way she'd come, decidedly chickening out. The Zane could get his own damn drink in any case.

Unfortunately, her movement caught his attention and he glanced up before she could duck around the corner. When he noticed the two cups she was holding, the corner of his mouth tipped up.

With no other options left, she headed toward the room, already in the process of handing him the squa.

He set the shing down and took the cup, quirking a brow. "Aren't you going to sip it in front of me first?"

"Funny." She grunted, settling against the doorframe. He'd made a habit of taking the first sip of all her drinks back in Inkwell, to show her that none of them had been poisoned. To get her to trust him. "What are you doing in here?"

"Keeping busy mostly," he admitted.

"What? Not enough excitement going on for you?" It'd been meant as a joke, but she knew the second his mood changed. Straightening, she retreated a step back into the hall.

"We should talk," he said, not attempting to follow her.

"Sure"—she motioned to her left—"later. I've got to go say hi to Fawna."

"Delaney."

"All right." If he wanted to talk so badly, she'd do it, but they wouldn't be discussing what she figured he hoped they would. "I need to know we're on the same team here."

"Of course." He took a step toward her, stopping when she held up a hand.

"I mean all of us. History leads me to believe you're not exactly willing to play nice with Ruckus."

"Nor he with me," he reminded her.

"Yes," she said, sighing, "I know. I've had this conversation with him, too, believe me. This is a weird situation, but we need one another."

"Did you purposefully come find me alone so that we might speak about him behind his back? So you could ask me if I intend to . . . What? Shoot him while you aren't looking?"

She didn't respond.

The next step he took forward was stiff. "Because you're right, and there are other things for us to focus on at the moment, I'll soothe your fears by promising not to kill the Ander. But I should also remind you, Delaney, that we had a deal. The past few days change nothing."

She bristled, but forced herself not to crack in front of him. Before his father revealed his deception, she'd agreed to cooperate with Trystan in exchange for her friends' freedom and safety. But now Gibus had been kidnapped and Pettus was dead. Truthfully, things had gotten complicated, and she didn't know how she felt about anything anymore. Except the Rex. That was crystal clear.

"I'd say a lot has changed, actually," she said. Then, without giving him the chance to counter, she started down the hall.

He didn't try to stop her, and she made it through the rest of the ship without bumping into anyone else. It wasn't long before she spotted the familiar path leading to the cockpit.

The mechanical whirs and beeps flooded out the open doors as she approached, heading up a slight ramp to get there. Inside, the room was all curved walls and ceiling, with different computer setups lining the way to the front, where the main controls were located. There were two seats there, and the one on the left was currently occupied by a tall blond woman.

Her hair was pulled back into a tight bun, and at Delaney's approach, she tilted her head, scanning her with fuchsia eyes rimmed in dark blue.

Fawna never dressed in Teller uniforms, opting instead to keep a more casual appearance. This made sense, considering the woman wasn't technically a member of the army, but a freelancer. She got to use Ruckus's ship in return for taking his jobs above any others. The two were good friends anyway, so the arrangement was more for show than anything.

"It's nice to have you back," Fawna said, smile stretching wide when Delaney dropped down into the empty leather seat next to her. "I hear we've got some rotten cargo. Need me to stop anywhere, drop it off?"

"If you're referring to the Zane"—Delaney leaned forward to peer out the large glass screen before her—"then no. He stays, actually."

"Hmm." Fawna clucked her tongue. "Gotten used to having him around, huh? Can't really blame you. All that muscle . . . and the hair . . . that smoky way he talks . . ."

Delaney stared at her, completely forgetting about the frozen scenery they were speeding past outside.

"Close your mouth, Lissa," she teased. "I've got eyes, you know. And just because I like the sound of his voice, doesn't mean I have to like the things he says with it. I don't. He's sort of got a reputation for being a bastard."

"I can't really argue with you there."

CHAPTER 5

Ruckus tried to ignore her, he really did, but it was difficult having Sanzie so close—and so cross with him—after all this time. Truthfully, he'd done his best to not think of her over the past six years. After a while it'd even started working. It was impossible not to notice the Sworn now, though, especially when she was burning hotter than a full-blown furnace.

And it wasn't the good kind of heat.

She'd come in and practically dropped the hot cup of dalla on the table before him, mumbling something about how it was from Delaney before stepping off to the side. He'd expected her to exit the room after that, but she hadn't.

Instead she'd lingered, typing away at her communicator as if she actually had something important to do. Which he was almost certain wasn't the case, because Trystan had gone off to handle any remaining issues with Inkwell almost an hour ago.

Ruckus had chosen a small room off the main cargo hold, a space where he tended to go over information on missions or, after he'd become Ander, to check up on Olena. He felt more secure close to the exit, where he could get off the ship as soon as possible if anything happened and he was needed elsewhere.

Unfortunately, the current occupant was someone he didn't want there. With an annoyed sigh, he tossed aside his shing and stood, making his way across the small room to where Sanzie sat against the wall.

Once he was a few feet away, she lifted her head, cocking her brow in silent question.

"We should talk," he said, hating that he had to, even if it was the smartest thing to do. It was obvious she was still upset, and they needed to clear the air before her anger got in the way of what they were trying to do here. "It makes the most logical sense."

"There's nothing to talk about," she disagreed. She brushed off her uniform pants in an attempt to avoid looking at him again, so she missed seeing his jaw clench.

"We aren't good to anyone if we're distracted," he tried again.

"If you're having issues with focusing, that isn't my problem." Finally she straightened, and didn't bother hiding the ire in her eyes this time. "If it's that you feel guilty, I'm certainly the last person who wants to help you alleviate that."

That, right there, proved what he was saying was true. She was angry, and the tension between them was thick enough to rival the tension between him and the Zane—almost. He didn't hate her the way he hated Trystan, and he also didn't blame her for her feelings. Not entirely, anyway.

She thought he'd abandoned her, left her out in Morray to die.

"It didn't happen the way you think it did," he said, his voice dropping slightly with the weight of memory. He could still picture that day, see his breath freezing in the air. Feel the way his frozen toes had sat in his boots. The fear he'd felt when he thought he'd lost her. He'd disobeyed orders and gone after her; only, he'd been too late.

She'd already been saved by the Zane.

"That doesn't matter." Sanzie stepped away quickly, angling herself toward the open doorway. "It was a long time ago."

"I don't want this to be a problem between us. We used to work well together."

"We used to do a lot of things together, Ruckus. It was a long time ago," she repeated a bit more vehemently. "We don't need to discuss it."

"Are you harassing my Sworn, Wux?" Trystan appeared in the doorway, lazily propping a shoulder against the frame. He glanced between the two of them casually. Too casually, the way a predator sized up its prey just before the pounce. "Or are we taking a trip down memory lane? Shall I participate?"

When neither of them said anything, he pulled a smaller shing from his pocket and held it out to Sanzie. "I just got off the coms with Ezran, telling him to send someone to Dominan's house to ensure he and his mother stay indoors until this is over. I don't feel as if simply avoiding the castle is enough. Can you ensure that order was followed?"

"Yes, Zane." Sanzie nodded, almost gratefully, then took the device and fled.

That left the two of them standing there, facing each other, Ruckus glaring, Trystan's gaze impassive.

"She doesn't need you to fight her battles," Ruckus stated when it became obvious the Zane wasn't going to speak first.

He feigned surprise. "I wasn't aware the two of you were about to do battle. What would Delaney think? She's actually pretty fond of the Sworn, chose her for the position herself, even. I doubt she'd appreciate you causing trouble where it doesn't need to be."

"Don't tell me what Delaney wants." Even though he knew the Zane was merely trying to get under his skin, he couldn't help but take the bait. It was a sore spot, obviously. Hadn't been before, but ever since Ruckus had seen the way she'd looked at Trystan lying in that hospital bed, he hadn't been able to shake this jealousy.

He hated it, hated that he felt it and that he felt it about the Zane.

But it was fine. It was only an emotion, and he could handle it. Once this was over, if they survived, the Zane would no longer matter anyway. Ruckus and Delaney would head back to Earth, where they belonged, and resume their lives. He knew that. Trusted it.

He had to.

"The only reason you're still breathing," Ruckus found himself saying, despite his thoughts, "is because we need you. As soon as that's no longer the case—"

"You'll what, Wux?" Trystan straightened, though he kept his hands in his pockets, where he'd placed them again after handing off his device. "Don't forget who we are. The fact that we love the same woman changes nothing when it comes to station. I am still the Zane, and you are still merely an Ander."

Ruckus felt the air leave the room all at once. He struggled not to show it, that he suddenly felt unbalanced, but he wasn't sure if he pulled it off. His skills at playing pretend only stretched so far.

"Yes"—Trystan pulled out a hand to smooth down his shirt—"you happened to be correct in this one thing. I do love her. Congratulations." He seemed to recall himself, stilling his motions to grin darkly. "Though, I suppose you actually wish otherwise, no?"

Back in his cell, Ruckus had goaded Trystan, egging him on by pointing out that he had legitimate feelings for Delaney. At the time, it'd been a smart move, exposing to the Zane that he wasn't merely doing this out of necessity or some misguided duty toward his people. His words had sent the Zane stomping angrily out of the dungeons. It'd felt like a small victory.

It didn't anymore.

"So you've admitted to yourself how you feel," he said, reining in the uncomfortable, foreboding sensation in his gut. "Good for you."

"Oh, I didn't just admit it to myself." Trystan chuckled, took a moment to search his expression, and then smirked. It was actually more insulting than his grin had been, because there was way too much satisfaction in the look. "She didn't tell you that, did she."

It wasn't a question, so Ruckus didn't bother giving an answer.

Not that he had the time to anyway. Just then the ship jolted, shaking them both off their feet.

Ruckus slammed hard into the wall, his left shoulder taking the brunt of the hit. His skull rebounded and he hissed, biting his tongue when the ship suddenly tilted in the other direction, sending him careening into the opposite wall.

The Zane swore and caught himself against the doorframe as the ship righted, and the siren blaring overhead signaled that whatever had just happened, it wasn't yet over. He moved back into the hall at the same moment Ruckus took a step forward.

"We're under attack," Trystan growled as they began to run.

Ruckus took the lead, winding them through the ship toward the cockpit. He wanted to find Delaney first, make sure she was okay, but she wouldn't be if they didn't figure out who was shooting at them and why.

His worrying wasn't necessary anyway. He spotted her the second he entered the cockpit, the knot in his chest loosening some at seeing she was all right.

She had the belt over her waist, keeping her safely in the seat, and when he went to her, pressing a palm to the back of her neck, she leaned into him. A silent way of saying she was fine, even with a flicker of worry in her green eyes.

"It started as soon as we entered Vakar airspace," Fawna told him. Her fingers were moving quickly over the control panel, flicking switches and turning knobs faster than his mind could process.

He'd never been a good pilot. It was one of the only things he hadn't excelled at in training.

"Have you identified where the threat is coming from?" Trystan questioned.

With a jerk, Ruckus realized the Zane was standing on Delaney's other side. That his hand was currently resting on her shoulder. He was staring between the scene outside and a small computer screen set into the controls, searching for signs of their attackers.

"I'd say Vakar, but things are a little tangled now that you and your dad have taken over the place," Fawna stated. "So, really, it could be anyone."

"Not what I meant," Trystan growled, but his attention was diverted as soon as Delaney shifted forward in her seat.

"Here!" She pointed to a tiny blip on one of the screens.

It was flashing various shades of green, and when Ruckus looked, he could make out a slightly darker dot trailing close behind them.

"He was using the mountains for cover," Fawna said, though mostly to herself. "Clever."

"As much as I agree," Trystan drawled, "perhaps we can admire their stealth at a later date."

"I'll get—" Ruckus came to an abrupt stop, realizing what he'd been about to say. Worry over the attack drained away to make room for the grief that swamped him. He'd been about to order Pettus to the back of the ship, to operate the cannons there, like he always did.

But Pettus was gone.

"Hey." Delaney sent the word through their fittings, twisting so she could place a hand on his chest.

It was enough to snap him out of it. To focus. He turned to the Zane.

"Contact Sanzie and get her to the rear cannons," he told him, trying not to dwell on the fact that Trystan nodded and complied without putting up a fight. He widened his stance in the small space between the two chairs, securing himself more, even as their ship shook a third time.

Now that Fawna was aware of their attacker's location, whatever had hit them hadn't done so with nearly as much force as before.

"She's inside the rear cockpit now," Trystan informed him a second later.

"There's a com link to the right—large purple button. Have her connect with us."

Trystan sent the order through his fitting, and a second later a spot on the console in front of Fawna beeped. She pressed it.

Sanzie's determined voice came through to them, a bit crackly but otherwise clear. "I'm firing up the weapons. Awaiting order to engage."

"As soon as possible," Ruckus said, then swore when he glanced at the screen.

Delaney must have noticed the same thing as he did, for she cursed almost at the exact same time. "We've got more company!"

Another two blips had appeared next to the one they'd already discovered. They were in the process of widening around them, taking position to cover their entire flank.

Ruckus watched the blips' maneuvers closely for a few moments and then gripped the backs of Delaney's and Fawna's chairs. "They're going to start herding us to the left."

"How do you know?" Trystan frowned and bent closer to the screen.

"I recognize the formation pattern." He caught the Zane's gaze briefly. "I came up with it."

A heat missile fired from one of the blips, and they watched it make a beeline for them. Everyone had to grip something as Fawna tilted the ship at a forty-five-degree angle in order to avoid getting hit. Even after she'd straightened the craft again, the ground beneath their feet continued to shake.

"How are those cannons coming, Sanzie?" Trystan called into the com, then grunted when another jolt sent him sprawling forward. He caught himself on the console.

"Almost . . ." They heard a sharp clicking from her end. "There!"

From the screen, they watched a trail of the same heat missiles fire out of their own ship. Sanzie let loose a string of them, tugging the cannon from one end to the other to cover their entire rear. It forced the three attacking vessels to disperse, giving Ruckus's ship a wider berth.

"It doesn't seem to be doing anything," Delaney pointed out, and she was right.

"They have shields," Ruckus explained.

"Why don't we?"

"We do," Fawna answered for him. "It's up now; that's why we haven't had a hole blown through the walls or anything. Yet."

"Comforting." Delaney started inspecting the controls in front of her, brow furrowing in deep concentration.

Which was a look that often made Ruckus feel a little wary, because it almost always led to some kind of reckless adventure or unknown. Like when she'd convinced him the elevator ride at that theme park Six Flags would be *fun*.

It had not been.

"Not sure I like where this is going, sweetheart," he confessed, even though she'd yet to allude to what she was thinking.

"I assume there are guns at the front of the ship as well, right?" she asked, either ignoring his comment or just too caught up in her head to have processed that he had spoken to her.

His money was on the first.

"How do you access them?" She glanced over at Fawna's section of the console, obviously making note of the differences. Then she reached below the lip of the console in front of her and smirked when she found a hidden button there. A second later the lights began flashing in front of her, and a panel slid out to cover her lap, securing her even more in her chair.

The controls popped out, a wheel that could control the guns attached to the front of the ship. There were six buttons in total, three on either side, placed for easy access while holding the wheel.

"Just like one of those driving video games," she said to herself with a humorless chuckle. "Okay, what now?"

"They're behind us," Ruckus started, "so that won't be—"

One of their attackers appeared directly to their left, swerving in front of them. The movement was so fast, they'd almost collided with them. Fawna only managed to dodge at the last second.

"You were saying?" Trystan drawled, somehow finding enjoyment in all this despite their situation.

Ruckus sent him a glare and then directed all his attention to the controls in Delaney's hands.

"Here," he said, tapping the first button on the right side of the controller. As soon as he did, panels on both sides of the front of the ship opened, and two large cannons lifted out. He bent over Delaney's smaller form, settling his arms lightly on top of hers so he could use his fingers to direct her thumbs over the other buttons. "The middle ones fire regular rounds. The bottoms let loose large ones. There aren't many of those, though, so try not to use them unless we have to."

When he pulled back, he tried not to openly smile at the scowl painted across the Zane's face.

Delaney twisted the wheel to the right, and the cannons outside quickly adjusted toward her target. Without hesitation, she pressed down on the middle buttons, and a round of fire shot off toward the attacking ship.

Before any of the zees could make impact, they came up against an invisible force field. As soon as one of the zees hit it, the force field glimmered green, and the zee fizzled in a spark.

"We've got to do something about those," Trystan stated, watching as the enemy remained totally unaffected. On the smaller screen, they could see Sanzie was still keeping the other two at bay, but it wouldn't be for long. Eventually they'd take the risk of getting closer and damaging their shields.

But there was no way they were going to get lucky enough for that to happen. Their attackers had already gotten a head start, had been slowly chipping away at their shield. If one was to fail, it would not be their attackers'.

"Do you have this?" he asked Delaney, and even after she nodded, he found it difficult to step away. Forcing himself to, he motioned with two fingers at the Zane, turning to rush down the ramp into the heart of the ship without waiting to see if he was going to follow.

"I assume that means you have a plan, Ander?" Trystan appeared at his side a few steps later, clearly nonplussed by their role reversal.

"Ever jumped out of a ship before?" Ruckus turned his head in time to catch the Zane's widening gaze, and chuckled. Without further explanation, he led them to a chamber off to the side that was rarely used. It housed most of their more advanced tech, the stuff that had been necessary during the war, but had since become next to obsolete.

Fortunately, because their treaty had been so tentative, the Basileus had ordered all military ships to keep their stash of weaponry on the off chance it might one day become necessary again.

Ruckus hadn't been the Basileus's biggest fan, but he had to admit that the man knew what he was doing at least half the time. Too bad the other half, all those bad decisions, were what had gotten Magnus killed in the end.

The door panel slid open as soon as Ruckus pressed his palm against it, and he entered before it'd fully disappeared into the wall. Everything was exactly where he'd left it, despite his leaving the ship and its running to Pettus and Fawna while he'd been away on Earth.

He shifted through a few things, moving toward one of the built-in metal closets, and then sighed in relief when he spotted what he was looking for.

He snatched two of the three packs hanging from hooks and tossed one to the Zane, angling his head down to hide his grin when the ship tipped at that exact moment, causing the pack to smack Trystan in the face.

All too quickly, the Zane righted himself, holding up the pack to see what it was. His eyes glimmered and he began unzipping the proper compartments, dropping to one knee so he could place it on the floor for better access.

"This is daring," he said while he worked, proving that he had in fact done this before, despite his words. "I'll admit to being impressed, Ander. Well done."

"Your compliments are making me uncomfortable."

"I was stating a fact," Trystan corrected, "not giving you a compliment. I do *not* enjoy your military prowess." That last part was said under his breath, and Ruckus was sure he'd misheard him.

Not caring enough to ask about it, Ruckus attached the last wire and then adjusted the straps, swinging the pack up and over his shoulders. He secured the belt around his waist, tightening it for good measure, and then turned to find the Zane was doing the same.

"You're aware," Trystan said as he finished, glancing up at him, "that if this goes horribly wrong—which is likely—we've just left Delaney unprotected, correct?"

"Don't worry." He turned to the camouflaged exit panel, lifting the lid that covered the touch pad. "If it comes down to you or me, I'll push you in the way of the zee fire and make sure I get back to *my* girlfriend safely."

He slapped his palm against the pad, and after a moment the loud scraping of metal on metal filled the room. The hatch leading to the outside began to ease its way open, the door at their back sealing tightly to prevent the change in airflow from affecting the rest of the ship.

Trystan stepped up to his side, watching as the gray sky was slowly exposed. "That would make you a cold-blooded killer, Wux." He tilted his head, caught Ruckus's eye. "Does she know you have that in you? She called me a monster; I wonder what she'd think if she heard the words that just left your mouth."

"Delaney knows who I am." Ruckus clenched his jaw, glad when the hatch finally opened the rest of the way and they could get on with this. Even though heights made him uncomfortable. "You know what to do?"

"Of course," he scoffed. "Who do you think developed this technology? Because I can assure you, it wasn't Vakar. We—"

Ruckus didn't give Trystan time to finish, instead opting to do what he'd wanted to do ever since he'd first met the Zane.

He pushed him out the window and watched his body plummet.

CHAPTER 6

Trystan was going to kill the Ander. No ifs, ands, or buts about it. This time he was serious. Ruckus Wux was done for.

As soon as Trystan managed to regain some control over his quickly falling body.

It'd been a while since he'd had to jump out of a moving vehicle—any moving vehicle—especially one as large as a ship. And, as he dropped, he was forced to admit that the Ander's ship was a pretty impressive size at that. No wonder they'd been targeted. How the hell had they expected to get away with entering Vakar in that monstrosity?

He reached for the latch at his right side, fingers fumbling to lift the flap of fabric meant to protect the controls from being accidentally hit. In his struggle, he ended up tearing the scrap of material loose, and the wind quickly tore it from his grasp. It fluttered away, disappearing in less than a heartbeat.

Placing his first three fingers against the controls, he pressed, holding down while the device did a quick scan of his body. The technology was brilliantly made—by a Kint—and was designed to digitally map a person's specs in under five seconds.

It was too loud for him to hear the beep signaling the scan was complete, but he noticed the flashing green light at his hip and pulled his hand away just in time for the machine to do the rest of its job.

He'd already opened the side panels on the pack on his back, to allow for a faster response time, and he held his arms straight out at his sides and spread his legs wider as material began to spool out.

It was a light shade of gray, like the surrounding sky, and covered in millions of tightly packed tiny rubber dots. The whole process took under thirty seconds, the soft material wrapping around his torso and up and down his limbs. Once his fingers were covered, it tightened, briefly impeding his ability to breathe as it adjusted around him.

The helmet came last, stretching up from the neck to encase his head in a clear plastic. Lights flickered in front of his eyes as systems came online, and then he felt the distinct pressure at the base of his skull, which indicated that the suit was connecting to his fitting. Doing so allowed him hands-free control, and with only a thought, he activated the jets in the soles of the gray boots he now wore.

They propelled him upward, and he scanned for the Ander. While it'd felt like he'd been falling for an eternity, it'd actually been under a minute. He spotted Ruckus wearing a similar suit, hovering at the side of his ship. When Trystan approached, Ruckus signaled toward the attacking ship on the right.

As much as Trystan loathed taking orders from someone technically beneath him, he gave the Ander a curt nod. This wasn't about struggling for alpha status, not when Delaney was currently on the ship being shot at.

The suits they were wearing helped camouflage them, so there was little fear that the enemy had spotted them. But they wouldn't protect from cannon fire, so Trystan gave himself a moment to assess a path before directing the suit toward the attacking vessel. He weaved and dodged, feeling the heat from some of the zees as they passed him. It would have been difficult enough without having to worry about Sanzie shooting from the opposite direction, but of course she was.

From the corner of his eye, he saw that the Ander was close to the other attacking ship. For optimal success, they needed to use their packs at close to the same time, so Trystan sped up.

Numbers raced across the screen in the corner of his visor, giving him updates on how high he was, how quickly he was approaching the oncoming ship. When he was less than ten feet from it, a beam came out to scan for the presence of force fields. Knowing there was one already in use, Trystan straightened his body so that he was in a somewhat upright position.

His hand dropped back to the control panel at his side, feeling out the triangular button at the bottom. As soon as the screen on his visor flashed that it had latched onto the force field, he pressed it.

He felt the pack at his back open at the top, and a good portion of the weight he'd been carrying lifted as a black box rose into the air and then slammed forward. As soon as it made contact with the force field, a bright burst of electricity hit it, and bolts of sharp yellow skittered around the entire ship, frying the wiring.

The protective shield flickered once, twice, and then vanished, leaving the ship vulnerable.

Sanzie must have been watching, for Trystan barely had enough time to dive out of the way before a large missile shot through the air toward them. The impact, and following explosion, forced him sailing backward, his body spiraling uncontrollably.

He allowed it to happen, let himself get swept away, dodging the raining bits of metal and debris now dropping to the ground from the destroyed ship on every turn. From the looks of things, the Ander had successfully deactivated the force field of his target as well, and even now Sanzie was taking it out of the sky.

Finally Trystan's momentum slowed and he was able to regain control. He twisted so that he was facing the final attacking Vakar ship. There was no sign of the Ander, but that was no matter. These suits had only been rigged with one power cell—the tiny EMP device that'd taken out the force fields. There was nothing he or Ruckus could do about this final ship.

Just hope that Delaney could handle breaking through the ship's shield on her own. And it looked like she was doing just that.

Even as Trystan thought it, the field around the final attacking ship began to flicker in places. Without the other two to help damage Ruckus's, it seemed this smaller vessel didn't have the fortitude to withstand so many zees at once.

Their shield gave way with a crackle, and the final zees Delaney was firing finally hit their mark. The ship struggled to maintain its balance for another precious second before a loud burst of one of the engines sent the vessel careening downward.

Trystan watched it spiral in the air, plummeting toward a patch of snow-covered ground. He remained where he was, flying at the side of the Ander's ship, long enough to feel like it was safe for him to head after the enemy without getting caught up in their gravitational pull. Because he'd already tipped his face toward the ground, he heard more than saw when Fawna changed their ship's trajectory to do the same.

He'd never say so aloud, but Ruckus had selected impressive people for his team. Vaguely, he wondered how much of their skill had been honed on the actual battlefield. Trystan had never encountered any of them during the war, or if he had, he had no knowledge of it. Though it was doubtful, seeing as how the Ander was well-known— so he would have recognized him. And those who went up against Trystan tended not to survive.

As Ruckus's ship passed him, he was forced to hang back, a bit annoyed. He was eager to get down there and check the enemy ship for survivors. Even more so to get back to Delaney. He'd known as soon as she'd figured out how to operate the controls that she'd handle the cannons on the ship just fine, but there was still a nagging thought in the back of his head telling him he had to see her to be sure she was all right.

The Ander appeared just as Trystan's boots were about to touch the ground, a little closer to the side of the ship. Before either of them could make their way toward it, the door at the side slid open, revealing a row of metal stairs unwinding to sink into the snow.

Delaney appeared at the top, breathing heavily, her eyes jumping back and forth between the two of them as both men trudged their way over.

The snow was up to their knees, and Ruckus stumbled just as he was about to reach the end of the stairs. These particular suits weren't exactly made with good traction.

She was at his side in a matter of seconds, wrapping her arm around his waist to help him tug himself free and get onto the first step. "Don't slip."

Trystan expected her to follow the Ander up, and he actually hesitated when she simply directed Ruckus halfway there before turning back. He was grateful for his helmet, because the glare from the sun, even as low as it was, probably kept the Ander, who glanced over his shoulder, from seeing his expression.

"Would you hurry up," Delaney called, and a thick puff of white burst past her lips as she did. "It's freezing." When her gaze dropped down to the snow, it was clear she was struggling with being near it.

Was she afraid because of what happened with Olena?

Before he could even think to ask, she surprised him again, stepping down to the final step to stretch her arm out toward him. Any trepidation was gone, replaced with determination, and a bit of irritation. Probably at having to retrieve them out here at all.

When he was close enough, Trystan grasped her hand, allowing her to help ease him closer to the stairs, and then onto them. The melting ice and snow the Ander had trailed made it a dangerous climb, and he slipped a few times, only to be immediately caught by Delaney.

They reached the top, and as soon as they were inside, she let go. He tried not to acknowledge how the loss of her touch stung.

"You." She waved a frustrated hand at the Ander, who was already stripping out of his suit. "So much for 'I won't be stupid if you won't be stupid.' That? That was stupid."

He must have replied through their fittings, because after a silent moment she snorted and vehemently shook her head at him.

"Don't even try that bullshit," she said. "You two"—she turned so she could address both of them with her angry glare—"drive me crazy. Next time one of you has a plan like that, I'm coming with." She held up a finger as Ruckus opened his mouth, silencing him before he could speak. "Nope. I know damn well Fawna could have managed to steer the ship and fire those guns at the same time. Trying to deny it will only piss me off."

"Unlike how you are now," Ruckus teased, "which is calm."

Trystan frowned, watching their exchange. Instead of getting more angry at him for his comment, Delaney actually started to smile. He was almost certain that if he'd said anything like that, he would have received another scathing remark for his efforts.

That realization pricked and he took a breath, hoping neither of them noticed the hitch there.

Which was of course wishful thinking—kind of like believing he'd be unaffected seeing the two of them interact. The sound immediately drew Delaney's attention, and the smile on her lips wavered.

"Ruckus," she said, looking at him, "since your suit's off, can you go check in with Fawna? When I left, she was scanning the enemy ship for survivors."

He hesitated, but to his credit he didn't glance suspiciously Trystan's way. "All right. I'll meet you back here as soon as I have an update. If there are survivors, we're going to have to get moving, fast." He disappeared quickly around the bend.

This was only the second time they'd been alone since the cave, and Trystan found he didn't know quite what to say. Actually, that wasn't really true; there was a lot he wanted to say, but their time was limited. The Ander would come back soon. The last thing he needed was Ruckus walking in on the two of them discussing emotions and feelings. He had a reputation as dangerous and uncaring to uphold. That was what was going to help keep them safe, after all.

Besides, he'd already tried talking to her about what had happened, and she'd changed the subject so fast, he'd practically gotten whiplash.

Delaney was staring at him, her lips slightly pursed. Her eyes roamed down the suit he was wearing, noting the puddle that was forming beneath his boots from all the snow he'd tracked in. "Can you take that off?"

"Want me out of my clothes now that the Ander is gone?" he couldn't help but ask, feeling a little bad about the remark when she dropped her gaze before regaining her composure.

"It looks like the cilla suits," she said.

Quickly, he began removing it, talking to fill the space between them and possibly distract her from the memories that were no doubt filtering through her head. "I believe they used the cilla suit as the model for this tech. Originally, only my people had them, but then Vakar stole the specs in the middle of the war, and suddenly evened the playing field. . . . For a short time, anyway."

He pulled his arms free and unlatched the pack from around his waist, slipping it off his shoulders next. When it dropped to the floor, it took down most of the material around his chest and waist, so that all he had left to do was peel the cloth from his legs. It took some effort because of how tightly wound around him it all was, but he didn't feel embarrassed with Delaney watching him balance on one foot then the other to do so.

"The problem with these are that, unlike the cilla suits, they can't be easily reused." He dropped the material in a heap and stepped away from it. "They have to be completely reprogrammed, which takes time."

"You were supposed to take it easy," she reminded him, luckily putting an end to his rambling. "Doctor's orders."

He scoffed. "I'm a Zane. I take orders from no one. Besides, I did what was necessary, and we made it out, didn't we? Our attackers are felled and we've lived to tell the tale. Just another day, really."

The main loading dock of the ship was spacious, making it more obvious how far she was standing from him. How badly he wanted to remove the space between them, take her in his arms, and hold her. Prove that she was all right, despite his father's attempts. If he'd just been a minute later, Olena would surely have killed her.

This was all a new experience, feeling things this strongly for someone else, and Trystan was actually a bit worried he'd screw it up by pushing too far, too quickly.

The realization almost made him laugh, because when had he ever cared before about ensuring someone else's comfort above his own? The truth was, though, he'd been doing that for Delaney a lot longer than just that night in the cave.

He thought back to that moment shared between her and the Ander. He wanted that. It seemed so easy between them, so simple. What could he do to get them to that place as well?

"Trystan . . ." She paused, then took a breath and set her hands on her hips determinedly. "How are you feeling, actually? I get you don't understand the concept of rest, being the Zane and all, but if you don't take care of yourself and something happens to you—"

"I feel fine, Delaney." He waited until she was looking at him again before adding, "Really."

When she didn't say anything else, he took a step forward, yet he didn't pay enough mind to exactly where it was he was placing his foot. Though the soles of his military-issue boots had more traction than the ones created by the suit, the puddle caught him off guard, and he slid, almost falling backward for the millionth time in the past twenty minutes alone.

Delaney rushed to him, latching onto his waist to help right him even as he caught himself on the wall at his back.

For a second they just stared at each other, and then she burst into laughter. Her body shook against his, and her grip on his hip eased, though she didn't remove her hands. When he laughed, too, she briefly dropped her forehead against his chest.

Before he could stop himself, he reached out, cupping her jaw to tilt her face back up to his. There were tears sparkling at the corners of her eyes, but the smile on her lips died down as soon as their gazes met.

He hated that he'd ruined the moment for her, but it didn't keep him from gently running the pad of his thumb across the rise of her cheek.

Footsteps echoed from the hallway, and Delaney pulled away, moving to renew the space between them. She crossed her arms and turned toward the door, and it was impossible for him not to feel dismissed by the move.

He opened his mouth to say as much, but the Ander walked back in then, a bundle of jackets in his arms.

"There are survivors," he informed them, handing one of the jackets over to Delaney. It was the red one Trystan had had specially made. Then Ruckus tossed the white one at him. "We should go have a chat. Maybe about the weather?"

"He makes jokes now." Trystan barely resisted the urge to roll his eyes as he quickly donned the jacket.

"Fawna will keep the ship running," Ruckus continued, "in case we need to make a quick exit. We counted half a dozen on the thermal reader. It's a tiny vessel, but there could be more hiding deeper within."

"We're just finding out who sent them, right?" Delaney zipped her jacket up and adjusted her fritz bracelet. Almost like they were going out for the evening—not about to encounter a group of trained Tellers.

"Chances are they recognized your ship," Trystan said. "It was put on the enemies' watch list as soon as Kint took over Vakar. I'd thought this course was off the beaten path enough to avoid detection, but perhaps I was mistaken."

It would have been smarter to have taken his Kint ship, he was realizing, but that would have meant leaving those who'd remained at Inkwell with no evacuation plan. All other military crafts were too small; at least his could hold more than half of the city's population, should it come to that. If they failed somehow, and there was a war, both Tilda and his father knew Inkwell was where he spent most of his time.

If either chose to get revenge against him, for one reason or another, that'd be the first location they'd hit.

"He admits he's wrong now," the Ander mocked. Then: "If that is the case, and they recognized us, we'll have to make sure they didn't send any communications out. If the Rex discovers my ship was on its way to Vakar, our cover story could be blown."

"Let's do this already." Delaney opened the hangar doors, a gust of icy wind slapping her in the face. Immediately her cheeks were stained rosy, but she remained collected. Any hint of that fear Trystan had glanced earlier was completely gone.

He'd always been impressed by her ability to absorb things, the way she could so quickly accept a situation, and, if not move on, plan out how to make it better. While he struggled with outside change, needing complete control in all things, she adapted. And if the way she'd handled things this morning was any indication, she'd finally decided to slip into her role as Lissa.

The corner of his mouth tipped up as he followed the other two back out, glad that he'd taken up the rear, so neither of them noticed him smile.

They'd landed in an empty field of white, which sprawled out in every direction. The sky above was just as void, gray and looming. Even though Inkwell was technically part of Vakar territory—though that went pretty much unacknowledged by the Kints who lived there—only this small section was experiencing winter. They hadn't made it far, which was why they'd yet to escape the frozen tundra.

Another fifteen minutes in the air and they would have begun to see green. The rest of Vakar had already entered its spring season, so temperatures would be warmer and it would be easier for them to travel on foot.

A thing Trystan was greatly looking forward to, since each step was a struggle as they slowly made their way around their own ship. The single enemy craft that had escaped total explosion came into view as soon as they rounded the nose. At least half of the Tellers that Ruckus had mentioned were already crowding around outside, their weapons drawn.

One of them fired, and the three of them darted back around the side of their ship. They hunkered lower, activating their fritzes as zees continued to ping at their backs.

"You go draw their fire; I'll stay here with Delaney," Ruckus said. "As soon as you've directed their attention elsewhere, she and I will make our move."

"Or," Trystan suggested, "you go, and I will stay. I'm larger, and therefore will make a better shield for her should any of them break formation and come this way."

"We have the same build," he argued.

"I am an inch taller."

"That can't be true."

"Can't it?" Trystan waved a hand out toward the snowy expanse. "You go, I'll stay, and should you perish along the way . . ." He lifted a single shoulder. "Let's just say, it's much easier to replace an Ander than it is to find another Zane."

"Especially one whose arrogance can rival your own," Ruckus bit out.

The sound of zee fire had continued during their discussion, but suddenly cries accompanied it. It was a second before he noticed, too caught up in his next barb for the Ander, but when he did, Trystan frowned.

It was clear Ruckus had caught on as well, and the two of them looked at each other for a moment before twisting around at the same time.

Delaney was no longer standing behind them.

Cursing, they shot around the nose of the ship a second time, their weapons raised.

And came up short.

Delaney had already dropped two of the Tellers, and was currently in the midst of a firefight with the remaining four. She retreated to avoid getting hit by one of them, dropping into a low crouch behind a snowbank.

"A little help here, guys," she snapped, her annoyance palpable.

Trystan rushed into motion, coming the rest of the way around their ship, already firing at the enemy. As soon as he passed her, he felt Delaney take position at his back.

"I've got the assholes on the left," she told him, a split second before she resumed shooting.

"I'll take right." Trystan kept his weapon aimed at the two Tellers there, one of whom had stopped shooting back. Either his weapon had jammed, or he needed to reload. Either way, the Zane wasn't going to give him the chance to fix his problem.

It was easy enough to take them out, hitting the Teller still with a working weapon in the shoulder first, and then landing a zee at the center of his chest. The next guy fell swiftly, and after a quick check to make sure they were really out, Trystan finally turned back to see Delaney had handled her targets as well.

Now that the initial threat had been neutralized, he took a breath, glancing over to find that the Ander hadn't made it very far from where they'd started. And he was frowning at them.

"Well?" Delaney's impatient voice drew Trystan's attention toward the enemy ship. A large hole had been ripped through the port, and she was standing next to it, her fritz held tightly in both hands. "Are you two coming or what?"

It must have been a rhetorical question, because without waiting for them, she twisted around and went straight through the torn gap and into the dark body of the ship.

CHAPTER 7

Delaney didn't exactly know where she was going.

She wound her way through the smaller ship, peering around corners before turning them, her fritz at the ready. Shooting those Tellers outside had been easy, especially on account of how annoyed she'd already been with the guys and their constant bickering.

Did it really matter which of them stayed to protect the "damsel"? She grunted, checked the right hall, and chose to head down it once she saw it was clear.

She could barely recall the last time she'd been a legitimate damsel in distress. Maybe the first time her parents had forgotten her at home alone? Or the time Tiffany Fogolstien had dropped that note in the hall telling their entire middle school class Delaney wanted to sleep with her best friend's boyfriend? A total lie.

But, no, she couldn't even count those occasions, because for the first, she'd hidden her parents' stuff in anger, and for the latter, well . . . Tiffany's friends talked enough shit behind her back, spreading all of her actual secrets, that Delaney never even had to lift a finger.

So, really, aside from the whole initial kidnapping thing—which, when she looked back on it now, she thought she'd actually handled fairly well—there wasn't a specific occasion when she'd ever fit the damsel-in-distress bill.

She'd known they'd follow close behind, yet she hadn't bothered to wait for them. They were both too stealthy for her to pick up on their movements, but she trusted they'd find her eventually. Besides, as stupid as heading in here alone probably was, she needed to prove to them things weren't going to be as they'd been.

Coddling her, keeping secrets, sugarcoating things . . . Yeah, none of that was necessary.

A soft murmuring ahead stopped her, and she shifted closer to the wall. She couldn't make out anything they were saying, but she was able to separate out at least two voices, both male.

Risking a step closer in an attempt to eavesdrop, Delaney steadied her finger over the trigger of her fritz just in case. All of that target practice, first with Ruckus, and then later with Trystan, had already come in seriously handy.

"Moving in?" Trystan's voice whispered through her mind like a phantom, and the timing, and suddenness of it, caused her to jump. *"Easy, Lissa."*

He rested a hand on her arm, and she turned to find that both he and Ruckus had snuck up behind her. The two of them standing in the hallway somehow made the space seem tighter, and for a moment all she could do was stare as she waited for her heart to settle its rhythm.

"What have you got?" Ruckus asked, speaking through their fittings, same as Trystan just had.

"Two of them. They sound frantic, but I can't make out what they're saying," she told them, one at a time.

"Let's go ask them to speak up." Trystan looked in the direction the voices were coming from. *"Shall we?"*

He breezed past her, walking as if he were heading into a corporate business meeting, and not into a room with a couple of unknown armed men. As he did so, he adjusted his collar, then sent a quick wink over his shoulder at her.

Delaney and Ruckus followed, though they left some space between them in the very likely chance this all went sideways. The hall wasn't wide enough for them to walk side by side, so Ruckus settled behind her, still close enough that she could feel the warm puffs of his breath fanning across her neck.

"Gentlemen," Trystan's voice called up ahead, and she picked up the pace just a little. "I'd like to discuss a few things with you."

Delaney moved forward just in time to see both of the Tellers lift their weapons and take aim at the Zane. Hers came up automatically, and she had them both on the ground before either managed to get off a shot of their own.

"Well," Trystan drawled, "that was a short conversation."

"Could you *not*?" she practically growled, shoving him out of the way so she could make it across the room toward the only other door. A quick glance showed it led to another set of halls. "They could have shot you, you idiot."

"I trusted you'd have my back," Trystan said, already standing behind her again.

With a roll of her eyes she entered the other hall, weapon trained ahead in case any other remaining Tellers had heard the commotion. Sure enough, not halfway down the new corridor, a Teller leaped from a side room.

The Zane shot him and they kept moving, with him checking all the rooms on their right, and her doing the same with the ones on their left. Five minutes later they finally arrived to what was probably the center of the ship.

There were two Tellers in the control room, distractedly talking among themselves. They hadn't noticed they had company yet.

"Let's not kill these ones, hmm?" Trystan suggested, smirking when she glowered. Still, he kept his fritz raised as he entered, moving off to the side to make room for her and Ruckus to follow.

Once they had the exit completely blocked off, Delaney cleared her throat.

The Tellers whipped around, but the second they saw weapons already trained on them, they hesitated with their own.

"Zane." The man on the left looked shocked to see him. "You weren't supposed to be here. If he'd known you were aboard that ship—"

The other Teller hit the one talking, shutting him up.

"He who?" Trystan questioned, angling his head at them. When neither of them appeared keen to answer, he grunted, took a wild guess. "My father."

"I know these men," Ruckus suddenly seemed to realize, moving to step past Delaney and Trystan. His eyes scanned them, his frown deepening. "They're Tellers in the Left-Center. You're Vakar. Did the Basilissa set this up?"

"That's a very good question." Something in Trystan's tone had Delaney looking at him. He was also staring, but the confusion that had been on his face earlier had morphed into something new. There was a calculation there, an intensity. It was the same look he got whenever he thought he'd figured out something particularly tricky.

He looked at her that way a lot.

"We aren't going to tell you anything." The one who'd quieted the other had his fritz pressed against his comrade's side in the span of a blink. He'd fired the weapon and turned it on himself before any of them could react.

Delaney watched as both bodies dropped to the ground in a heap, a pool of blood already spilling out around them. "Holy shit. He just . . ."

Trystan cursed.

"Did you send for them?" Ruckus switched things up, drawing

the Zane's attention away from the corpses. "When you took control of Vakar, did you send for troops from other areas? To help reinforce the capital?"

He shook his head. "That wasn't necessary. I brought a small Kint army along with me. Your men were left wherever they'd been stationed."

"Where's the Left-Center?" Delaney wanted to get off this ship. The hole in the side was letting in a lot of the chill, and the temperature kept dropping.

"An area near the western border that separates Kint and Vakar," Trystan explained, though it was halfhearted. Distracted, he crouched down to get a better view of the Tellers.

"Okay, so who would want a group of Vakar Tellers to attack us?" Delaney glanced around the room, trying to find anything that could help give them answers.

"We should check their com-log." Trystan straightened and made his way across the room, carefully avoiding contact with the bodies. "Maybe we'll find something. And we can make sure they didn't report us."

"And if they did?" Delaney waited where she was as the two of them began accessing the various computers in the room. She hadn't had enough lessons with the tutor Trystan had hired for her to be able to read their language. Maybe that was something she should consider changing.

"No one's come for us yet," Ruckus said, clicking away at a counter that looked like a giant keyboard with five times as many keys.

"They didn't get any messages out. But—" Trystan swore and pulled away from the computer he'd been searching.

"What?" Delaney moved closer.

"Tars," he said. "They were Tars."

"I thought you handled the Tars." Delaney frowned at Trystan. "Back in Kilma."

"It was a setup," Trystan told them, smoothing his hair back in frustration. "One organized by my father."

To get him away from Delaney. Made sense. She took a deep breath, tried to think past the anger and the lingering fear she still felt about that entire situation. Dwelling wasn't going to help them figure this out.

"He was using them."

"Still is, apparently." Ruckus abandoned the console he'd been searching and joined them. "But from the sounds of it, they knew who they were attacking. Do you think the Rex knows?"

Delaney held her breath while Trystan thought it over. If his father did know, they were screwed. In order for this to work, they needed to be the ones to tell Tilda about Olena. If the Rex beat them to it, who knew what kinds of lies he'd spin?

"If he knows I'm alive and Olena is dead," she said, "that means you aren't safe, Trystan."

"He doesn't know. If he did, he would have sent a lot more than one measly ship after us. No"—he shook his head—"this was a co-incidence. He must have left the Tars with instructions to attack should they ever see the Ander's ship. My father knows that Ruckus had friends in the Vakar army, and in the palace."

"You think this was just a precaution?" She wasn't sure if that made her feel any better.

"They didn't receive any orders, or send any messages," he re-minded her. "And they're too far for their fittings to have worked. That means they were operating on old orders."

"The one thing we know for certain is that the Tars are working for the Rex," Ruckus pointed out.

"Back in Kilma, all the Tars I spoke to clearly had no idea about my father's plans," Trystan said. "They'd been used. If they have been working for my father this whole time, I don't think they're aware of it."

Leave it to the Rex to manipulate a group from behind the sidelines, having them do all his dirty work so he could keep his hands clean. Had he been responsible for everything the Tars had done, or just a few events here and there? How far did his reach with them go?

"Delaney is cold. You should take her back to the ship," Trystan said after a moment of silence, scanning the circular room. "I'll do a final search to ensure we're not missing anything. We can discuss what to do with this information later."

Ruckus lifted a dark brow. "You want us to leave you here? Alone?"

Trystan scowled and flung out his arms. "In a destroyed, empty craft? Enlighten me, Ander: What is it exactly you think I'm going to do? What nefarious plot have you imagined I've come up with in the past five minutes we've been standing here?"

"All right." Delaney so didn't want to deal with this, especially because, as he'd said, she *was* cold. Already it was getting hard to feel her stiff fingers. "But be back in ten."

The Zane held her gaze a moment, and then nodded.

"I mean it, Trystan. If I have to come back out here to find you, I'm going to be pissed."

"Go." He angled his chin toward the hall at her back. "I'm right behind you."

Ruckus clearly didn't like it, but when Delaney took his hand, she didn't really leave him much choice but to go with her.

"HERE, LISSA." Sanzie handed her a mug with steam coming out the top. The liquid within was a pale pink.

"Thank you." Delaney smiled at her, and then blew across the top of the pra, eager to take a sip and warm herself. The heating system on Ruckus's ship had finally kicked in to full power, and even though she hadn't been inside long, already she could feel herself begin to thaw.

They were in the cockpit, with her seated next to Fawna while Ruckus stood nearby. He'd been uncomfortably quiet on their way back, but Delaney hadn't pressed him to speak. Eventually, he'd tell her what was wrong, and besides . . . It probably had something to do with the Zane.

"Take this," Sanzie grumbled, practically tossing the mug she held in her other hand at Ruckus. She refused to meet his eye, and kept the tight expression firmly in place.

"All clear." Trystan chose that moment to arrive, making his way up the ramp and into the cockpit with an easy gait. He'd stopped to change into a different set of clothes, and had left the coat off. "Have we come up with any solutions to our possible problem?"

"I'm scanning the area for any other nasty surprises," Fawna answered without turning from her controls. "Unfortunately, I can't check more than a few miles in any direction. We're still far enough from the capital city and the palace that it could pose an issue."

"We could stumble into another ambush without even realizing it," Delaney figured. Great. "We need to get to Tilda. Soon."

They only had until tomorrow, and then Trystan had to get back to Carnage or risk tipping off the Rex. She was still trying to work out a way they could avoid having him go at all, hating the thought of him with that asshole, but so far the only thing she could come up with was gaining the Basilissa's support. If they were able to do that, perhaps Trystan wouldn't have to go.

"Can you get us into Varasow?" Ruckus moved closer to Fawna, checking her screens as the scan continued. There were a couple of clusters of heat dots, similar to the ones they'd spotted too late earlier.

Delaney counted them, seeing that there were at least five areas they needed to avoid. They'd gotten lucky before, and there was no guarantee they'd get lucky again. There was also no way of knowing if those blips were Vakar ships, or if they were secretly being run by more Tars.

She took a deep sip of her drink, needing a moment to separate herself from her thoughts. The fact of the matter was, they didn't have any choice but to continue forward. There was no one else on this planet they could go to, no one who stood even a remote chance against the Rex. And Tilda deserved to know what had happened to her daughter, the one she'd done so many awful things in the name of.

All of that pain and suffering, for nothing. With Olena dead, the Vakar throne was once again without an heir.

"I can," Fawna was answering Ruckus, and Delaney came out of her head just in time to catch her words. "On the outskirts, in any case. If the Zane is correct, and we were attacked because they recognized the ship, it's too risky going farther in."

Ruckus nodded. "Set us down as close as you can to Varasow, and we'll foot it from there." He glanced at Delaney and Trystan. "It's going to put us behind schedule, but this is the best we can do."

"Agreed." Trystan turned to her, then noticed what she was holding, plucking the mug from between her hands. When he saw what was inside, he made a face, but risked a sip anyway. A second later he licked his lips and handed it back. "Surprisingly, that wasn't awful."

"You've never had it before?" she asked, glad to have it back to keep her hands warm.

"Pra is traditionally a Vakar drink—" he started to explain.

"We're going to need to change your hair," Ruckus interrupted.

"Excuse me?" The switch in topic caught her off guard.

"He's right." Trystan scowled. "Being a redhead will give you away."

Seeing as how she was the only one currently on the planet who had red hair. Crap. She fiddled with a strand, twisting it around her finger. This wouldn't be the first time she'd had a physical change in order to survive Xenith. Before, though, they'd had the device to help make the alteration easy.

"I don't suppose you guys keep a bottle of hair dye on this ship?"

"It's not as popular a custom here as it is on Earth." Ruckus shrugged apologetically. "We'll have to wait until we're in the city. There's a place we can go; it's just a matter of getting there undetected."

"What about you two?" The Ander had been marked as a traitor after his rescue attempt, and the Zane, in his royal uniform, would be impossible not to recognize.

"I have an idea."

CHAPTER 8

A couple of hours later Fawna dropped them off in a forest on the edge of what was supposedly Varasow.

As the capital of Vakar, Varasow was home to the Ond family, and housed many spectacles—or so she'd been told. It wasn't large in comparison to most cities on Earth, but it had a vast population. As they approached, Delaney ran the numbers through her head, figuring that at least a fifth of the Vakar people had to live here.

She was tucked beneath a heavy hooded jacket, a deep forest green. The hood shielded her face so that only her mouth was visible. It also had the annoying side effect of making it practically impossible for her to see anything herself, and she had to be carefully led forward by one of the guys. At least through the forest she'd been able to keep the hood tipped back enough, but now that they were closing in on the city, there was too great a risk she'd be spotted.

"This was a terrible idea," Trystan grumbled from her side for the hundredth time since stepping off the ship. He was helping to lead her, his hand at her elbow, and though he was gentle, it was impossible not to note the annoyance simmering beneath his surface.

"You look fine," she tried—also for the hundredth time—but he growled.

"I *look* ridiculous."

Ruckus had pulled out a set of dusty old clothing, non–military issue, and given it to the Zane. He seemed to get a real kick out of the fact that they were still in traditional Vakar greens and blacks. All they were missing were the gold embellishments.

Ironically, it wasn't that he was going to have to dress in the colors of his enemy that bothered Trystan. Nope. The holes and crooked collar on the shirt made him cringe, as did the permanent stains on the black pants.

He'd asked Ruckus what the purple blotches had been caused by, and had received only a laugh in response. Delaney sort of felt bad for him, but there was nothing that could be done about it. He needed a disguise, and this was as good as any. Especially since Ruckus had donned clothes in a similar style.

"It's only until we take care of my hair," she reminded Trystan. They'd decided having the Zane walking around dressed in his royal uniforms would draw too much attention. It wouldn't be a big deal once she was no longer a redhead, but until then, they didn't want to risk being seen and him having to explain who the strange hooded woman with him was.

Especially if word somehow got to his dad.

Trystan was carrying a bag over his shoulder with three sets of Kint uniforms for them to change into as soon as they'd taken care of her hair.

"Ruckus is going to have to pretend to be one of your guards," Delaney said, "and you don't see him complaining."

"I am not complaining," Trystan mumbled, automatically discrediting his words.

"Almost there," Ruckus called, and with a start Delaney realized he'd somehow moved ahead of them.

Damn hood.

"We'll be entering the city in roughly three minutes," Trystan told her, not that he needed to. Though it was late in the afternoon, the city sounded very much alive.

With her head down, Delaney tried to match all the sounds she heard to something familiar, but was only able to with a few things. Talking people, for one, were obvious. She made out snippets of conversation as they moved deeper in, distracted some by the changing ground beneath her feet. They'd been walking over grass up until this point, but now everything was black marble. It glittered gold wherever the light hit, like someone had dumped a vat of the metal into the mixture.

"Everything's always so glittery," she murmured, thinking about the snow they'd just left behind and how it shared a similar property. She'd meant the words for herself, but being as close as he was, Trystan caught them.

"We lay our streets with white marble instead." There was a hint of wistfulness in his voice. "And it sparkles silver. It's also less dangerous. It's hard to see puddles when the ground is black."

"Or ice."

"Yes, well . . ." She felt him shrug, his arm brushing up against hers with the movement. "Their cold season is very short. Less than three weeks, actually. They do get a lot of rain, but with temperatures as high as they usually are, it's not often they have to fret over the streets freezing."

She wished she could see the rest of it. There were beeps and blasts of air, metal clinking against metal. When they passed beneath a particular building, she could see green neon lights reflected in the surface of the marble at her feet. They moved on before she could make out whether it was an image or words.

As interesting as the sounds were, the smells were even more so. There were so many of them, some coming quickly and leaving just as fast as they passed by, others lingering even once they'd turned down several streets—she assumed they were streets; all she knew for certain was they kept going without stopping once.

At one point there was a coppery, buttery smell in the air, and she actually tipped her nose up a bit to try to catch a better sense of it.

At her side, Trystan chuckled. His hand slid down from her elbow, the tips of his fingers trailing against her skin in the process.

Because Vakar was a lot warmer than Kint had been, their new clothes were short sleeved. The hooded jacket she wore covered the mark on the inside curve of her elbow, but it stopped halfway down her forearm.

When his hand finally reached hers, he pressed their palms together, weaving their fingers together.

"Shakalla," he said, and she frowned.

"What?"

"It's what you're smelling. Shakalla."

For a second Delaney debated whether she should pull away, but in the end, she decided against it. She couldn't see where she was going and he was leading the way. It made sense to hold hands.

"Is that a food?" she asked to distract herself, tilting her head when he chuckled a second time.

"An animal, actually. And not one enjoyed during consumption."

That was . . . gross. She'd been intrigued by the smell of someone's pet?

"I believe we are here." Trystan tightened his hold on her hand briefly as they came to a slight stop. The marble reflected an awning covered in bright white twinkle lights, and the side of a building with many windows.

The reason behind Trystan's hesitation became apparent when the sound of a door opening was followed by another hand reaching for Delaney's free one. As soon as it did, the Zane let her go.

"Come on," Ruckus's smooth voice said as he led her beneath the awning and into a stuffy room ripe with the smell of sharp chemicals.

He didn't stop at the front, instead winding his way through rows of chairs with metal bases.

Delaney caught sight of a few feet, and on the ground a scattering of hair in various shades. She blinked, a bit surprised by how much the place resembled a hair salon back on Earth. She'd known he was planning on taking her somewhere they dyed hair, but after mentioning that it wasn't a thing his people generally did, she'd pictured something less . . . well, normal.

They made their way to the back and then to the left, where the corridor narrowed so that they had to move in single file. At the end, Ruckus opened a door, and they entered a brightly lit room.

"Wait here." He let go of her hand and stepped away, the sound of his footsteps receding far enough that she would have gotten nervous if not for the sense that Trystan was hovering close by.

"He's speaking to someone," Trystan whispered as he leaned down. "A woman."

She did not like the tone of his voice, the way his words had lifted. If she'd been able, she would have glared at him, knowing full well he was just trying to cause trouble.

They needed to have a talk, a real one. She no longer had to pretend she was betrothed to him; in fact, for the first time since she'd stepped foot on Xenith soil, she didn't have to pretend to be anything. Hide, yes. Sneak around, of course. But pretend to be someone else? To want something else?

It was as liberating as it was terrifying, knowing that from here on out everything she said or did was completely up to her. If she went along with one of their schemes, it was because she wanted to. It put her and Trystan on a level playing field, another new situation for them.

"He's returning," Trystan said then, abruptly cutting into her thoughts. It was obvious he was addressing Ruckus when he added more tersely, "Well?"

"She's going to let us use the room," Ruckus explained. He reached out and eased Delaney to the side, allowing a smaller body to pass and exit the space. "Nala doesn't know how long she can keep her employees distracted, though. We'll have to make this quick."

"And Nala is trustworthy?" Trystan asked, not sounding convinced. "You're positive?"

"I'm staking our lives on it, aren't I?" he snapped. "Just guard the door, Zane."

For a tense moment no one moved, but then Trystan's hand touched the small of Delaney's back. "You'll call me if you need anything?"

Suddenly she was sort of glad for the hood. She didn't have to see Ruckus's expression in that moment.

I mean it, Delaney, Trystan continued privately, through their fittings. *Leaving you alone makes me uneasy.*

"I'll be fine with Ruckus," she told him aloud, hoping he'd get the point. "But, yeah, if something goes wrong, you'll know. We're in this together, right?"

"Of course, Lissa." His voice firmed. "I'll be just outside the door."

"Perfect," Ruckus said.

As soon as the sound of the lock clicking into place reached Delaney's ears, she tossed the hood off her head, taking a deep breath of fresh air. That thing was stifling. She blinked, allowing her eyes to adjust to the bright white lights that were set in the corners of the room and aimed toward the center, then paused when she got a good look around.

It wasn't exactly what she'd been expecting, not that she'd had a clear picture in her mind of what a back room in a business on Xenith would look like. But this . . . This wasn't it. The ground was the only dingy thing about it, the stone faded and a dull gray. The rest of the room was all flash and smooth lines. The walls and ceiling were polished jade, as was the single counter that sat in the right corner.

It had a sink with a mirror over it, and a metal chair, like at any salon on Earth.

The rest of the room was lined in gold shelves stuffed with different products Delaney couldn't place or pronounce. She assumed they were shampoo and the like. When Ruckus had said he knew someone who could provide them with cover while they altered her appearance, she'd figured he'd meant a military friend, or something like that.

Given Trystan's reaction, whoever Nala was, she was not from the Vakar army.

She glanced up at Ruckus, then immediately reached out and gripped his hand comfortingly. He looked wrecked. His dark brown hair was mussed, and there were purplish-blue blotches beneath his eyes. There was also a weariness there she hadn't seen in a long time, not even when he'd been locked up in the Inkwell dungeon. The events of the past few days were taking a serious toll on him.

"Military personnel don't tend to visit this part of the city, hence the clothing," he explained softly, before she could point out his appearance. "I met Nala when we were children. We grew up in the same sector. Only a few people knew I even came here to get my hair cut, so I don't think the place will be monitored. We should be safe. As safe as we can be, anyway."

"Tilda will listen to reason," Delaney assured him, squeezing his hand.

"You don't know that." He shook his head. "You don't know her like I do, sweetheart. There's a reason she's a regent on this planet, and it isn't because she's made of sunshine and rainbows."

The corner of Delaney's mouth quirked up at that. Mariana was always using that phrase; he must have picked it up from her. Somehow that was both saddening and reaffirming, because it meant that the life they'd had back on Earth really was worth doing everything to return to. Even taking out the Rex to ensure they were returning to something they could keep.

"The Basilissa was born into the role," he continued, even as he led them over toward the station in the corner and eased her into the chair. "When she married Magnus, it was a political merger, but he took her last name and the two of them eventually developed a love between them. Losing him couldn't have been easy for her."

"And now her daughter's dead, too." She didn't even want to try imagining what that might feel like.

"*And*"—he moved between her and the closest shelf—"we have no idea how she's going to react to that news when she first hears it. This is dangerous, for everyone involved. If she goes on a rampage without hearing us out, and ends up killing Trystan, we've got a war. If she blames you, tries to hurt you, and either the Zane or I kill her, we've got a war. We have to be delicate here, Delaney. Choose our words carefully."

She sighed and slumped back in her seat, watching his reflection in the mirror as he shifted through the bottles, clearly looking for something specific. "You're asking if I know what I'm going to say to her yet."

The bottles and jars were all different shapes and sizes. Some were made of glass; others appeared to be plastic. The colors on the outside also varied, though they were mostly warm tones, like yellow, red, and orange. Delaney also spotted a few pink ones, but she couldn't read any of the labels.

Ruckus found what he was looking for, snatched the light-orange bottle from the shelf, and came back over to her. At some point, he'd picked up a pair of plastic gloves as well, and he set the bottle on the counter in front of her and tugged them on while he met her gaze in the mirror.

"Do you?" he asked it casually enough, but given his speech, and the way his mouth thinned out in preparation for bad news, she understood how concerned he really was.

She couldn't blame him.

"I'll come up with something. I always do."

He paused while untwisting the cap on the bottle. "You sound like the Zane."

"Do not." She so did.

"You know nothing's changed for him, right?" Ruckus grabbed a sheet of plastic off the counter and unfolded it over her shoulders. Gently, he lifted her hair and spread it out across the back of the plastic. Then he reached for the now open bottle and squeezed a glob of inky goo into his right palm. "Tip your head back."

She stared up at the ceiling, saw him rub his hands together over her before he moved to bunch the ends of her hair between his palms.

"He thinks this is going to end the same way he always has," he continued when she didn't say anything. "The only thing that's different is now he wants to help us stop his father. After that, he'll become Rex, and he intends for you to become his Regina."

"Ruckus . . ." Did they really have to talk about this? They'd yet to do anything in regard to stopping the Rex. For all they knew, they wouldn't reach that end for another month—or six, not that she wanted to think about that possibility—which meant they had time before they actually had to worry about what Trystan thought was going to happen.

"I saw the way you two worked together," he said. "You cleared that ship like you've been a team for a long time."

"You know we had to do the compatibility test." She and the Zane had literally had to work as a team against a group of enemy forces as they made their way through a maze, all to prove to their coordinator that they'd make a good couple.

Reminding Ruckus that she'd undergone a series of steps in preparation to marry someone else probably wasn't the best idea.

"Say we stop his father," he said, running his hands through her hair all the while, "and he becomes Rex, Tilda remains the Basilissa, they agree to keep Earth out of Xenith affairs from now on. . . . Where does that leave us, Delaney? If the two of them decide they still want you to rule, what can we do to stop them from making that happen? Even if I'm reinstated and no longer considered a traitor, I'm only an Ander."

He was the youngest Ander in all of their history, she wanted to point out, but he didn't give her the chance.

"I don't have the power or the authority to stand up to regents. They won't listen to me, especially the Zane, and if anything, what just happened to Olena will give me less credibility in the Basilissa's eyes, not more. If Trystan decides he wants to keep you, that he wants you here, on this planet, and Tilda agrees, there won't be anything I can do."

"That's not true," she said, feeling a lot like she was in that hood again, unable to tip her head back and see the way he was holding her hair. Maybe he'd done it on purpose, brought this all up now because she couldn't meet his gaze. "If it comes to that, you'll find a way to get us out. I know you will."

"How can you?" he said, his voice rising an octave. He pulled back and spun away.

She straightened in her chair and swiveled so she could watch him over her shoulder. He was pacing, clenching and unclenching his gloved fists.

"How can you have so much faith in me when I've done nothing to prove it should be there?" he demanded. "I'm the one who took you from your home the first time, do you remember? I brought you onto my ship, and I'm the one who made you pretend to be Olena."

"The Basileus and the Basilissa are the ones who made me keep pretending," she said.

"But it was my idea!" He took a step toward her, thought better, and spun away again. "Damn it, Delaney, it was my idea! And even if it hadn't been, they ordered you to stay, and what did I do to stop them? To help you get off the planet even when you begged me to let you go? Nothing. I did nothing."

"You couldn't." He hadn't had a choice; neither of them had.

"That's my point!" He flung a hand out. "I was powerless to do anything to protect you then, and when Trystan came and took you that second time—" He had to stop, catch his breath. Then he said, a bit quieter, "When he took you the second time, that was my fault, too.

"I made you do the Uprising," he continued, and because he was still turned away, he missed her flinch. "Even knowing our laws, our traditions, I let you go out there, say the oath, take the mark. . . . I basically handed you to him on a golden platter."

Her eyes snapped open. "I'm not a *thing* you can give away, Ruckus."

Seeming to see his mistake, he shook his head. "That's not what I meant. I'm sorry. It's just . . . you should be angry with me. You have every right to be. To hate me, even. I might not have meant it, but I helped them trap you. I'm the reason you're here and not on Earth, where you should be. The reason you have to hide . . . *again*."

He motioned angrily toward a small handheld mirror on the counter before her.

She picked it up, finally taking a look at what he'd been doing with the goo from the bottle.

It wasn't finished, but he'd been in the process of dying her red hair a dark brown, similar to his own. The bottom half was already done, though the strands were shiny and slick, still covered in the gooey black substance. A portion toward the top had dried, showing her the color it would be at the end, once he'd finished her roots.

Delaney looked into her own eyes, her very green, very single-toned eyes, and any frustration she'd been feeling moments prior drained away.

They were both on edge, both scared and feeling guilty. One of their friends was dead, the other kidnapped, and the only guaranteed ally they currently had was the Zane, who, only days ago, was Ruckus's number-one enemy.

"I'm angry," she admitted, forcing herself to lift her gaze to his. He flinched, but she continued. "I am. I'm pissed that this happened to me, and yeah, I'm upset that you let me go through with that ceremony without explaining what it really meant in the long run.

"But . . ." She stood and then turned so they weren't looking at each other through a mirror, so he could see the truth on her face. "I don't hold you accountable, Ruckus. I don't blame you, and I definitely don't think it's your fault I'm here. Like you said, you're an Ander, and you were just doing your job."

"My *job*," he protested, "ensured you ended up on this planet a second time."

"No." She shook her head and stepped toward him, frowning when he immediately retreated. "You were supposed to keep me alive, and you did that. You were supposed to help avert a war. And you did that. Anything that came after, Olena screwing up, Trystan figuring it out, the Rex taking over . . . you had nothing to do with any of it. It's on them, Ruckus. Anything that isn't here"—she waved a finger between his chest and hers—"is on someone else."

He angled his head. "What does that even mean?"

"It means I was there, too, remember? I know you only did what you thought you had to. We didn't really have any other options."

"But . . ." He searched her face. "You're angry?"

"Yes." She was. That couldn't be helped right now.

Because he hadn't been up-front with her. Maybe if he had, nothing would have changed. Probably wouldn't have, in fact. At the time, getting Uprisen was her best bet at avoiding more assassination attempts. It hadn't worked, but that wasn't his fault, either.

"Is that something we're going to talk about?" he asked when she didn't elaborate.

"You couldn't have known how it was all going to go," she said again. "From now on, promise you won't leave anything out, no matter how unimportant or obsolete you think it could be. I need one hundred percent honesty, Ruckus, at all times. Always."

There was more to say, but she'd meant it before. They really didn't have time for it, and neither of them were exactly in the right state of mind. He looked like he'd been awake for months, and when she saw her reflection, she didn't look much better.

He eased his body as close to hers as he could, so that she could feel the heat of him. He had to be careful not to touch her with his hands, or let her still-goo-covered hair touch him, but that small bit of space somehow didn't matter. The corner of his mouth turned up in a somewhat sad, yet reassuring smile.

"Always."

CHAPTER 9

rystan hadn't stopped staring since they'd stepped out of the back room. He even weaved his way through the main floor, dodging moving customers and chairs that had been pulled out too far without once taking his eyes off her.

"Cut it out," she sent through their fitting, trying not to let on how uncomfortable his attention was making her. *"It's just hair."*

"It's brown," he said, emphasizing that second word like he was talking about garbage instead of a color.

"Yeah, which was the plan." When he still didn't look away, she sent him a glare. *"What? Would you have preferred I'd been made a blond?"*

He scowled. *"I would have preferred you to not have been altered at all."*

Delaney didn't know how to respond to that, so took the opportunity to observe her surroundings. As she'd thought originally, the room was set up much like hair salons were back on Earth, with two rows on either side. Each station had a chair, a mirror, and a large enough counter space to hold plenty of products. The colors were a mix of metallics and different shades of green—not too surprising—and there were at least five women currently helping out the same number of customers.

It was how they were doing it that really caught her attention, though. Unlike back home, none of the stylists were using scissors. Or combs. They each had a single device, shaped like a helmet three sizes too large, which was propped up on a stand to the right of each chair. A computer screen faced outward, toward the middle aisle, so Delaney got a good look at all of them as she and the guys passed.

The stylists were inputting different instructions, some using one finger to tap away at the screen, others two or three. A digital image of whoever was seated in the chair was displayed, and the picture altered every time a button was pushed.

Delaney paused when the stylist she was currently walking by tapped one last time and then pulled back. The machine was wheeled behind the chair, and then lowered over the person's head. The stylist asked if the woman was comfortable, and once she received an affirmation, hit a large triangular green button on the side.

The sound the machine emitted wasn't loud at all, more like a low buzz. Sort of like a bee was flying around Delaney's head. It wasn't anything compared to the sound of multiple blow-dryers that would have been heard in a salon back home.

Realizing that she was no longer with them, Ruckus turned and came back, glancing between her and the machine.

"They don't dye hair. Only cut and style it. If you'd needed a French braid, we could have used one, but . . ." His voice filtered through her head, and when she looked at him, he shrugged. *"I told you, people here don't really change their hair color. That's more an Earth staple. Don't ask me why."*

She'd been about to, so the fact that he'd caught her made her smile. "Don't hate me for saying this, but blue kind of suits you."

They'd changed into their Kint uniforms before leaving the back, coming out to find Trystan had changed while waiting for them in the hall. Everyone knew that his Sworn was female, so the hope was that anyone who did spot and recognize him would just assume he was walking around with Sanzie and another Teller.

Ruckus grimaced and flicked at the hem of his navy shirt. "It's awful, I hate it, we'll never speak of this again."

She laughed, but made no promises.

Trystan was tapping his foot impatiently by the door, scanning the streets through the large windows at either side. He barely spared them a glance when they joined him, pushing the handle and stepping out onto the walkway.

As soon as her feet hit the marble ground and she looked up, Delaney gasped.

Buildings towered overhead, far higher than she'd ever imagined. She'd visited New York City once when she was younger—one of the few business trips her parents had decided to bring her along on—and she remembered feeling so small, thinking the skyscrapers went on forever.

That was nothing compared to this. And it was almost every building. There were a few, like the one they'd just exited, that were regular sized and clearly only housed one or two floors at the most, but they were hard to spot among the giants. The streets were also larger, about twice as wide as back home, and lined on either side with a row of flashing pale yellow lights. The glow wasn't too bright or distracting, just light enough not to miss.

Those lights, along with the slight dip downward, were what helped differentiate the sidewalk from the road. They were both made from the same type of marble, and it would have been difficult to tell otherwise.

Above, carefully spaced out between buildings, was another street of sorts. The same lights that lined the ground hovered some hundred or so feet in the air, making paths for flying cars. She'd seen one of the cars before, so knew they existed, but it was different actually witnessing them in the air. The speeds they traveled were baffling—she wasn't sure how they managed not to crash into one another, especially when they took sharp turns around the corners of buildings.

The only thing not spectacular about them was the fact that it seemed like they only came in three colors: silver, gold, and a metallic black.

The rest of the capital definitely made up for it, though. Lights flashed from every structure, some projecting moving images onto the sidewalks in front of them. A hologram of a strange animal with two heads similar to a cat's, though on a body more closely resembling an eagle, flickered directly across the street. It blinked its wide blue eyes at Delaney, even as a Vakar man walked through it. The image became a little blurry, but that was it.

Spirals of color twisted around some of the larger buildings, starting at the top or bottom and making their way to the opposite end. There were shots of gold, green, red, and even purple.

"They help larger ships dock on the roof," Ruckus explained when he followed where she was looking. "They also help keep other crafts from flying into them when the weather is bad. We don't get a lot of snow here, but we do have a fog problem around the end of every year—"

"We need to eat," Trystan interrupted, his eyes taking in their surroundings as well, though for a different reason. What trouble did he think they'd run into? Was he looking for Tellers from the palace? "And even with hair like that, you won't blend in with that expression, Delaney."

She snapped her jaw shut, and her stomach chose that moment to rumble angrily. When he finally tugged his gaze away from the streets long enough to set a smug look on her, she rolled her eyes and motioned down either side of the sidewalk they were on.

"Which way?" Even though she wanted to keep staring, take everything in, she forced herself to turn to Ruckus and not allow her eyes to wander.

He thought it over for half a second and then pointed to their left. "There's a place a couple of blocks from here. They've got good food."

"Won't we run the risk of stumbling on Tellers from the palace?"

Trystan asked, proving that was exactly what he'd been searching the crowds for. It was sort of comforting, to know he was always paying attention, even when Delaney allowed herself to get distracted.

They might not be actively hiding now, but that didn't mean they wanted anyone walking up to them and asking the Zane questions about what he was doing.

"No." Ruckus shook his head and started off. "There's a place that's just as cheap closer to the palace. That's where we tend to coagulate after shifts. It's rare for any of us to come this far into the capital, not unless we have a reason."

They turned a corner, and a woman dressed in a strange black coat lined in gold practically slammed into Delaney. Trystan yanked her out of the way and into his arms just in time. He caught her against his chest, glaring over the top of her head at the woman, who stumbled a bit when she looked at him.

She was in the process of apologizing, but Trystan started forward again, taking Delaney with him. Once they'd rounded the corner, he let her go, yet still keeping close. For the rest of the walk, everyone who came within a five-foot radius of her got the same terrifying warning glare.

"Now who's drawing attention?" she asked from the corner of her mouth, shaking her head when he merely grunted.

On her other side, Ruckus wasn't exactly being any friendlier. Though his glare wasn't as frightening as the Zane's, and he was more careful about who he set it on, the tense air around him gave away that he was dangerous.

"Chill out," she told them both.

They traveled the rest of the way in silence; fortunately, the trip wasn't long. At a four-way, Ruckus pointed out a small building that was practically being squished between two skyscrapers. It was another one of the few single-floor structures, but there were a decent amount of people crowded around outside it.

"Kind of looks like a diner," Delaney mused as they waited to cross the street. There were crosswalks here, but instead of hanging from wires, the lights seemed to hover in place on their own. There also weren't three of them, just one, triangular and about the size of a Frisbee.

The light shifted from a steady purple to a flashing bright orange, and Ruckus took her hand and led her across.

"When you took me to that one back home," he told her, "it reminded me of this place."

"How adorable for you," Trystan drawled sarcastically behind them.

Inside, the smells hit her with as much awe as seeing the city for the first time had. It was a heady mixture of sweet and salty and tangy, so that she could never quite put her finger on any one scent for longer than a moment before it altered.

Trystan took one look around, and then stepped back toward the door. When she frowned at him in silent question, he smiled reassuringly. "I've got to go find us a Kint ship. Eat—I'll return as soon as I've completed my task."

"You're going to do that now?" Ruckus moved in closer so it'd be harder for the three of them to be overheard. The place was packed with enough bodies that there wasn't much space between them and prying ears.

"The sooner I get a ship and transport the bodies onto it, the sooner we can confront the Basilissa and get this over with."

"Hey." Delaney eased herself between them, facing the Zane. She lowered her voice. "You said you were hungry."

"I'm eager to get us what we need."

"Fine, then we'll go with you."

"You can't do that." He shook his head. "Trust me, I would much rather not leave you, but I'll have to get close to the palace, find a Teller I trust, and procure a Kint ship without drawing too much attention to myself. It'll be harder to do with you two. I'll move more quickly on my own."

They needed a Kint ship so they could fly directly into the palace's landing zone—Delaney knew that. They'd talked about it. They couldn't exactly bring Ruckus's there without someone seeing and alerting the Rex.

She also knew the real reason he didn't want her to come along wasn't because she'd get in the way. They'd agreed on the plan to get a Kint ship. They hadn't talked about separating in order to do so. Wherever he was going, he thought it might be too dangerous to bring her along. That made her uncomfortable.

He lifted a hand to her face and traced the left line of her jaw, stopping at her chin for a second before pulling away. "I'll be fine. There's no cause for concern."

"Trystan," she sent to his mind, hoping to prompt him to explain, but he'd either caught on to the fact that this was a tactic she used, or he was simply too hell-bent on keeping this secret.

He shook his head again. "I'll return shortly."

"And if we aren't here?" Ruckus asked.

"Then you meet me. Where we parked your ship. I'll try to have the new one loaded and ready to go when you arrive."

Ruckus eyed him. "I don't like this."

"Don't you?" He quirked a brow. "I would have thought you'd like the idea of being left alone with Delaney. For a time." He glanced at the food lines, thought for a moment. "Use my code to pay."

Ruckus's spine stiffened. "I don't need your money, Zane."

"We don't know if they're tracking your accounts," Trystan shot back. "Why risk it if we don't have to? Use my code." He rattled off a string of numbers and letters quickly before he could be argued with further.

Sighing, Ruckus gave a curt nod and then flicked his fingers toward the door, clearly dismissing the Zane.

Trystan's jaw clenched, but surprisingly he didn't take the bait. Instead he let his gaze linger once more on Delaney, and then he stepped back out onto the sidewalk and disappeared among the crowd.

APPARENTLY, money wasn't something carried around on Xenith. It wasn't even something one needed a card or a phone app for. She let Ruckus choose the food, unsure what any of the words or symbols meant, and after placing their order, all Ruckus did was enter Trystan's code into a little bar at the bottom of the screen. Within a second it was paid for and done.

They picked up their food at a window inside, near the section where they'd ordered from a large touch screen. As far as she could tell, there weren't any actual employees up front, though the cooks could be seen in the way back.

They ate quickly, and Delaney tried not to watch the door the entire time. She didn't want to give Ruckus the wrong idea, and she trusted that Trystan could handle himself, so it was stupid to be worried.

By the time they were finished and had stepped back out onto the street, it was getting dark. Now the lights everywhere lit the place up like Christmas, and Delaney took another moment to admire it before allowing Ruckus to lead the way to their next destination.

"We don't have time to see as much as I'd like to show you," he told her as they walked, "but there's one place we absolutely have to stop at."

"Yeah?" She was only half listening, too distracted by their surroundings and the various people milling around. Most of them were garbed in shades of green or gold, though some wore black and grays or whites as well.

In Inkwell, the cold had kept everyone in long sleeves and long pants, but not here. While it wasn't hot out, it was warm enough that people wore short dresses with high heels, or sleeveless shirts that zipped up the front. Almost everyone held a shing in their hand. Some wore small devices in one ear, a tiny screen attached to it and placed over their eye. The device was clear, so the person could still see, but there were pictures and moving words flashing across as well.

"Here." Ruckus pulled up short in front of a massive building with green tinted windows. Then he took her hand and entered.

They passed through the circular lobby, straight down a narrow hall to a set of double doors. They opened automatically at their approach, exposing a bustling marketplace within.

"You thought the rest of the capital was impressive," he whispered in her ear as he bent down. "This place puts all that to shame."

He was completely and totally right.

The room was huge and dome shaped, with a curved ceiling. At the center, there was a large gap that exposed the night sky.

A swirling pattern of stars peered down at them, a mixture of greens and pinks and purples. The sky at night was one of the few things from her first experience on this planet that she'd enjoyed. She'd even looked forward to it. She would walk out onto her balcony—Olena's balcony—and just stare up and breathe.

"I thought you'd like it." Ruckus grinned at her, and when she smiled back, he shot into the crowd, tugging her quickly after him. Unlike back on the street, he didn't seem to be concerned with the people here or how close they got, and he squeezed the two of them between clusters of bodies with ease.

Music came from every direction, some tunes upbeat and lively, others calm and melodious. People danced around tables, and others laughed, their arms linked as they traveled between booths. Occasionally someone could be spotted not having a good time, either frowning or walking away from a seller while shaking their head, but for the most part, everyone here seemed to be enjoying themselves.

She pulled on Ruckus's hand to get him to slow, and then leaned up to practically scream in his ear. "What is this place?" It was too loud between the music, the movement, and all the other chatter for them to talk at a normal volume, and it only got louder the deeper in they went.

"Zephra Viya," he called back. "Loosely, it translates to the Dust Market."

"The what?" She pressed her cheek against the side of his arm, stepping out of the way of a man swinging a long swath of crimson silk. He winked at her as he passed, even though he seemed old enough to be her father, but she smiled in return and didn't miss a step.

Ruckus repeated himself, and she had to admit it was the perfect name for such a place. The market was thriving and full, colorful and crowded, yet didn't overload the senses. Vendors were set up in rows, and there were too many to count, branching off and connecting at seemingly random intervals, so that there was no real method.

Delaney lost their way back within minutes, but she didn't really care.

It was hard not to feel giddy, not to be excited when everyone else seemed to be feeling the same. They placed odd instruments to their lips and played, or stroked their fingers across ones that had strings but weren't even close in appearance to guitars.

And the food . . .

There were tables covered in different edible items, some in baskets, others stacked up or hanging from awnings by metal wire. They passed strange bits of meat, and weird-looking fruits. One booth smelled like oranges and honeysuckle, another like rich spices and buttered mashed potatoes. Despite the fact that they'd only just eaten, Delaney's mouth began to water.

Ruckus glanced back at her and then detoured off to the right, toward a booth that displayed tiny golden balls on glass shelves shaped like steps. He nodded to the beautiful Vakar woman who stood on the other side, then tapped Trystan's personal number on the small screen that had been set on the edge of the table.

The woman smiled at him, tucked a strand of her mahogany hair behind one ear, and then seemed to notice he wasn't alone. The look she gave Delaney lacked the flirtatious note in the one she'd set on the Ander, but it wasn't unkind.

Ruckus plucked four of the small golden balls, gave another nod, and then turned Delaney back into the ever-moving crowd.

Delaney linked her arm through his so he could use both hands to unwrap the golden balls, exposing a smooth dark-blue globe no larger than a marble. When he brought it to her lips, she opened her mouth and let him place it on her tongue.

Guilt over the fact that Trystan had done something similar only a few weeks ago hit her, but it didn't linger. The bitter taste, followed by a wash of sugary sweetness, distracted her, and her eyes widened.

"You like it?" he asked, then laughed when she nodded.

"Give me another."

After what could have been a half hour or only ten minutes, they reached the center of the market. He told her just as they were about to turn the corner into it, watching her face as she searched for differences, a reason why this area warranted being pointed out.

She didn't have to search long. A few steps in, it started.

Delaney pulled them to a stop, too stunned to go any farther, and tipped her head all the way back. Glitter was falling from the sky. It drifted down through the gap in the ceiling slowly, and so thinly that it'd been hard to see until she was directly in it. She held out a hand, watching as it drifted onto her palm. Within moments, she was coated in a fine sheen of burnt gold.

"Stardust." Ruckus pointed upward, at one of the bright swirls of green. A galaxy much farther away than it appeared, and one impossible to see from Earth. "We've got a few comets that pass by and break apart in our atmosphere. The dust falls this time of year in a few places around Vakar, but this is the most popular location because it falls in a larger radius here. By the time we leave, it'll be falling over the entire marketplace. That's why some of the vendors, like those selling food, have tents over their tables, and others do not. The dust adds a special sparkle to certain items. When it falls on them, vendors sell more."

"It smells like"—she sniffed the air, a little bit enthralled by it all—"grapefruit, Earl Grey tea, and . . ." She smiled, realizing why he'd brought her here. "Storm clouds."

Back on Earth, Ruckus had developed an odd affinity for thunderstorms. Whenever one came, he'd stand outside in the rain and the wind with his head tipped back and his eyes closed. Eventually she'd drag him back in, worried he'd make himself sick, but even then he'd open one of the windows a crack and sit close enough so he could lean toward it and smell the air.

She'd asked him about it, but he'd merely shrugged and mumbled something about how it reminded him of home. She hadn't understood, because as far as she knew, Vakar didn't have thunderstorms, and she'd never smelled anything like one during her stay there.

Now she got it.

And why, even though he loved coffee so much, he always ordered a side of tea and let it sit untouched on the edge of their table.

"Come on." He urged her forward, a knowing smirk on his face. "There's something else."

CHAPTER 10

At the very center of the marketplace, there was a station different from the others. It was circular and made out of stone. From a few feet away, it looked almost like a shallow fountain, only deep enough for the water to go up to a person's waist. But upon closer inspection, it obviously served a different purpose.

There was no water within, only a dozen or so men and women dressed in all black. They must have been there for a while, because instead of the thin sheen of glitter that Delaney and Ruckus were covered in, they were caked in it.

The women let their hair hang loose, and it had a metallic sheen. Even the men's. Their skin held the same glow, a slight sparkle whenever they turned at a certain angle. And every single one of them was busy talking to a customer outside the stone wall, which was about three feet thick, serving as a table between them.

The surface of it was smooth, a dark granite, and covered in piles of stardust. As they approached, Delaney watched two people take up a handful of the stuff, then hold it over a large bowl set before the vendor they were dealing with.

"It's tradition," Ruckus said as she watched them drop their handfuls of dust into the bowl, "for couples to come here to celebrate their relationship. There's no set date, because this event happens around the same time every year, so it's not like your various anniversaries back on Earth. More a general celebration, with a token."

She glanced around, noticing for the first time that there were many couples in this section of the marketplace. They had the stone circle surrounded, in fact, most already doing the same as the ones she'd been watching. She glanced back at them, curious to find out what came next.

The vendor had done something, but Delaney had missed it, and she didn't get to see what was pulled from the bowl, either, because Ruckus was already urging her away.

Her annoyance faded quickly, however, when she realized he was only moving them to an empty section of the circle. They stopped in front of a male vendor whose hair shone like milky moonlight. His eyes were the color of peaches, rimmed in a crystal blue, and when he smiled, his skin glowed like glittery porcelain.

"Hello." The vendor nodded at them, his hands folded on an empty spot on the table. A similar bowl sat before him, and now she could see that it wasn't completely empty. There was a small metal protrusion at the very bottom, with a charcoal-colored wick.

Ruckus leaned in and whispered, "I promise this is a ceremony that holds no unseen consequences."

In too good a mood to let the reminder bother her, Delaney gave him a half smile and returned her attention to the counter. There were already small piles of dust made, a couple dozen in fact. Aside from size, some being larger or smaller than others, they all looked exactly the same. Like an hourglass had broken, and spilled golden sand everywhere.

"All right," she said, because she knew he was waiting for a verbal response, and then she reached toward one of the piles. "Do we just . . . ?"

"Yes." Ruckus chose as well, letting go of her hand for the first time since they'd entered the market so he could use both of his hands to scoop up the dust.

It felt like snow when Delaney lifted it, even lighter than glitter, practically weightless. She tilted her hands and it flickered and spread, coating her palms and the bottoms of her fingers. She probably would have kept staring at it if Ruckus hadn't motioned for her to drop it into the bowl, like she'd seen the couple do earlier.

The sides of their hands brushed when they turned them over, spilling the dust into the black bowl. It fluttered down, mixing, until there was a decent-sized heap at the bottom.

Ruckus eased her back a step as the vendor reached for a switch on his side of the table. A second later the wick at the bottom ignited, sending up a burst of purple flame that instantly consumed the dust.

It was so bright, it was hard to look at, and Delaney had to glance away. She turned her face into the crook of Ruckus's arm and inhaled, smiling slightly when his personal scent briefly chased away the smell of the area. When he nudged her, she found him watching the vendor work, and forced herself to turn back.

The light had dimmed and no longer hurt her eyes, and the vendor had slipped on a pair of inky gloves covered in some slick material that reminded her of oil. Without hesitation, he put his hands into the fire, and began working the melted-down dust material. He molded it with ease, compressing it and moving it around to get it from all sides.

"The usual, miss?" The vendor glanced up from his work to catch her gaze.

"Um . . ."

"Yes," Ruckus answered for her, "thank you."

With a nod, the vendor shifted the material between his palms one last time, then pulled it hastily out of the bowl. He dropped it into a smaller bucket at his feet that Delaney had to lean halfway across the counter to see.

"First time, miss?" the vendor gave her a friendly smile. "I assure you, I do some of the best work here at Zephra Viya."

After a moment, the vendor stooped down and retrieved the item from whatever liquid it had been soaking in. His grin broadened when he got his first glimpse of it, and he turned that look on her with a wink.

"The best I've ever done, if you ask me."

"Do you flirt with all of your female customers?" Ruckus asked, though there was a teasing note to his voice. He wasn't the least bit upset by the other man's comments.

"Oh, I don't have a preference, sir." The vendor's eyes slipped suggestively down Ruckus's body.

Delaney laughed, receiving another wink from the vendor, who then reached into a shelf on the inside of the stone circle. She caught a flash of gold.

Ruckus tapped a code into a touch screen that Delaney hadn't noticed, and then curled his fingers at the vendor.

With a slight bow, the vendor placed the item he'd just created into Ruckus's hand. "Lovely doing business with you. Please"—he looked to Delaney—"come again."

Linking their fingers, Ruckus tugged her away from the stone station, though he didn't lead them back the way they'd come. Instead they circled around and to the right, heading off into a darker section of the marketplace. True to what he'd said earlier, the dust had started falling over more of the area, so that even when the center was far enough behind them and she could no longer turn her head to see it, the golden stuff still fell.

"What is it?" she asked, a bit impatient to see what he was holding. That whole experience had been fascinating, and more than that, it'd been distracting. She hadn't thought of their poor circumstances once since they'd entered the market, and she wanted to stave off those dire thoughts for as long as possible.

Her reality had been pretty bleak for a while now. What was wrong with wanting a little pretend? Right now they were just another couple enjoying the Dust Market, partaking in an old tradition their parents probably would have.

Ruckus pulled her into a tiny alcove between two unoccupied tents, out of the way of the crowd. Then he brought his hand up between them and slowly opened it to show her the small charm he'd been clutching.

It was a tiny square with flattened corners—an octagon, really—and such a dark shade of green it was practically black. Tiny bits of golden glitter sparkled within, just enough to make it look like a smattering of stars in an inky night sky. It was roughly the size of her thumbnail, and for a second she wondered how two handfuls of dust had only managed to make something that small.

There was a tiny golden loop set into the top of it, with a thin chain strung through. By the time she noticed, Ruckus was already urging her to turn around.

She felt his fingers at her neck, and a second later recalled what he'd find already hanging there. She blanched, making to pull back, but he stopped her with gentle hands on her shoulders. The guilt felt like a living thing swimming in her gut, and already an explanation was forming on the tip of her tongue, even though she knew it wouldn't be good enough.

There was really no good way to explain why she hadn't taken off the necklace from the Zane. Especially since, if she was being honest, *she* didn't even really understand why she hadn't.

"It's okay," Ruckus reassured her quietly, comfortingly. "Really, Delaney. I've known this whole time you were wearing it. It's okay."

She frowned, turning to stare at him questioningly over her shoulder. "I didn't—"

"I don't need an explanation. This isn't about him. It's about you and me." He held up the tiny stone. "May I?"

She nodded and then faced forward once more, inhaling when the cool tips of his fingers brushed against her skin.

He lifted the new necklace, deftly latched the clasp, and then adjusted the pendant. As soon as he was done, he stepped back, giving her a chance to look down at the small stone resting higher than the circle pendant that was still tucked safely beneath her Kint uniform.

Delaney ran her thumb over the smooth surface of the stone and turned to meet his gaze.

In the darkened section of the marketplace, he looked fierce, like a real Ander, the one she'd first met in that alley months ago. His relaxed features were the only difference.

The sounds of footsteps and hundreds of conversations happening at once drifted to the background. For a moment it was as he'd said, just the two of them, in a sea of strangers on a world that neither of them really belonged on.

"We've touched stars together," he murmured then.

"What?" She tipped her head back when he came forward, his fingers trailing across her forehead to tuck a strand of hair behind her ear.

"The star-stone"—he motioned to it—"that's what it means. 'We've touched stars together.' It's a reminder to hold on to the good moments, no matter what happens or changes in the future. Couples who come here don't always last, sometimes they've only even been together a few days, or weeks, or they're young and experimenting, not really looking for a bondmate. But this experience"—his eyes swept over the bustling market—"this is something they'll always have, together."

"Remember the good," she said, catching on, "even if there's eventually bad."

His brow furrowed. "There's always going to be a little bad, Delaney. Someone's always going to make a mistake, be it a big one or small one. I think the important thing is to hold on to moments like this, where everything feels *right,* even if it's only for a minute or an hour. Hold on to these moments and figure out if having another is worth the risk of forgiving some of the bad."

"Ruckus." She got the feeling that this was about more than just showing her the Dust Market. That, really, this was an extension of the conversation she hadn't wanted to have at the salon.

He shook his head before she could say as much, however, denying it. "That's just what the stone stands for. But, no matter what happens"—he tried to cover up the fact that his gaze dipped down to the hidden silver circle still around her neck, but failed—"I'll always remember this. I'll always remember *us.*"

TRYSTAN HAD THE ship ready and waiting by the time they made it back through the forest. Since they'd already spent most of the night in the city, they boarded the Kint craft and took off for the palace almost as soon as they spotted it.

Sanzie disappeared down a side hall after letting them know the opposite direction led to the front of the ship. Delaney and Ruckus weaved their way to the cockpit, where the Zane was waiting for them in the pilot seat.

"Has the Basilissa been notified of our upcoming arrival?" Ruckus asked, moving toward the front of the room to skim over the computer readings.

"She is aware," Trystan confirmed. "Though she doesn't know what for yet, just that I have something important to show her. Until I can convince her to board, preferably alone, it's best you stay inside. We don't want to risk anyone recognizing you. Even with the new hair."

"You really hate the hair." Delaney dropped down into the passenger seat.

"There are quite a few things I'm currently not very fond of—"

"I'm going to check to make sure everything is secure," Ruckus said, interrupting their banter. Without glancing their way, he turned on his heel and left.

Delaney watched him go and then sighed. "He's going to see Pettus."

"I'd imagine so," Trystan agreed, flicking at a few switches on the console before turning in his chair to face her. At her pointed look toward the controls, he shrugged. "Autopilot. I want to know if you're all right."

She frowned. "Don't I look all right?"

"Just answer the question, Delaney," he drawled, but the corner of his mouth tipped up despite his obvious efforts to keep it from doing so.

"I'm fine." She was struggling to hold back her own grin now. "How are you?"

His eyes narrowed. "I feel like you're mocking me."

"Trystan . . ." Absently, she rested a hand on his arm. "It's barely been two hours since you left us at the restaurant."

"A lot can happen in two hours."

"Sure, but we're both here now, aren't we?"

"What did you two do without me?"

Delaney shook her head. "Let's not pretend I didn't already catch you noticing the necklace. If you've got a question, just ask it so we can move on to the important stuff."

She almost regretted being so forward, but the palace wasn't too far off, and once they reached it, who knew how the rest of their night would go? Truth be told, she was relieved to find him unscathed as well.

His gaze dropped down to the charm, not bothering to pretend to not be looking any longer. "Did you enjoy Zephra Viya? I hear it's quite a sight, especially this time of year. Were there many couples present?"

116

"There were, and it was amazing. We don't have anything like that back on Earth; I could probably spend an entire day there, just looking. You've never . . . ?"

"No," he replied. "I've never had a reason to."

He'd never been in a relationship before that warranted it, he meant.

"They have a lot of other stuff," she said, only partially noting that her voice had dropped. "You'd enjoy the food. I didn't get the chance to try much of it, but I liked what I did."

"There's that." He eased closer. "But the true purpose of Zephra Viya, the heart of the market, is for lovers."

"Trystan . . ." She didn't like where this was going. "Don't."

"You made me a promise, Delaney."

"Back when the Rex approved, and I had no other choice." Finally she realized that she'd been touching him, and pulled back, straightening some in her seat. The renewed distance did nothing to help clear her head, however, and she could tell by the clenching of his jaw that she'd annoyed him. "Admit it: Things are different now."

"Not that."

"Everything is," she insisted.

He paused, canted his head. "Including us?"

"Of course." Hadn't she just said that? "Your father never really approved of you marrying a human anyway, and Tilda—"

"That isn't what I mean," he cut her off, and she wasn't sure he'd even been listening to her anyway. "We've been different since the cave. I can't be the only who's noticed. I'm *not* the only one. The Ander—"

This time she stopped him. "I don't want to talk about Ruckus with you."

"Because you know I'm right." He waved a hand at her throat. "You just returned from the most romantic location Vakar has to offer, your boyfriend is just downstairs, and yet you're here. With me."

"I'm giving him space to grieve his dead friend," she said. "But yeah, he *is* my boyfriend."

"Aren't you lucky, then? You have a boyfriend and a betrothed." Trystan grunted, pulling away and returning his attention to the console. His fingers moved across it, undoing the autopilot feature as swiftly as he'd set it. Once he'd taken hold of the controls again, he glanced her way, catching her gaze.

"Last I checked, Delaney, only one of those is a person you promise to spend the rest of your life with."

CHAPTER 11

Ruckus hadn't meant to stumble upon her; he'd just wanted a moment alone with his friend before they reached the palace. But Sanzie was in the lower-level cargo hold when he got there, standing directly between two tables that held what he assumed to be Pettus's and Olena's bodies.

Pausing in the doorway, he debated whether or not to turn back. He'd already tried to talk to her, and she'd made it clear she wasn't interested. While he still wanted to settle things between them, if only for history's sake, now probably wasn't the best time to get into it.

"Are you going to stand there all day, Ander?" Sanzie called, forcing him out of his contemplation. As soon as he entered the room, she pointed at the body closest to the door. "This is Pettus."

Pettus and Olena were wrapped securely in body bags, and strapped down on the tables. He moved to Pettus's side but didn't open the bag. He'd gotten a good enough look when they'd found him outside in Inkwell, not far from where Olena had fallen.

"You and he aren't that different, you know?" Sanzie said a moment later. At his frown, she continued. "You and the Zane, and I'm not just referring to the fact that you're in love with the same woman.

He cares about his people, too. Actually, probably more than you do. He's not a bad person."

Ruckus shook his head. "You want to do this now?"

"I don't want to do anything," she stated. "I was merely making conversation."

"Liar." He took an angry step forward before thinking better of it, glad the table was between them, at least. Calming himself, he stilled, inhaling slowly. Once he'd settled some, he said, "You hate me, I get it. It makes sense, considering what you believe happened—"

"I *know* what happened," she growled.

"No." He forced himself to ease his tone, to not give in to the urge to yell at her. "You don't."

"You left me there!" Apparently she didn't feel the need to do the same. She even went so far as to slap a hand down on the table.

"That's not what happened," he disagreed. "I went looking."

"And broke protocol?" She snorted. "Don't lie to me. You wouldn't have done anything to risk your position, and the big promotion it was going to lead to. You *left* me there. To die. If it weren't for the Zane, I would have."

"Sanzie." He held her gaze pointedly, hoping after all this time she'd still be able to read the truth in his eyes. *"I came looking.* I broke off from the rest of the squad, but I didn't stand a chance of finding you alone. I tried, but there was too much ground to cover, and by the time I even caught sight of your ship, it'd been too long."

He could picture it now, the smoke billowing up from the hull, the way it'd been tipped and half-buried already in deep snow. Remembered thinking there was no way she'd survived the crash, and the feeling of hopelessness and loss that had swept through him when he had.

"I was at risk of dying out there, too. If Fawna hadn't found me when she had, I probably would have. I was too frozen to say anything to her, so she didn't know to look for you. It happened so quickly, and I passed out as soon as she had me in the ship."

"I didn't hear from you for weeks," she reminded him, but he caught the inkling of uncertainty in her eyes.

This was something they should have talked about six years ago, but she'd never given him the chance. He'd tried, on multiple occasions. Once she'd joined the Kint army, it'd been nearly impossible to get in touch with her, especially without one of them getting caught. He hadn't wanted to risk the Zane finding out and accusing her of being a spy. Then the war ended and he'd tried again, only to be refused communication.

"It took me eight days to recover," he admitted.

"I never heard anything about that."

"Fawna helped me cover it up. She knew if my commanding officer found out what I'd been up to, that I'd gone on an independent rescue mission against orders, I'd be cut. She staged the whole thing, told him we were on a secret job. As soon as I'd healed and come to, explained to her what had happened, she'd already gotten word that you'd made it out alive. And that you'd defected and joined the enemy.

"That's how she became my pilot. How we became a team. Neither of us meant to hurt you, Sanzie. Her, especially. You've got to know that. Every time you refused one of her calls, or sent back her communications unopened, you wounded her."

The two of them had been best friends practically their entire lives, even before Ruckus had met them and joined in on their friendship. Before he and Sanzie had become something more, however brief it'd been.

"I thought you'd betrayed me," she said.

"We both tried to explain." He took a breath, allowed some of his own hurt to slip through. "You're the one who wouldn't listen. *You* left us."

For a moment he thought she was going to let it go, that they'd slip back into the icy silence. The next thing he knew, she was standing at his side.

"Do you have any proof?" she asked, the twinge of continued accusation there clearly forced.

"Why would I lie?"

"To get me to turn on the Zane, perhaps?"

He waited until she met his gaze. "You know me better than that."

She hesitated. "Do I?"

"Yes."

"We weren't together long," she said, "but you meant a lot to me, and I've spent years believing I didn't mean as much to you."

"You did." He rested a hand on her shoulder before he could think better.

She fiddled with the zipper of her uniform, lost in thought for a moment. "This can't change things for me."

"I understand."

"Do you?"

"Yes," he said. "You're a Sworn, and a Kint. You admire and respect the Zane. I didn't tell you any of this to try to get you to return to Vakar. I've wanted to tell you the truth for years, and now I have. What you do with it, that's up to you. But I understand, Sanzie. I've always understood."

"We're about to land," Delaney's cool voice sounded from the doorway, shocking them both. It was pretty clear by the closed-off expression on her face that she'd been there long enough to overhear.

Guiltily, Ruckus dropped his hand from Sanzie and opened his mouth to explain, but Delaney stopped him.

"Trystan is waiting for you in the cockpit, Sanzie."

The plan was that the Zane and his Sworn would exit the ship first, and if Tilda was alone with only a handful of Tellers, then he'd lead them on board and insist she enter the room in which they were currently standing—alone. That was when they'd tell her the truth.

Sanzie kept her head ducked, bowing slightly to Delaney as she passed. Once she was out in the hall, she turned and quickly glanced at Ruckus before disappearing out of sight.

"That's funny. I could have sworn we just had a conversation about being honest. Why didn't you just tell me that you two dated?" Delaney asked. "That you were on the team she thought abandoned her all those years ago? She told me about that. It's half the reason she's Kint now."

"I didn't—"

"I heard." Even though she'd come to inform him it was time to get ready, she made no moves, remaining still across the room, staring him down.

The last thing he'd intended was to hurt her, especially when the goal had been to ease the tension between him and Sanzie, not form a wedge between him and someone else—especially Delaney, of all people. He could have told her before, but the timing had never felt right, and she'd had enough going on already.

"I was going to say something once we'd figured out what to do about the Rex," he said. "My past relationship didn't seem important, in comparison."

"It is to me. Especially when I find you two touching in a secluded room."

"I had my hand on her shoulder," he pointed out, unable to help the slight bite to his words. "Last I checked that was a lot more appropriate than holding hands or hugging. What's more, I don't do those things with someone else when I think you aren't looking."

She bristled, but he saw her pale slightly, despite her defensive posture. "I've never kept anything from you. Trystan—"

"Is in love with you!" She flinched at his outburst, but he was too distracted to contain himself. "Yeah, he told me. The real question is, why didn't you? See? I'm not the only one keeping things to my-self after all. At least what I had with Sanzie is in the past."

"There's nothing going on between Trystan and me," she told him, her voice dropping.

"I want to believe you."

"So believe me." Almost as soon as she said the words, she tilted her head, and he gave a humorless chuckle. She was clearly receiv-ing a communication through her fitting, and seeing as how he wasn't the one sending it. . . .

"Trystan says we're landing now," she confirmed.

He sighed, suddenly exhausted with this whole situation. All he wanted was to get on a ship and head back home, to Earth. To their cruddy apartment with her hilarious best friend and their room with the lock on the door. He'd taken his denzeration to be with Delaney, and he loved her, but he'd also developed a fondness for her home world. There, he didn't have to worry about organizing Tellers, or putting a spoiled royal family first.

He didn't want to be an Ander anymore, he realized with a start. He just wanted to be Ruckus Wux. Boyfriend of Delaney Grace.

Ruckus turned, prepared to tell her as much, but at that very mo-ment they felt the ship slow and lower. There was still so much to say, about Trystan and about Sanzie, but he bit his tongue and silently motioned toward the other side of the room. They'd decided earlier they'd wait here, out of sight.

Delaney opened her mouth, but must have thought better of it. Then she settled more comfortably across from the door to wait in silence.

DESPITE WHAT HAD happened between Trystan and his father, Kint still held control over Vakar. Therefore, there was no real reason for Tilda not to simply board at Trystan's insistence.

That was the hope, in any case.

Delaney tried not to look at Ruckus as the two of them waited, keeping a slight distance from the tables housing Olena's and Pettus's bodies. They'd only been there for about five minutes before they heard someone approach. She needed to stay on task, focus on what was most important here. Ruckus and Sanzie having once dated several years prior was not it.

Though, she couldn't help but feel a tad bit betrayed—again—by it all. First she finds out he kept information about the Uprising from her, and now this? She understood the need to keep a secret, and logically, sure, she could see how their past relationship might not have seemed very important to him.

Except what she'd just walked in on had been intimate, much more than just a basic apology.

The Basilissa's voice reached them first. "What is it exactly you need to show me, Zane?"

"You'll see," came Trystan's steady reply, a moment before his frame came into view.

Tilda and two Tellers, both Vakar, accompanied him, and Delaney frowned. The plan had been to get Tilda here alone so no one else would know about her or Ruckus. On the one hand, she understood why the Basilissa would refuse to go anywhere alone with the Zane, would insist on bringing protection of some sort, but . . . Delaney couldn't help but feel suspicious. And for good reason.

Because she was watching so closely, she noticed the moment the Tellers shifted their armed wrists.

"Trystan!" Delaney shouted in warning before she'd fully processed what was going on.

Trusting her, the Zane leaped to the side, spinning around to face the small group. Doing so allowed him to just avoid being shot with the Teller's fritz.

She and Ruckus were so distracted watching the Zane, neither of them noticed the other Teller raising his weapon.

Ruckus didn't have enough time to evade, taking the hit and slamming back against the wall. A flash of blue flickered over his body, and he momentarily convulsed before stilling.

"It's a stun round," Trystan quickly assured Delaney, at her side in a matter of seconds, stopping her from dropping down to touch the Ander. "He's just unconscious. He's all right, Delaney. He's fine."

"For now," Tilda said, drawing their attention back her way. At either side, the two Vakar Tellers still had their fritzes aimed on them, but neither attempted to fire again. She was staring at Delaney with wide eyes, then seemed to notice the two body bags. "I was told you would be in one of those."

Trystan stiffened at her side, and then practically growled through their fittings, *"My father."*

They should have expected the Rex to blow it and alert Tilda of Delaney's "death" before his son could make it to Vakar. They'd stupidly believed he was really going to allow them to tell the Basilissa in person.

"She refused to board unless she could bring Vakar guards with her," Trystan stated. *"I should have realized something was amiss, but I saw no other way than to allow it."*

They'd needed her on the ship. How was he supposed to guess she was onto them already?

"I'm sorry," Delaney said to Tilda, hoping to convey how truthful she was being with the tone of her voice. Now that this meeting was finally happening, things were escalating much more quickly than she'd hoped. Even knowing he was okay, she was struggling against the urge to check on Ruckus, forcing all of her focus onto the Basilissa.

"Open it." Tilda flicked a wrist toward the body bag closest to them. Then, when neither of them immediately leaped into action, she motioned for the Tellers to take a threatening step closer. "Open it!"

"Let us explain what happened," Delaney urged, though she walked toward the bag as she did. "This is the Rex's fault. All of it. You know that. Olena tried to kill me on the Rex's order."

"Don't say her name," she snapped, already focused on the bag before Delaney had even reached for the zipper.

Olena's body was exposed bit by bit. Delaney tried not to prolong it, opening the bag as quickly as she could while avoiding coming off disrespectful. The Lissa's face was pale, her lips a slightly off shade. She did not look like she was taking a long nap. She looked dead. There was no mistaking it.

Seeing her again caused Delaney to shiver, memories of standing out there in the snow, of thinking she was going to die, flooding through her mind against her will. Her eyes trailed over to the other table, where Pettus was, and her heart clenched as bile rose up the back of her throat. No part of her wanted to mourn Olena; she'd gotten what she deserved. But if they wanted to gain Tilda's alliance, they couldn't exactly show distaste for her deceased daughter.

A strangled sound slipped past the Basilissa's lips then, and Delaney looked up just in time to see her point a finger toward the Zane, a clear order for the Tellers.

Without even realizing what she was doing, Delaney activated her own fritz and stepped back, blocking Trystan with her smaller form. Even when the two Tellers at the door set their weapons on her, Delaney didn't waver, keeping hers aimed directly at the Basilissa's heart.

"Get out of the way, Miss Grace," Tilda practically growled, the tears flowing freely now. "Or I will let them shoot you."

"They do that and I take you out with me."

Tilda's eyes widened a fraction. "You're defending him now? I entered this ship with the full intention of avenging my heirs. If you're to be believed, his father is the reason my daughter is lying there on a table. Move so that I can take from him what he has so callously stolen from me."

"We need Trystan." She felt the Zane shifting behind her, and stepped farther back so she could press herself to his front in silent warning. If he moved, she'd just move with him. He didn't have to say anything for her to know he wasn't liking the fact that she'd put herself in front of him like this.

"My daughter is dead!" Tilda took a threatening step closer. "After everything I've done, everything I've sacrificed, she was murdered anyway. What happened to the promise your father made me?" She directed this last part over Delaney's shoulder. "He swore she would be protected!"

"He lied," Trystan said. "He's the one who ordered Olena to take Delaney into the woods. What happened after that is ultimately on him. He's the one who put your daughter in danger."

"Why would he do that? Why try to have her killed? Delaney is the heir, exactly like you wanted. I did *everything* you wanted."

"My father tricked me, just as he tricked you. He never intended mutual rule."

"He's been playing you," Delaney told her. "Order them to stand down, and we'll tell you everything that happened."

"I can guess well enough on my own, Miss Grace. One"—she motioned between Ruckus and the Zane—"or both of them killed my daughter to protect you. Am I close?"

"This isn't her fault." Trystan gripped Delaney's hip, clearly ready to shove her out of the way if he had to.

"No," Tilda agreed, "it's yours, and your father's, for orchestrating all of this."

"We want to stop him, same as you."

"I want to kill him," she said. "After I'm done killing you."

"Think about your people." Delaney was running out of time to get through to Tilda; that much was obvious. "Murdering Trystan will only put them in greater danger. The Rex will declare war."

"Let him." She laughed, but the sound was grating, turning into a sob at the end. "I gave up my people for Olena once. I'm more than willing to do it again."

"I don't believe that."

"Then you're more naive than I thought."

"You really want Vakar to know that you'll abandon them? For revenge? Think of all those families, Tilda. All of those daughters still alive. You'll just hand them over to the Rex? You're the Basilissa; you have a duty."

For the first time since they'd started this, Delaney saw a hint of doubt flicker through the other woman's eyes.

"You want to get back at the Rex for what he's done here—well, we want to help you. Trystan has a strong hold with the Kint people, and a good portion of the Kint army. If the two of you combine resources, we should be able to come up with a way to stop the Rex. Take from him the one thing that actually matters: his crown."

"How will that be putting my people at risk any less, Miss Grace? What you're suggesting also leads to war."

"Not if we can expose him before he finds out he no longer has the two of you on a string." And, thanks to this conversation, she thought she might have an idea how to go about that. "We discovered the Rex is the true source behind the Tars. If we can find proof that he's in league with them, a well-known terrorist organization, we can get him dethroned."

"There's no way the Kint people will stand for that level of betrayal," Trystan quickly agreed. Part of him was probably a little annoyed he hadn't thought of this himself.

Tilda narrowed her eyes at them, thought it over. "He's to blame for the Tars? How do I know you aren't lying to save yourselves?"

"Why would we come all this way and risk this much on a lie?" Delaney asked.

"So you returned my daughter's body in, what? The hopes that you could convince me not to kill you both, and agree to yet another convoluted peace treaty? I suppose you've thought about what happens if we are successful in removing the Rex from his throne?"

Delaney couldn't cover up her frown fast enough, and when Tilda saw it, she laughed, and this time the sound was sharp and mocking.

"He really has you convinced he'll make a better Rex than his father, doesn't he?" She shook her head. "I help you now, and as soon as another End gets crowned king, Vakar and Kint are right back where they started before we came to a peace agreement."

"That's not true," she insisted. "Trystan doesn't want a war any more than you do."

"You'll forgive me, Zane, if I find it hard to trust that." Tilda canted her head, lips pursing. Whatever turmoil she was feeling over Olena, she was trying hard to pack it away, to think clearly.

Which could either work in their favor, or against it. Delaney wasn't really sure which way the scales were tilting. The Basilissa no longer looked like she was about to tear them limb from limb, though. There was something cold and calculating in her eyes now.

"I want peace," Trystan said. "I'll give that to you in writing, if you want."

"Your father and I had an agreement in writing," she stated, "and you see how well he held up his end of the deal. No, I'm unwilling to believe you'd give up your life's ambition. Not without a little collateral to ensure it."

"My goal has always been to do what is best for my people."

"And as Miss Grace has so delicately pointed out, as the Basilissa, that needs to be my defining goal as well." Tilda paused for a brief moment, then pulled her shoulders back and exhaled slowly. By the time she was done, the tear tracks on her cheeks were the only remaining indication she'd been a wreck only a few short minutes ago.

"I want to protect my people, but I also want revenge for my daughter. No matter what happened in Inkwell, one thing is very clear, and that is that ultimately, the Rex *is* to blame. Therefore, I am willing to join forces, Zane, but not until I have assurances that if we are successful, Vakar will be safe from Kint."

"Of course, Basilissa." Trystan bowed his head slightly. "You have my word."

"Oh, it's not your word I'm looking for." Tilda set her gaze on Delaney unblinkingly.

A pool of anxiety welled in her chest, but before she could even think of something to say, the Basilissa continued.

"Most of my family was destroyed during the war," Tilda told her. "Olena had no other close relatives who could vie for her place. There's no one of blood relation who could announce an official claim to my throne, which means the Zane can decide to fight it. He might be agreeing now not to go to war, but you and I both know he'll take Vakar without hesitation once I'm gone and there's no one left to stand in his way."

Delaney wanted to deny it, but it was true. Trystan wouldn't find fault in taking Tilda's throne. He wasn't a bad person, but he was still the Zane, and he had been raised by the Rex. He wouldn't see a problem with taking over, would more than likely think of it as him helping Xenith get stronger.

Kint was more advanced, had larger numbers . . . proof that his kingdom was already flourishing in ways Vakar struggled to achieve. In Trystan's mind, combining the two would merely mean providing strength to what was once his enemy.

Knowing his line of thinking made it impossible for her to argue with the Basilissa's concerns. The fact that the Zane didn't say anything to deny those concerns further solidified them.

"Except for you," Tilda added.

Delaney's breath caught in her throat, and she felt Trystan's hand on her hip tighten in mutual shock. "Excuse me?"

"I refuse to allow Kint to take full control of my kingdom, to put my trust in the word of an End. Who's to say he won't claim Vakar and change our ways to suit his? That's typically how takeovers work, and I won't have that."

"I don't understand how I—"

"Yes, you do." Tilda had her Tellers deactivate their fritzes. "You will agree to remain my heir. You are Uprisen, the people already expect it, and more important, the Zane is in love with you. If we are successful in removing the Rex, I will train you in the Vakar way, and groom you to take my place as Basilissa. When the time comes for me to step down, you and the Zane will go through with your betrothal, ensuring equal hold in both Kint and Vakar."

"*Delaney* . . ." Trystan's voice filtered through her head, but she couldn't listen to him right now. He'd already made it pretty clear what he expected from her, hadn't he?

"If you mean what you say, that you truly want peace, this is the only way to get it." Tilda smiled, but there was no mirth in it. "Or I suppose you could shoot me after all. Unless you agree, I won't help you, and without me, you stand no chance of stopping the Rex. You and I both know once he's conquered my planet, he'll come for yours next, Miss Grace."

Part of her was wondering how the hell she'd ended up right where she'd started; the other half, however, wasn't as surprised. Somewhere deep down, she'd sort of known something like this was a possibility. No one walked away from a deal with the royals completely free.

Or in her case, it seemed, free at all.

If she agreed.

That was the one clear difference this time around. Tilda wasn't going to force her, and the Zane had remained surprisingly silent after his one attempt. Whether or not he'd try to force her hand later was yet to be seen, but for now, in this moment, the choice was entirely up to Delaney.

Inadvertently, her gaze swept toward Ruckus.

Staying on Xenith was a major life choice, without adding to it the fact that she'd be agreeing to marry Trystan.

"If you're struggling with the decision," Tilda said a bit smugly, "think of all those families, Miss Grace. The Rex won't show mercy to either of our people."

No, he wouldn't. But if this all worked out, the Rex wouldn't be around to threaten Earth much longer. With him out of the way, Delaney could leave without fear or guilt that her home world was in danger because of it. Trystan and Tilda would be upset, of course, furious even, but she doubted they'd take it out on an entire planet.

Ruckus had already mentioned escape; he'd help her get away. Especially since leaving was sounding like the only way they could be together. They could do it as soon as the Rex was dethroned, while everyone was distracted.

Though the idea of sneaking off without any sort of explanation to Trystan bothered her. . . . Delaney swept those misplaced emotions to the side. He'd be fine without her, the king of Kint, exactly like he'd always wanted. Eventually he and Tilda would come to some sort of agreement that didn't include Delaney giving up her life.

"All right," Delaney heard herself say, slightly detached, distracted by her racing heart. "You have my word."

CHAPTER 12

D elaney."

She tried not to start at the sound of Trystan's voice, having not heard him enter the room. It'd only been a few hours since the incident with Tilda, not nearly enough time for her to process everything that had taken place.

Everything that she'd agreed to.

Ruckus was lying on the bed, still unconscious, and she'd taken an empty seat next to him. They'd been brought here almost immediately after the Basilissa had agreed to help them, led through the palace by the same two Tellers who'd witnessed their whole exchange. As of now, the plan was to keep their presence quiet, to minimize the chance word would get to the Rex.

Sanzie, who'd been left outside the ship during their meeting, was on the other side of their door, the only person Trystan trusted to guard them.

Delaney also hadn't been able to meet the Sworn's gaze, so she was glad Sanzie had remained outside the room and out of sight. She knew she didn't really have a reason, or more important, a right, to be angry or jealous toward her. Even more so now that she'd made this major decision while Ruckus had been unconscious and unable to participate in it. But knowing that didn't make ignoring her feelings about it any easier.

It wasn't even so much that she was jealous, per se, more that she was hurt. There weren't many people on this planet she felt close to, and she didn't want to lose Sanzie's friendship. This lie made it hard for her to be in the same room as the Sworn now, and she hated that. Staying upset wasn't an option, though, not when they needed to be a strong unit.

When it became apparent Trystan wasn't going to take the hint and leave, she sighed, dropping an arm onto the edge of the bed so she could rest her head in her palm.

"Not right now," she said, watching the steady rise and fall of Ruckus's chest. They had no idea when exactly he'd wake up, only that it should be sometime within the next hour. She was trying to prepare herself for when he did, and what she'd say. How she'd explain she was bluffing and still intended for them to leave together. The Zane absolutely could not be present for that conversation.

"Tilda set those terms, not me," he pointed out, which only made her quirk a brow.

"So you're not happy about it at all then?" She snorted when he didn't reply. "I can't talk about this right now, Trystan. I need to think."

"I didn't come here to pressure you about that, in any case," he said, clearing his throat. "I need to go. My father will be expecting me by tomorrow night, and now that we've secured Tilda's aid, I'll leave at least knowing you'll be safe here."

"Are you joking?" Delaney was up and around the bed in a matter of seconds, instinctively grasping his wrist. "No way. You can't go to Carnage."

"I have to. We can't afford not to keep up appearances. While I'm gone, you and the others can work on a way to expose my father's connection to the Tars. I'll try to find some evidence in Carnage while I'm there. If he's kept any, that's where it'll be."

"It isn't safe."

"My father doesn't know about Olena, and he's already expecting me. We'll be in more danger if I don't go. We have the advantage, but we won't for long." He paused, took in her expression. "You're concerned for me, even after what Tilda made you promise?"

Delaney closed her eyes and took a deep breath. Things were happening too quickly. They'd only just arrived and now he was running off to meet his father, the most dangerous man on the planet. Getting Tilda to agree to help had felt like a win, despite what Delaney had agreed in exchange for it, but if anything happened to Trystan, none of this would matter.

"Kint won't follow anyone but you," she said.

"But the majority of them still won't if my father remains the Rex. You knew I was going to have to leave as soon as we brokered this deal with Tilda."

Yes, of course she had; they just hadn't discussed it. Logically, she knew if Trystan didn't go, his father would come looking, probably starting here since he was aware of his son's visit to the Basilissa.

"I didn't think it'd be this soon. We only just got here. What if Tilda changes her mind, or—"

"She won't." He eased his wrist free from her hold and ran his hands up her arms comfortingly. "You made a very compelling argument, Delaney. Offering her a viable solution in the form of exposing my father's ties with the Tars was brilliant. Sanzie will be here, just in case. And you've proven you can more than handle yourself."

Not against an entire palace full of Tellers. She would have said as much if she hadn't just processed his other comment.

"Sanzie isn't going with you?" She shook her head vehemently. "You can't go alone."

He tilted his head, the corner of his mouth tipping up slightly, though it was obvious he was trying to hold back the smirk for her benefit.

"Yes, okay, fine," she snapped. "I'm concerned about you going to Carnage to confront your psycho dad. Happy?"

Trystan cupped the side of her face. "You're tempted to demand I stay; I can see it in your eyes."

"Would that work?"

He clucked his tongue. "You don't give me orders, Lissa. Though I will admit, watching you give them to others is a sight."

"Trystan"—she placed her hand over his, not even caring that she sounded desperate—"don't do this. You remember I almost just watched you die? I don't want to do that again."

He was quiet a moment, and then whispered, almost too low for her to hear, "Kiss me."

She froze, her mind blanking, her feet freezing to the ground. They'd only kissed once before, during the Claiming ceremony, and that had been because they had to. The guilt she'd felt afterward had been all-consuming; the only reason she'd been able to shake it was the fact that, the day after, she was distracted by the Rex's betrayal and Olena's attempt to kill her.

But, looking back on it, it wasn't hard to recall *why* she'd felt so guilty. It hadn't been because they'd kissed; they hadn't had a choice in the matter, after all. It was that she hadn't exactly hated it.

Trystan took in her expression and let out a sound from the back of his throat, part disappointment, part arrogance. Like he'd known that was the reaction he was going to get when he'd asked her.

He ran his thumb beneath her eye, then eased close enough that he could press his lips to the center of her forehead. He left his mouth there a breath too long, but she couldn't shift her toes, let alone convince her body to move away from him.

When he retreated, she felt the loss of his warmth, and kind of hated herself for noticing it. Silently, she watched him walk to the door, reach for the handle.

Just before he turned the knob, he glanced back, his cornflower-and-crimson-red eyes catching hers.

"You've got to decide, Lissa," he told her. "That's what I remember."

Then he left, and the words he'd spoken while they'd been in that cave played through her mind like a war drum beating after him.

"I decided I love you," he'd said. *"Now you need to decide."*

RUCKUS LISTENED TO their exchange, pretending to still be unconscious. At first he'd told himself he was doing so to give them some semblance of privacy, but that wasn't the truth. Part of him, the part that hated the fact that she still wore that Claiming ring around her neck, had wanted to hear for himself how they reacted to each other when they didn't think anyone was listening.

It was wrong, and deceptive of him, but he couldn't help himself. Ever since he'd seen her hovering over the Zane's hospital bed, he'd known something was different between them. Then, after tonight, how things had gone, he feared they'd never get back to where they'd been, that Earth and their home there was a dream he was foolishly clinging to, one that he'd never have again.

So he'd stayed still, his eyes closed, his breathing even, and had listened in on their conversation. They'd kept their voices down, but in the silent room he was able to make out every word.

He'd been about to give up the ruse, however, when they began arguing over whether or not Trystan should go—Ruckus still didn't one hundred percent trust that Trystan wouldn't cut another deal with his father, but he knew the Zane had to get to Carnage before the Rex grew suspicious—but then he'd gone and ordered Delaney to kiss him.

In the following quiet, Ruckus had actually feared she was doing it, had strained to hear and almost opened his eyes, torn between needing to see and not wanting to. When the Zane had made that disappointed sound, giving away that she hadn't done it, he'd felt a wave of relief so strong, it actually made him feel more guilty for eavesdropping.

It was a while after the Zane left that Delaney returned. From the sounds of it, she was sitting next to the bed, though he still didn't open his eyes to be sure. She took his hand in both of her own, bringing it up so she was clutching his arm close to her chest.

Through her clothing, he felt the press of the metal from her necklaces.

He thought about how uncomfortable she'd gotten when he'd exposed that he knew she was still wearing the Claiming ring. He'd hated the way it'd made him feel, knowing that she was concerned he'd get angry or jealous. He *was* jealous, but that was his personal issue to work through, not hers. The last thing he wanted to do was burden her with anything else.

Which was why he hadn't asked her to take it off. Why he'd waited so long to even bring it up. He'd seen it the last time she'd come to visit him in the dungeons on Inkwell. She'd tried to hide it by tucking it beneath her shirt, but he'd recognized the outline of the ring, known immediately what it was.

It bothered him that she hadn't told him about it herself, but he understood why she'd felt the need to keep it a secret. He'd been locked in a cell, after all, and she'd been doing everything she could just to keep her head above water. So he hadn't said anything, knowing that she'd tell him eventually, when the time was right.

And once he was free and they were together again, he hadn't drawn attention to it because what would be the point? He saw the way she looked at the Zane, even though she tried so hard to hide it.

He saw, and it cut him every time he did. But getting angry wasn't going to help anyone, especially when it was also obvious she was torn by the way she felt toward Trystan. He hated it, hated the idea that she could feel anything for the Zane, but he was also grateful, in a sense, that she'd had that support while dealing with the Rex.

Ruckus was grateful that he knew Trystan wouldn't let anything bad happen to her, that he had in fact risked his life and his station on numerous occasions in the past. How could Delaney *not* have developed feelings after all that they'd been through?

He felt a bit slighted that she'd fallen for the guy who'd thrown him in a cell, but being in there had given Ruckus a lot of time to think. And to come to grips with the fact that he was as much responsible for Delaney being dragged back to Xenith as Trystan was. He'd let her do the Uprising ceremony. Hadn't fought against the Basileus when he'd suggested it. Hadn't explained things to Delaney. Hadn't batted an eyelash, in all actuality.

She shifted, and the necklaces pressed more closely against him. He could have asked her to remove the Claiming ring, and he had actually intended to do just that when he'd brought her to the Dust Market. He'd hoped to replace it with a symbol of his own, the starstone. As soon as he'd seen her reaction, however, he'd changed his mind.

There was a reason she hadn't taken the Claiming ring off, and while he wanted her to take it off, he didn't want it like that. He didn't want her to do it out of guilt, or obligation. Didn't want her to make a decision because he'd asked her to make one, because he'd made it feel like an ultimatum.

But he also wasn't sure how much longer he could endure this. He needed to hear her deny the Zane's claim, to toss that ring aside in place of his. It was stupid, to need reassurances from his girlfriend, yet after everything that had happened . . .

He needed to know, once and for all, if he'd lost her.

Just as he opened his eyes, the door across the room opened again, and he turned to watch the Basilissa enter.

"Good. You're awake, Ander." She gave him a curt nod—no apology for having knocked him out in the first place, but okay—and then immediately turned to Delaney. "The Zane just departed, which means we need to start discussing how you expect this plan of yours to work."

"What's going on?" Ruckus slowly eased himself into a seated position. When he faltered some, Delaney rushed to help, only pulling back slightly once he was propped against the headboard.

He'd gathered from her conversation with the Zane that the Basilissa had agreed to help them, and it was nice that he wasn't waking up in a cell somewhere. But he hated that he didn't know any of the details on how they'd managed to convince Tilda to be on their side.

"Someone needs to fill me in. Now."

"They've told me the Rex is behind the Tars." The Basilissa caught his eye. "Is this true, Ander?"

"Yes. A ship attacked us just outside the border. They were Tars."

Tilda quirked a brow. "You mean to tell me you didn't have a plan prior to that?"

His plan had been to get off this planet before the Zane ever woke up, but Delaney had had other ideas. After that, in truth, the best he could come up with was simply keeping them alive long enough to *eventually* get them off Xenith.

"The Rex is holding Gibus hostage, and he's created the Tars for some unknown reason. Unfortunately, we weren't able to gather more details on what exactly that was. We knew we needed your help," Delaney said.

"Because you had no one else."

"Because you're the ruler of Vakar."

Tilda hummed and glanced between the two of them.

"Exposing the Rex's connection to a terrorist group is the only plan we have," Delaney reminded her.

Ruckus spoke up. "That'll work. We just need enough proof to shake the Kints' belief in him as their king. Having the support of the Vakar ruler will help press the issue. Many have been waiting for a reason to denounce him for a long time now, as you well know."

"Yes," Tilda said, her lips twisting in a scowl, "the Zane is better liked by his people. I am aware. That changes nothing. His father will have to undergo a trial, no matter how great the proof against him. During that time, those still loyal to him will stop at nothing to clear his name."

"Which, again, is where you being the Basilissa comes in handy." Delaney had a hand on Ruckus's shoulder, and he could practically feel how nervous she was through their connection, despite the fact that her voice never wavered. "When that time comes, you make it public and perfectly clear that you're siding with the Zane. You want Trystan on the throne, it's time for a change, you've always known the Rex can't be trusted. . . . Say whatever you have to in order to convince them. Most of Kint doesn't want war, either."

"I give them a clear way to avoid that," Tilda said, and nodded her understanding. "And it helps sway them into denouncing the current Rex."

"Exactly."

"It could work, Miss Grace. But . . ."

Delaney tilted her head, waiting, and when Tilda didn't follow that up with anything, prompted, "But . . . ?"

"How do we get proof?" Ruckus answered for the Basilissa.

"Precisely, Ander. *How* is the real issue here. I doubt the Rex has information that can connect him to the Tars just lying about. Even if that's the real reason the Zane has gone home, it won't be easy, if even possible, for him to find what we need. Does he even know what to look for? *Evidence* is a pretty vague concept."

Delaney ran a hand through her hair in frustration, dropping down on the edge of the bed next to Ruckus. "So you're saying this plan actually sucks."

"I'm saying that, until we have something concrete we can hold over the Rex's head," she corrected her, "this is all working theory. *Can* I side with the Zane against his father once their people are more susceptible to that notion? Of course. *Will* they take the bait to avoid more bloodshed? Probably."

"Why couldn't you just do it now?" Delaney asked. "The two of you joining forces could be enough."

"It isn't," Ruckus told her. "If Trystan even tried it, he'd risk losing a vast majority of those loyal to him. A Zane siding with the enemy in order to steal the crown? It's not very respectable."

"Right," Delaney practically growled. "Tradition."

She was no doubt thinking about how that was what had gotten her stuck in this mess a second time. Tradition was the stepping stone Trystan had used to make her the official Vakar Lissa. Ruckus wasn't sure he'd ever forgive himself for his hand in making that possible.

"We can't just sit here hoping he finds something while he's in Carnage, then," Delaney said after a moment of silence. "He wanted us to figure out how we'd get the information to the public. I'm guessing that won't be too complicated."

"There are news outlets I trust," Tilda told them. "As for filling your time and being useful, your files have been left untouched, Ander. I know you've kept a large amount on the Tars and their past transgressions. Perhaps, now that you're aware of their connection to the Rex, you'll be able to spot something you overlooked before."

He thought about it, nodded. "That's a good idea."

"Unfortunately, the palace is still under Kint control. It isn't safe for you to be roaming the halls, and I certainly cannot reinstate your status without drawing too much suspicion."

She was right: He couldn't risk using any of his old access codes on the off chance the Rex had men monitoring the palace's systems.

"You have friends here"—it was clear this wasn't a question—"and you can give a list with a few names to Sanzie, and I'll get in touch with them. If they aren't currently in the palace, I'll send for them immediately. They'll be able to move freely, and can bring whatever files you need directly to you in this room."

Delaney had stiffened some at the mention of the Sworn, and it took all of Ruckus's strength not to look her way. Tilda was clever, would easily catch on that something was off between them, and besides, this wasn't the time to continue their talk about his past.

Or Delaney's.

Her parting conversation with the Zane was still fresh in his mind, and he wasn't exactly happy about it.

"I suppose since the Rex alerted you about my 'death,' it's not safe for me to be walking around, either," Delaney said, frowning when her words caused the Basilissa to appear perplexed.

She glanced between the two of them. "I assumed that had been kept from him, along with news of my daughter. If the Rex is aware he no longer has a foothold into Vakar, we have a more imminent problem on our hands."

"What do you mean?" Delaney slowly rose from the bed. "The Rex is the one who told you that I was dead, isn't he?"

"No," she said, shaking her head. "We received a coded message yesterday morning. In it, I was told that both you and my daughter had been murdered. When the Zane radioed in that he was approaching the palace and had something to show me, I assumed he was bringing me both of your bodies."

"That's why you brought along Vakar Tellers and had them shoot without asking questions," Ruckus surmised. "You had their weapons set to stun to avoid causing a political issue should the information end up being bad."

"If he was truly bringing me the bodies of my heirs," Tilda confirmed, "then I was willing to hear him out before killing him, yes. But then I saw Delaney, clearly alive and well, and that there were still two body bags on the tables . . ." Her voice trailed off, and neither of them pressured her into continuing.

"You knew Olena was dead?" Delaney asked, cutting into the silence. The panic in her tone caught Ruckus's attention. "You're certain that's what the message said? Not that she was injured and in surgery? In critical condition?"

"I knew she was dead, Miss Grace," she replied tightly. "The fact that I'd had the information hours before your arrival, and therefore was able to process it, is the only reason you were given the chance to speak to me at all."

"But the message, it came from Inkwell, right?"

"Delaney." Ruckus reached for her, grasped her hand, but she didn't tear her gaze off the Basilissa. It took him a moment, but he figured out what she was getting at fairly quickly.

The only people who'd known about Olena's death had been in Inkwell. While he'd been unconscious, she and the Zane must have assumed the Rex had been the one to expose them, but he'd only been told about Delaney. He'd thought Olena was still alive. If Tilda had received a message stating otherwise, it meant someone in Inkwell had betrayed Trystan.

"Actually, no," Tilda said. "We traced the message back to Carnage."

Delaney was moving for the door without a second thought, forcing Ruckus into motion in order to stop her. He caught her before she could open the door, and she spun on him with a hiss that surprised him.

She looked terrified and furious all wrapped into one.

"We have to stop him!" She tried to shake off Ruckus, but he held on to her arms tightly.

"Who?" Tilda asked, but it was clear Delaney wasn't paying attention to her anymore.

"It's too late," Ruckus said, trying to calm her down in the process. "He's already taken off."

"So contact his ship!"

"The one he brought us here on isn't registered to Vakar systems. We'd have to ask the Kints to look up the vehicle number, ultimately alerting them that something was wrong."

"Something *is* wrong!" Finally Delaney shook him loose, but she didn't try for the door again.

"I'm sorry to say"—Tilda held up a hand—"I'm unclear as to what is going on."

"It's a trap," Delaney snapped.

"For?"

"The Zane," Ruckus answered, watching as the breath stuttered out of Delaney, an almost lost expression flickering over her face.

"The Rex knows about Olena," she said. "Trystan is in danger."

CHAPTER 13

His father met him on the tarmac.

Which immediately had his hackles rising.

The Rex was many things, but an attentive father wasn't one of them. Yet here he was, waiting with his hands folded in front of him, watching the ship Trystan had managed to procure at the last minute hover above the landing zone and then slowly lower.

He was doing a fairly good job of hiding the fact that he was still angry at his son's delay—only years of experience allowed Trystan to see through it—and smiled broadly as soon as the Zane stepped from the ship and headed his way. The Rex even went so far as to wave, moving to clap his son on the back once he was close enough.

"I had thought you'd leave it until the last minute. When I heard you were arriving earlier than expected," the Rex said, leading them toward the stairwell that trailed from the roof to the innards of Carnage Castle, "I had to come see for myself."

He had to find out why, he meant. This whole show was made to put Trystan on edge, make him wonder what his father was up to. Of course, the fact that he was trying so hard to mask his lingering irritation also meant this was supposed to distract the Zane.

From what? That was the question, and until he figured it out, the only thing he could do was play along.

As soon as they started down the stairs, the familiar smell of the place assaulted his nose, and Trystan almost gave up his steady facade. There were very few things on the planet he hated more than that smell: a mixture of salt, smoke, and musk that always reminded him of home. And how much he detested being there.

"My business with Tilda concluded sooner than I thought it would," Trystan said, forcing himself to ignore the disgusting scents and focus on reading the Rex's physical cues.

"You mean the Basilissa grew tired of your moping." He clucked his tongue, his arm moving to wrap around the broad width of Trystan's shoulders. He tugged him closer. "Son, I know it must have been very upsetting, losing your human, but she's meaningless in the grand scheme of things. You'll see. Once you're on the Vakar throne, you'll thank me."

So he still believed Delaney was dead. Trystan sighed internally. That was something good at least.

"She wasn't just a human," he sneered, making sure to add an extra layer of outrage to his tone. He wouldn't be expected to grieve openly—the Rex had trained him to be "stronger" than that—but a reaction was required to sell this ruse. It was a thin line. Too much, and he'd give himself away, exposing that Delaney lived. Too little, and he'd do the same.

The Rex was clever.

"Of course not, son." He tightened his arm in what was probably meant to be a comforting squeeze. "She was *your* human. I know."

"Don't patronize me," Trystan growled, and this time he didn't actually have to fake his anger.

"Never," the Rex said, ultimately doing so again. "You look like you could use some rest. I was hoping to have you attend the meeting with the council at my side, but no one should see you like this. When was the last time you slept, Trystan? Please don't tell me you've been up all night, crying over her corpse? How morbid."

"I wouldn't expect you to understand," he replied thickly. "You didn't shed a single tear for Mother."

It was probably too far.

The Rex paused with one leg hovering over the last step. They'd gone down several flights and were finally on the right floor, but instead of continuing, the Rex swiveled his head slowly until he was staring at Trystan darkly.

The deceased Regina was something they never spoke of. Ever. It was a silent rule made the moment after her lifeless body had been discovered in the royal chamber. Neither of them had ever broken it before, and for the life of him, Trystan couldn't imagine why he'd been so foolish as to do so now.

"Apologies, Father." He bowed his head, keeping his eyes downcast on the tips of the Rex's polished boots. "I don't know what came over me."

The Rex still had his arm around Trystan's shoulders, and for a moment, it seemed like he might move his hand over and strangle the Zane. He seemed to surprise them both when he suddenly flashed a half smile instead and dropped down the final step, dragging his son with him.

"You're forgiven, this once." The threat at the end was clear, though the mirth never left his eyes. "Losing someone you care for is never easy; however, we're Ends. We don't dwell on such trivial nonsense. The planet keeps turning, and we continue on. But you must have come to that conclusion on your own, or else, why would you be here? Isn't that right?"

It was a trap, a poor attempt to gauge a reaction and see if Trystan was hiding something. Knowing this, he kept his expression firmly in place, making sure not to flinch or twitch, or even alter his gait as they moved down a long hallway. He kept his gaze firmly ahead, pretending not to be bothered by his father's intense stare at his side.

"'The Crown before the Common,'" Trystan stated, repeating the bullshit creed his father had taught him as a child. It was even scrawled across a tapestry in his father's bedroom, though few others ever saw it.

For good reason.

"Exactly." The Rex patted him one last time and then finally let go of Trystan. "I knew I could count on you to see reason."

They'd walked a little more than halfway down the hall, and now paused at a set of silver doors. The walls themselves were a pale blue, the floors carpeted in a deep navy. This section of the castle was made to look lavish, with all the expensive trimmings and even small square tables with plants drifting in glass bowls filled with water. It was meant to be relaxing, nonthreatening.

Like pretty much everything else involving the Rex, it was a lie.

Trystan could see it, clear as day. He'd known his father wasn't the best choice for ruler, that he didn't always keep the safety of the people in mind. He'd known he was manipulative, and controlling. But making the Zane believe they were on the same page, that he could finally have one thing that he wanted without fear of his father taking it . . .

Delaney was right: The Rex was a monster. And unless you could befriend them, monsters needed to be put down. He and his father would never see eye to eye; Trystan realized that now.

Which only left them option two.

"Now, as I've stated, I don't think you're in any shape to meet with the council." The Rex ignored the two sentinels at the doors, who were waiting to open them. "You should go straight to your rooms. Get some sleep. When you wake, freshen up and we'll meet again for dinner. How does that sound?"

Like literal hell.

"Perfect, Father," Trystan said, clasping his hands behind his back respectfully. "May I ask, why is it you're meeting with the council? I might not be in the right sorts to attend, but surely I should be privy to what's taking place."

"There's damage control to do. We must prove to the people that Olena is the right option." He glanced pointedly up and down the hall. "Which reminds me, where is Lissa Olena?"

"Back in Inkwell," he said. "She wasn't well enough to travel."

"You were meant to keep me updated on that. We never even received a report from you. I still don't know how this happened."

"Apologies, Father. In the rush to get the information to Tilda in person, it slipped my mind. Teller Pettus managed to get control of a fritz and shot Olena twice. Once in the abdomen, once in the left shoulder. The doctors have managed to secure her, and report that she'll live through the ordeal." He made sure to add a twinge of distaste to his tone at the end there.

"Don't sound so thrilled about that, son," the Rex drawled. He chuckled and then turned toward the sentries. "Do you need an escort to your rooms?"

"That won't be necessary, Father." Trystan bowed and then moved away, careful not to glance back as he heard the double doors opening and his father greeting the council members within.

He turned the corner, playing the part he always did—mirroring the Rex and ignoring the Tellers he passed, heading in the direction of his rooms.

HE NEEDED TO figure out the reason the Rex was angry, especially since he believed Delaney was dead and Olena was alive. Trystan was here, wasn't he? That should have been enough to placate his father, but no, there was something else going on.

It was possible he was still upset about having been disobeyed, Trystan mused, placing his palm on the keypad at the left of the door once he reached his rooms. As soon as it opened, he entered, coming to an abrupt halt just within the doorway.

They were exactly as he'd left them, the open lounge area all polished marble flooring, tall dark-blue walls, and wide windows. The silver pillows on the couch were placed at the exact angles he'd set them, and the coffee table before the couch was clear, aside from the statue of his favorite animal, which he used as a centerpiece. He had a similar one back in his rooms in Inkwell, and the memory of Delaney standing there, inspecting it, hit him like a ton of bricks.

This place was empty, hollow. It needed Delaney.

He needed her.

He'd been careful not to dwell too long on the promise Tilda had forced his Lissa to make. Though he'd been standing behind her at the time, he knew Delaney well enough to know she wasn't pleased with having to agree to marry him.

Again.

But that was a topic they'd discuss at a later date, once all of this was finished and he knew they were safe. Until then he needed to keep his own feelings about the matter—and about how she clearly still didn't want to be betrothed to him—carefully locked away.

The whole way here he'd tried not to think about her, or how he was leaving her behind. He knew the Ander would keep her safe, but he would prefer to be with her himself, so he could be sure she was protected. Yet they'd needed more information, fast, and try as he might, this was the only solution he could come up with under such short notice.

Forcing his feet forward, Trystan passed by another empty side table to the left, and the circular glass table set before the floor-to-ceiling windows directly across the main door. The room branched off at either side, one leading to his bedroom and bathroom, the other to his study. He took the latter.

His study was almost the same size as the lounge area, which made sense, because when he was here, he spent more time in this room than any other in the entire castle. Bookshelves lined the walls, volumes carefully sorted by color, and aesthetically displayed with trinkets and statues between them.

Trystan didn't bother sparing them a glance, moving to his desk at the far end. He didn't sit in the large leather chair, either, opting to lean over, already tapping on the clear glass panel that took up most of the desk's surface.

The device hummed to life beneath his fingertips, a row of blinking lights greeting him before his home screen appeared. He inputted the sequence that would ensure no one could trace what he was doing or spy on his screen while he was doing it, before he ran a search through the castle's systems. As soon as that was accomplished, he got down to business.

His father had Kint's top specialists create the firewalls that kept the castle computer systems safe. Of course, in his need to have the smartest child on the planet, he'd also hired those same people to teach his son, not realizing they would teach him everything he'd need to know to teach himself how to hack. Which meant Trystan could easily infiltrate the system, and had been doing so since age thirteen.

Trystan knew the Rex had a private computer, one not connected to the rest of the castle's systems. If he was keeping damning evidence, that was probably where it was, but Trystan wanted to cover all his bases before taking a risk like that. There'd be no explaining his way out of trouble if he got caught in his father's study, the only place, aside from his parents' bedroom, that he was forbidden from entering without the Rex present.

Needing to know if anyone else was in on it, Trystan ran a full search through all communications that had been sent and received by the castle in the past seventy-two hours. He supplied a few specific keywords to look for, in order to weed out what had to be thousands of messages. While that process began, he clicked open a new screen, pulling up video footage of the hallway directly outside the conference room his father was in, and then the corridors surrounding the Rex's study.

When the latter popped up, he frowned, momentarily confused to find security had been more than doubled. At least half a dozen Tellers roamed the halls, boxing the study off.

In all his years living here, he couldn't recall there ever being that much security placed on one room. It drew unwanted attention. The Rex had to have something to hide for him to go to such lengths in what was meant to be his own highly secured castle. Did he expect someone to try to break in? Try to search through his things?

But why, and who? The only known enemies the Rex had were Vakar, and he currently believed he had Tilda eating out of the palm of his hand. That left the Tars, whom Trystan now knew his father secretly ran, and Ruckus's little ragtag group, who he'd left back in Varasow.

Actually, that wasn't entirely true. There was someone else he hadn't considered.

A few keystrokes later, and he had a separate search running through the castle's security cameras. The screen flicked through different images, almost too quickly to be processed, but Trystan had done this multiple times as well, and knew what to look for and what not to bother focusing his attention on. He slammed his palm down a split second before the image he was currently looking at could change, pausing it.

It was grainy and in black and white, but he could easily make out the Sutter his father had taken from Inkwell. Delaney's friend Gibus.

He was bent over a worktable, fiddling with some metal device. His face was set in intense concentration, even as his right foot tapped out a rhythm Trystan couldn't hear. These cameras didn't have any sound, which often came in handy for him. When he'd been younger, it meant if he'd gotten caught, he could easily make up some story as to why he was where he wasn't meant to be.

Just as he was about to check the location, a soft ding drew his attention to his first search, and he quickly tapped over to his original screen. There were three communications that matched his search parameters. It was honestly a bit surprising that there were even this many. Leaving behind a trail was sloppy, but then again, having the most secure systems in Xenith meant sometimes the Kint got a little lax with protective protocols.

The first one he looked at was a useless outgoing message that had been flagged due to a vague mention of the Tars as a whole. The second was more interesting, giving him pause as he read through the somewhat cryptic message.

It was only three words—*Confirmed. They're here*—but something about it gave Trystan a poor taste in his mouth. He checked the location from which the message had been sent, and felt himself start to worry when he saw it'd come from Varasow late last night.

Around the same time he and the others would have landed in the palace.

Quickly, he flipped to the final message, hoping that his suspicions would be proven wrong. Instead he sucked in a breath when he read the single word.

Secured.

The message had come from Inkwell.

Trystan had put the entire castle on lockdown, leaving behind a couple dozen of his most trusted Tellers. If his father had sent another retrieval team after him, he should have received word from his men. Unless they'd been caught off guard and overrun.

He tried to rack his brain for any other possible explanation, but came up with nothing. No, his father must have sent more Tellers to Inkwell, either before or after their conversations about Trystan's trip to Vakar. They'd taken the castle there, and had silenced his people before they could get word out to him. The fact that he'd taken a random ship, and that his shing had cracked during his and the Ander's skydiving escapade, would have made it difficult in any case. Especially since he'd only discovered that it'd been broken after departing from Varasow, and hadn't had the chance to get a new one.

He needed to check on his people, see if any had been able to escape in the ship he'd left behind.

Fear for Dominan and the boy's mother forced Trystan to pause and take a deep breath. There was nothing to be done about that at the moment, and he had other, more pressing issues.

The Rex knew about Olena.

Putting the two incoming messages together was proof enough to convince Trystan, especially when he took into account his father's odd behavior. He'd seen his son more worn down than he was now plenty of times, and not once had that been reason enough for him to suggest he shirk his duties. The Zane being in the castle but not attending a council meeting? That would certainly cause more gossip than if he'd gone in there looking tired.

This was a setup.

He glanced at the computer screen once more, scanning the tightened security around his father's office, everything clicking into place. The Rex wanted him to try something; that was why he'd let him go off on his own as soon as he'd gotten there.

Did he know Trystan had discovered his connection to the Tars? Or was there something else he was hiding that he didn't want him to see? Why hadn't he used his knowledge of Olena's death against him already? Everyone was in jeopardy now, including those currently in the Vakar palace.

If the Rex knew his hold over Tilda and her crown was gone, he'd be plotting a way to regain control. By any means necessary.

Cursing, Trystan spun away from his desk, running both hands through his hair until he could tightly cup the back of his skull. His options had dwindled, and he needed a better plan for how to proceed.

If he tried for the study, surely he'd get caught. He could do it, play into his father's hands if only to see where the Rex intended to take this. Perhaps Trystan would be able to glean important knowledge from it, even. . . . But if he couldn't get away? He'd be putting Delaney and his people in greater danger.

Which meant giving up on the mission. He barely resisted the urge to slam a hand through the wall. He did not come all the way here for nothing, and he refused to let his father win.

Still scrambling to come up with a solution, he turned back to the computer, and paused when he spotted the window displaying Delaney's Sutter.

The one who'd been in his father's clutches for a few days now. And who was clearly working on something for him . . .

The beginnings of a new plan started to take root, spurring him back into action. Trystan hit a few more buttons to bring up the location of that specific camera. After finding that the Sutter was being held on the opposite side of the castle, in the South Wing, he quickly wiped any trace of what he'd been searching, and shut down his device.

A smaller version rested in a drawer, and he grabbed it before exiting the study to head back to the main door.

While this wing was supposedly private and unwatched, he didn't trust that his father wasn't having him spied on. It was the type of thing the Rex would do, especially considering he knew he'd been lied to.

The only reason he could think of for his father not to have openly confronted him was that he was waiting to see how far his deception ran. Not attempting to break into his study was a good way of throwing his father off, especially if he was successful in retrieving the Sutter, making this appear like it'd been nothing more than a rescue mission.

Either way, he couldn't still be here when the Rex's meeting concluded. If he was, he risked being detained, and he needed to get back to Vakar and warn Delaney and Tilda that his father was onto them.

Trystan activated the device in his palm and loaded the program that would allow him to access the security cameras. Once it was open, he inputted the North Wing and waited for the feed to appear. Sure enough, there was one camera set down the length of each hall on this floor. They were meant to only be operational in times of an attack, so clearly his father didn't trust him.

Knowing that the footage would be carefully monitored, Trystan ran through his plan one last time to ensure there weren't any obvious kinks. When he couldn't find any, he rotated his shoulders and pressed his palm to the keypad at the side of the door, hitting a single button on his device afterward. Since it connected to the main computer, it was easy enough for him to hack in and download everything the castle's security cameras had recorded over the past hour. Once he had the video footage, it was a simple matter of rewinding. A programmed thirty-second loop of the feed began to play, and he darted out of the room and ran left.

A few feet away from the turn, he hit another button, altering the camera footage in the next hall so that it would start to loop. His count hit thirty seconds as he turned the corner, having just made it before the original looped footage ended and returned to regular record.

This had been a game he'd played as a child, a way to sneak up and spy on his father during council meetings he'd been too young to attend. Or even—more often than not—to sneak to the kitchens in the middle of the night to satisfy a sugar craving.

Because of this, he knew to adjust the loop to thirty-five seconds as soon as he passed the East Wing, and again to forty when he entered the South.

Trystan traveled the castle this way, taking the most secluded corridors, which he knew were more than likely empty. Twice, he had to duck into side rooms to avoid a set of passing Tellers, making sure to switch back to the regular footage so that the security guards watching the feed would see their fellow Tellers and know all was secure. Both times, he was forced to wait until they'd evacuated the hall completely before reactivating the loop.

Unsurprisingly, the South Wing was guarded, and Trystan slowed as he approached, watching the four Tellers there through the camera feed in the corner of his screen. He continued to count off the seconds in his head as he assessed the situation, coming close to the end of his forty seconds.

He adjusted the timer for the next loop to two minutes, hating that he had to pull the prerecorded footage back that far. It left a lot to chance. One guard simply having scratched their head in a strange way could alert whoever might be watching this area that something was going on. But he wouldn't have enough time to deal with the Tellers, make it down the hall, and grab the Sutter unless he took this risk.

Activating his fritz, he made sure the setting was on stun and then took a deep breath. Three seconds before his time ran out, he hit the loop button for the hall with the guards, and twisted around the corner. He fired before they could say a word, catching them by surprise. It was necessary; every single Teller in this place was linked to his father through fittings. If one of them managed to get a message out, Trystan wouldn't even know until it was too late.

He had to trust he hadn't given any of them enough time for that. They dropped faster than he could blink, and quickly he moved deeper into the hall.

The Sutter was being held in a room on the right, and he rushed toward it. As he approached the door, he pulled up the feed from inside the room, cursing when he noticed that there were now another three Tellers within, watching the Sutter from the back wall.

With no time to come up with a different plan, he quickly unlocked the door and shoved into the room, taking the occupants by surprise.

The door closed again behind him and all three Tellers were down on the ground in a split second. His fritz still hovered in the air from when he'd raised it to shoot them, and he didn't bother dropping it when he turned to stare at Delaney's wide-eyed friend.

"Sutter Gibus," he said calmly, "you're coming with me."

CHAPTER 14

Um." Gibus glanced over Trystan's shoulder, and when he seemed to realize no one else was coming, he frowned. "No?"

Trystan growled. "You'd rather stay and remain my father's prisoner?"

"Your prisoner, his prisoner . . ."

"I'm not taking you prisoner," he snapped. "I'm rescuing you!"

Gibus blinked, obviously waiting for the punch line. "I'm sorry?"

"You should be, for wasting precious time. We need to go."

Gibus still didn't seem convinced.

"Delaney sent me." That wasn't entirely a lie . . . not really. Besides, what did it matter if he had to lie to the Sutter anyway? There was only one person he cared about telling the truth to, and she'd more than understand his reason for fibbing here.

"She's alive?" There was so much emotion in those words, Trystan almost felt jealous.

Almost.

"Yes. I'm counting on you knowing something about my father's plans. Tell me you do?" He'd gotten to the Sutter, and he'd get them both safely out, but he needed to know if the man knew anything useful. If not, Trystan was going to have to come up with a new plan, a way to get to his father's study after all. He couldn't leave here without any information.

He hated having to operate so spur-of-the-moment with all this, but against his father, taking the time to carefully construct a viable plan was out of the question. If Trystan was going to get away with this, he needed to keep moving.

"Of course," Gibus said, finally getting into motion as he began shoving things into a bag. "Who do you think perfected the device for him?"

Trystan pulled back. "What device?"

"You don't know?" His eyes widened. "Clean Slate, that's what it's called."

So Trystan's assumptions had been right; the Sutter would be useful.

"We don't have time for this conversation right now, or for you to pack. We need to go before—" The sound of pounding feet outside cut him off and he cursed, pulling up the footage on his device. Since there was clearly someone out there, and the Tellers he'd knocked out had been discovered, he stopped the remaining twenty seconds of the loop so he could access the live camera feed once more.

"They must have been doing a sweep of the castle." It was hard to get a handle on his frustration as he watched two new Tellers checking the pulses of the ones outside the room.

"Anything you haven't already packed stays. We've got to leave—now."

"How?" Gibus eyed the exit, obviously fully aware it was now blocked off.

"We're going to go through that door there."

Gibus followed his line of sight toward a door in the far right corner and frowned. "That's a supply closet."

"Among other things." Without further explanation, Trystan strode across the room and yanked the door open. It wasn't deep, and was cast in shadows with no light switch, so he had to feel around the back wall before finding what he was looking for. A tiny indent no bigger than his pinky.

He slipped his fingernail in and popped off a panel to expose an opening large enough for them to enter—so long as they bent at the waist.

"That has not been here this entire time," Gibus said, and swore at Trystan's back.

Trystan didn't bother pointing out that it wouldn't have mattered if he'd known about it. A Vakar Sutter wouldn't exactly have many friends in Kint, let alone Carnage Castle. If he'd managed to find the hidden escape hatch, it would have only led him to more trouble once the Rex caught up with him.

"Let's go. And close the closet door." He walked through first, listening for sounds in the empty corridor ahead of them, as well as to the Sutter following at his back. "This passage stretches around this side of the hall, and will lead us to the end of the South Wing."

"Is that where we are?"

"Yes."

Gibus was silent a moment as they practically crawled forward, and then said, "Did she really send you?"

"In a sense," he admitted. "I came for information and realized you're our best chance at getting what we need. Delaney knows where I am, and she's been talking about rescuing you nonstop the past few days so . . . This seemed logical."

"Two birds, one stone." When the Zane gave him a confused look, he chuckled. "It's an Earth phrase."

"I really must update my hebi. I don't do well with much of their slang." And Delaney used it frequently enough that that was a problem. He wanted to be as close to her as possible, even if that meant adding nonsense to his translator.

Ruckus didn't seem to have the same issue.

They were coming close to the end of the passage, so Trystan pulled up the camera footage there, letting out an irritated curse when he saw that the entire area was now crawling with Tellers.

"What's wrong?" Gibus asked, attempting to poke his head around the Zane's larger frame to see for himself.

"The discovery of those bodies has caused a complication." He paused, taking a moment to come up with another plan. There were two other exits, and he quickly checked the halls, noting that the one outside the nearest door was currently empty.

Without a word, Trystan began moving again, bringing them straight to it. He fiddled with the latch and then pressed a palm against the wood, turning to the Sutter. "Once we're out there, be very quiet."

He checked the screen one more time to ensure the hall was still empty, only to discover that the connecting one no longer was. If they entered, they'd be completely blocked off. Unless . . .

Not giving himself time to reconsider, Trystan grabbed the Sutter and rushed into the hall. Quickly, he crossed to the other side and lifted a metal slab set in the center of the wall. He motioned to the other man to get in, and received an incredulous look in response.

"You aren't serious? We're going down a garbage chute?" Gibus frantically shook his head. "Are you mad? We'll be burned alive before we even reach the bottom."

Trystan ground his teeth, the sounds of approaching steps already echoing toward them. Twisting the device around so the Sutter could see the screen, he showed him that he'd already disabled the heating mechanisms in the garbage disposal, which would allow them to slide down safely.

To avoid polluting the planet, trash on Xenith was incinerated the moment it was tossed out. Most places, like homes with children, had preventive measures included to avoid a child accidentally falling in or hurting themselves. While there hadn't been a child in Carnage

Castle since Trystan had grown—he avoided bringing Dom here like the plague—those measures were still programmed into the system, and all he'd had to do was access them.

"Well then." Gibus nodded and then without any more complaints, grabbed the edges of the chute, pulled himself up, and entered feetfirst. The sound of his body sliding down the metal was a faint whisper of fabric, soft enough that there was no worry of it being overheard on other floors.

With not a moment to spare, Trystan followed suit, needing to pull his shoulders in tightly in order to fit. The clanging of the chute door was unavoidable, as he was already sliding away from it. The surface of the chute was kept slick and shiny, so he dropped quickly, one second at the top, the next hitting the bottom with a heavy thump that knocked the wind out of him.

A thick cloud of dark ash puffed up around him, and he noted that the Sutter was already coughing loudly a second before he joined in. It was hard to see through the black cloud, but he struggled to move in the direction he believed the room's door was, slipping a few times in charcoal piles as he did and trying not to think about what he was now covered in.

The room was on the basement level of the castle, circular, and visited only once every month, by someone whose job it was to clear out the ash and soot. Fortunately, there was only about a foot of it to wade through, so the door was still visible once Trystan got close enough to it. His hand gripped the metal handle and twisted.

"Hurry up," Gibus urged, suddenly at his back. He was rubbing ash from his eyes, smearing black marks across his cheeks. It was thick in his curly sable hair as well, and had stained his lab coat.

The lever wouldn't budge.

Trystan clenched his jaw and adjusted his footing. Just as he was about to get nervous, the handle gave, creaking as it finally twisted to the left.

The two of them toppled forward, spilling out onto the main floor along with a pile of ash. When they stood, they left smeared handprints and footprints on the ground, too many for them to take the time to clean up.

"Looks like there's no covering our tracks," Gibus stated, poorly attempting to dust himself off. All he did was make the mess worse, and Trystan rolled his eyes.

Holding up a hand to keep the Sutter from moving forward, he pulled the device from under his arm to check the screen. He needed to rub away soot first, but surprisingly it was pretty clean, enough that he could check the single stairwell that led down to this level.

The room they were standing in now was empty save for a couple of heavy-duty shovels and three large wheelbarrows. Its only purpose was taking care of the trash, so other than those tools, the space remained untouched. They didn't have to worry about guards down here, so Trystan took a moment to catch his breath and consider their next move.

This was far from his original plan, which had been to sneak through the secret passages to the garage. If they left like this, they'd trail ash with them. But there weren't any rooms nearby, nothing on the level above that would contain fresh clothes. . . . They were just going to have to take their chances.

"Wait." Gibus stopped him just as he went to take his first step forward. "If you didn't know about Clean Slate, what information did you come here for?"

"My father's working with the Tars," he said, then headed toward the metal stairs that led up to the next level.

"And the plan once you got proof?"

"Use it to stop him." Without waiting, he started up, checking the screen every other step to make sure they were still clear above. The stairs led to an open floor plan with three doors. He made for the one on the left, the one that would take them to the main garage.

When they entered, his eyes took in the room quickly, darting to the back at one of the vehicles closest to the door.

"Get the garage door open," he ordered Gibus as he ran over toward a car, already accessing its controls using the device in his hands. The doors clicked and the headlights flashed on before he'd even reached it. He slipped into the driver's seat and connected his device to the control panel at the center.

There was no steering wheel, no pedals like on Earth cars. He'd gotten a good look at a few of them the last time he'd visited, while searching for Delaney. He'd had to drive one, even, in order to get to her at the beach.

The sound of crunching metal at his back clued him in to the fact the Sutter had successfully opened the garage door, and he quickly clicked away at the device, taking over the control panel with ease.

Gibus slammed into the side of the car, jolting Trystan, then yanked the door open and dropped into the passenger seat, a bit out of breath. A second later he explained why.

"We've got company."

Trystan's head whipped over toward the exit and he swore. A group of Tellers was making their way into the garage, weapons drawn and aimed in their direction.

"Hold on," Trystan ordered, then brought the car to its highest setting. A dangerous gamble, seeing as how they were still in a contained space, but they didn't really have the luxury of bringing the engine to a slow purr, as was recommended.

The garage door wasn't all the way open yet, and he debated whether they'd have time to wait it out. As if in response, a zee cracked against the bulletproof glass of the car, followed by another, and another.

Trystan hit the black button on the center console, and the car shot backward so quickly, they were both thrust forward and then slammed back against their seats. The rear of the car busted through the bottom of the garage door, scraping against it, and he had the fleeting thought that his father was going to be livid that he'd ruined the paint job.

Which was idiotic. Because, really, that was the least of their concerns.

As soon as they were out on the road, he pressed his palm against the center of his device and spun the car around so they were facing forward. Tapping his middle finger increased their speed, and they rushed forward, even as he moved his pointer and activated the thrusters at the sides of the vehicle.

The car shot into the air like a cannon, shaking them roughly as it did because he'd rushed the process. A few alarms rang, and lights on the dashboard flashed in warning, but within a minute they'd calmed and the car had leveled itself off.

"They're getting ready to follow!" Gibus yelled. He'd twisted around in his seat and was staring out the back window.

"No," Trystan said, hitting another few buttons on a side program he'd already started on his device, "they are not."

All at once, the engines of every vehicle within the garage shut down. They got a fleeting look at the Tellers struggling to figure out what was wrong before the dented garage door dropped like a lead weight with a loud bang, sealing them inside.

Gibus let out a celebratory whoop, and righted himself in his seat.

The corner of Trystan's mouth turned up.

"If you ever repeat this, I will deny it"—Gibus held up a finger—"but that was fantastic!"

Trystan grunted, mostly to cover up the fact that he wanted to chuckle and agree.

"So," the Sutter said, and settled more comfortably in his seat, "where are we going?"

"I have a few places the Rex doesn't know about." Of course, he'd never had to hide after committing treason, but . . . first time for everything. "We'll stop at one of them first, lie low. I'll have to find a ship, something untraceable, and then once it is safe, I'll take you to the others."

To Delaney.

Who better be okay.

If *anything* happened to his Lissa, he'd burn all the royals to the ground.

CHAPTER 15

We're doing everything we can, Lissa."

"That isn't good enough!" Delaney spun away from a Vakar Teller, Verus—one of three who'd been waiting in the study when they'd arrived forty minutes ago. So far, they'd been absolutely useless. "There's got to be a way we can get in touch with him."

They'd tried Trystan a dozen times through his shing—the only device not connected to the ship he was on—but he'd yet to respond. They were way too far away for their fittings to connect, and contacting the Rex was completely out of the question. The Zane was in danger, and there was absolutely nothing she could do but stand here twiddling her thumbs.

"How far is Carnage from here?" she asked, pacing in front of the fireplace. It was as far from the cluster of people as she could get, and she needed space to think.

The Basileus's office, now Tilda's, looked exactly as it always had. A fire was even going in the hearth, filling the room with the smell of burning wood and sugar. It used to be enough to give Delaney some semblance of comfort, but her worry for Trystan was too great.

Ruckus was currently leaning against the edge of the desk, the

Tellers nearby. He had other followers, those loyal who'd worked under him during his time as Ander, and even those who'd fought with him in the war and trusted his judgment. The tentative plan was to get a message to them that he was alive and planning something with Tilda. Have them start looking into the Tars themselves, wherever they were currently stationed. They had to be delicate with who they shared this news with, which meant going through the list Ruckus had given Sanzie and checking up on their previous actions to be certain they were trustworthy.

Fawna and Sanzie had already started on this, working while the rest of them tried to figure out how to help the Zane.

"Depends on what kind of ship he took," Ruckus answered. "I didn't get a great look at the model. K-20 series, that's all I know for sure."

"Could have taken a K-24 ship," one of the Tellers suggested. She thought his name might have been Julius, but she hadn't been paying much attention when they'd been introduced. "They're fast, but inconspicuous."

"He needed to be there by tonight," she reminded them.

"If he'd taken a K-26, he could be there now, depending on what time he left," one of the other Tellers, Shellus, told her.

Great. Basically they had no idea where Trystan might be, and no way of getting ahold of him to warn him. Why did it always feel like she was juggling the aliens around her? Trying to find one, or save another? Why couldn't they all just stay put and get along and—

She cut that train of thought, realizing how stupid she sounded. And how ridiculous she was presently being. Trystan was a big boy. He could more than take care of himself, and freaking out about what *might* happen wasn't going to be useful to anyone. She'd just gotten Tilda to agree to help them, which meant there were about a dozen other things they could be discussing right now.

But the Zane was still more important than any of it.

She sighed, ignoring how doing so drew Ruckus's attention, and closed her eyes. Tipping her head back, she gave herself a moment to think and calm her racing heart.

"How positive are we the Rex knows the truth?" Julius asked, and though he was directing the question to Tilda and Ruckus, Delaney replied.

"Pretty positive. If someone from Carnage had the information, they had to have gathered it from a source who'd already delivered the news to the Rex. He found out somehow. Had probably sent another team after the Rue before Trystan even called him."

It would be just like the Rex, to lie to his son and give him a false sense of security. Of course he'd let Trystan believe that he was willing to wait a day before seeing him.

"Rantan might have had some protocol to follow that we weren't aware of," Ruckus said. "Something we missed."

"Either way, the Rex knows, which means Trystan is walking into a trap." She paused. "Or is already in the middle of one."

Delaney glanced out the window and saw that it was late in the afternoon, nearing dark. By the time Tilda had tracked down these three Tellers, and filled them in, so much time had passed. A whole day, gone, and they had little to show for it and another issue to add to the growing list of things she wanted to scream about.

"If he can find proof to expose his father," Ruckus pointed out, "his risk will be worth it."

"And if he doesn't?" Tilda posed the question everyone was thinking. When no one immediately said anything, she set a pointed look on Delaney. "As much as you dislike it, there's nothing we can do until we hear from either the Zane, or his father. Our best option is to proceed with what we do know to be fact. We need to find a link between the Rex and the Tars.

"I CAN HAVE the research delivered to you, back in the rooms," Tilda continued, pulling open a drawer to remove a shing. She fiddled with it for a moment and then turned it around and held it out toward Delaney. "If you could press your palm to the center, please."

She frowned, but did as asked, holding her hand there until the device beeped. She watched as the Basilissa clicked away at the screen for a few more seconds, and then took it once Tilda passed it back over.

"I trust the Ander can teach you how to use it," Tilda said, and waved at Ruckus. "It's fairly simple. The digital research files should be sent to you within the next fifteen minutes. I'm not sure if you'll find anything useful, but you might. I'll have the Tellers here retrieve any paper documents in the Ander's office. Go over them, and we can reconvene tomorrow morning. In the meantime, I'll continue to try to reach the Zane, as well as attempt to gather more information myself."

"If you were the Rex," Delaney prompted, "how would you do it? He knows Olena is dead, and therefore his hold over Vakar is in jeopardy. If you were him, how would you ensure you didn't lose control?"

Tilda stared at her a moment and then pulled back. There was a glimmer in her eyes that briefly reminded Delaney of the look Trystan got when he was scheming.

It wasn't like she'd gone into this trusting the Basilissa—she hadn't. After everything that had happened during her time here, Delaney knew better. But she was counting on Tilda's anger over Olena, and her pride at wanting to keep her kingdom, to override any negative emotions she may or may not feel toward Delaney herself. Negative emotions she didn't even have a reason to feel, considering it was partially her fault Delaney had been pulled into this in the first place.

"He's yet to contact me directly about my daughter's death," she began. "My best guess is he's preparing a lie, coming up with a way to put the news to me where the blame is placed solely on an outside force. Initially, I would have said you, but seeing as how everyone seems to believe you died out there as well, it's probably going to be the Ander. Turn me against my own, promise to help me get justice for my daughter . . ." She lifted a single delicate shoulder. "That's how I would do it, in any case. We'll have to wait and see how the Rex chooses to handle it."

"Do you think we'll be waiting long?"

"There's really no way to tell."

"If we don't hear from him soon, you'll have to reach out to him. We can't stay in the dark forever," Ruckus said, causing the Basilissa to lift a brow.

"Oh, will I?" She clearly wasn't pleased.

Delaney jumped in before things could get ugly. "Yes. We don't have time for postulating. We're all on the same team here."

"But some of us still hold higher stations than others," Tilda reminded them coolly. "Don't forget how this all ends, Miss Grace."

Ruckus sent her a questioning look, but she pretended not to notice. When and how she told him about the deal she made was her business. It was a decision she got to make. The Basilissa couldn't take that from her.

So, instead of clarifying, she crossed her arms and turned to the three Tellers who still hovered on the sidelines, quietly watching.

"You two are going to get the rest of the files, while Julius helps us go through the digital information."

"I'll let Fawna know to send any information she retrieves from our allies to my shing," Ruckus said. "I think it's best that she still remain with the ship."

"Already planning another speedy exit, Ander?" Tilda canted her head, watching him coyly.

The reaction was a bit surprising to Delaney. Could the Basilissa be upset that he'd chosen to go on his denzeration last minute? It made sense. He'd been the only one capable of controlling her daughter— for the most part—and he'd left to follow Delaney to Earth.

"Just trying to be prepared, Basilissa," he replied curtly.

"To get the Lissa away, should anything happen."

It wasn't a question, but he answered anyway, straight-faced and pointedly. "Yes. She's my top priority. If a threat were to arise, I'd do everything in my power, limited as that may be considering I'm only an Ander, to get her to safety."

"Hmm." It was impossible to tell if Tilda was annoyed by that statement. She wasn't pleased, in any case. "How times have changed."

CHAPTER 16

They'd parked the ship in the hangar, not bothering with subtlety since they were in an unmarked vessel that couldn't be traced back to him.

Of course, if his father's spies did take the time to investigate, it'd be simple enough for them to discover Trystan as he strolled through the palace with the Sutter close on his heels. They'd been met at the doors by a set of Vakar Tellers who'd taken one look at him and bowed their heads.

His father must not have labeled him a traitor yet, since they'd taken him to the Basilissa without hesitation once he'd ordered it. He'd been counting on the Rex being reluctant to admit his own son had betrayed him.

Tilda was in the middle of a meal, seated at the long table, in the same room where they'd once had breakfast with Delaney. Only, this time she was alone.

Trystan glanced at the empty place mats in front of all the other chairs, unable to stop the stray thought that it was sort of sad. Dwelling on that meant dealing with the fact he'd had a hand in her misery, so he dashed those thoughts away and straightened his spine.

"Where's Delaney?"

The Basilissa lifted a brow at his tone, slowly easing the utensil she'd been eating with down onto the table.

"She's currently unavailable, searching for information with the Ander," Tilda said.

He was in no mood for this.

"Let me make myself perfectly clear," he growled threateningly. "If you do not bring me to her right now, I'm—"

The doors at the left opened suddenly and there she was.

Trystan was already moving toward her before she'd even fully entered the room, sweeping her up into his arms. He pulled her off to the side, out of the way of the others still entering, so he could inspect her, make sure she was whole and unharmed.

Her hair was still that muddy brown, and she appeared to be exhausted, but aside from that, she seemed all right.

Relief hit him so hard, he actually forgot himself and exhaled, tightening his hold on her and urging her back against him in another embrace. He'd been so afraid that Tilda had done something to her, or that his father had somehow managed to, had already plotted out a dozen ways to get revenge if that had been the case.

"Trystan—"

"Wait." He sent the plea through their fittings, refusing to budge when she went to pull away. *"Just a moment longer. I need this."*

It looked like she might argue, but then she settled against him, resting her cheek on his chest and bringing her arms up around his waist. With a sigh, she practically melted into him, and he would have done anything to keep her there.

So of course the Ander had to ruin it by greeting the Sutter. Loudly.

At the sound of Gibus's name, Delaney's head whipped up, and she separated from him enough to glance around his body. Her eyes went wide and she broke out in a massive grin, which at first had another flare of jealousy going off inside him. Until she rested her smile on him.

"You found Gibus." She sounded so happy, it was infectious.

He smirked at her. "Rescued him from an evil king and everything," he joked. "If my knowledge of Earth lore is accurate, that's the type of thing princesses go for."

She laughed, pushing up onto her toes and planting a chaste kiss to his cheek so quickly, he couldn't mask his surprise. Not that she noticed. As soon as her feet hit the ground once more, she was off, rushing to the Sutter. Gibus caught her when she leaped at him, and she laughed again.

Trystan was so busy watching her interact with Gibus, he didn't notice Ruckus moving up to him until he was practically at his side.

"You saved Gibus." The Ander took a breath and then held out his hand. "Thank you."

It was on the tip of his tongue, to say that he hadn't done it for him. To make another snide remark, and attempt to put him in his place. But something stopped him, and instead of saying anything at all, Trystan found himself accepting, pressing his palm quickly against Ruckus's. They both pulled back as soon as it was done, clearing their throats uncomfortably.

A quick glance around showed no one had seen the exchange, at least.

"Have I missed much?" Trystan asked a second later, once the silence between them had grown too uncomfortable to withstand.

"Only absolutely nothing," Ruckus told him with a chuckle, and it was such a Delaney-like thing to say, Trystan was forced to look back at him. "We've been combing through everything we have on the Tars, all the communications we've managed to intercept over the years, et cetera, but so far none of it implicates the Rex. What about you? Did you find anything useful? Aside from the Sutter, of course."

"As it turns out," Trystan said, lifting his voice a bit so that he could draw the attention of the rest of the room, "the Sutter can help speed things up for us."

"What do you mean?"

Delaney pulled away from Gibus, dragging him after her as she moved closer to Trystan. She either didn't notice that Tilda was moving over as well, or didn't care. Whatever had taken place between the two of them in Trystan's absence, obviously she didn't fear for her life where the Basilissa was concerned.

"My father's apparently been working on some type of new technology," Trystan explained. "He had Gibus helping him."

"I tried not to," Gibus stated, "sincerely. It was difficult, however. The Kints have some . . . very interesting methods of torture I'd rather not revisit." He shivered, forcing a half smile at Delaney when she touched his elbow comfortingly. "It isn't really 'new,' not to the Rex. He's got research going back years. Once I studied the progress they had made, the solution became fairly simple. It was impossible not to let on that I'd developed a theory."

Ruckus frowned. "A theory about what? You were only with them for a few days. How did you manage to solve something in that short of time that they couldn't?"

"I'm brilliant." Gibus even went so far as to roll his eyes.

"Get to the point, Sutter," Trystan ordered tersely. They'd had this conversation already, and he wasn't interested in hearing the other man boast again. All he really wanted to do was sweep Delaney away, somewhere they could be alone. He wanted to know what she'd been doing, what had happened in his absence. If she really was all right or if she was just saying that in the presence of the Basilissa.

"The Rex knows he's been slowly but surely losing the loyalty of his people to the Zane," he began. "Since publicly choosing a human as his betrothed, this became even more apparent."

"The Kint *like* that I'm not one of them?" Delaney frowned.

"Not exactly. They like that his willingness to bind himself to you, a human, implies he's serious about wanting to avoid war. They've taken it as proof that Trystan won't rule the same way his father has been. Obviously, this was the exact opposite reaction he'd expected, and the Rex took notice of this. His solution was to restart development on the Clean Slate project."

"Which is?" Ruckus waved a hand, clearly losing patience now as well.

"A device that can completely wipe away a person's memory. It'll leave basic knowledge, like how to count, or how to shoot a fritz, what your name is . . . but actual memories of your life or your childhood, what you had for breakfast? That stuff gets erased."

There was complete horrified silence for a moment, and then Delaney asked, "How is that even possible?"

"Our fittings." Gibus tapped the back of his neck where the device was inserted.

"They're already programmed to interface with the brain," Ruckus mumbled, just loud enough for them all to hear as he worked it out in his mind. "They open passageways so we can communicate telepathically."

"Exactly!" He snapped his fingers.

"But they only allow you to send messages," Delaney said. "You can't poke around somebody's brain with it."

"See, here's the thing," Gibus told them. "The Kints have a prototype in which you can. A person has to be hooked up to it, their fitting connected to the machine. Our brains are basically just computers: We have preprogrammed functions and controls. Clean Slate translates all our internal data and displays it on a computer monitor. After that, it's as simple as copy and delete."

"Simple, huh?" Delaney quirked a brow, not bothering to mask her disgust.

"Okay," he conceded, nodding, "it's a bit more complex, but there's no point in my getting technical. You won't understand anyway. You aren't Sutters."

"As mentioned," Tilda spoke up, "you were only with him a short time. He couldn't have tested it on many people in such a small period. Correct?"

"Yes," Gibus agreed. "They were very close to completion on the machine by the time I was brought there. Because of that, it was an easily solved problem for me, so testing began the same night. Only about fifty initially joined the program. The first dozen or so died during experimentation. After that, there weren't many volunteers left."

"Be honest," Trystan said. "How many of them were really volunteers to begin with?"

Gibus glanced at his feet. "I did what I could to refuse to help. I didn't want to do it. The science behind the device was brilliant, but the results . . . all those people . . ."

"How many?" Ruckus asked. "How many people made it out?"

"We only had six subjects considered successful. They were taken away after I did a checkup. I don't know where they are, or what's being done to them."

"He can't just expect to go around erasing people's minds without anyone noticing," Delaney pointed out.

"I don't think he intends to," Gibus said. "My guess is he'd use it more sporadically, on the people who truly stood in the way of his goal."

"Seizing complete control of Xenith." Tilda sighed. "He plans to use this on me."

"That seems most likely," Trystan told them, "considering he knows that Olena is dead."

"What about Delaney? Does he know about her?" Ruckus asked.

Gibus shook his head before Trystan could answer. "He thinks she's dead."

Ruckus thought it over and then glanced at Trystan, catching his gaze. "You believe that?"

He'd been playing with that since leaving Carnage, wondering the same thing. Knowing the cost if he was wrong. "He's arrogant. Enough to believe Delaney must be dead in order for me to rebel against him the way I have. He probably thinks that both she and Olena died out there."

"Good." The Ander ran the backs of his fingers absently over his jawline and the hint of dark stubble growing there. Another reminder that they'd been on the run . . . and that Trystan didn't look much better.

He barely resisted the urge to reach up and feel the shadow on his own face, already detesting the fact that it was there. It was unbecoming of a Zane to allow his appearance to be unkempt. He needed to remain distinctly polished at all times.

Which was all nonsense his father had ingrained in him. Yet, even knowing that, Trystan couldn't help the anxiety that came whenever he thought about how he hadn't shaved. How there was a scuff on the tip of his right boot, and how the tear at the bottom of his shirt seemed to be staring at him judgingly.

"He must have been planning out this Clean Slate program for a while now. Only, he's just now putting it in motion, and we've given him a reason to use it on the Basilissa." Delaney began pacing. "If the public found out—"

"There are very few of us working on this," Gibus interrupted. "And from what I saw, I don't think I was the only one who was a prisoner. If personal bodily harm didn't work, threats were made against our families. No one on this project would dare risk leaking anything."

"So we get the evidence ourselves." When they all turned to her, Delaney shrugged a single shoulder like it was no big deal. "We've gone through practically all the information you guys have collected on the Tars the past few years and come up with nothing. Trystan wasn't able to get his hands on anything in Carnage, and for all we know, proof of that doesn't even exist. But *this*. We know where everything about Clean Slate is being held."

Before any of them could speak for or against her suggestion, she was turning to the Sutter.

"Did the Rex mention anything about Earth?"

His father had started work on this long before discovering Olena was dead. Actually, even before he'd come up with the plan to betroth the two of them. Which meant he couldn't have intended merely to use this as a last resort, should the betrothal not go through. No, he had to be planning on using it whether or not he kept control of Vakar.

Not for the first time since discovering all this, Trystan wondered how much his father had planned on revealing to him. Had he intended to keep it a secret up until the last possible moment? He'd never mentioned it before—that was for certain.

And how was that, even? He had more control over the Kint army than his father did. They trusted him, were loyal to him, more so than a Rex who never bothered fighting among their ranks. The army might not even make up half of the Kint population—meaning the majority of people would side with his father simply because he was the Rex, and Trystan was only Zane—but few civilians were allowed into Carnage Castle.

If there'd been any kind of word about this project, it should have found its way to Trystan's ear. He'd always known that his hold wavered the closer to his father he got, but he'd still been foolishly under the assumption he'd held enough sway that the Tellers would have leaked the information, despite the Rex's wanting it kept on lockdown.

Apparently he'd overestimated himself. Part of him had always avoided going back home because his father was surrounded by those most loyal to him, but still. Perhaps he'd disengaged with Carnage too much.

But he'd also never intended to overthrow his father. Even after finding out the Rex wanted to marry him off. Being that he was already the Zane, already held power, he'd just figured he'd wait it out. Once he was Rex, he could do as he pleased without having to worry about his father stepping in.

Because as much as he hated the man, he *was* still his father.

"He didn't tell me anything specifically," Gibus was answering Delaney's question, and Trystan forced himself to concentrate and tune back in.

"It's safe to assume he'll find a way to use this to his advantage on your planet as well," Tilda said.

"We should focus on stopping him on our planet first," Trystan suggested. "If you only managed to get it working a few days ago, I don't see how he could hope to use it on the Basilissa anytime soon. Let alone a political influence on Earth. He'd need to get ahold of them and implant fittings first. Besides, they don't operate the same as we do; their planet isn't run by merely two leaders. Even if he happened to get his hands on one, it wouldn't matter. Our technology is more advanced, it's true, but they have strong enough weapons that a full invasion would still take days, if not weeks, to accomplish. He wouldn't attempt this so soon after gaining full rule over Xenith."

"You're giving us weeks now?" Delaney smirked. "How sweet."

"I've realized humans have more tenacity than I previously gave them credit for," he replied smoothly, shifting closer so their arms noticeably brushed.

"Well, that's gross." Gibus made a face at the two of them and then, before Trystan could get angry, took a quick glance around the room. "Where's Pettus? I figured he'd have joined us by now. Do you have him out on some crazy errand or something?" This last part he directed to Ruckus, who was back to actively glaring at the Zane. "If so, please tell me it's for food. We haven't eaten since yesterday, and I'm starving."

Delaney's eyes went wide, but the Ander spoke before she got the chance.

"You didn't tell him?" Ruckus's tone was accusatory, and Trystan gritted his teeth.

"There wasn't exactly a good opportunity for it while we were on the run, no."

"Tell me what?" Gibus frowned, but the fear in his eyes was apparent.

Delaney stepped over to him, wrapping an arm around his shoulders to gently lead him off to the side of the room. Her voice was soft as she explained comfortingly, and even though they'd moved too far and were speaking too low for Trystan to make out the Sutter's response, it was obvious when he deflated in her hold that he wasn't okay.

She sunk down to the ground with him, easing onto her knees at his side as he sat. She whispered something, held him tightly, and let him cling to her.

The whole ordeal reminded Trystan of the night she'd held him like that, when he'd first told her about his mother. How odd the sensation had been at first, yet how welcome.

No one had ever comforted him like that until Delaney.

For some reason, that made him feel more alone than he ever had.

CHAPTER 17

Delaney and the others were participating in something that apparently Tellers did whenever they lost a comrade. A method of honor created during the war. It was a small remembrance ceremony, though probably only because their presence needed to be kept secret.

Pettus had been well-liked. There had to be a ton of people who wanted to honor his death. Maybe they already had, in their own way, when they'd found out the news.

The mourners moved to a private sitting room, one with a large floor-to-ceiling window that let in lots of light. It sparkled against the rich green carpet, and flickered off the gold paint on the walls.

Ruckus stood closest to the window, sunlight filtering in on him. In his hands, he held a piece of cloth. When he shifted it and began tearing strips off the bottom, Delaney recognized that it was from a Teller uniform. One of the thinner ones, which were sometimes worn beneath green vests or jackets.

Once he'd gotten a piece of cloth free, he handed the shirt over to Gibus, on his right, and then began tying the strip around his right wrist. He murmured something under his breath as he did, lost in the moment and far away.

Gibus followed suit, then handed the shirt to Verus. Julius and Shellus were next.

Trystan was standing between Shellus and Delaney, a guest appearance that seemed to catch the rest of the party off guard. His spine was straight and stiff as he took the shirt and ripped a strip free.

But when he brought the piece to his wrist, he hesitated. The Zane glanced up, over to Ruckus, and waited, silently seeking permission to continue.

After a quiet moment Ruckus gave a curt nod, watching as Trystan secured the two ends around his left wrist and tied them together. As he did, he spoke the same words, though a little louder than the rest had.

It wasn't hard to catch on that it was for Delaney's benefit.

"Though you have returned to the stars from which you fell, you will travel with me always." Trystan finished and passed the tattered shirt over to Delaney, who took it tentatively.

"The words are a farewell." Ruckus's voice entered her head and she looked at him as she readied to rip a strip off. *"We tie a strip of their clothing to the wrist of our nondominant hand, to avoid interfering with our fritzes, and after a week, wherever we are, we take it off and leave it. The extra days give us time to say good-bye, prepare for letting go."*

It was sweet in a sad way, and made sense. During the war, they didn't exactly have time for a big flashy ceremony. But they could get their hands on a shirt, or something that belonged to the deceased. She wondered what they did if they couldn't find a clothing item. And what people's wrists looked like after a large battle, where many were killed instead of just one or two.

Were there other rules for that? A different way to honor the dead, or did they tie bits of material up to their elbows, carrying all those deaths with them?

She understood leaving it behind after a week, too; at least, she was pretty sure she did. The person traveled with them for seven more days, living on somehow that way, hopefully getting farther from the place their life was lost. Then they were given someplace new to rest in the form of a piece of them, or their old belonging in actuality, being left behind.

The *always* made sense, because even though they left behind the symbol, during their weeklong journey they'd somehow made peace. The memory of the person was carried on, as well as the memory of where that tiny bit of them had been left. A new memory, to wash away the recollection of their last dying moment.

Delaney repeated the words that Trystan, and the rest of them, had said as she tied the cloth off. Once she was done, she handed the shirt back to Ruckus, who placed it on an end table at his back.

"That's it." Ruckus sighed, but no one immediately broke away from the circle, all of them lost in their thoughts.

The room was silent for a long while. Gibus seemed to be taking it the worst, with bloodshot eyes and shaking hands. He kept crossing them over his chest, then uncrossing them, unsure how to stand and unable to hold still for longer than a few heartbeats.

The Rex had to pay for all the pain he'd caused.

Whatever it took to keep him from doing this to anyone else, Delaney would do it. There was so much more at stake here than her happiness, or even revenge for Pettus. The Rex needed to be stopped to protect all of those other people he'd had yet to hurt. The ones on Xenith and Earth alike.

AS BADLY AS they all wanted to pretend they could grieve forever, they couldn't. The next morning Julius was sent to sneak Delaney and Ruckus through the hallway, and Sanzie met up with them on the way, with Shellus accompanying her. They were led to the study, where Tilda and Gibus were already waiting.

They both looked up when the door opened, and the first waved at them to hurry inside.

"The Sutter was filling me in on more details about this device," the Basilissa said as soon as they were securely inside the room. "The Rex plans on creating a mobile one."

"It would make the chair obsolete," Gibus elaborated.

"How far away from that is he?" Ruckus asked, moving over to the desk where the two of them were standing. He crossed his arms, frowning at the possibility. He'd donned his old uniform this morning, the more formal of the two with the long sleeves, and the gold trim flashed a bit in the room's bright lighting.

"It's hard to say," Gibus told them. "Longer than previously expected, since I'm not there to help build it anymore."

"You're just telling us about this now because . . . ?" Trystan growled.

"I was too busy explaining to your feeble minds how the machine worked before," he snapped back, then blanched a little. "Apologies, Basilissa." He glanced at Ruckus. "Ander." Then Delaney. "Lissa."

When he pointedly left Trystan out, the Zane rolled his eyes. The move would have been laughable coming from him, under different circumstances.

"How would you like to proceed?" Tilda asked them.

"We should assume the Rex hasn't yet done it." Ruckus sighed. "But be cautious."

"Even if he hasn't found a way to do it *yet*," Trystan said, "he will. If we let that happen, we'll have no chance of overthrowing him."

"We can't wait around any longer," Delaney agreed.

Ruckus quirked a dark brow. "I wasn't aware that's what we were doing."

"You know what I mean." She leaned her hip against the edge of the desk. "We're out of time. We have to get into Carnage Castle now."

"Yes, but," the Sutter said, shaking his head, "wouldn't he have moved everything? Knowing that I'd escaped, he wouldn't risk leaving all of that in the same location. I could lead anyone straight to it."

"Sure," she agreed, "but this machine is huge, right? Too big to just move on a whim, especially now that his top Sutter has left the project. I think the risk of breaking or damaging it far outweighs the possibility that you'd be stupid enough to go back."

Ruckus tapped his fingers against the side of his arm in thought. "The Rex does think we're either dead or we've run."

"Exactly," Delaney said. "And the last place he'd expect you to go is here, when Kint still has control of the place."

"Even if he did," Trystan joined in, "there's no way my father would suspect Tilda would help out. She might harbor a fugitive, but actually plot against him? His arrogance wouldn't allow him to foresee that."

"What about you?" Ruckus asked. "You rescued Gibus; I believe that qualifies as a statement. He knows you're against him."

"He knows I'm upset," Trystan corrected. "I made sure he believes that it's because of Delaney's death. He'll consider this a tantrum—rare, coming from me, but hardly surprising given the circumstances."

"You don't think he's worried you'll actually turn against him?" Delaney frowned. "He's not taking you seriously."

"He never does." He sighed, then turned back to the Basilissa. "Has he contacted you yet about Olena?"

"No," Tilda stated bitterly. "He has not sent a single word about it."

"Which means he still doesn't know there's a leak at Carnage." That could work for them. Delaney couldn't think of anyone, other than those currently in this room and Fawna back on the ship, who would lie to protect her. Yet that was exactly what someone had done by telling the Rex they'd seen her dead body. "Do you know anything else about this person?"

"I don't," Tilda said. "I told you before, the message was encrypted. I don't have any friends in Kint, especially not at the castle."

"You have spies," Trystan argued, though he put it plainly, not the least bit upset by the possibility.

Tilda held his gaze, but didn't confirm anything.

"Seriously?" He glanced around at the others, settling on the Ander. "Is that really true? You don't have even one spy in the capital?"

"We were in the middle of a peace treaty," Ruckus said between gritted teeth.

He scoffed. "I've had several embedded in your ranks since the moment the war ended."

"You—"

"Really not the time," Delaney said, stopping them before it could turn into a full-blown fight. "Back to me and my idea, please. Thank you. Between Trystan and Gibus, we should be able to narrow down the device's location. Anywhere you think your father might have moved it," she said to Trystan, then to Gibus, "and where it was before, on the off chance he left it there."

"All right," Sanzie said from where she sat on the edge of the couch a bit farther from the rest of the group. "We'd still need a way to access it, and I doubt they're going to let us walk through the front doors."

"I assume you have a way to get us inside the castle and avoid detection, Delaney?" Trystan said. "Otherwise you would not have brought it up."

"I do," she agreed. "The largest threat is getting caught by your father, so, seems like the logical thing to do is get rid of the Rex first."

"Isn't that the whole reason behind the plan?" Gibus asked.

"She means remove him from the premises," Tilda said, clearly picking up on what Delaney was thinking. "Preferably out of Carnage altogether."

"Yeah," Delaney said, crossing her arms, "and as far away from it as possible, in case we trip an alarm or something."

"I can easily disable the alarm systems," Trystan stated, and she didn't bother explaining that wasn't quite what she'd meant. Though it was good to know there would be legitimate alarms and that he could take care of them.

"You've got loyalists inside the castle, don't you?" Ruckus questioned the Zane then.

"Not as many as I would like," he admitted.

"He has plenty outside the castle walls, however," Gibus said. "I met a few of them on our way here. They helped us get a ship so we could ditch the car and make it here in a timely manner."

"My father is unaware of who stands by me," Trystan continued, "but he does know I hold more sway over the army than he does. He's careful about who he allows nearby, and that includes who he allows inside his home."

"But he won't be there," Delaney pointed out, "not if we're successful, in any case. Could you sneak in some of your people then?"

He cocked his head, thought it over. "I might be able to change the list—the one that contains all the Tellers' names who work at the castle any given day of the week—to include a few extras. I can also easily hack into the system to allow them to enter from a side door. I'd need to get word out as soon as possible, though."

"You have a way to do that?"

"I've ordered everyone to leave channels open and await my call," he informed her, tapping the new shing in his back pocket for emphasis.

"We don't need many people on the inside," she said. "Just enough to help us out if we get spotted by the Tellers who work for your father."

"Technically," Ruckus reminded her, "they all work for his father."

"You've been in battle," Trystan told him. "You know firsthand how hard it is to respect a leader who refuses to get his hands dirty."

"All the Rex ever does is get his hands dirty."

"Touché." He grunted. "But you've never, and will never, see my father out fighting alongside his Tellers. It did not go unnoticed during the war. Especially when he refused to visit a particularly nasty area after a legion of our own was slaughtered by yours."

"Let me guess. You did?"

"I did."

"Could you call him away?" Delaney addressed the Basilissa. "Get him to leave Carnage and meet you somewhere, anywhere that'll give us enough time to get in and get out."

"He won't be summoned," Tilda said. "I'd have to have something important to him in order to draw him out. Something more important than his pride."

"Or something that plays into it," Trystan speculated. "Tell him you know about your daughter's death, and that you want to meet and renegotiate the terms of Kint's hold over Vakar."

Tilda pursed her lips. "That would certainly get his attention."

"Make it clear that you aren't interested in dissolving our . . . alliance, but that you insist on hearing about Olena's assassination from him, and that you want to come up with new terms."

"What exactly does she have to bargain with?" Ruckus asked. "There's nothing to use against him to renegotiate. Her heirs, both the one by blood and the Uprisen one, are thought to be dead."

"They can still proceed with a merger of the two houses," Delaney stated, catching Tilda's gaze in the process. She'd spent all night thinking the idea over, and had honestly felt stupid for not coming up with it sooner.

It took them all a second to catch on, and Trystan was the first to vehemently reject the idea.

"Absolutely not." He held up a hand before she could say anything else. "I know you meant that Tilda would bond with my father, not me, but it still isn't happening."

"She wouldn't really," Ruckus tried to explain, obviously more on board with the idea, but the Zane shook his head hard enough that his perfectly smoothed hair fell out of place.

"And if we aren't successful?" he asked. "If we fail to find proof, and he agrees to the merger? What then? He won't wait like Olena and I had to, or even like Delaney and I. There'd be no cause to, not when they are both already rulers of the people. He'd insist on the ceremony being done immediately, before hold of Vakar could slip through his fingers a third time."

"Careful, Zane," Tilda said, far too lightly for someone in her current position. "It's beginning to sound like you're concerned for my well-being."

He clamped his jaw shut so hard, Delaney actually heard his teeth snap against each other.

"Relax. This could work." She placed a hand on his shoulder and sent her next comment through their fittings. *She won't end up like your mother, Trystan.*

"I know that," he said out loud, and only she knew that he meant it as a response to her last statement.

Tilda was watching them closely, but had yet to give away how she was feeling about the suggestion. Surely the irony wasn't lost on her; she planned on forcing Delaney to marry the Zane, after all.

At the thought, Delaney inadvertently glanced at Ruckus. They'd yet to be alone since Trystan had gone to Carnage, always surrounded by the Tellers and Sanzie. When he'd asked her how she'd convinced Tilda to help them, she'd only had time to mumble something about the Basilissa understanding that doing so was best for her people. Then they'd been interrupted by the others.

Guilt over the partial lie had been eating away at her, but she'd been unable to tell him about it when they had company, considering she also planned on explaining she'd agreed that they'd still leave Xenith. She knew she'd have to find a way to talk to him in private. Especially since Trystan was back and could say something to give it away before she got the chance.

"It's decided then," Tilda said suddenly. "I'll contact the Rex as soon as we're ready to proceed."

"You'll need to pick a meeting place where you can contain him," Trystan declared, though it was obvious he still didn't like this part of the plan. "As soon as we've obtained proof of his treachery toward Kint, we'll release it. He's going to try to run. If he gets away, he'll regroup with those loyal to him. And, as Rex, he'll have access to weaponry I do not. I won't be able to stop him from releasing the bombs."

"The ones that destroyed that Vakar city years ago?" Delaney asked, ignoring the surprised look he sent her. Ruckus had told her about that during her first stay on Xenith. He'd also mentioned the possibility of something worse being created by the Kints. "Or the other ones?"

Trystan had the good sense to drop his gaze. "The other ones."

"So our intel on that was true." Ruckus cursed. "How bad is it?"

"Bad." The Zane ran a hand through his hair, smoothing back the blond locks he'd shaken loose. "He could destroy the entire western coast if he chose to."

"What?" Delaney wasn't sure exactly how large that particular coast of Vakar was, or how many people lived there, but it sounded horrible enough that she was mostly positive she didn't want to know.

"That's absurd!" Tilda exclaimed almost at the same time, true fear entering her eyes.

"I assure you," Trystan disagreed, "it is not. He's been working on this for a while. His secrets have always been of the deadly variety. I only found out about these particular weapons last year"—he glanced at Ruckus—"maybe even around the same time you did. There was nothing I could do to stop their production."

"Did you even try?" Ruckus chided him.

"If I'm being honest, not very hard. Our peace treaty was shaky at best, and despite how terrible those bombs are, they had the potential to protect my people. Unlike my father, that's my top priority."

Part of Delaney was horrified, but the other part understood. He was a Zane, and he had responsibilities she could only dream about in her worst nightmares. Besides, the fact that he'd brought it up now, that he was warning them about it, meant he had no intention to use them himself.

He was here, like the rest of them, to help avert a war and prevent bloodshed. Not cause more of it.

"You find proof and release it to the public," Tilda told them, though she kept her eyes locked on the Zane's, "and I'll make sure the Rex doesn't get away before he can be judged."

"I'll inform Fawna of our plans," Ruckus said, but Delaney waved him off.

"Sanzie can do it." She smiled at the Sworn, trying to lighten some of the blow that would no doubt cause.

From what Delaney had gathered, her issues weren't just with Ruckus but Fawna as well. She and the Ander had sort of cleared the air, but for this plan to work, everyone needed to keep a clear head. Which meant Sanzie and Fawna couldn't come to blows in the middle of it.

"Excuse me, Lissa?" Sanzie's dark brows winged up.

"Is that going to be a problem?"

The Sworn glanced around, settling one final glare on Ruckus before she stood and gave a curt shake of her head. "No, Lissa. Not a problem at all. Our fittings aren't connected. I'll have to use a communicator."

"I'm sure Julius won't mind taking you to one."

The Teller, not really understanding what was going on, shrugged and moved off to lead Sanzie out of the room.

As soon as they were gone, Delaney noticed the dry look Ruckus was giving her.

"What?" she said. "It's not meddling if I've given an order, right? Isn't that your alien logic? Certainly got me to do all kinds of stuff I would have rather not."

He opened his mouth, but ended up closing it again and sighing instead. It was hard to argue with the truth.

"Looks like she's getting the hang of being Lissa, Ander." Trystan chuckled. Without waiting for a reply, he started away, heading after Julius and Sanzie without so much as a glance back at the rest of them.

"Well," Gibus drawled, rocking on his heels, "I guess that means we're finished?"

"We've got our tasks," Tilda stated matter-of-factly, as if excusing the Zane's abrupt departure.

Delaney was barely listening to them, too caught up in Trystan's parting words. He'd always believed she was going to continue being Lissa at the end of all this, had made that assumption and hadn't bothered keeping it a secret. From anyone.

She really needed to talk to Ruckus.

"Once you've contacted the Rex," Ruckus was saying to the Basilissa, not noticing Delaney's sudden discomfort, "let us know the meeting time so we can plan accordingly. We want to get this done as soon as possible, but who knows when he'll claim to be available next?"

"He's not usually one to make time for anyone," Tilda agreed. "I'll set up a communication with him now. You're right: The sooner we do this, the sooner we can eliminate the threat and move on with our lives."

CHAPTER 18

Ruckus and Delaney had left the study to allow the Basilissa time to prepare for her call with the Rex, but once they'd gotten to the room, Delaney had gone straight for the Tar information to resume going through it.

Ruckus spent the first hour packing up a few of his personal items for the eventual trip back to Earth. He'd had to leave a lot behind the last time, especially since he'd thought it'd been for his denzeration, but now that he knew better, there were a lot of things of significant value he wanted to take.

It was crazy to think about how he didn't intend to return.

Delaney was still typing away at the shing when he'd finished, having not glanced his way once during the entire process. She hadn't even wondered what he was doing.

"Delaney?" He dropped one of the bags onto the end of the bed and moved closer to the couch where she was sitting. "Delaney?"

She made a noncommittal sound from the back of her throat, but it wasn't good enough for him.

"*Delaney!*" He sent it through their fitting, keeping his face schooled so she wouldn't see his guilt when doing so caused her to jump a little. "I called you, but it was like you didn't hear me."

"Sorry." She clutched the device in her lap, only relaxing her grip when she noticed his gaze immediately drawn there. "What's up?"

Moving over, he dropped down next to her and took the shing away. He placed it on the end table at his back and then he settled closer to her, crowding her space some so that she'd have to give him her full attention. "What's wrong?"

She frowned at him, feigning ignorance. "Um, the fate of the worlds as we know it literally rests in our hands? Just for starters."

"That's not it." He brought his knee up so it pressed against her thigh, needing contact to settle the odd feeling in his gut. "We never got the chance to talk about what you overheard between Sanzie and me, not at length."

She paused for a moment and then shook her head. "I'm still a little upset that you kept it from me, but honestly that's slightly hypocritical at this point."

Ruckus stiffened. "So it's about Trystan. This thing that's bothering you."

He hated having to bring the Zane up as much as he hated how bitter he sounded when he did.

"What? No. Well, sort of, I guess. But it isn't just about him. I didn't tell you the truth when you woke up. Tilda was there, and I didn't think it was a good idea to say anything in front of her, especially since I'm hoping there's a way around it."

"Around what?" She'd completely lost him now.

"Tilda thinks I'm staying once this is over," she confessed.

For a second he was sure he'd misheard, but when she didn't take the words back, he slowly stood.

"Explain," he whispered intensely, done leaving room for interpretation. "Delaney, explain."

She dropped her head in her hands and groaned, then brushed them back through her hair, stalling. Which was something she'd apparently been doing this whole time. How long had she known she wasn't going back to Earth? Or, more aptly, how long had she believed she wasn't?

No one was going to force her into anything she didn't want. Never again. As angry and confused as he was right now, he knew he'd never let that happen.

"It was the only way Tilda was willing to take the risk and help us," she said. "I had to agree to stay on as Lissa."

He swore and spun away.

"You were unconscious and there were fritzes pointed at us," she rushed to explain. "We'd come all that way, and without Tilda's help we stand no chance of stopping the Rex, ever. She needs an heir, and I'm already Uprisen so . . . as much as I hate it, her forcing the issue made sense."

A humorless chuckle slipped its way past his lips and he turned to her. "That's not what you thought over a month ago when Trystan fed you the same bullshit line."

"I didn't have a choice," she reiterated. "It was the only way to get her to not shoot Trystan and me as well."

"And we couldn't let the poor Zane get hurt, now could we?"

"That isn't fair." Her expression darkened.

"Neither is you staying here, Delaney! I'll get you off the planet," he said, his mind racing over the possible ways he could do it. "All we really need is the opportunity to do it when Tilda and Trystan aren't looking. Fawna will pick us up. We just have to make sure we're quick about it, so that by the time anyone notices, it's too late to stop us."

Delaney was quiet a moment and then asked, "What about when we get back to Earth? Originally I figured we'd just make a run for it, too, but . . . they know where I live, Ruckus."

It was the "I" part of that statement that had him freezing, lifting his head to look at her. Because wasn't it where *they* lived? Together?

"We'd have to leave everything behind," she continued, either not noticing his stricken look, or believing it was still because of her promise to Tilda. "Go on the run. Do you want to live that way? I know you like Earth because it's simple. Running . . . that won't be. We wouldn't be returning to the same life we left. You know better than anyone, they won't let us get away that easily."

"Trystan won't, you mean."

"It wasn't his call," she insisted. "Tilda is the one who put me in this position."

"And I suppose the Zane fought for your right to choose, huh?" He was so upset, he didn't even consider taking the harsh words back when she noticeably flinched, unable to stop himself from continuing. "Why are you even defending him right now? Have you forgotten what he's done? He's half the reason you're here, Delaney! He kidnapped you! He threw me in a cell!"

"I know." Delaney took a shaky breath. "But he's on our side now."

"He's not on *our* anything!" He stopped, another thought hitting him. "If you're going to pick up being the Lissa, that means you'll have to go through with being his bondmate, too, doesn't it?"

She stood from the couch, but he threw both hands up to stave her off. There was too much going on in his head right now, and her touching him wasn't going to make any of this easier for either of them.

"I'm not saying no to the two of us leaving," Delaney said. "I'm just pointing out that things will be different if we do. Are you sure that's what you want?"

"Isn't being together what you want?" he asked.

"This is your home, Ruckus. If you left with me this time, you really would be marked a traitor. You could never come back. Never see your friends again . . . Before, you had the option to return to your life here, to pick up being an Ander—"

"Tell me this conversation really is all about me," he cut her off. He didn't want to, but another reason was niggling at the back of his mind, one he could no longer ignore. "That it has nothing to do with the Zane. I'm not the only one who'll have to say good-bye to people here, Delaney. Don't think I haven't noticed the way you look at him: It's different. Maybe you're the one who doesn't want to go on the run."

"Stop bringing him into this. You're the one who keeps bringing him up. If I don't want to run, it's only because I don't want to abandon the people here, and I didn't think you would want to, either."

He stared at her pointedly, waited for her to realize how ridiculous her words were. He'd given up everything, walked away from responsibility, once before already. For her.

"I'm sorry," she said, shaking her head. "That's not . . . Look, I just want to make sure we don't leave a huge mess behind. If I were to go, we'd need there to be a reason for Trystan and Tilda not to follow. And, come on, you can't honestly tell me you'd be fine with leaving your planet in chaos? You'd need to see that Vakar is safe just as much as I do."

Did he want anything bad to happen here? No, of course not. But he hadn't felt a connection to Vakar for a while now, maybe even before meeting Delaney. As Ander, he'd been forced to watch over a spoiled Olena like some babysitter. Needed to follow orders and regulations dictated by others.

He'd felt more at home on Earth than he had on his planet in a long, long time. Fawna, Gibus, and Delaney, those were his people. As long as he knew they were safe . . . He could leave. He'd do it with little more than a brief glance in the rearview mirror.

Apparently, she wasn't the only one who'd changed these past few weeks.

"The thing is, Delaney, I wouldn't." He took a step back, toward the door, ignoring the voice screaming in his head not to. The one telling him to move to her, not away from her, despite it all. But she wasn't the only one who didn't deserve to have their choices taken from them.

He also had every right to choose what he wanted.

"Ruckus."

"When this is over, and we've stopped the Rex, I'm leaving. Earth is where I belong. And I think you need to figure out exactly where it is you belong before we continue this conversation. Until then . . ." He couldn't keep the disbelief over his own words from slipping into his tone. "I think we need to take a step back from each other."

She froze.

Part of him wanted to recant, but he ignored that impulse. He refused to stay here, on a planet that was no longer his, watching as she slipped further away. Already, he was seeing her become someone else, the girl she'd been on the ship when he'd first taken her slowly but surely fading away.

"Are you . . . breaking up with me?" she whispered, and it was clear it was a struggle for her to do so.

He squeezed his eyes shut in a poor attempt to avoid seeing the tears he'd spotted in hers. "I think, until we stop the Rex, it's for the best."

"And after that?"

He opened his eyes to look at her again, held her gaze, and forced himself to say, "After that, we see where we stand."

No matter what she chose, his feet would be planted firmly on Earth soil and he knew it.

DELANEY SQUEEZED HER hands into tight fists in her lap, trying to calm her racing heart. Ruckus had gone some time ago, quietly shutting the door behind him like he hadn't just shattered her. Like he was fine.

No, that wasn't fair. He had every right to be upset after what she'd kept from him. Of course she should have told him sooner, should have found the time to do so despite everything going on. Part of her hadn't wanted to, though, knowing it would result in an argument. But she'd never . . .

He'd really just broken up with her.

Recalling his parting words caused her breath to hitch, and she dropped her head into her hands. It was a breakup, but with the possibility of reconciliation. All they had to do was stop the Rex, and then the two of them could talk about their relationship and where to go from there.

For Ruckus, that was obviously back to Earth.

For her . . . Stopping the Rex wouldn't magically solve all of Xenith's problems, would it? There would be things that needed to be dealt with, like putting Trystan on the throne in his father's place, and making sure Tilda accepted that, even without Delaney around to ensure it. She'd meant it when she'd told Ruckus she couldn't just leave knowing everyone here might still be in trouble.

Though, he also had a point. This wasn't her planet, and she didn't really belong no matter what kind of alien ceremony she partook in. Why *shouldn't* she run back to Earth with him once they'd dealt with the Rex? Especially if that was the only way she didn't lose Ruckus?

Had she already lost him?

A light knocking sounded then, and the door opened a second later. Her head whipped up, but her chest tightened when she saw it wasn't Ruckus. Of course it wasn't. He never made a decision lightly; he wouldn't change his mind and come back so soon after.

"Delaney?" Trystan was in the room and on his knees in front of her a second later, reaching for her.

"Don't." She pulled away, blinking through the tears in a poor attempt to stop them.

He sat back on his heels, dropping his arms at his sides. "You're crying."

She'd only just realized that herself. Wondered how long she had been. If Ruckus had seen. If he'd still . . .

"Did you need something, Trystan?"

"Delaney." His voice was low, soothing. "If there's something the matter—"

"Did you need something or not?" she snapped, instantly regretting it. Ruckus said she was different around Trystan, and maybe he was right. But that didn't mean she had to take what was going on between her and the Ander out on him. "I'm sorry. Sorry."

He hesitated, as if waiting to see if she'd continue. When she didn't, he shifted on his knees, getting back to his feet. "I came to ask you to attend something with me. I see that perhaps now is not a good time."

"No, it's fine." In actuality, she wanted to curl into a ball and cry for a week straight, but that wasn't possible.

The only thing she could do right now was keep going, moving forward. Ruckus wouldn't talk to her about their relationship, past or future, until they took care of the Rex, just as he'd said. Dwelling on it in this moment made no difference, would in fact only make her more miserable. She could use a distraction, and no one was better at being that for her than the Zane.

Delaney rubbed the tears out of her eyes, took a shaky breath, and stood. She knew he didn't buy the forced smile she gave him, but he didn't press the issue. "What did you have in mind?"

CHAPTER 19

Trystan couldn't help but stare as he and Delaney stood off the side of the square, watching as other masked citizens wandered through the festival grounds. A few already held various food items he'd heard about, but had yet to try himself, and others were clutching prizes won from games that had been set around the area.

Everyone wore a mask in either black or gold, and there were booths set up at every exit and entrance, distributing them to those who came without one. Knowing it'd be unwise for them to be seen outside the palace, Trystan had procured masks for himself and Delaney prior to their leaving.

"This is a festival?" Delaney drew his attention back her way, and he glanced down to find her taking in their surroundings with as much interest as he'd just been.

Some of the tension he'd been feeling dissipated, and he let out a small sigh. She'd been in a terrible mood an hour ago when he'd gone to ask her to come out with him. She'd yet to mention why, but he assumed it had something to do with the Ander, as he'd been absent from the room.

Trystan hated seeing her cry, wanted to press the issue, but he knew better. She wouldn't appreciate him prying, and to be honest, he didn't want to think about her and the Ander in any case. Not today. Really not ever, but especially not today.

"They put it on every year around this time, to celebrate what you witnessed in Zephra Viya. People travel from all over to experience both the market and the accompanying festival. Is it very different from your Earth ones?" He took another look around, tried to picture how things might be done on her planet, but couldn't. It'd been hard enough for him to imagine what a true Vakar Viya festival would be like.

A large part of the public grounds that attached to those of the palace had been given over to the event, with high walls made of gold tarp stretched around the area to create a sort of enclosure filled with all kinds of frivolous oddities. The space was huge—it would probably take them hours to see everything—but they'd yet to move far from the main entrance.

This had been his idea, but now that they were here, it was a bit daunting, and he couldn't really decide which way to go first. On the right, it appeared as though a path led through an area selling edible items, while the one on the left led toward fair games—most of which he'd never played. He wanted them to enjoy themselves, not force her to watch him struggle to understand some frivolous game involving fake fritzes and water.

"Well, at a fair there are typically more colors," Delaney said, pointing toward one of the game setups and the onyx-and-yellow tarps that made up its walls. "But I've never been to an official festival before."

"It'll be a true first for both of us, then." He smiled when she finally glanced up at him.

"It's not my first time wearing one of these." She tapped the gold mask that he'd tied securely to her head before leaving the palace. It covered the top half of her face, and was a dull gold, instead of flashy and eye-catching, chosen in the hope it would help them avoid drawing attention. "We had a masquerade once at my boarding school. It was fun."

"You were upset when I arrived at the room earlier," he said, unable to hold it in any longer, inwardly cursing himself when that had her immediately looking away. "We don't have to talk about it. Just reassure me you're all right."

The corner of her mouth tipped up, but he could tell it was forced. "I'll be fine. Why did you want to come here so badly, anyway?"

Allowing the change in topic, he took a step forward, opting to head down the wider middle path that led deeper into the festival. Once she'd fallen into step at his side, her eyes on him while she clearly waited for a response, he blurted out, "It's my birthday."

Delaney came to an abrupt halt, forcing him to follow suit. "Today?"

"Yes." He nodded and turned to face her. "Even though it's Kint tradition, I don't typically get to choose what my new experience is. In the past, my birthdays were either spent wherever the war took me, or wherever my father needed me to be. As I've never been to the Viya festival before, I thought it'd be something nice for us to do together."

"I'm sorry I haven't been very good company." Determination raced across her face and she straightened her spine. "If this is for your birthday, we have to do it right. So, what did you want to see first? Was there anything specific? How"—she twisted on her heel to take in the various paths—"do we even find anything amid all this?"

Her sudden change in mood, the fact that she was so clearly going to try to enjoy herself for his benefit, had him grinning.

"There is one thing I believe we'll both enjoy." He motioned her forward once more. "I asked around before we left the palace, and was told it was usually placed somewhere near the center. I was leading us that way, but if you're hungry, we can eat first."

"No, let's go." She waved him onward, and the two of them started making their way through the crowds again.

Some people were dressed more causally than others, the flashiest thing on them their gold or shiny black masks. Others wore elaborate outfits, with more metallic trim than Trystan had ever seen, or deemed necessary, and his relief at finding plain outfits for both Delaney and himself was renewed.

Even with their faces covered, going out dressed as Kint Tellers would have drawn unwanted attention, so he'd ordered basic sets of black clothing delivered to their rooms. Since black and gold was the theme here, it seemed appropriate, and they fit in perfectly, so he knew it'd been a smart choice.

"I think—" He stopped abruptly when Delaney's hand suddenly clutched at his arm. Instinctually, he followed her line of sight, expecting a threat, so was surprised when he noticed the two young boys she was staring at.

They couldn't be older than eight or so. Both wore gold from head to toe and held bags no doubt filled with treats from the stalls. He couldn't figure out what about them had caught her attention, until he noticed the way they huddled together.

A Kint Teller wearing his uniform was standing nearby, purchasing a small plush toy, probably for his own child. The two Vakar boys were watching him and whispering, their fear made more apparent when the Teller turned to pass them and they noticeably flinched.

Of course, the Teller saw it, too, picking up the pace so he wasn't near them for long. The man hung his head as he did so, clutching the stuffed toy tightly at his side.

"They hurt his feelings," Delaney said, though the words were clearly meant for herself.

Trystan watched the retreating Teller, noting it was true. The stares and whispers had never personally bothered him before, but he knew it was hard on some of the Kints who'd been stationed in Vakar.

"Children don't know any better." He rested a hand over hers where she still touched his arm, causing her to realize and pull away. Trying not to let it bother him too much, he motioned them forward. "Our destination hopefully isn't much farther."

She was worrying her bottom lip, turning once to glance over her shoulder back where the boys had been. But they were gone now.

"You seem upset again," he pointed out, and she quickly shook her head.

"Explain why masks are traditionally worn to this."

"Isn't it fortunate?" He'd thought so earlier when he'd been trying to think up something new and possibly exciting they could do. "Everyone who enters is required to keep their face covered, so there's no chance anyone will ask us to remove the masks and discover our identities. Because the festival is celebrating the falling of stardust, the masks are meant to symbolize that, like the stars in the sky, we're all merely pieces of a grander puzzle. That one day we'll fall and turn to dust as well."

"That's kind of morbid," she said.

"I don't think so." He shrugged. "There's comfort in getting to forget who you are for a bit. People can set aside their daily worries and be whatever they want for a change at this festival. Like . . ." He leaned in closer and discreetly pointed toward a man across from them in a black mask. "He might be an ex–war hero who is recognized wherever he goes, and constantly reminded of his past. But here, with his face covered, he doesn't have to be that."

He pulled back and shrugged. "People travel from all over Xenith to experience this with their friends and family, to dress up and relax. I think it's more romantic than morbid."

"Did the big, bad Zane actually just call something romantic?"

She mock gasped, making sure to keep her voice down even as she continued to tease him. "How mushy of you. Although, it does happen to be an event meant to remind people they'll one day die, so I guess I shouldn't be too surprised."

"That isn't the point of it at all," he said. "Sure, centuries ago, when this festival was first created, it focused more on that aspect. But over the years things have changed, so that this is more a celebration of life and all its possibilities, than of death."

"Cherish the good times even if there are eventually bad," she murmured, and if he'd been farther away from her, he wouldn't have caught it.

"Exactly. This whole thing is meant to be done with people you care about—to make new good memories to recall later during darker times. Keeping your identity a secret is more a choice now than an actual rule. You still have to cover your face, but most people don't really take the hidden identity thing seriously anymore. Couples even wear matching masks now, to openly show others that they're together."

He frowned when he realized she was looking at him oddly now, couldn't understand why at first until he remembered. When he'd ordered two masks brought to him, he'd insisted they be, if not identical, at least as similar as possible.

The unpolished gold one he wore tied around his head practically matched hers perfectly.

"We're here," he said as they turned the corner, grateful for the distraction. It was stupid to feel embarrassed; he'd made his stance on their relationship clear. She knew how he felt, so revealing he'd wanted to experience this with her *as a couple* shouldn't make him uncomfortable. And yet . . . "What do you think?"

She blinked at him, and then thankfully turned to take in the giant black tent they stood in front of. It was covered in gold glitter that looked a lot like the actual stuff from the Dust Market, and the center flap had been left open only a few inches to expose a swath of darkness within. There was a sign painted to the side, but of course she couldn't read it, and he didn't want to translate.

"What is it?" she asked after a moment.

"Would you like to go find out?" He reached for the side of the opening, gently easing the material away so she could enter.

Delaney only hesitated for a split second, then stepped forward so they could walk through together. Inside, the main tent connected with another, leading straight back, and they passed through the dark space, unable to see much of anything.

"Apparently, they're light sensitive," Trystan told her, unable to see her expression, but he felt it when she eased a bit closer to him.

"What are we talking about here?"

Already in the process of pulling the next slit in the tarp open, he didn't bother answering. Once he'd gotten it back enough that they could both see within, the two of them simultaneously sucked in a breath.

"What *is* that?" Delaney moved the rest of the way into the room, leaving him behind.

Glass enclosures lined the walls, leading down to the end of the tent where the exit was. Each unit housed one to three tiny animals, the only light source in the room being a pale white globe set in the very center of the ceiling. There were a decent amount of other people crammed inside the tent, but everyone kept their voices hushed respectfully, knowing that the animals had a sensitivity to noise as well as to light.

The animals weren't very big—he could easily hold one in the palms of both hands—and they had inky black fur that glimmered silver every time the animal turned and caught the white light. In the wild, the effect would resemble moonlight bouncing off the surface of water sources or waxy leaves. The animal's four long, pointy ears, two on either side, sat at the top of its head, with two long antlers between.

"Those look like the stems of roses," Delaney said, pointing to them. "Dark green with deep red-tipped thorns. Is that for camouflage?"

"Yes."

"And the tail?" It was long and thin, almost three times the length of the small creature. "Climbing?"

"In the wild, they live in trees during the day. At night they come down to roam the forest grounds and hunt," he explained.

"I want to know everything." It was impossible to miss the enthralled note in her voice.

"It's called a luxvia." Trystan went to stand next to Delaney, bending down to get a closer look at the sleeping creature on the other side of the glass. "I've never seen one in person before."

When he neared the creature, it blinked slowly, opening its dark red eyes to meet his gaze before stretching a bit and then instantly going back to sleep.

He clucked his tongue. "Well, I feel wholly dismissed."

Delaney laughed and sidestepped so she was in front of one of the more awake luxvias instead, watching as it used its claws to climb up the side of a small tilted branch. A few had been added to each enclosure for that very purpose.

"We don't have felines on this planet, but I recalled that these looked somewhat similar. Is that accurate?" he asked, worried he'd said something wrong when she gave him an odd look.

"Why were you looking for something feline?"

"When we first met," he reminded her, "you expressed an interest in cats."

Her eyes widened. "I . . . That's true. I do like cats." She cleared her throat. "And these do sort of look like tiny ones. Just, you know, with thorn antlers and shimmery fur and four ears instead of two."

"So," he drawled, "nothing like an Earth cat at all, actually."

"Not even a little." She laughed and reached over to rest a hand on his arm. "But these are really cool, and I'm glad you got to see them for the first time on your birthday, since you're so interested in animals, too."

"I'm what?" Now he was the one confused.

"You know." She waved absently at him with her free hand, her attention already back on the luxvias. "All those creature statues and figurines you've got at Inkwell. They're, like, the only items other than books you have in your room, Trystan."

She'd only ever been in his private room once, and it hadn't been for very long. He'd known she was looking around, but he hadn't considered that she'd actually been paying attention to his things. Sadly, with how casually she'd just spoken about it, he got the feeling neither had she.

He was about to point that out when a laugh on the other side of the room had her looking for the source.

A Vakar woman was showing her young daughter one of the luxvias, her green-and-gold uniform making it clear that she was a Teller, probably off duty just in time to take her child to the festival, but not change her clothes.

"Trystan." Delaney's voice had lowered, and he glanced back at her quickly to find she was still distracted by the mother and daughter. "Those kids outside . . . they were too young to have been old enough to remember the war, right?"

"That's probably true," he said, instantly knowing where she was going with this. Why it'd bothered her.

"Yet they were afraid of that Kint Teller. Really afraid."

He sighed, eased a step closer to her. "I'm sure they've heard stories, from their parents or from friends. We haven't been at peace for long; you know that."

"Are Kint children just as afraid of the Vakar?"

"I'm honestly not sure," he was forced to admit. The only child he'd been around was Dom, and aside from his one visit to the palace, he'd been kept away from most Vakar people. "That bothers you?"

"Doesn't it bother you?" she asked. "You've got a peace treaty, but everyone is still afraid of everyone else."

"It'll take time to overcome the past," he said. "And unfortunately, we haven't had the best rulers around to help with that. My father is hardly a comforting figurehead, as you've witnessed firsthand."

"Magnus wasn't much better in that regard," she replied.

"No, he wasn't."

She was quiet for a long moment, watching right up until the mother and daughter finally pulled away from the cages and disappeared through the exit at the other end of the room.

"Delaney—" Trystan reached for her, but she seemed to snap out of it just before his hand could make contact, spinning away so she could walk backward toward the door the pair had just gone through.

"It's your birthday," she said, plastering a smile on her face. "Let's go have fun. Knowing you, you have an entire itinerary planed out, so we should get moving. What did you want to see next?"

He wanted to press her on what had just happened, on the cause of her sudden change in mood, but she was still smiling at him, clearly trying hard to appear excited about all this. He couldn't bring himself to ruin that for her. Later, if the opportunity arose, he'd ask then, but for now, if she wanted to forget about whatever had been troubling her, he could go along with that.

"Actually," he said, following her, the two of them turning toward the door once he'd reached her, "there's this festival dessert I've always wanted to try."

She laughed, the sound loud and unforced, catching him off guard with how real it was. "Of course there is."

Delaney shoved the tarp opening to the side, exposing the bustling festival grounds once more, and then reached back with her free hand to take his. Because she was already turned away, she missed his shocked expression, which only grew when she tugged him out of the tent, keeping their palms tightly pressed together.

"Which way?" she asked once they were standing among the crowd again, tilting her head in every direction as if she'd figure it out on her own. When it took him too long to respond, she glanced at him and quirked a brow.

The look snapped him out of it, and he cleared his throat, glancing around their surroundings now as well. After a moment, however, he was forced to confess, "I don't know."

"Well then." She tugged him to the left, taking off at a brisk pace. "Guess we're just going to have to walk around until we find it."

CHAPTER 20

The Rex had agreed to the meeting with Tilda, but had insisted it be today, despite the fact that she'd only made the call yesterday. When she'd tried to set the meeting place, he'd firmly demanded that he come to her in Vakar.

They were scheduled to meet at the palace in just under three hours, so Delaney and the others were on their way to Carnage Castle. To avoid the risk of flying past the Rex's ship while headed there, they'd had to take a detour, extending their trip by a good seventy minutes or so.

Which shouldn't have been too much of a problem, as Trystan had assured them that Ruckus's ship was faster than the Rex's preferred mode of transportation. Once he'd described how flashy his father's model was, it'd made sense. Of course the Rex's ego wouldn't allow him to arrive anywhere in a dull metal craft like the Ander's, no matter how much faster said craft would get him to his destination.

No, instead he'd had a ship custom-made with chrome paint, flashing blue lights on the descending ramp, and the Kint symbol painted in navy on the side. Pretty much the opposite of discreet, but then, that seemed in character as well.

He was the Rex. He wouldn't expect anyone to dare attack him, in the sky or otherwise.

They'd timed it so they'd arrive near Carnage Castle only five minutes or so after the Rex had gotten to the Vakar palace. If Trystan was correct, his father should have taken most of the Tellers along with him. They'd act more as a show of strength than in any guard capacity—the Rex was apparently physically capable of defending himself. Either way, that worked in their favor. Fewer of them at the castle meant an easier time sneaking through it; they'd chosen to dress in Kint colors to appear less conspicuous if spotted, though the hope was to avoid it.

Delaney took a glance around the room at the others. They were packed in front of the ship. Ruckus was currently leaning over Fawna, giving instructions. Gibus was seated in front of a separate computer panel, doing something with a row of keys and buttons Delaney couldn't follow, and the Zane was by the entrance.

He had a shoulder propped against the open archway, his arms crossed over his chest. He turned his head slightly when Julius and Verus approached from behind, walking up the ramp, but he didn't bother turning to look at them.

Even though Ruckus had many other loyal Tellers, they'd opted to only bring two—Julius and Verus—and had left Shellus with the Basilissa. If something were to go wrong, he'd been instructed to contact them immediately. It wasn't a very strong fail-safe, but it was the best they could do. Especially under such short notice.

Delaney glanced at Ruckus. They'd caught each other's eye once or twice already, and each time had been awkward. She just wasn't sure what to say, or how to act around him, especially not on a crowded ship. It was hard to tell if he was having the same problem, or merely keeping his distance.

Sanzie, who was standing off to the side with her, tightened the strap of her pack, cinching it at her waist with a huff. The entire time, her face remained impassive.

Delaney sort of envied that about her. That her poker face was so good. She'd been struggling to contain her own tumultuous emotions. Ruckus had barely spoken two words to her, and Trystan had been busy listing all the possible places the Rex could be hiding the device.

Trystan's distraction was something she should actually be grateful for, since she'd been trying so hard not to think about his birthday.

The festival yesterday had been an amazing experience, and aside from a few uncomfortable moments, she'd actually had a lot of fun. With Trystan, specifically. Which wasn't something she wanted, or had the time, to dwell on. Especially since she hadn't been able to shake the fear she'd seen in those Vakar children.

Of course she'd known about the unrest between Xenith's people, but hearing about it and seeing it firsthand were completely different. Watching those kids, scared simply because that Teller was Kint, had made her realize that stopping the Rex wasn't the end-all to Xenith's problems. There was still so much trust to build between the kingdoms, laws and rules and compromises to iron out. How long would all of that take?

More important . . . Could she really sneak off knowing the kind of mess she'd be leaving behind?

"We never got the chance to speak, Lissa," Sanzie said then, breaking through the quiet and pulling Delaney from her thoughts.

Delaney sighed. "Why didn't you just tell me about you and Ruckus?"

"I didn't think it was my place."

"We're friends, aren't we?" She wasn't sure when exactly she'd started viewing the Sworn as such, and not just as Trystan's second-in-command, but she did.

"I . . ." For a moment Sanzie looked taken aback, then she licked her lips and nodded. "Yes. I would like for us to be."

"Good." Delaney smiled, but before she could say anything else, the Sutter leaped up from his chair.

"Finished!" Gibus exclaimed. In his hands was a black metal band, which he brought over and passed to the Zane. "I've programmed it to your specifications. This should allow you easier access to the mainframe computer."

"*Should* is not a comforting word, Sutter." Trystan inspected the band, flipping back and forth the clear glass piece that attached to one end. He brought it up to his head, securing the two ends around the tops of his ears. When he flipped the glass panel again, it was directly over his right eye. He pressed at a spot directly behind his ear, and a row of lights lit up on the inside of the glass.

"What exactly does that thing do?" Delaney asked, curiosity getting the best of her. She moved closer, watching as the lights changed and fuzzy images took their place.

"Hey!" Fawna yelled from her seat. "Get out of my systems, Zane!"

Trystan didn't reply, merely tapped the same spot a second time, shutting the band off. The lights disappeared and he shifted the glass off to the side. "Everything seems to be in working order."

"*Seems* is sort of like *should*," Gibus said. "Don't you think?"

"The gorud connects remotely to computer systems and devices nearby," Sanzie began explaining, much to Delaney's relief. "He can control it by interfacing his fitting with it first, allowing him to communicate with it."

"We're approaching Carnage now," Ruckus told them, coming up on her side. Then he turned to Sanzie. "You have the recorder?"

"Right here." She patted the straps of her bag.

The plan was to split up into two teams once they got to the castle, in the hopes that one of them could successfully discover the location of Clean Slate. One team would follow Gibus to its last known location, while the other would go with Trystan to search areas he thought his father might hide something.

A member of each team would carry a video recorder, no bigger than an iPhone back home, so that they could record what they found.

Once they'd all reconvened on the ship, and were safe, they'd broadcast the footage across Kint.

"For this to work," Ruckus reminded them, "we need unwavering proof. It can't just be a video of some strange-looking machine that we claim has the ability to wipe people's minds. Gibus said there were test subjects—search through the computers for footage. While you're at it, keep an eye out for anything that looks like it can connect the Rex to the Tars."

They'd agreed that finding and destroying the device was their top priority—they couldn't let the Rex keep something so dangerous—but that finding proof to use against him, and ultimately to prevent him from rebuilding the device, was also important. If they could just get their hands on *something*, whether it be legitimate evidence on the Clean Slate project, or on his involvement with the Tars, that was all they'd need.

Having convinced herself this would work as much as she was able, Delaney relaxed her shoulders and took a deep, calming breath. She could do this; they all could. Her gaze trailed to the left, landing on the Ander.

And once it was done, she could finally figure the rest out.

"My men on the ground have the side hangar secured," Trystan said. "We should be able to land undetected."

"There's that word again." Gibus wagged his finger until the Zane shot a glare at him. Then he immediately dropped his hand and suddenly became interested in a speck of dirt on his shoe.

"Don't linger," Trystan called over to Fawna. "As soon as we're off, get the ship back in the air. You remember where I instructed you to land? That's the only safe location. My Tellers will keep others from stumbling upon you. With any luck, we'll be able to take a few cars once we have what we need, and then meet you there within two hours. Three, at most."

"I know where to go," Fawna confirmed. "You should all prepare for landing. We're about to be over the castle . . . now."

She kept the ship as steady as possible, but they wavered on their feet anyway. Delaney ended up bumping into Ruckus, who grabbed her, stilling her against his side. As soon as the ship evened out again, he let her go and stepped away.

It stung, but now wasn't the time to dwell on boy drama.

The ground shook once more as the ship landed, the engine roaring loudly before dying down to a soft purr filling the air. Fawna flicked a few controls, activating the cameras on the outside of the craft so they could take a look at the hangar first.

"All clear," she announced a second later. "You guys better get to the loading bay. I don't want to rely on Trystan's contacts being able to keep us under the radar for long."

They began departing, heading down the ramp quickly and then through the corridors. Sanzie was the only one who hesitated, glancing back over Delaney toward where Fawna still sat, prepared to fly back out.

"Be careful," she stated.

Fawna seemed surprised for a moment, only able to nod silently.

It must have been enough, because the Sworn left. She didn't explain as Delaney followed her down to meet with the others.

As soon as they turned the corner and entered, Ruckus reached out and pressed his palm to the panel at the side of the doors. They opened and a staircase formed, leading down into a hangar.

The one back in Inkwell and Vakar had been larger, Delaney noted as she descended the steps. Which made sense. Trystan had planned on having them enter here because there was less space for his Tellers on the inside to keep covered. He had people messing with security camera feeds, as well as the detection systems on the roof of the castle.

Julius was the last to exit the ship, and as soon as his booted feet touched the ground, the stairs caved in on themselves and retracted. The ship didn't linger, lifting back into the air once they were all clear.

They'd decided who would go with whom before leaving Vakar. Since Gibus and Trystan each had to lead their own search party, the rest of them had to be divvied up accordingly. The Zane had refused to go anywhere without Delaney, and despite the fact that he wasn't really speaking to her, Ruckus had said the same. Verus was joining them.

That left Sanzie, Julius, and a Kint Teller who Trystan claimed they could trust. Seeing as how the Teller was one of the ones who'd helped keep them hidden when Fawna had flown the ship in, that seemed legitimate.

Still, when someone suddenly entered the hangar, Delaney acted on instinct. She pushed Trystan out of the way and had her fritz in hand and aimed at the intruder before anyone else had even noticed his arrival.

"Hold," Trystan ordered, gripping her shoulder.

She lowered her weapon, watching the Kint Teller as he approached.

His hair was a darker shade of blond than the Zane's, and a little longer. When he was close enough for her to make out his eyes, she noted they were an odd olive green rimmed in fuchsia. He was wearing the traditional long-sleeved Kint uniform, like the rest of them.

"Zane." He angled his head toward Delaney, making a partial bow. "Lissa. The others are still in position. I've been informed that they'll only be able to keep the cameras in this room occupied for another seven minutes before detection that they've been tampered with becomes a high risk."

"This is Warran," Trystan said. Then to the Teller: "You'll be on Sanzie's team."

"Sworn." Warran nodded at Sanzie. "It's good to see you again."

"We should get moving," Ruckus pointed out. "Everyone, make sure to keep your fitting channels open. The first team to find something should immediately alert the others. And remember, no one comes back here. We're meeting in the garage on the other side of the castle. Once we're all together again, we'll make our way to where Fawna has hidden the ship nearby."

At the exit to the hangar, Delaney paused and glanced at the other team members. They were already headed to the right, down a long corridor that stretched to the South Wing, the opposite direction of where they were going. That was where Gibus had last seen the device, so it was the best place to check first.

"Come on." Ruckus nudged her to the left. "The faster we do this, the faster we can get everyone out safely."

She turned back to find that Trystan was already at the end of the other hall, and had slid the gorud's glass panel over his eye. At his side, Verus had his fritz activated, his back pressed against the wall in preparation to move.

Lights flickered across the screen and then Trystan motioned to them with two fingers. "I'm in the system. Shutting off the hallway cameras now. All right, let's move."

They passed down the corridor on their right as quickly and as silently as possible. He stopped them with a raised hand when they were close to the end, clearly taking care of the next camera with the gorud. After a beat, he had them moving again. The process repeated itself a few times, moving them deeper into the heart of the castle.

Even though they were moving slowly enough, Delaney didn't really have time to look around. She processed that most of the floors they were treading over were made of white marble with streaks of silver, and that a lot of the walls were various shades of blue, but that was about it. She was concentrating on her next step too much to pay attention to anything else, let alone home decor.

It would have been nice, though, if she'd had the chance to explore, get to see the place Trystan had grown up. It was strange, trying to picture a younger version of him sneaking through the halls the same way they were now. Coming up with ways to avoid his father.

"Is this how you got Gibus out?" she asked after twenty minutes of silence had passed. Unsurprisingly, she wasn't the only one extremely focused on the task at hand.

"It is," Trystan said, then waved to the left, indicating it was clear for them to head that way. They were halfway down the hall when his arm shot out, simultaneously stopping her and just about knocking the wind out of her. "Tellers are heading down the other hall."

Their group stilled, the tension so thick, it was like a heavy weight pressing down on all of them.

After what felt like forever, but was really only a minute at best, Trystan let out a breath. "They turned down the corridor adjacent to us. We need to hurry."

They moved, slipping back into that anxious silence as he navigated them through the castle. The place seemed to go on endlessly, and it was a while before they even reached their first checkpoint.

It was a room hidden within another that appeared to be a plain old sitting area. The door was set into the wall, a hidden panel made to look like just another piece of it. Trystan had it opened easily enough, and they entered cautiously.

"There's nothing here," Verus was the first to announce as they took stock of the room. It was slightly larger than a supply closet, with a couple of different outlets on the walls. But aside from some dusty old machines that clearly hadn't been touched in years, it was empty.

"Let's head to the next possible location," Ruckus said, and they slipped back out, shut the hidden door behind them, and continued on.

The next two places Trystan thought to look were fruitless as well, and they'd yet to hear anything from the other team. Everyone was starting to grow impatient. There were only a couple other rooms the Zane thought might be capable of housing the device. If they didn't find it in either of those, plan B was to go straight to his father's study and search for a link to the Tars.

Apparently, the security level surrounding that area had been heightened since Trystan had been there last, and he assumed it'd only gotten worse once he'd broken Gibus out, proving to his father he wasn't on his side. Because of that, it had to be the last thing they did, in order to avoid setting off some kind of alarm and giving them away.

"At least we haven't been shot at yet," Verus mused as they traveled down yet another blue, white, and silver hall, obviously trying to lighten the mood. "The Rex really must have taken the bulk of the Tellers usually stationed here with him. Lucky for us."

Delaney turned to reply, but Trystan came to an abrupt stop, causing whatever she'd been about to say to die on her lips.

He tapped the button on the back of the gorud, his movements becoming more frustrated with each passing second. It became apparent why he was annoyed when she realized the screen in front of his eye was no longer lit up.

"What's the problem?" Ruckus asked, keeping his attention locked on the end of the hall. They'd stopped pretty close to it, not leaving much escape room.

"There's a glitch," Trystan growled back, still trying to get the gorud to work. His free hand reached for his back pocket, where he'd slipped a shing earlier. "Keep watch. I've brought the handheld, but it'll take me a moment to switch over to it."

The whole reason they'd decided to use the gorud was so that the Zane's hands could remain free, saving them precious time. He was the only one who could activate the palm scanners at every door, after all, and he was also one of their best shots. Having to hold the device meant they'd be at yet another disadvantage.

And no matter how slight that disadvantage might seem, Delaney was smart enough to know it could make all the difference.

"How is that even possible?" Verus questioned, facing away from them so he could watch their backs. "Gibus said he worked on it. He doesn't make technical mistakes."

"Well," Trystan drawled, already working on the handheld, "he did this time."

"Has it powered off?" Ruckus risked a quick glance over his shoulder at the Zane before returning his gaze to the end of the hall.

"That's the odd part. It hasn't. It's just not wor—" Trystan's body jolted, his jaw clenching shut hard as his shoulders rocked forward with so much force, he ended up slamming into the wall. The device in his hands clattered to the floor loudly, his fingers shaking rapidly.

It looked almost like he was being electrocuted, and Delaney rushed to him, catching the back of his head in her palm just as he was about to slam into the wall. His large form slipped down until he was sitting on the ground, still shaking.

It had happened so fast, the others had only just turned around to see what was going on. They both emitted sounds of surprise, but Delaney's only concern was the Zane.

His eyes kept blinking, and he was twitching, like spasms were still racing through him.

Acting on impulse, she reached up and tore the gorud off his head, tossing it to the other side of the hall.

As soon as the device was off, he went still, sagging so that she had to press against his shoulders in order to keep him from curling in on himself. His eyes had closed, and his body was limp in her hold.

"Trystan!" She shook him, momentarily forgetting they were

supposed to stay quiet. It was like being in that cave all over again, and she couldn't hold back the sudden onslaught of fear.

"What just happened?" Verus had both hands in his hair and was staring wild-eyed down at the unconscious Zane. "I've never seen a gorud do that before!"

Ruckus grimaced, kneeling next to Delaney so that he could help her hold Trystan up. He felt for a pulse, pressing his fingers to the side of the Zane's neck. "He's breathing, in any case. So whatever happened, it didn't kill him."

"What are we going to do now?" The Teller glanced up and down the corridor. "If we're caught here, the Rex will be alerted immediately."

"If he wasn't already." Ruckus frowned, staring down at the Zane as he contemplated something.

"Help me get him—" The sound of skittering metal had Delaney quickly turning to the end of the hall. A gray circular object was rolling toward them, too far away for them to do anything about what was coming.

She had just enough time to grab on to both Trystan and Ruckus before the orb stopped moving and instantly exploded in a blinding rush of bright white light.

CHAPTER 21

If someone knocked her unconscious one more time, so help her . . .

Delaney came to, angry. Unlike most other times she'd awoken, she recalled with perfect clarity exactly what had happened just before she'd passed out. There was so much for her to be pissed about here, not least of all the fact that she was currently being dragged across the ground like a bag of garbage.

Two people were holding her by the wrists, tugging her down the hall. Her arms were burning, giving her the impression they'd been at this for a little while. Overhead, the lights blared down, momentarily making it difficult to really see the Tellers and their uniforms.

She allowed her head to sag backward, trying to make it seem like it was slumping naturally—not that anyone was looking—and caught sight of the others being handled by their own sets of Kint Tellers.

The ones who had Verus were at the lead, with Ruckus and his captors close behind. There was no sign of Trystan, which renewed her panic. He must have been taken somewhere else, but why? If anything happened— She cut off that train of thought, forcing her racing heart to calm down. Being frantic right now wouldn't help anyone. No one was speaking, all the Tellers moving down the corridors as if in a trance. She tested the hold on her wrists, carefully flexing them a little to see if doing so would elicit a reaction. Squinting, she risked staring up at the Tellers holding her, feeling an inkling of hope when they didn't react to her minor movements.

First things first, getting away from these guys. Then get the others and figure out what the hell went wrong. Obviously the gorud had malfunctioned, somehow electrocuting Trystan, but . . .

She frowned to herself.

Kind of convenient that these Tellers had been waiting just around the corner from them. There was the chance her loud exclamations had alerted them to her and the others' presence, but she somehow doubted it. It seemed too coincidental, for one. Besides, Trystan had kept a careful monitor of the halls, and would have said if they'd had company nearby.

Unless they'd arrived after the gorud had shut down on him . . . ?

There were too many variables to work through, and she certainly wasn't going to get any answers in her current condition. She brought her attention back to the matter at hand: how to get out of this.

She could easily break the hold of the Tellers dragging her, but that would leave the other four to deal with. She'd taken on more than six soldiers before, but that had been with distance, and either Trystan or Ruckus, aiding her. Aiming and firing her fritz would be too difficult in these close quarters, especially with her friends still unconscious and unable to get out of the way of loose shots.

Tipping her head back once more, she watched as the ones dragging Verus approached the end of the hall. She and her captors were a good four or five feet away from Ruckus. If she could wait until the rest of them had turned the corner, she might stand a better chance.

If she was quiet about it.

How the hell was she supposed to silently break away and take out two Kints?

Delaney inhaled slowly between her teeth, still watching ahead.

With no idea where they were being taken, this might be her only opportunity.

Verus disappeared first, the tips of his boots scraping against the marble. It was difficult for her not to tense up in preparation, but she somehow managed, counting the seconds to distract herself as, little by little, Ruckus's body slid around the bend as well.

She waited ten seconds after he'd disappeared out of sight, and then shot into action before she could second-guess herself. With one hard yank, she had both of her wrists free, and had already twisted onto her knees by the time the two Tellers sprung around. Dropping onto her butt, she kicked with all her strength, delivering blows to each of their guts.

They stumbled back a step, and she leaped for them before either could slam into a wall and give her away. Wrapping her arms tightly around the neck of the one on her left, she used his body to boost herself up, tightening her legs around the waist of the other. Then she pulled all of her weight backward, so that she toppled and brought them with her.

They fell forward, and she just barely maneuvered her body into the space between them at the last second, avoiding being crushed. Still, the one on the right landed on her shoulder and she bit her lip hard to keep from crying out.

Quickly, she got to her feet, activating her fritz in the process. They were still on their stomachs, but were making to get up. Before they had the chance, the weapon formed and her finger found the trigger. She shot them in their backs with a stun round, pausing for a beat to make sure they'd stay down.

When she didn't hear the sound of approaching footsteps, the breath she'd been holding eased past her lips.

She moved to the end of the hall and peered around the corner. There was no sign of the others. Glancing up, she tried to catch sight of some of the security cameras, but they were well hidden in this part of the castle.

Not having any choice but to risk it, she darted down the connecting hall, popping around to check down the other.

They weren't there, either.

Delaney swore. She'd not only lost Trystan, but now Ruckus as well. What if one or both of them got hurt? What would she do then? She could either keep going and risk not finding them and getting more lost—or running into more Tellers—or . . . With another curse she backtracked, entering the hall where she'd left the two unconscious men. Slowing when she got to them, she realized she probably shouldn't leave them out in the open.

There were doors at either side of her a few paces away, and after randomly selecting one, she began to drag them each into the room. It cost her a few precious minutes, and her arms hurt even more once she was done, but hopefully it'd prevent anyone from stumbling upon them in the hall and also buy her more time to find the others in the long run. Heaving slightly, she forced herself to continue on, trying to find her way back to where she had been knocked out. It took her two wrong turns, but surprisingly they hadn't been taken as far as she'd initially believed when she'd woken.

Her eyes scanned the hall as she entered, catching sight of the discarded gray ball, which she assumed was no longer a threat, until finally she spotted the gorud where she'd tossed it earlier.

It was up against the wall, clearly out of the way; the Tellers obviously hadn't seen it. Rushing over, she snatched it up, fiddling with the screen before she'd even fully looked at it.

Pressing the button on the side caused the lights to flicker back to life, a row of blue dots trailing across the screen before a different pattern appeared with a row of tiny boxes.

She was already lifting it over her head when she hesitated.

Why was it working now when it'd shut off on Trystan earlier? Also, after seeing what it'd done to him, was it even safe for her to use? Maybe the fact that it was on was only a further malfunction. It was a risk; if she got knocked out *again*, she doubted she'd wake up in time to help anybody. And if she was found here alone in the halls, who knew what someone might do to her.

But what if it'd done more than merely knock Trystan out, and he was in serious pain somewhere? And there was no telling where those Tellers had been taking Ruckus and the others. They could be getting tortured or some other horrible thing she didn't want to think too hard on, for fear she'd lose it.

Delaney steeled herself, determination pushing its way past the rest. Same as before with the Tellers, she didn't really have a choice here, even if it could all backfire. She'd already wasted so much time finding the damn thing, it couldn't be just so she'd chicken out at the last second and not use it.

Delaney settled the band around the back of her skull, securing the ends over the tops of her ears. Her finger pressed against the button at the side once more, and she braced herself for the worst.

There was an odd tingling at the base of her head, sort of the same sensation as the one she'd felt when her fitting had first been implanted. It didn't hurt, exactly, and was over rather quickly. A second later she propped the screen over her right eye and watched as the boxes lit up, waiting for her instruction.

The others had described the device as being a hands-off computer, taking its commands from her fitting. She didn't understand the written language the gorud used, but she could easily picture the symbols of the code Ruckus had had her memorize. The one that would contact Fawna.

Hopefully.

Delaney focused all her energy on the first empty box on the screen, envisioning the first symbol of the code. She broke out in a huge grin when the image actually appeared and the second box began blinking in its place. Three more to go.

Her excitement died when all the boxes were filled and nothing seemed to be happening. She waited, holding her breath, and after a few moments, deflated. It must still be damaged from before. She was lucky she hadn't been electrocuted like Trystan.

She was about to rip the thing off her head when suddenly it beeped at her ear. Almost immediately after, a string of words began playing across the screen, heading left as the sentence formed. It appeared to be in Kint, though for all she knew, it could have been Vakar.

Having come too far to give up now, Delaney accessed her fitting, forcing her next thought into the device the same way she would if she were trying to talk with Ruckus through it. The only difference was, she tried picturing what she was trying to say, sending a message stating that it was her.

No sooner had she finished the thought, the words began changing on the screen, first dissolving, then replaced with new ones.

Ones in English.

Delaney? It's Fawna. Where are the others?

She sagged forward, the relief hitting her hard enough that she had to rest her palms on her knees. She couldn't believe that'd actually worked.

Taken, she thought, hoping it would send. *Can you help me find them?*

A moment passed where she assumed Fawna was attempting to try, then:

Can't. Can only access the gorud from this distance, not the computer's mainframe in the castle.

Delaney sighed, then ordered, *Do that then.*

Another pause, followed by the message: *Done. I can now see everything you do.*

Great. At least she wasn't alone, but still. The hope had been that Fawna could use the gorud the same way Trystan had. She'd managed to figure out how to turn it on and type a message, but Delaney doubted she'd be able to learn how to hack into some high-tech supercomputer in time to help the others.

Nope. She needed a new plan. But what?

I'm going to go looking, she sent to Fawna, then started back the way she'd come. *Stand by.*

Standing by, came the quick response.

Delaney went silent and, aside from a small row of lights indicating it was still on at the top, the screen cleared. It was easy enough to backtrack to where she'd woken up, and she silently sped through the halls. Once she was at the turn where she'd lost them, she slowed a little, debating which way to go.

The path forked to the right and left, and she had no idea where either way led.

The gorud beeped quietly at her ear again, and then a message scrolled across.

Blueprints Zane sent earlier indicate kitchens to the left, labs to the right.

Unless they planned on cooking Ruckus and Verus dinner, she doubted that was the way they'd go.

Sending a thanks to Fawna, she went right. At the end of that hall, she received another message, this one telling her which way led to the lab rooms. Apparently they were on the same page, both deciding that was the most likely place for them to be taken.

Following Fawna's leads, Delaney swiftly made her way through the castle, losing track of time as she did. She didn't run into anyone as she traveled, though that could also mean she was going in the wrong direction. Wouldn't they want to keep prisoners secure?

She was about to turn the next corner when Fawna sent a message for her to stop. She halted, waiting for an explanation.

Lab rooms are down that hall. Move with caution.

She settled her nerves and then peered around the edge of the wall.

A single Sutter was headed down the other direction, away from her. They went around the far corner, and after waiting to see if the person would return, Delaney entered the hall.

Moving down the center, she kept low, noticing all the windows set into the doors lining either side. When she came to one, she popped her head up enough to catch a glance inside, and then kept going. All of them seemed to be empty.

She'd come to the end, with only three rooms left, when she heard the sound of a chair scraping against the floor. It'd come from the room closest to her, and she eased up to it and took a quick peek.

The room was rather large, with the first half by the door empty. On the other side, farther down, were two Sutters and three Tellers, all staring at the same man trapped between them.

Gibus.

DELANEY WATCHED AS Gibus was roughly shaken by the closest Teller, then shoved toward the other two Sutters, who moved out of the way to avoid being bumped into. He hit the edge of a table with enough force that the metal clanked against the floor. It was hard not to notice him shaking when he righted himself.

The door had to be soundproof, because they were talking to him now but she couldn't hear a thing. Gibus was clearly agitated. He was waving his hand in the air, indicating something on the rectangular black device one of them was holding. It sort of reminded her of an old walkie-talkie.

Which is when she noticed the cell in the way back of the room.

It was hard to make out the people inside from this distance, but she didn't have to get a good look to know who had to be in there.

They must be threatening the others to get him to help them, she sent to Fawna. That would explain why he wasn't in the cell with them.

Delaney took another glance at the other occupants in the room, noting that none of them seemed to be watching the entrance—or even facing it, for that matter. She searched for a control panel on the wall, then blinked when she realized there wasn't one.

Taking a chance, she lifted a hand to the doorknob, twisting slowly so as not to make any noise. When it clicked open, she held her breath, easing it toward her a crack. No one immediately sounded an alarm, and it didn't sound like the ebb and flow of conversation within the room had altered in the least.

Confidence growing, she opened it a little wider, so there was just enough room for her to slip inside. Then she eased the door shut at her back and, hunched over, rushed behind a large counter. There were some odd machines on top of it, but she didn't bother inspecting them, all her attention riveted on the prisoners in the cell.

It wasn't just Ruckus and Verus, either. Sanzie was there, propped against the stone wall, breathing unevenly, as well as one other person who had his back to her.

The Sworn looked terrible, and was clutching at her right side with a hand that had fingers bent at odd angles. There were bruises forming along her jaw and beneath her eyes, and a thin trail of blood had trickled and dried at the corner of her mouth. Whatever had happened, she hadn't gone down easily.

A quick perusal of the rest of the space showed there weren't any others. No Trystan, and either no Julius or no Warran—assuming the man whose face she couldn't see was one of them.

On your right!

Delaney had been so caught up trying to see if Ruckus was hurt, she hadn't been paying enough attention to the others in the room.

She sprang to the side, tucking herself out of sight against the counter just in time to avoid being seen by one of the Tellers.

The man crossed the room, opened the door, and disappeared without once glancing back. Which was good, because if he had, he would have spotted her for sure.

She sent a quick thank-you to Fawna for the heads-up, and then shifted back around to face the rest of the room again. Even with one fewer Teller to deal with, she doubted she could attack and take them all out before at least one managed to sound the alarm.

Ideas? As she waited for Fawna to reply, she took stock of the rest of the supplies in the room. There were two computer systems set up at either side, each flashing and emitting strange noises. No one seemed to be paying any mind to them, so she figured they must be unimportant.

Instead they were still talking around that weird walkie-talkie, one of them even vigorously shaking his head at something Gibus had just suggested.

Get the Ander's attention, Fawna suggested.

Duh. In her rush to stay hidden, she'd completely forgotten that the gorud still allowed her to use her fitting the same way she usually would. The only remaining problem was it appeared as though Ruckus was still unconscious. If only she'd had her frequencies linked with Sanzie's, this would all run so much smoother.

She could either wait for him to wake up—which could be forever—or she could try to wake him herself.

Settling on the latter, she began calling his name in her mind, directing the thought at him as loudly as possible. She was practically screaming it internally, and somehow hoped she wasn't also sending it to Fawna and the ship. Though it probably would just come up as symbols on the pilot's computer screen.

After the third time calling him, she saw his leg twitch, and increased her efforts. Her head was actually starting to hurt from the strain by the time he shook himself and sat up. She watched him blink in confusion and then glance around himself. A second later panic filled his eyes and he scrambled to his feet.

"Delaney?" his voice sounded frantic in her mind, and he ran his gaze around first the cell and then the rest of the room.

"I'm here," she told him then, *"but don't look. They don't know. We need to create a distraction. Can you do that?"*

He hesitated but then gave a swift nod. Realizing he didn't know where she was or if she could see him, he sent back, *"Yes."*

"Good. In three . . . two . . . one!"

Ruckus slammed himself against the front of the cell hard enough that the glass rattled. Before Delaney could ponder too long why they weren't using an electric cell like the ones back on Inkwell, he began screaming at the Tellers.

"What the hell is going on here?" He brought his palms up to the wall loudly. "Let me out of here! Gibus!"

"Quiet," one of the Tellers snapped. "As long as Sutter Gibus continues his work on the portable version of Clean Slate, none of you will be harmed."

"It was a trap," Sanzie told the Ander. "They knew we were coming."

They'd hoped Trystan's dad would assume—and smartly so—that Tilda wanted nothing to do with the Zane, considering the death of Olena was partially his fault. But he must have reconsidered the alliance when the Basilissa had called him to set the meeting so soon after Gibus had been freed by his son.

Knowing they wouldn't be able to stall for long, Delaney made sure the rest of the people in the room were also watching the cell, and then stood from her hiding place. Moving as quietly as possible, she darted past other counters and machines, making her way toward where the remaining two Tellers stood off to the side.

They obviously weren't part of the science party going on with the Sutters and were only there as guards. That worked out nicely for Delaney, because it meant they were already slightly separated from the herd.

The room was large, but it was still just a room, so right when she was about to reach the Tellers, one of the Sutters on the other side turned his head and caught sight of her. He lifted an arm and let out a warning.

Fortunately, she'd spotted him as well, and already had her fritz aimed. She took the first Teller down before he could get his weapon out, but the second sent off a round of zees that she only barely escaped from. She felt the heat sear her right arm as she dove out of the way, rolling on the ground toward the center of the room.

Back on her feet, she fired again, taking the last Teller out. Not waiting for him to fall, she turned her weapon on the two Sutters, just in time to catch one of them headed toward a control panel on the wall.

Delaney shot her in the back with a stun round, then hit the last remaining obstacle in the shoulder.

Gibus let out a long, drawn-out breath, his shoulders slumping forward. "Thank the stars."

"Can you get this door unlocked?" she asked, motioning toward the cell.

"It might take me a minute," he said, rushing over to one of the computers. "Hold on."

"You don't look very good." She eyed Sanzie, biting her tongue when Ruckus immediately spun around and dropped to his knees next to the Sworn.

The worry on his face was palpable.

"You're bleeding," Ruckus said to Sanzie, reaching out to wipe a smear off her chin.

"They're just flesh wounds," the Sworn grunted. But she didn't pull away.

Delaney forced herself to turn around, step closer to Gibus. "How much longer?"

Gibus grunted something about not being sure, his fingers rushing over the keys as his eyes scanned the screen. More Tellers could arrive at any moment, and they needed to get out of there before they did.

"There's no use," Sanzie told her. "Leave us. Go find the Zane."

"We have no idea what we're dealing with here," Ruckus argued.

"All of us remaining in this room hardly helps anyone," she snapped back.

"Wait." Gibus drew their attention his way and then slammed a button before grinning up at them. "Got it."

The door emitted a slight hiss and then clicked open, the Ander shoving it out of the way before Delaney could even think about reaching for the handle. A second later his arms were around her, holding her close as he breathed a sigh of relief against the side of her head.

CHAPTER 22

What happened? Are you hurt?" Ruckus asked, his arms tightening around her.

"I'm fine." This was the most contact they'd had since they'd broken up, and selfishly she wanted the moment to last a little longer. Knowing she'd found him, that he was safe, was a relief, and she wanted them all to get the hell out of there before anything else bad happened.

But not before they also found Trystan.

Which meant, as nice as this was, they didn't have time for it.

Delaney pulled away and turned to help the others out of the cell, frowning when she realized the unconscious Teller facing the wall wasn't Julius or Warran.

Sanzie had thrown Verus's arm around her shoulders and was in the process of hefting him up when she noticed Delaney's look. She dropped her gaze and explained, "They didn't make it. They died fighting back."

Verus was starting to come to, blinking rapidly.

Leaving him to the Sworn, Delaney motioned at the single person still in the cell. "Who is that, then?"

"Ezran," Sanzie said, right before the man in question moaned and rolled onto his back. "Apparently he's been in Carnage a long time. Like, since before we ever reached the Vakar palace. Presumably, he's how the Rex found out about Olena's death."

"Lot of good that did him," Ruckus mused, "considering his current state. Some reward for being honest."

"It's because I wasn't honest enough." Ezran's voice was rough, and he coughed after speaking. Twisting onto his stomach, he groaned and painfully lifted himself onto his hands and knees. He was clearly injured, though aside from a few scrapes and bruises, it was hard to tell where or how badly.

"What should we do about them?" Sanzie asked, pointing toward the Sutters and Tellers littering the ground. "We should do something before we start listening to Ezran's excuses."

"They are not—"

Delaney held up a hand, silencing him when he went to argue. "Tie them up, and make sure there's no chance of any of them getting loose."

"Is that thing turned on?" Ruckus tapped his forehead, indicating the gorud Delaney still wore. "If so, I could try tapping into it from here, using one of these computers. Though"—he glanced around—"I doubt any of this constitutes actual evidence."

"All raw data is stored on the Clean Slate's main computer," Gibus told them. "However, some of the device's blueprint was copied here so that work on the handheld version could be done. It's protected behind a ton of passwords and firewalls, but I might be able to access it."

"First, get into the security feeds and find Trystan." Delaney ignored the look Ruckus gave her. She understood how important uncovering this information was; she did. But so was finding the Zane.

Gibus went about following that order, while the others began moving the bodies out of the way.

Delaney guarded the door to the cell, making sure Ezran didn't try to escape—not that he appeared physically capable of doing so—

while the other three hurried to secure the Kints. As soon as it was done, she crossed her arms and glared down at him where he still sat on the ground.

"Explain what you're doing here, Teller," she ordered, trying to emulate the cold way Trystan spoke whenever he wanted someone to spill their secrets as quickly as possible.

"I was the one who informed the Rex of Olena Ond's demise," he acknowledged, "but only because his men were going to kill us otherwise. The group that'd been out delivering messages to the people to stay indoors survived, as well as those who'd boarded the Zane's ship. But those of us within the castle walls . . .

"I told the Rex what I could to avoid the same fate." He at least had the decency to sound ashamed by that fact. "Only, I kept the truth of the Lissa a secret. It was simple enough to convince the Rex's Tellers that Delaney's body had been destroyed by the elements. They'd arrived late in the day, and temperatures had already plummeted to dangerous levels. No one wanted to bother risking their life for a dead girl."

"So the Rex really does think I'm dead?" That was something.

"He did." He licked his lips and sighed. "But that's why I'm in this cell now. One of his spies discovered otherwise. As soon as the Rex realized I'd lied to him, he had me beaten and tossed in here."

If his father knew that Delaney wasn't dead, Trystan was in bigger trouble than she'd feared.

"Why didn't he just kill you?" Ruckus asked.

"He hoped I still had information about your group, and the Zane. Especially with his forces currently on the way to Varasow."

Delaney stilled. "What do you mean by forces? He took the Tellers who are usually stationed in this castle—that's it, right?"

"Well, yes, but that's not enough to stop the attack, so I assume he's calling in more of the Kint army to provide backup." He glanced between her and the Ander, clearly confused by their frowns. "You two do know about the Tar attack, correct? The Rex received word that they were planning to attack the Vakar capital."

"What?" Ruckus shot forward. "When?"

"Now."

"The Tars are under the Rex's influence," Delaney explained to Ezran before he could say anything else. "Why send them to Varasow? And why bring his own men after them?"

The Rex had demanded the meeting be at the Vakar palace; they should have guessed it was because he had something up his sleeve.

Sanzie had been busily typing away at one of the main computers during their talk with Ezran, and now she let out an excited sound and tapped the screen in front of her hard enough that her nail made a clicking sound against the glass.

"I've found him!"

Delaney darted to her side, bending to stare at the screen herself. It was footage from a hallway security camera, and showed an unconscious Zane on a stretcher. Four Tellers were carrying him, and she watched as they turned a corner and disappeared.

Before she could ask where they'd gone, Sanzie tapped more keys, and a second later a new hallway flashed across the screen. The angle was different this time, showing them heading toward the camera before vanishing out of sight. The Sworn traced their path through another five feeds, until finally the men came to a room with double doors, entering with the Zane.

They didn't come out again.

"There aren't any cameras in that room." Sanzie cursed, even going so far as to slam her palm against the tabletop. "None of what we just saw was in real time, either. This all happened a half hour ago. Who knows what's been done to him in that time frame?"

"Do you know where that is?" Delaney pointed to the now closed doors they'd gone through, trying not to allow the same panic the Sworn was feeling to infiltrate her defenses. Clearheaded, that was what the guys were always telling her. The one constant in both Ruckus's and Trystan's lessons.

She couldn't allow herself to lose focus, or allow fear to get in the way. That was how people got killed. That was how she'd let people get killed. And there were way too many people counting on them right now for her to do that.

"In the far corner of the North Wing," Sanzie read off the screen. "About fifteen minutes from here, give or take." She stood, fast enough that the chair shot back a few inches.

Delaney stopped her from moving farther from the computer. "You're not coming."

Sanzie opened her mouth to argue, but snapped it shut again when she received a pointed stare.

"I need you to stay here and work on getting a message out to Vakar. We need to warn Tilda in Varasow," Delaney said.

"They could be there already," Ezran reminded her, but she ignored him.

It didn't matter. If there was even a slight chance the attack hadn't started yet, then they needed to try to get word to Vakar before it was too late.

"You can't go out there." Ruckus grabbed her by the elbow, not roughly, but firmly enough to convey how he really felt about the idea. "It's too dangerous. For all we know there are Tellers everywhere."

"And if I run into any," she reassured him, "I'll handle them. We know where Trystan is. I can't just leave him."

"You don't even know how to use that thing." He motioned to the gorud.

"Connection's down anyway," she said. "I haven't been able to access the computer's mainframe." At his frown she elaborated. "Fawna's been helping me. She'll help me now."

"If it's not connected, she can only see what you see," he stated. "How is that helpful?"

"You'd be surprised. Besides, we haven't gotten what we need. I'm sure there's a record button on this thing she can show me. We can still complete the mission."

"No way. Gibus will look here and copy any information on the device's development. It's not a lot, but it's what we can get."

"Ruckus—"

"Then I'm coming with you," he said, changing tactics determinedly.

She took his hand, squeezed once. "You know you can't. You have to stay here and help get ahold of Tilda. Vakar needs you."

"You need me more," he argued.

"We don't know that. Could be the only thing waiting for me is an unconscious Zane. Maybe they just put him in there until the Rex gets back. We all know he'd want to deal with his son himself. It's probably nothing."

"We don't know that," he fed back stubbornly, and she sighed. "I've already lost Pettus. I'm not about to lose you, too. Besides, I don't recall putting you in charge."

"Don't you?" She quirked a brow, waiting for him to catch her meaning. She felt a little bad when guilt flashed quickly over his face, but she didn't take the words back or offer an apology.

"You all made me Lissa," she continued when he didn't say anything, tightening her hold on his hand. "Now let me do my job."

His hands were suddenly in her hair, guiding her to him, even as he bent to meet her halfway. When he pressed his mouth against hers, her eyes shut of their own accord, and a rush of warmth flowed through everywhere they touched.

"I'm not trying to stop you," he said stubbornly, pulling away in the process, "but if you're the Lissa, I'm your Ander, which means I'm coming with whether you like it or not. We can stand here arguing all day, or you can just get onboard."

For a moment she was blank, not sure what to say or feel. Then she took a shaky breath and gave a curt nod. He was right, after all: It was safer if the two of them went together, and the others could handle contacting Varasow without him.

"We get Trystan, and then we get out." Steeling her shoulders, Delaney tapped the side of the gorud, making sure it was still on, and then headed for the door across the room.

You still with me, Fawna? she asked, visualizing the words.

A second later Fawna's response came through, actually making Delaney smile a bit despite what she was about to do.

Yes, and next time, remember that before *you make out?*

CHAPTER 23

He felt like he was dying.

Trystan woke with a sharp ache at the front of his skull. Before he'd even opened his eyes, he was squeezing them tighter, instinctually trying to avoid more pain. It felt as if someone had been rummaging through his head, an altogether unpleasant thing to wake up to.

Once the pounding had abated, he risked movement, shifting slightly. He was sitting in a chair, the material beneath him uncomfortable and rather solid. The details of what had happened were a bit fuzzy, and he struggled to sort through them as he flexed his arms and legs.

And realized they were bound.

His eyes popped open and he swore, tugging at his wrists even though it was clear he wasn't going to be able to get loose. Metal bands secured them to the arms of the chair, and another band stretched across his chest, preventing him from leaning forward to check his legs. Not that he needed to. He could feel the ties on his ankles.

"You have got to be kidding," he stated, giving one final tug for good measure.

The events leading up to his obvious capture filtered back, causing him to grit his teeth. He'd been in one of the halls with Delaney and the others when the gorud had suddenly stopped functioning. Then . . . He thought it might have electrocuted him, which was puzzling, because he'd never heard of that happening to anyone before.

The Rex chose that moment to appear, entering from the opposite side of the room, directly across from where Trystan was being contained. His dark blond hair was perfectly smoothed back, and there wasn't so much as a wrinkle anywhere on his uniform. The only thing not impeccable about him was his scowl.

A Sutter entered directly behind him, keeping a pace back. She was one of the heads of the Kint bioengineering department.

"What did you do?" Trystan growled, giving one final tug on his restraints before forcing himself to settle down.

"Used the gorud to overload your fitting just enough to knock you unconscious without causing permanent damage. It must have slipped your mind that I have access to your frequency. I'm disappointed in you, son," the Rex finally said, when he was only a few feet away. It'd taken him a while, since the room was actually pretty large.

There were multiple projects set up in different corners, and even a few placed oddly at the center of the room. Trystan didn't recognize any of it, but that only meant it was probably more dangerous, not less so. Some of the various machines were recognizable, yet he couldn't even begin to guess what his father's Sutters had been working on in here. The space was all whites and silvers, with specks of color in the forms of wires sticking out from within machines, poking from behind some foreign objects.

He'd been placed in a section surrounded by computer towers, stretching at his sides and, he assumed, behind his back. When he tipped his head, he could just make out the top of a few of them, and the flashing lights they emitted.

Despite the size, however, they were the only three there. A quick assessment told him the room had been cleared rather quickly, everyone else made to drop what they were doing and exit without the time to properly put things away or shut things off. The Rex had made this all happen in a rush.

Whatever happened next, it wasn't going to be pleasant.

"Likewise, Father," Trystan drawled, slipping into his nonchalant Zane persona with ease. "You're moving against the people's best interests. I was told your ship left for Vakar. You must have gone through some trouble to ensure no one realized you weren't actually on it."

The Rex snorted. "Their best interests? Honestly, what's come over you? What's best for them is what I say is best for them. Nothing more, nothing less."

"How is working with a terrorist group good for them?" he asked, watching as his father ambled toward one of the computers attached to the tower on his left. "Your subjects have always been loyal. There's no reason for you to have done this."

"Oh, they've been loyal, all right," he agreed, then lifted his steely gaze. "But not necessarily to me. You think I haven't known about your little side projects? Haven't noticed you lurking, always sneaking off at odd hours, returning in a better mood than when you left? I'll admit, for a couple years I actually thought you were seeing a woman, someone I wouldn't approve of, sure, but still, just a woman. Nothing to be concerned about."

Trystan struggled not to let on that he knew exactly what his father was talking about, and where this conversation was leading. He'd believed himself so careful, all this time, going to speak with the army members on his side. Keeping them hidden, and out of the Rex's notice.

Until he'd brought Gibus straight to them, that was.

He clenched his hands into tight fists but kept his expression blank. Whether or not his father was telling the truth now—and he really had already known about Trystan's loyalists—didn't matter.

He'd exposed them, confirmed their existence, when he'd asked for their help getting him and the Sutter out of Kint.

"But," his father continued, "you've been plotting against me for some time now, haven't you, son? Why else would you need a bunch of secret networks? A hidden communications link within my own systems?" He clucked his tongue. "Clever. I'd be proud if its purpose hadn't been to be used against me."

"That was never its intention," Trystan said. It was most likely futile, but if there was a chance he could convince the Rex he had it wrong, he had to try.

"Are you trying to protect them?" His father canted his head. "There's no need. They've already been dealt with, right before my men headed off to deal with that lecherous Basilissa. She's unworthy to wear a crown, so you and I are going to take it from her, like we've always planned."

"You're lying." There's no way the Rex could have done what he claimed, not unless he'd taken out more than half of the Kint army. But that didn't rule out the group who'd aided Trystan and Gibus.

There was little doubt in his mind that those were the people who'd been "dealt with." Anger warred with disgust, but he banked those emotions down, still intent to come off cold and disinterested. Showing he cared about something was only going to further his father's attempts to destroy it. He might not have been able to protect those men already dead, but he could try to keep the Rex's interest from trailing toward the others.

"I'm not the liar here, son," he sneered, a spark of fury entering his eyes. "Or did you forget?"

The Rex entered a sequence into the computer, and one of the screens a little ways away from Trystan came to life. Across it, an image of an unconscious Delaney being dragged down the hallway greeted him in bright Technicolor.

"You reported she was dead," the Rex stated, watching closely as

Trystan felt his defenses begin to crack. "She doesn't look dead to me. Not yet, anyway."

His gaze shot to his father's before he could stop himself, and he tugged at the bindings around his wrists hard enough to shake the chair beneath him.

With a laugh, the Rex flicked another button, and the image on the screen changed. This time, it was an aerial shot of Varasow—Trystan recognized the streets he'd walked with Delaney and the Ander. Instead of the calm, bustling city they'd been in, however, there was chaos. People were screaming and running in every direction, causing cars to crash into one another, or veer off sharply and slam into buildings.

The reason for their panic became apparent when the camera swept down a different street, immediately highlighting the mass of Tellers swarming the place.

Tars didn't have a uniform, no designating symbol or marker. They'd avoided it in part because most of them were Kint, but mostly to avoid detection. Being that they were a secret terrorist organization.

Which was why it was so strange that the people attacking the city were carrying flags with their name scrawled across it in big bold letters. It was impossible not to realize they were Tars, and not just because of the signs, either. They'd all worn the same color, a rich purple with a navy capital *T* stitched over the left pectoral.

They were shooting people in the streets, firing their fritzes at anything that moved, including a few holograms. It wasn't hard for Trystan to figure out their plan, that they'd surrounded the city, creating a barrier preventing anyone from leaving, and were now moving inward.

Toward the Vakar palace.

"What have you done?" The words slipped past his lips, shock making him unable to hold them back. As the capital city, Varasow was home to a fifth of Vakar's population. Thousands of people lived there, and now every single one of them was about to die. This was exactly the type of thing he'd always tried to avoid, even during the war.

He'd known his father was capable of great horrors, but this . . . This was surprising, and that only pissed Trystan off because, really, he shouldn't be surprised. There'd only been one other occasion when the Rex had done something this drastic and awful—when he'd chosen to drop that bomb, demolishing an entire Vakar town in under six seconds.

Trystan had been disgusted then, excusing himself as soon as he'd been able. He hadn't told anyone, but he'd gone straight to the bathroom and thrown up.

"Me?" The Rex glanced pointedly at the screen, feigning ignorance. "Those are clearly Tars attacking. I have nothing to do with them. All of Xenith knows that. But don't fret, son; I'll send help." He grinned. "As soon as they've reached the palace and taken care of the Basilissa for us."

"There is no us," Trystan growled. Absolutely no part of him wanted to be linked to *this*, not even in conversation.

"Ever since that human got involved," he stated, "I agree. She's done something to you, made you forget your place. Your purpose."

"I'm the Zane." He couldn't lean forward with the bar across his chest, but he tried. "I'm meant to protect the people!"

"No!" His father's voice boomed across the room, causing everyone—including Trystan—to jump a little. "You are meant to do as you're told. Always have been. Why else do you think I bothered with offspring? I reared you to help me achieve greatness, and that is what you're going to do, whether it damn well pleases you or not!

"Now." As quickly as he'd snapped, he pulled himself back together, smoothing a hand over his hair and adjusting the bottom of his shirt. "Back to the matter at hand."

Trystan shook his head vehemently. "I am not helping you destroy a city, Father. You've gone too far." He angled his chin toward the screen. "You think too little of them. They'll figure out it was you, that you're the one who sent the Tars to Varasow."

"Oh? And how is that?" He grunted arrogantly. "My own son couldn't figure it out, and he had years to do so. I'll give you one better; *they* didn't even know. I formed the Tars, gave them purpose, and not a single member of that organization had the slightest clue who was the master of their creation."

Trystan stilled. That wasn't possible. . . . Though, the more he thought about it, the more it actually made sense.

They'd been winning the war, but not nearly fast enough to appease the Rex. So he'd decided to test out a new weapon, bomb one of the smaller towns on the coast of Vakar. The test had been successful— so much so, the Basileus had been open to peace negotiations without hesitation.

Which must have been his father's real goal the entire time. He hadn't used that weapon to help end the war and save lives. He'd done it to manipulate the Vakar royal family into making a deal—binding Trystan and Olena to combine the two houses.

He'd already admitted to Delaney back in Inkwell that even *that* had been a half-truth. His intentions hadn't been equal rule, but an easy takeover. The plan had been to blindside Vakar once Trystan was bound to their heir. An untimely demise for the old Basileus and Basilissa, an event that would force Trystan and Olena into the roles far sooner than anyone expected. After that, the Rex would use his son's forces, combining the armies of Xenith, and invade Earth.

Trystan had promised Delaney that he'd talk to his father, work out a way Earth could remain as it was, in peace. What a fool he'd been. All of this playing out right in front of his eyes, and he'd been blind to it.

But then, that had been part of the plan, too, hadn't it?

"You knew the idea of bonding with Olena would keep me distracted." Bile rose up the back of his throat and he swallowed it down. The screams coming from the still-playing screen were faint, the volume turned low, but he wasn't looking at that anymore. His father had his full and undivided attention.

"To the rest of the world you might be a conundrum," the Rex began, "the mysterious, aloof Zane. But a father knows his son. I knew you'd find tying your life to that spoiled girl beneath you, that you'd focus all your efforts on finding a way to avoid having to go through with it. The Tars were an out you could detach yourself from."

"There wasn't meant to be an actual out, though," Trystan said, and received a bitter look in return.

"No, there was not. You were meant to keep distracted, miss all the signs, not see my true intentions. Until, of course, it was too late and you and Olena were already bound. Then, what choice would you have but to join your forces with mine?" His expression darkened further, like he had a bad taste in his mouth. "That disgusting human came along and ruined everything. Well, *almost*. I've gotten us back on track, mind you. Possibly ahead of my initial schedule. Part of me even thinks I should be thanking her."

"That's the new plan, then? Pretend Kint Tellers save Varasow from the wicked Tars?"

"Sneer at it all you like. Sometimes the simplest strategies are the most effective."

"Say it does work," Trystan offered. "How do you intend to get ahold of Vakar without having me bound to anyone? Olena is dead, and the Uprisen heir is currently in holding. Do you just expect Vakar to be so grateful, they roll over and pronounce you their new king?"

He'd slipped that bit about Delaney in there, unable to resist attempting to find out *something*. She just had to be alive. If she was, he could still figure a way out of this and get to her.

He almost slumped in his chair when his father didn't react to his phrasing, or jump to correct him. That was a good sign he hadn't killed her.

"Of course not." The Rex waved him off, stepping back over to the main computer, where the Sutter had been working for the past five minutes. "I only need them to let their guard down. Just a few weeks, days if we're lucky, and I'll have them all begging me to take over if that's what I please."

"By using the device?" He made a big show of rolling his eyes, grinning on the inside when he saw how negatively it affected his father.

"This device is a work of genius," the Rex ground out past clenched teeth. "Proof is right before you. Don't you recognize any of the Tars on that screen? You should. You're the one who procured them for me in Kilma."

Trystan frowned, turning back to watch the mayhem still unfolding, despite how badly he didn't want to. He couldn't make out any of their faces; the camera was too far away for that. He wasn't really supposed to, anyway. It was just another point his father was trying to make. And he'd made it.

"You said you formed them—why?" There were a few reasons he could think of, but he wanted to know the whole story. "Just to further my distraction?"

"Things aren't always about you, son." He tsked in disparagement. "No, they served a greater purpose in the long run. A group for the world to hate more than they hated us. Somewhere else for them to look while I worked tirelessly on getting us right where we are now. Close, so close, to our final goal."

The Rex might have set the Tars in motion, but he hadn't been their actual leader. Once they'd served their purpose, distracted the world with attacks, drawing attention away from all the horrible things Hortan End had done during the war, he'd found a new use.

Having met some of them in that warehouse, Trystan knew first-hand they believed they were working for the good of the entire planet. They wanted to protect the integrity of the royal families and the thrones. That was why they hadn't wanted a twit like Olena having a say in Kint politics. Why they'd later rallied against Delaney, a human. They'd been labeled terrorists, sure, and they'd executed attacks, had tried to kill.

But not whole cities.

The people of Varasow were innocent; it was out of character for the Tars to attack the way they were, same as wearing a uniform was.

"You used the device on them, didn't you?" Trystan's gaze roamed across the screen, counting. There were way more Tars invading than he'd arrested in that warehouse. His father must have used them to get the rest of their numbers, trapped them. "All of them?"

"Only on the handful of leaders you'd procured for me," the Rex said, pride apparent in his tone. "Took a few rounds of trial and error, we lost a couple, but it was worth it, wouldn't you say? Look at them go." His eyes glazed over a bit. "Doing exactly what I instructed them to do. The final task I created them for. The genius of Clean Slate is, I can strip away a person's sense of self, but leave behind basic knowledge and information. The Tar leaders who survived the tests recalled they were Tars, and what their purpose was. They just didn't remember they never took direct orders from me before."

"You're a monster." Trystan couldn't play the game anymore, couldn't pretend like he was unaffected or like he cared at all for the man standing before him. "If I weren't tied down right now, I'd kill you myself."

The Rex's eyes narrowed, and for a moment it looked like he was going to activate the fritz around his wrist and shoot him. Then the storm in his eyes settled and he motioned toward the Sutter. "We'll proceed now."

Trystan tensed up when the woman approached him, not liking

where he thought this was heading. After that major confession, there was really only one way this could go, and it wasn't with the two of them shaking hands and letting bygones be bygones.

"Once this is through," the Rex said, moving in front of him so that he was hovering over his son while the Sutter began plugging things into the computer at his back, "everything will return to the way it was. I'll have the dutiful son I deserve, and you will no longer have disgraceful feelings for a human."

The Sutter reached over the back of the chair, pressing Trystan's head forward. He struggled against her hold, but the binds kept him from being successful. There was a prick at the base of his skull, and a slight burning sensation as something thin and metal was placed over the spot his fitting had been implanted.

"I'll wipe your memories, all those ideas about rebellion and that misplaced animosity, and we'll start fresh. I'll have to take more than I did with the Tars, of course. There's a lot you'll need to be reminded of, but I can't risk leaving something behind and having you turn against me a second time, now can I?" The Rex grinned.

"Father." Trystan wasn't sure if he was pleading with or cursing the man.

"Don't worry." The Rex bent down so that he was in the Zane's line of sight. "The technology is flawless now. No nasty side effects. I wouldn't murder my only heir. Even unbound to a Vakar Lissa, you're still far too useful for that. After all," he said, leaning a little closer so that Trystan could see the cruelty flicker in his eyes, "you've got more sway over the Kint army than I do. That'll come in handy when it's time to order them to prepare for invasion."

He tried not to let the words sting, but it was impossible.

His father didn't care about him any more than he did the computer he was currently hooking Trystan up to. Hell, since he'd spent years trying to perfect the device, he probably cared about the damn thing more.

"We are ready to proceed, Rex," the Sutter said, and Trystan squeezed his eyes shut, bracing himself.

"Unless this part was important." Delaney's bold voice suddenly filled the room.

The Sutter was shocked enough that her hold faltered, and Trystan was able to lift his head to see Delaney standing there between two computers, one of which was still playing the attack on Varasow.

She was holding her hand up, waving something in the air. It took a moment for him to realize it was a set of wires with a port at the end.

His Lissa glanced at it, then at the Rex, and said fearlessly, "It sure looks important, don't you think?"

CHAPTER 24

What the hell was she doing?

As far as bad plans went, this one totally took the cake. Even as she stood there, painstakingly keeping the grin plastered to her face, she knew it. This was a horrible, terrible idea.

She was supposed to wait for Ruckus. They'd separated when they'd entered the wing, and were going to come from either side of the hall, taking out any Tellers they met on the way, so they wouldn't be hit with any surprises.

But of course, when she'd gotten to the door, the biggest surprise of all was standing over Trystan, gloating. The Rex was supposed to be gone, yet there he was. . . . And seeing what he clearly intended for his son, Delaney knew that unless she was willing to watch Trystan get his mind erased—which she definitely wasn't—she needed a new plan.

Sending one last command to Fawna, she'd taken off the gorud and hidden it from sight. Fortunately, as per usual, Trystan was holding everyone's attention, making it easy for her to slink her way into the room.

Once she was close enough, all she'd had to do was wait for the

Sutter to turn her back, and then she quickly snuck around to the other side of the supercomputer behind the Zane. She'd spent a good minute trying to figure out what looked most important—partially wishing she hadn't taken off the gorud, so Fawna could help her—and then had just started pulling. Most of it she'd left on the ground back there, but the wires in her hand she'd kept.

Slipping back around to the head of the room without getting noticed was just as easy. Something told her everything from here on out wouldn't be.

"Miss Grace," the Rex said as he spun on her, glowering. "Always turning up at the most inopportune times. Imagine my surprise when I heard you'd somehow cheated death. Again."

She lifted a single shoulder. "Sorry to disappoint."

"I'm going to need that returned"—he angled his chin toward the wires—"immediately. Afterward, since you're here already, you can watch."

"You hurt your son?" She shook her head. "No, thanks."

"No." He chuckled. "I meant you can watch him kill you. That'll be the first order I give him. A test, if you will, to ensure the device has worked and erased all memory of who you are. I'll tell him you're the enemy, and recalling that I am the Rex, and he is the Zane, he'll attack without hesitation."

"How many people did you murder trying to get this thing to work?" she asked. "Don't they count for anything? Weren't they your people?"

He waved his hand in the air, seemingly unthreatened, though she caught the step he slid closer. "Fodder. They served their purpose, and their Rex."

"And their families?"

"*Delaney.*" Trystan's voice entered her mind, sounding strained. "*What are you doing?*"

"*Trust me,*" she sent back. Now that she'd momentarily saved him from the machine, the rest of her plan required getting the Rex to play along, without letting on that that was what he was doing.

"*Do you have a way of getting us both out of here unscathed?*" he asked, and when put that way, she was forced to tell him the truth.

"*Nope. But Ruckus is coming. Eventually.*" She held her ground. "*Just give me a minute.*"

"*I don't believe we have that kind of time, Lissa.*"

"*Working on it.*" Kind of.

"Their families should be honored that I gave meaning to their loved ones' pathetic lives," the Rex said then, cutting into their private conversation. "Everyone on this planet has one purpose, and one purpose only: serve *me*. They did their jobs, and now the rest of my Tellers will do theirs."

Delaney heard the sound of the doors opening behind her and felt a shiver skitter up her spine. Without even having to turn to see for herself, she knew it wasn't Ruckus entering. Things had just gone from bad to worse.

"*Shoot the Rex!*" Trystan demanded, tugging at his bonds. His struggles only caused the chair to shake a bit. There was no way he was going to get himself out of that.

"*Can't,*" she returned. "*I don't think we got enough!*"

"*Enough* what? *Damn it, Delaney!*"

She wanted to explain, but there was no time for that.

Tightening her grip on the wires, she activated her fritz and spun on her heel, already aiming for the entryway. Her stomach clenched painfully when she realized there were at least a dozen Kints flooding the room, spreading out to block the only exit.

It wasn't like she could leave anyway, with Trystan still in that chair, but that didn't make it any less frightening being trapped.

They'd come in prepared, with their own weapons drawn. Not

wanting to give them the chance to open fire, she began shooting as she dove for cover behind the computer next to the large screen still displaying the attack on Varasow. Zees pinged against the metal, ricocheting off, and for a moment she was so distracted by the obvious threat, she forgot all about the others.

The Sutter darted across the room, headed straight for her. The woman didn't have a fritz, however, so had no way of defending herself when Delaney finally caught sight of her and lifted her own.

She pulled the trigger quickly, watching as the Sutter's body jerked and then dropped forward. Her forehead whacked sharply against the solid ground.

"Delaney!" Trystan's warning came too late.

She glanced up to find that she was surrounded, with twelve fritzes aimed directly at her head. Her mind raced to come up with a way out, but as far as she could tell, there wasn't one. If she tried to fire, they'd kill her.

"You've been bested, Miss Grace," the Rex drawled, almost like he'd read her mind and wanted to rid her of that final thread of resistance. "Deactivate your weapon and place the wires on the ground, carefully."

"If I do that," she said slowly, eyeing the end of the fritz closest to her face, "you'll use that thing on Trystan."

"If you don't," he stated, clearly losing patience, "I'll simply have them shoot you, and use it on him anyway. Do you really want the last memory my son has to be of your death?"

"Are you seriously trying to play on my compassionate nature right now?" It'd been pretty stupid, thinking she could waltz in here and solve everything on her own. Especially considering the only part of her plan that had so far run smoothly relied heavily on Fawna.

Barely resisting the urge to glance at where she'd placed the gorud earlier, Delaney began doing as the Rex said. Her fritz caved in on itself with a wave of her middle finger over the sensor at the bottom of the metal band. As it did, she lowered her palm until it was pressed flat to the ground.

"Just because you don't have a heart," she added as she forced herself to let go of the wires, "doesn't mean you have to take advantage of those of us who do." She canted her head at him, pretending to think. "Or maybe it's the opposite. Maybe the reason you're going through all this trouble is because you're jealous."

"Excuse me?" His eyes narrowed.

"What's wrong?" She tsked. "Jealous of your own son? It's gotta suck, huh, finding out that *your* army would rather follow him. That it's his name they whisper in the dark, chant on the battlefield. How many of them, do you think, are just waiting for the day he can take the throne and they can all be done with you?"

"Delaney . . ." Trystan was glaring at her now as well, though she only risked sparing him a glance, unwilling to take her eyes off the Rex for long. *"Whatever this supposed plan is, I do not approve."*

"Duly noted. Next time, when I'm the one tied to a chair, you can come up with the plan. Deal?" She didn't give him a chance to respond, and opened her mouth with the intent to lay it on the Rex some more.

An explosion at the doors forced her jaw shut, the blast practically knocking the Tellers closest to it off their feet, and they stumbled and slipped. Two of them accidentally pulled their triggers, sending off rounds of zees pinging against the surrounding computers and metal contraptions.

One sailed straight toward Delaney, and she only had enough time to curl in on herself to avoid a direct hit. It grazed the side of her leg, just above her knee, and she let out a startled cry at the sharp pain. The last time she'd been shot with a legitimate alien bullet, she'd been on Earth.

After, she'd passed out. Now she couldn't afford to.

A cloud of pink smoke flooded the room directly after the doors exploded, engulfing half the Tellers in less time than it took to blink. Sounds of a struggle soon followed, though it was impossible to see what was going on through the thickness of the smog.

To avoid getting caught up in it herself, Delaney abandoned her position against the computer, clenching her jaw against the pain in her leg as she put pressure on it. A tendril of the pink cloud drifted closer, and she accidentally breathed it in. The coughing started immediately, her throat suddenly on fire as she stumbled forward, away from the rest of it and toward Trystan.

The burning was so intense, she almost didn't notice when strong arms banded around her waist, lifting her into the air. She had a split second to register it was not a friendly hold, before whoever had her threw her like she weighed nothing. Her body spiraled, and she closed her eyes, already knowing what was coming.

When she landed, it was on her right shoulder, and the momentum sent her rolling until she slammed back into one of the computers at Trystan's right. Her skull whacked back against it, dazing her, but that was nothing compared to the sensation still going on in her throat.

She struggled onto her hands and knees, hacking, barely able to see through the tears in her eyes. Trystan was screaming her name, but she couldn't tell if it was through their fittings or aloud. Her hands clawed at the collar of her shirt, not that it would do any good, and she'd just sat back on her heels when a shadow stopped in front of her.

Through blurry vision, she saw the Rex lift a fist, and she braced herself a second before he brought it down across her cheek.

If it'd been difficult for her to see before, it was impossible now. The world momentarily winked in and out. Her face was pressed to the floor, the chilled surface surprisingly soothing to her skin, while the rest of her felt like it'd been completely doused in kerosene and set ablaze.

When she finally managed to peel her eyes open again, it was to find three Kints pulling the Rex away. He struggled for only a second, glaring down at her furiously, before he twisted and followed of his own volition. They ran directly into the pink cloud, which was just starting to dissipate around the edges.

Delaney was wheezing, her throat not just burning anymore but closing up as well. She tried moving once, not sure if she'd managed to even twitch her finger, and then gave up.

Because she was already facing that direction, she saw the single figure step from the cloud, though it took her mind longer than it should have to process it wasn't one of the Rex's men coming back to finish the job.

The guy was wearing a black mask over his face, similar to a gas mask, though with flashing lights and strange circular buttons running up the right side, from chin to brow. He was dressed in Kint colors, but the way he moved was familiar, so she didn't even consider attempting to fight him off when he rushed to her side.

He dragged her hurriedly onto his lap, tugging something small from his pocket and shoving the end of it past her lips. Without explanation, he pressed down on the side, tightening his arm around her when she jerked as a burst of icy air shot down her throat.

The racking coughs started again, and he shifted so that now she was bent over his other arm, staring at the floor as her body shook. It didn't last nearly as long as the first time, and the pain eased away and then disappeared altogether.

"I trust you had a good reason for not waiting for me as planned?" Ruckus said then, and she twisted her head around to watch him pull the mask off and toss it to the side.

"If what I did worked, then yeah."

"Well, we're just lucky I happened to stumble upon a room filled with weapons. These certainly came in handy." Helping her to her feet, he glanced over toward the doorway, where the pink smoke had all but disappeared.

Discarded on the ground were the twelve Tellers who'd been about to shoot her.

Ruckus let her go and rushed toward the same computer console the Sutter had been using. After he inputed something Delaney couldn't follow, the chair holding the Zane emitted a loud beep.

The metal bands holding him down slid away, disappearing into the arms, legs, and sides of the black metal chair, exposing raw welts and cuts on his wrists from his struggles.

Trystan heaved himself out of the chair, wavering. Once he'd gotten his balance, he pushed back the Ander, grabbing on to Delaney. His hold was hard enough that she almost had trouble breathing a second time, but he let go before that became an actual issue.

"What the hell was all that about?" he demanded, pulling away enough to openly glare down at her. "If the Ander hadn't shown up just in time, my father would have shot you for the things you'd said to him! It was reckless, and uncalled—"

"Actually," she cut him off, and then quickly disentangled herself from his hold. She'd planted the gorud between two of the main computer towers, and went to retrieve it. In order to fit, she'd had to squeeze it in at an angle, but even with the device on its side, what had just happened should be clear on camera.

Before explaining to them what she was doing, she settled the gorud back on her head and sent a message to Fawna, holding her breath while she waited for a reply.

"Delaney—" Ruckus sighed when she held up a finger, silencing him.

As planned. It was a brief return message, but it was all Fawna had to say for an all-consuming relief to sweep through Delaney.

She dropped her hands to her knees and let out a breath, wincing when it caused her shoulder—and really, the rest of her as well—to twinge in pain. When she straightened again, the guys were staring at her, their impatience clear.

Right.

"We got it all on tape," she told them, still trying to catch her breath after all of *that*. "I had Fawna record everything after I entered the room. It's on record."

"Proof." Ruckus looked a bit awed.

"But how much of it?" Trystan asked. "How much did you catch?"

"Enough, hopefully." She shook her head and planted her hands on her hips. "We aren't done, though. Varasow is still under attack, and we need—"

"To stop my father," he finished for her with a growl. Without waiting, he headed toward the door, propelling himself forward. "Leave him to me. This ends tonight."

She sent Ruckus a pointed look, and then the two of them rushed after him. They caught him at the entrance, just in time to push through into the hall with him. The three Tellers she'd shot earlier were still there, unconscious, and she paid them little mind as she stepped over their bodies.

"Do you even know where you're going?" she demanded when the Zane didn't say anything.

"He'll retreat to the hangar," Trystan explained, clearly positive in his assumption. "Board a ship and go. He isn't aware that you recorded his confession. For now he'll attempt to carry out his plan."

"Which is?" Ruckus asked, moving briskly at their sides. He had his shing out, and was probably conveying all of this to Sanzie and the others.

"Arrive at the Vakar palace just in time to save the day." Trystan clenched his hands into tight fists at his sides. If flexing his wrists like that hurt, he didn't show it, though Delaney couldn't imagine how it wouldn't. Some of his wounds were bleeding.

"We don't have enough men on the ground to cut him off," Ruckus stated. "If the Rex makes it to a ship—"

"We won't be able to stop him." The Zane nodded curtly. "I'm aware."

"He got a head start." Delaney didn't want to be the bearer of bad news, but she wasn't really sure how they hoped to catch up in time. "There's also the issue that he's got a ton of Tellers with him, and we don't."

"Survivors?" Trystan directed his question to the Ander.

"We're down two."

"Brilliant."

"We should focus on destroying Clean Slate," Delaney said, waiting until they'd both paused to frown at her. Under different circumstances, she might have teased them over the fact that they wore the exact same expression and had the same pissed-off military poses. As it were, she kept that little gem to herself.

"Think about it," she continued. "We're too late to stop the Rex from leaving. But we can ensure no one gets to use this device on anyone else."

Trystan shifted angrily on his feet. "My father almost killed you. He almost turned me into a slave. I let him get away now, and he's only going to try it again. Proof be damned. You really think he's going to let the rest of the world stop him? No, I can still—"

She grabbed his arm when he went to turn away, tightening her grip when he would have stubbornly yanked himself out of her hold.

"Protect the people." She held his gaze, unwavering. She'd caught that part of his speech to his father. Hoped he understood she was referencing it now, using it as a reminder. "Do your job, Zane."

He let out a low growl in the back of his throat and tore his gaze from hers, only to look back a second later. His shoulders were still stiff, and there was so much rage coming off him, she could practically taste it. But when he spoke, all of that was contained, tucked beneath the icy demeanor he'd always been so perfect at projecting.

"Of course, Lissa," he said coolly, and then began heading back the way they'd come. It didn't take long, since they hadn't gotten very far in the first place, and the room was exactly as they'd left it, complete with downed Teller bodies everywhere.

"Any chance they're going to wake up soon?" Delaney asked, toeing one of them in the side as she passed. She'd had more than enough surprises for one day. Having enemy Tellers suddenly spring out of a deep sleep and attack *so* wasn't in her cards.

"That smoke is lethal without the antidote. I didn't see another way to stop them all at once," Ruckus confessed.

Not wanting to dwell on that, Delaney turned away, easing up to Trystan's side where he was already typing on one of the main computers. The keyboard didn't look anything like the ones on Earth, and she hardly recognized the symbols, so she didn't bother trying to be useful there. The weird sentences and patterns flowing across the screen were just as foreign.

"I'm hacking into the mainframe," he explained, understanding she'd want to know without her having to ask. "The device has been kept on a different server, cut off from the castle's main systems, so I wasn't able to do this remotely."

Ruckus, who'd been watching the attack on Varasow, which was still playing on the screen, turned away. He went to the computer at the other side of the chair, flicking his fingers over the keys. After a moment he cursed and pulled back.

"We've been cut off from the outside," he said. "All communications are down."

Delaney tapped the button at the side of the gorud she was still wearing. The lights hadn't gone away, so she'd been under the impression everything was still running smoothly. Now she sent the question to Fawna, waiting to see if they'd lost the connection to her as well.

Still here, played across the screen over her eye, and she glanced between the two of them.

"We've still got Fawna."

"Unless the lovely pilot can access these particular computers," Trystan stated, not breaking from his work, "I don't see how that's very helpful."

"What about the others?" Delaney asked Ruckus. "We're still getting feedback from them, right?"

"Looks like," he replied, checking his shing.

"We should be able to meet up with them soon, Ander." Trystan smirked devilishly and pressed one last button before leaning back to stare at the screen. "Done."

"With?"

"I've just written in a virus to ensure all data on the Clean Slate project is unrecoverable. It should only be a few minutes before everything is erased for good."

"Just like that?" Delaney had to admit, she'd expected it to be a bit more complex.

He scowled. "I'll have you know this was actually quite difficult. I just happen to be very skilled."

"We still have a problem," Ruckus said. There was a dire look on his face that neither of them liked seeing. "Sanzie was unable to get a direct message to the Basilissa before outside communications were shut down."

"I don't see why that matters." Trystan motioned to the screen playing the attack. "Clearly she's aware now."

"Yeah, but . . ." Delaney shook her head. "That means she doesn't know the Rex is coming . . ."

"Specifically to kill her." Trystan caught on, and swore for the millionth time that hour alone.

CHAPTER 25

'll tell the others to get to the garage," Ruckus told them as they entered the hallway. They'd waited to be sure the data on the computer had been erased, and were now on the move again. "We'll meet them there and head to the ship as fast as possible. We might still be able to make it to the Basilissa before the Rex does, considering how fast my model is."

Before anyone could comment on that, Trystan slowed a step, cocking his head. A second later he grunted and continued at a quicker pace, leading them through the castle determinedly.

"It appears Sanzie is attempting to get the communications systems back online," he explained when Ruckus gave him a pointed look. "If she can, we'll have access to the computer's mainframe again, and the security feed from the cameras."

"Here." Delaney removed the gorud and handed it over. "You know what you're doing with this thing, and you've got a better chance of keeping it safe. I had to get Fawna to help me do something as simple as hit record."

"But it was your idea to do so in the first place," Trystan said, taking the device anyway and slipping it over his head. After adjusting the screen in front of his eye, he tapped the side button and waited a moment before adding, "The pilot is very rude."

"Fawna?" Delaney asked. "What'd she say?"

"Something about returning the gorud to you because I'm a . . ." He made a face, then shook his head curtly. "It doesn't bear repeating."

"If Sanzie can get the block down," Ruckus began, "Fawna should be able to access the mainframe herself and do a wider check of the castle grounds. It'd be nice to know just how many Tellers are still in the building."

"Agreed."

Delaney blinked at both of them, then grinned when they frowned. "Look how much progress we've made. And all it took was the three of us almost dying. About four times."

Trystan let out an annoyed sigh before turning to Ruckus. "I suppose I should thank you for showing up back there."

Ruckus seemed surprised, but he nodded, a clear indicator that this was the only response he was going to give the Zane.

"How are you?" Delaney asked, carefully checking around a corner as they reached it.

"You mean considering my father just tried to wipe my memories?" Trystan shrugged.

"It's all right to be upset about it," she sent through their fittings, knowing she'd only make him feel more uncomfortable if she did so out loud in front of Ruckus. *"What he was willing to do to you . . . That was absolutely awful. If it'd been my dad trying to do that to me, I'd be a mess right now."*

Trystan hesitated, and just when it seemed like he might respond, a light on the gorud flashed, distracting him from whatever he'd been about to say.

"Sanzie's done it," Ruckus said, staring at his shing. "She's trying to access the cameras now."

"I'm already on it." Trystan's eyes flickered from right to left as he half focused on the screen. He kept his pacing even and continued to lead them without difficulty as he did, obviously not having a problem multitasking. "The next two halls are empty. We should be able to make it straight to the garage without issue."

"That's because most of the Tellers have already gone, or are on their way, to Varasow." Delaney hated that she was actually worried about Tilda. After everything the woman had put her through, she'd kind of hoped she'd hold more animosity toward her, and yet . . . "How much farther to the garage?"

"Just around the corner."

Sanzie met them at the end of the hall, before the entrance to the garage. As soon as she spotted them, she disappeared into the room, and they picked up the pace, finding her working the controls for the large door at the other end.

"We're all set to go," she told them as they approached. "Gibus stored what information was on the computer about the Clean Slate project on a shing, then we destroyed the source."

"He what?" Ruckus swore under his breath.

"In case there's a way to reverse the process," Sanzie said, coming to the Sutter's defense, and for a moment the two of them glared at each other before Trystan cleared his throat.

"We need to get going. The Lissa and Ander stay with me," he told the Sworn. "Your group leaves first. Head straight for the ship."

"Yes, Zane." She nodded once in a partial bow and then turned on her heel.

Verus and Gibus were already in the back of one of the cars, and Sanzie rounded to the driver's side and practically jumped in. Before she even had the door fully closed, they were speeding off toward the garage exit. The metal gate was still down, but it began to lift as they approached.

"This way." Trystan urged them forward to the second car, which was already running. It was sleek and silver, and would be cramped with the three of them, but it appeared to be fast.

At the side of the vehicle, the Zane tossed open the door, waiting for Ruckus to get into the back seat.

Delaney slid into the passenger seat without much thought, realizing what she'd done a second too late. It wasn't like she'd actively chosen to sit next to one of them over the other. She just preferred the front of the car.

Ignoring the look Ruckus sent her, she tried to focus on what Trystan was doing instead as he entered the vehicle and began activating the controls with his nimble fingers. He worked quickly, having their destination programmed in and the car shooting forward in under a few seconds.

Just as they started moving, a handful of Tellers swarmed the garage, coming from the castle. Trystan glanced at them in the mirror, but he didn't hesitate. He grabbed the controls and angled their vehicle through the still-parked cars, straight for the now open exit doors.

"Looks like they caught up with us," Ruckus stated.

Of course the Rex was going to try to stop them from going after him. She glanced at the gorud. If anything happened to that before they got it to Fawna, all the evidence she'd just recorded would be gone.

"Hold on," Trystan suddenly warned, then pressed a triangular button on the console. There was a loud buzzing right before an icy-blue force field formed over the outside of the vehicle.

Trystan swore, drawing their attention upward, and when Ruckus saw his narrowed gaze, he twisted around to check out the back.

Two cars were following, preparing to attack.

"Battle vehicles," Trystan explained to Delaney, who was also staring back at their pursuers. "They come with built-in herri-fritzes on the sides that let off larger, faster, and therefore more effective rounds than the smaller handheld fritz weapons."

"The force field won't hold for long!" Ruckus warned.

Trystan twisted the car to the right, then the left, just as one of the enemy cars sped up to their side. The move had him slamming their vehicle into that one, and as soon as he'd righted the car, he did it again. Their force field buzzed upon contact, ripping paint from the other car and shocking it in defense every time they touched. By the third impact, the momentum was enough to send the enemy car flying off the road.

Delaney watched as it flipped, then rolled behind them, so that the second car had to jerk to the side to avoid a collision. As soon as it'd straightened out, however, the car started firing its herri once more.

One of the shots clipped the side of their vehicle, going straight through the force field, which flickered out before returning, weaker this time.

"We aren't going to make it!" Ruckus said.

"Yes," the Zane growled stubbornly, "we are!"

"Can Fawna meet us?" Delaney suggested, gripping the headrest tightly as the Zane took another sharp turn.

Ruckus cocked his head, clearly sending a message, and then clenched his jaw a second later. "The others are boarding right now. She can't move until they're safely inside."

As if in reply, another zee smacked the back of their car, breaking through the force field. The zee connected with the metal bumper, tearing chunks away in the process. The glass of the back window cracked.

Bits and shards rained down, and Ruckus hissed as a few cut through his bare arms.

"Are you okay?" Delaney was about to hoist herself into the back seat, but he lifted a hand to stave her off.

"Don't come back here; there's too much glass."

"Update, Ander!" the Zane demanded, his eyes still scanning ahead. "Brace!"

No sooner had the warning been delivered, another zee shot straight through the opening where the window had been. It sailed between the front seats, and ended up slamming directly into the side control panel. Sparks flew and there was a burst of bright light.

When Delaney opened her eyes, the Zane was putting out a small fire with his bare hand, hissing upon contact with the flames. Eventually he extinguished it, so that the only remainder was a smoky tendril twisting out of the now destroyed controls.

Fortunately, it hadn't fried the entire system—they were still driving—but the rest of the force field that had somehow held up around the front and sides of their vehicle was gone.

"Incoming!" Trystan yelled.

Ruckus shifted and pulled his left arm free, twisting so he could take aim out the back. He planted his finger on the trigger of his fritz and began firing randomly.

"Not what I meant!" the Zane said, causing Ruckus to frown.

A high-pitched whistle sounded above them a second before a large object dropped from the sky, plummeting downward over the enemy car. They swerved in a desperate attempt to avoid getting hit, but there was no escaping one of those.

The missile hit the side of the car and exploded, the whole thing going up in a burst of white and yellow bright enough to blind someone. Delaney ducked and squeezed her eyes shut a second time, the residual blast rushing through the window, practically shoving her off the seat and out onto the ground.

When everything settled again, she risked a look back: She saw billowing smoke and the charred remains of the enemy car.

Trystan brought them to a stop, jerking them a second time with how quickly he slammed on the brakes. He was out and yanking open the passenger door without explanation, though the sight of the ship currently hovering nearby was answer enough.

Ruckus was only a step behind as the Zane tugged Delaney out of the vehicle and raced across the road, to the field where Fawna was lowering the ship for them.

The stairs dropped right as they reached the ship, and they rushed on, greeted by Sanzie in the cargo hold.

"We need to broadcast the video footage from that"—Delaney waved at the gorud while the doors sealed shut behind them—"now. Preferably everywhere."

"The Ander and I can access Vakar and Kint media," Trystan said, already moving toward the door.

"Tell Fawna to go as fast as she can," Ruckus ordered Sanzie as he went to follow the Zane, touching the side of her arm gently as he passed. Without waiting for a response, the two men disappeared around the corner, leaving the Sworn and Delaney alone in the loading bay.

Sanzie stared off after the guys, an odd expression on her face.

They'd gone off together without hesitation, a far cry from how they usually were.

"Thank you for finding us earlier, Lissa," Sanzie said. She waited until she had her attention before adding, "And for getting the Zane."

"You don't have to thank me. I wouldn't have just left him behind." Delaney wasn't sure why she felt the need to clarify that, especially since the Sworn knew that well enough already. Maybe Sanzie had noticed how badly Delaney had wanted to stay with Ruckus when she'd found them earlier.

She'd also seen them kiss after. . . .

Just because they managed to get proof of the Rex's crimes against Xenith didn't mean they were in the clear. Delaney didn't have time to dwell on that kiss with Ruckus, what it could mean or how she felt about it.

"Come on," she said, motioning to the opposite hallway, which would lead them to the cockpit. "Hopefully we can still make it before the Rex reaches the Basilissa."

CHAPTER 26

The palace was already under heavy fire by the time they arrived, and Fawna struggled to get the ship close enough to the back hangar of the palace. She'd already told them she wouldn't be able to actually land, so they were getting ready to rush out of the loading bay as fast as possible.

"Are you sure he can do it?" Sanzie asked Ruckus, using her hand to support herself against the wall as the ship lurched for the tenth time in the past few minutes.

"The Zane got the proper Kint channels open, and Gibus understands Vakar systems better than I do. He'll transfer the files from the gorud; it's really just a matter of how long it'll take him to do so."

Apparently, the data was fairly hefty, and needed to be carefully copied from the gorud, since acting as an actual video camera hadn't really been its intended purpose. The record button had only been added so users could take clips of blueprints and security feeds and transfer them onto their shings for shared access.

Not film a ten-minute confession.

The sooner they could get it out there, the better, but they had no way of knowing exactly how long it would take.

"Fawna says she's lowering us into the hangar now," Ruckus told them, reaching forward to hit the control panel for the doors. A gust of wind shot through the slowly opening gap, making it hard to hear his next comment. "Get ready to jump!"

The four of them moved closer together, and Delaney ended up between Ruckus and Trystan, her arms bumping against their sides as the ship descended. Since this wasn't a frequently used section of the palace, and Fawna had been able to give the proper code to the Tellers who controlled the hangar's access, it didn't look like they'd be met with any hostility.

"Now!" Ruckus ordered once the ground was only ten or so feet beneath them. He grabbed Delaney's hand and jumped with her. A second later the other two followed.

It was hard not to notice the Zane staring at their clasped hands, his gaze lingering even when Ruckus let go to ready his fritz. When Trystan glanced up and found her watching, she quickly looked away.

As soon as Delaney, Trystan, Ruckus, and Sanzie were on the ground, Fawna lifted back into the air with Gibus and Verus still in tow. The plan was that the Sutter would work on getting out the broadcast while they went to find the Basilissa and the Rex.

"Come on." Ruckus gripped his fritz and took the lead, exiting into the hall and moving left without hesitation. Since his fitting was connected to the royal family, he was able to contact Tilda, and knowing that was the plan, the others followed silently.

"Seems like they haven't broken in yet," Trystan noted, sticking close to Delaney while Ruckus and Sanzie slipped ahead.

Delaney watched the Sworn lean toward the Ander; she could tell Sanzie was speaking, but she couldn't make out the words, though they were only a few paces behind. It was good that she'd gotten a chance to clear the air with Sanzie before all of this, no matter how brief their talk had been, but she still needed to figure things out with Ruckus.

"Delaney?"

She glanced at the Zane, recalling what he'd just said. Outside, they could hear crashes and shouts, coupled with the occasional explosion. It was obvious the Tars were trying hard to get into the palace, but he was right: It didn't seem like they'd succeeded yet.

"Hopefully we get to Tilda before they do," she said. Then he called ahead to ask, "Tilda is still secure, right?"

"Yes," Ruckus confirmed a moment later, probably having contacted the Basilissa to be sure. "She's waiting for us in a safe location. We just need to keep moving."

Their group slipped into silence the rest of the way. Right now getting to Tilda was the main goal. Just because they'd yet to see the enemy didn't mean there wasn't the chance the Rex was already inside, looking for her himself.

Finally they turned into what appeared to be a dead end and then came to a stop. There was a window overlooking the back of the palace, and a single small table pressed against the right wall.

Ruckus reached for the drawer there, twisting the golden knob to the right twice, and then once to the left, before his fingers dipped beneath it. There was a soft click, and he stepped back.

A section of the wall shifted free from the rest, retreating half an inch inward before sliding off to the left. As it disappeared, it exposed a fairly empty room within. There was a single chair in the corner and a monitor attached to the center of the wall. What appeared to be a news feed was playing across the screen, showing the attack still taking place in the city.

Tilda and two Vakar Tellers were the only occupants, and as soon as they spotted Ruckus they rushed toward them.

"Where's Shellus?" Delaney asked, noting he wasn't with them.

"After making sure I was secure," Tilda explained, "he went to help defend the front entrance."

"We need to get you to safety, Basilissa," the Ander told her, already motioning her toward the other end of the hall.

"I'm not going to hide out while they break down my doors," she argued, though she moved after him, same as the rest of them. "While my people are dying in the streets. I need to—"

"You've already called for reinforcements, I presume?" Trystan cut her off, lifting a fine brow when she turned to glare at him.

"Yes, but some of them are traveling from opposite coasts. It could take them hours to arrive. Something needs to be done in the immediate future."

"And you have an idea for that?" he asked. "A suggestion?"

She obviously didn't.

Delaney stepped in, not wanting to deal with a royal argument at a time like this. "Okay, I think the point's been made. Tilda, we need to keep you safe. The Rex intends to kill you."

"What could he possibly hope to gain from that?" she asked. "Vakar won't follow him. He can try to take my people, will maybe even be successful where Varasow is concerned, but he'll never get my throne. Especially if he murders me."

"We're pretty sure he plans on framing the Tars for that," Delaney explained. "On the outside, he's got his Kints fighting alongside your Tellers. As far as the populace will be concerned, he came to your rescue in your greatest time of need, but was too late to actually save you."

"They'd hardly fall for it overnight," Trystan added, obviously disgusted by the notion, "but you have to admit, it would be a solid plan."

"Would be?" The Basilissa listened intently as they explained what Delaney had recorded back in Carnage. They were only halfway through the story when the sound of zee fire filled the opposite corridor.

Looked like the Tars had finally broken into the palace.

"You two," Ruckus said, addressing the Vakar Tellers, "stay with the Basilissa." Then to Tilda: "You and Delaney, head to the maze tunnels. Even if someone manages to follow, they'll never be able to sort their way through that. Once there, wait for us."

"Us?" Trystan scowled. "I'm not leaving Delaney alone."

The sounds got closer, followed by shouts.

"We don't have time to debate this," Ruckus insisted. "You and I need to cut them off before they spot the Basilissa and inform the Rex of her location. That's got to be why they're this deep into the palace when the majority of the fighting is still going on outside. Unless you want Delaney to come do that with us?"

Trystan opened his mouth to argue, but Delaney stopped him with a hand at his elbow.

"It's fine," she said. "I'll keep Tilda safe; you guys keep them off our trail. We're a team, remember?" Logically, she agreed this was their best play: Split up to keep the Basilissa safe. But it wasn't any easier for her to let them walk away, knowing they'd be going to fight and she wouldn't be there to help.

"I'll remain with the Lissa, Zane," Sanzie put in when he didn't respond fast enough.

"You're injured," he pointed out.

"Just some bruising. It's nothing that will stop me from doing my job."

Obviously, he still didn't like this plan, but he nodded anyway. As soon as he'd turned, he seemed to think better of it, spinning back on his heel to reach for Delaney and draw her in. His lips pressed lightly to her forehead, lingered just a little too long.

"Zane." Ruckus sounded angry, but he didn't try to pull them apart.

"Be careful," Trystan told her.

"You too." She glanced up at him, and then over to Ruckus, who was watching their exchange with an enigmatic expression.

"Don't do anything stupid, right?" she asked through their fittings.

After a brief pause, Ruckus gave a single curt nod to her and then flicked a wrist at the Zane. "Let's go."

For a moment Delaney watched them head away, wrestling with the sinking feeling it caused. She didn't like the idea of being separated from them any more than they did. Didn't like the added worry it caused.

"They're highly trained," Tilda said, and Delaney was embarrassed to find her and the others all looking at her. Watching her stare after Trystan and Ruckus. "They can take care of themselves."

"Of course," she agreed, once she'd processed the Basilissa's words. Clearing her throat, she deliberately turned to face the other direction.

"We're heading to the same location we stayed in the last time the palace was under attack," Tilda told her the second they'd started back into motion. "Do you remember?"

"Kind of hard to forget." The halls even seemed familiar as they moved through them. Once they made it to the entrance, they'd enter a square room with a door on each of the four walls. Every side would appear identical, with no indication as to which one led to the center where the safe room actually was. Only the most highly stationed Tellers knew how to navigate through it, along with the Ander and the royal family.

If Delaney wasn't mistaken, they had just entered the hallway where Trystan had stopped Ruckus and her the first time. The group moved swiftly, focused on making it to the door at the other end.

Maybe that was why none of them noticed the open door to their right until a string of zees shot out.

Delaney sucked in a breath as the two Vakar Tellers dropped, and quickly drew her own weapon up toward the opening, shooting without hesitation as three Kint Tellers emerged. She moved to step in front of the Basilissa at the same time Sanzie was repositioning herself in front of Delaney.

The Sworn took out two of the Tellers before a zee hit her in the side and she jolted, dropping to one knee from the force of it.

Delaney aimed and fired as she rushed forward, shooting the remaining Teller before he could get another shot in at the Sworn. She glanced down at Sanzie, sure to keep her fritz up and aimed at the open room in case anyone else was in there.

"Crap." Her eyes widened when she noticed all the blood seeping through the material of Sanzie's uniform. "That looks—"

"Worse than it is," Sanzie cut her off, pressing her palms against the wound.

"You aren't fooling anyone." The Basilissa eased down next to the Sworn, gently moving her hands aside to check.

Delaney hesitated, knowing they weren't yet safe but wanting to see for herself that Sanzie was going to be all right. Realizing she couldn't waste more time, she forced her attention back to the open room, moving toward the doorway to check inside.

It was just a small space, maybe a storage closest or something, and from her view in the hall, it didn't seem like there was anyone else within. Tentatively, Delaney took a step closer, eyes scanning the far corners, where stacks of boxes took up space. Just as she was about to call it all clear, a hand shot out from the side, latched onto the wrist with her fritz, and yanked.

Delaney stumbled, off-balance, and slammed forward into a solid body. She was pulled into the room and shoved around so she could face the hall. A second later she felt the cold press of metal against her forehead, and froze.

"I knew you couldn't stay away, Miss Grace." The words were hissed directly over her head, and though she knew who she'd find there, she still felt her heart plummet when she risked glancing up.

Directly at the Rex.

"And you brought me the Basilissa." He leered at Tilda, who was standing just outside the door now, her eyes wide. "How very helpful of you."

"Go," Delaney said. At least if Tilda got to the end of the hall, she'd stand a chance of disappearing into the maze.

"Take a single step," the Rex growled, tightening an arm around Delaney's waist and pressing the end of his fritz more firmly against her forehead pointedly, "and I shoot her. You've already got me to contend with; I doubt you also want to make an enemy of my son."

"Don't listen to him. Trystan will understand." Delaney wasn't really sure she believed that herself, to be honest, but she wasn't stupid. "He'll shoot me anyway," she added, changing tactics, but he slammed the end of his fritz against her skull, affectively shutting her up.

"You're wasting your time, Rex," Tilda said, holding up both hands. "Soon everyone is going to know you're behind this attack; killing us won't stop that."

"What are you talking about?" He grunted. "The rest of my Kint reinforcements will arrive long before your Vakar do. They'll fight the Tars, and the world will see me as a just ruler, more than an appropriate candidate for taking your late husband's place."

"And Trystan?" Delaney couldn't help the rush of fear for the Zane.

"Has proven to be a failure, more unworthy of being Zane than I imagined, let alone a king. And after this year's events? I've imagined it quite a bit. If only I'd had another son, but of course, Trystan's mother was too weak for that. Useless."

A growl came from the hall, and a second later Sanzie had twisted around on the ground to aim through the doorway, firing off a zee before anyone could react. It was aimed high enough that there was no chance it would accidentally hit Delaney. But pulling the trigger even that once with her injury seemed to take a lot out of the Sworn.

She slumped back against the Basilissa's legs almost immediately after.

The shot caused the Rex to retreat a step, distracting him enough that the press of the fritz on Delaney's forehead eased up.

Without hesitation, she pulled back her elbow and jammed it into his side. The shock, more than anything, had his arm loosening around her waist, and she dropped to her knees just as his finger tightened around the trigger.

She felt the burst of heat overhead, knew that she'd just barely avoided being shot. Not having the time to dwell on that fact, she forced herself into further action. Twisting onto her butt, she brought her feet together and kicked out, landing a blow to the Rex's gut.

He'd been about to aim for her again, but he ended up stumbling backward, the fritz suddenly pointed up at the ceiling.

She leaped for him before he could regain his footing, shoving him so that he hit the wall with a resounding thud that sent the contents of a metal shelf clanking. She'd barely had enough time to position her finger over the trigger of her own weapon before he'd recovered.

The Rex stretched out his leg and brought it around, knocking her off her feet. As she fell, he stood, turning so that his back was to her. He grabbed her left arm, pulling it over his shoulder, and then propelled her over him like she was a bag of flour.

Her body slammed into the ground, with him still gripping her wrist, and in one swift motion, he twisted, pulling her shoulder from its socket.

Delaney saw blinding white light, the pain excruciating, and might have even momentarily blacked out. When he let go, her arm dropped uselessly at her side, the burning made worse when she hit the ground, jarring the injury further. Unable to use the hand with the fritz, she panicked, quickly searching the room for any other kind of weapon as she forced herself to sit up and move away from the hovering Rex.

He looked on as she did, clearly finding her a non-threat, taking his time reactivating his fritz and adjusting the settings.

"I was really looking forward to having my son present to watch you die, Miss Grace." He sighed heavily, like it was a real letdown that she'd ruined this for him. "But I suppose gifting him your corpse will have to do."

Suddenly Tilda was there, flinging herself at the Rex in a blur of motion, momentarily blocking Delaney's body from his line of fire.

It lasted only long enough for Delaney to struggle to her feet before she watched as the Basilissa's body jolted and stilled.

A second later Delaney's good arm came up instinctually to catch Tilda as she stumbled back. They both dropped to the ground, her doing her best to keep the Basilissa from taking much of the impact.

There was a wound at the center of Tilda's abdomen, blood already leaking through the silky green material of her dress.

"What did you do?" Delaney didn't bother keeping the horror from her tone. Her uninjured arm was keeping the Basilissa in place against her chest, but she couldn't even move the other to try to help stanch the blood flow.

"I couldn't save Olena. . . ." Tilda's voice was weak, but the corner of her mouth turned up slightly. She let out a stuttered breath, and then the fingers over her wound noticeably relaxed a split second before her entire body did.

Delaney blinked down in shock, her arm tightening around the Basilissa's shoulders as if that might somehow help. It'd happened so fast, her mind was still racing to put all the pieces together. Because there was no way Tilda had just sacrificed herself in order to protect Delaney, a human.

"She couldn't save you, either." The Rex's sneer drew her attention from the deceased Basilissa. There were scratch marks down the right side of his face, huge welts already puffy and dripping crimson drops of blood. Unfortunately, he only seemed to be more pissed than he'd been a moment prior.

As much as she didn't want to, Delaney forced herself to prepare to abandon Tilda's body, searching for anything she could use to defend herself. Her eyes landed on a silver bucket only a foot away, and before she could overthink, she grabbed it and spun around, tossing it at the Rex with all the strength she could muster.

Which was arguably not much, but the object flying at his head caught him off guard enough for her to jump to her feet and dive behind one of the metal shelves. She pressed her good shoulder against it and shoved, watching as it toppled toward him.

He noticed it too early for it to be a real threat, stepping out of the way so that it clattered uselessly to the ground.

She'd gotten herself caught in a corner, with him and the fallen shelf blocking her path to the door. Stepping to the right brought her closer to the exit, but she'd still have to leap over the shelf, which would involve giving the Rex her back.

So not happening.

As her mind scrambled to come up with a way out, the Rex recovered from her pathetic attacks. Out of the corner of her eye, she saw him raise his fritz, and by then it was already too late.

The shot hit her in the right thigh, the momentum forcing her back against the wall for the millionth time that day alone. She barely felt the impact, however, too distracted by the searing pain caused by the zee. She'd never taken a direct hit before, and the sensation was excruciating, easily bringing her to her knees.

Instinctually, her hand pressed against the wound, where blood was already starting to seep out of her.

"Originally," the Rex said, taking a menacing step closer, "I planned on making this quick, but after all the trouble you've caused, you no longer deserve that mercy."

The pain in her thigh was overshadowing the pain that still pulsed in her shoulder, and she desperately struggled to get her fingers working again. It was her only chance, activating her fritz and shooting him before he could get the kill shot off.

"How dare you come here and think yourself worthy of my son," he stated, and for once she was actually glad that he was so loquacious. He was completely unaware his berating was buying her time. "That *you*, a human, could undo my plans. Really, Miss Grace, you're hardly that clever at all."

Finally her fingers twitched and she almost let a sound of joy slip past her lips. Her fritz appeared in her hand just as the Rex lifted his own, and she gritted her teeth against the pain and swung her arm around in front of her, pulling the trigger.

She hadn't had time to aim properly, so her shot ended up going through his left arm. The hit caused him to jerk, throwing him off by a few inches so that when he fired, the zee ended up missing her heart, his intended target.

Not that it felt any better where it did land.

The zee pierced her flesh, only a few centimeters from her dislocated shoulder. If she hadn't already used the last of her energy trying to shoot him that one time, she certainly would have lost it all now. Her arm dropped and she sagged back against the wall, her vision blurring. She could just make out that the fingers pressed to her thigh were stained red, as was the front of her shirt over where the new zee wound was.

She'd never suffered from blood loss before, but it wasn't hard to figure that was what was happening to her now. Another thing that didn't matter, because through her blurry vision she could make out the Rex furiously cursing her.

His next move seemed to come in slow motion, giving her ample time to think about how stupid she'd been taking him on in the first place. And how much she didn't really regret it, not if it meant the others had enough time to get that damning video broadcast. As badly as she didn't want to die, she'd rather he didn't get away with all the horrible things he'd done.

And at least her death would mean he'd no longer have anything to use against either Trystan or Ruckus.

Thinking about them hurt in a different way, and her breath caught in her throat. She wished there was something else she could do, but she didn't even have the energy left to open her fitting and send a message.

After what felt like a week, the Rex had his fritz on her one final time, and she debated whether or not she wanted to close her eyes, look away. Stubbornly, she kept them open, and lifted her chin, ignoring how even that tiny motion sent her whole body screaming in agony. How he seemed to flicker in and out as she struggled to fight off unconsciousness.

Yup, definitely suffering from blood loss.

Which is why she thought she might be seeing things when another blurry figure suddenly appeared in the doorway. The world winked in and out, and when she was able to focus again, it was to find Trystan standing next to his father, a hand pressed against his side. She frowned, and it took her a moment to figure out that he was holding a knife there.

CHAPTER 27

Trystan had expected for them to be safe in the maze rooms, so Sanzie's unconscious body in the middle of the hallway had sent him into a panic.

When he'd rushed toward the room, and seen Delaney bleeding out, the fritz aimed at her head, he'd reacted without thought. The lizard-shaped knife came easily out of its hiding place in his boot, felt hot in his palm as he shifted it in his hold. One second he was in the doorway, and the next he had one hand wrapped around his father's neck, the other gripping the knife he'd just buried in the Rex's side.

He'd just stabbed his father.

He'd. Just. *Stabbed.* His father.

Sure, he'd secretly fantasized about doing something just like this before, but that was all it'd been. A daydream. This was . . . He had to glance down at the handle, prove this was real, that it'd really happened.

It was the Rex's sudden movement that pulled him out of his shock.

Trystan's hand was still at his father's neck, but that did nothing to stop the Rex from lifting the fritz. Realizing that the Rex was going to try to shoot Delaney again, despite the fact that there was a knife between his ribs, the Zane quickly adjusted their positions. The Rex ended up shooting the wall across from the door, with Trystan now safely blocking her from his father's view.

"Enough," he growled when the Rex struggled to get loose.

"'The Crown before the Common,'" his father sneered, grabbing at Trystan's elbow. He tried to shove his arm, and therefore the knife, away, but only managed to budge both a centimeter at best.

It'd been a long time since either had bothered testing who was strongest. Since forcibly taking over had never seemed a legitimate solution in Trystan's mind, he'd never considered who had more brute strength, especially when all his memories involved his father's heavy hand.

Now, however, he used all his energy to keep the knife buried, catching the Rex's furious look. Trystan leaned forward so his father wouldn't miss his next words. Wanting him to understand. For once.

"She is my crown."

The Rex didn't bother verbally replying to that. Instead he pulled his arm back, and it was easy enough for Trystan to figure out that he was going to turn the weapon on him now.

Unceremoniously, he yanked the knife free of his father's side, grabbing the Rex's wrist so that he could redirect the fritz away from his head. That left his hand safely off his father's neck, and without preamble, he drove the four-inch blade straight through it, directly beneath his jawline.

Blood sprayed across Trystan's face as the Rex jerked violently in his hold, but Trystan refused to let go. He couldn't stop thinking about everything his father had done. He'd driven his mother to taking her own life. Had made his childhood a living hell—when he'd bothered paying attention to him. Tried to erase his memory, tried to murder the woman he loved.

Turned that fritz on him.

His father had never cared about anything but power, not the people he was sworn to protect, and certainly not his own flesh and blood. Growing up, he'd gone out of his way to make Trystan feel inferior. Like he was never smart enough, strong enough, dressed well enough. He'd spent his entire life tiptoeing around the Rex, pretending like he wasn't a pawn when that's exactly what he'd always been.

He could see that now. It was in the way he couldn't let a hair stay out of place longer than a heartbeat without feeling panic. In the way he used his size and his station to get what he wanted. The look he turned on people who tried to disobey him.

How he believed, with no uncertain wavering, that he had the right to take Delaney from her home world simply because he was a Zane.

Being the Rex's son had almost cost him everything. But he was done.

Trystan forced himself to meet his father's frantic gaze, watched as the fury there turned to panic and then pure, undiluted fear. Watched as all of that was swept away, replaced with nothingness.

He held on until the Rex's gaze had dimmed, his body had gone lax, and the blood spurting from his neck had turned to just a trickle.

Then, leaving the knife where it was, he let go.

He let it all go.

Someone was calling his name.

Trystan's father's body was lying on the ground, motionless, and a numb feeling rushed through him. He took a moment, staring down at him, waiting for some kind of emotional reaction to flicker through the shock, but nothing came. When he heard the soft voice call for him again, he finally dragged his gaze away and over toward the sound.

Delaney was pressed against the wall, one hand covering her thigh, the other unmoving at her side.

He was kneeling next to her in a matter of seconds, reaching out to inspect her wounds. There was a significant amount of blood loss, but neither fritz shot seemed to be fatal, so long as they hurried and got her medical attention.

"I need to get you to the med wing," he told her, trying to figure out a way to lift her while causing her the least amount of pain.

"Trystan," she struggled to speak, "the Rex . . ."

"I don't care about the Rex."

"I'm sorry."

"Stop it. Save your strength."

"Should we just leave him?"

"I don't care." And he really didn't. The only thing that mattered was making sure she was all right, and she most certainly wasn't currently.

"And Tilda?"

"I'm going to pick you up," he told her. "It's going to hurt."

She cried out when he lifted her, her head dropping against the curve of his shoulder. "Trystan—"

Someone was running down the hall, their steps reaching them and cutting off whatever she'd been about to say. Holding her the way he was, Trystan wasn't able to easily access his fritz, and he was in the process of figuring out how to put her back down gently when the Ander raced around the corner.

The first thing he saw was Sanzie, and Ruckus dropped down next to her, the panic on his face apparent.

"She's all right," Trystan reassured him, watching as he reached to check for a pulse.

"It worked—" At the sound of Trystan's voice, Ruckus finally turned to look into the room, blanching the second he noticed the blood on Delaney.

Trystan tightened the grip around his Lissa. "Grab Sanzie. We have to get them to the med wing."

Surprisingly, Ruckus complied.

DELANEY WINCED AS she adjusted into a more comfortable sitting position on the bed. It'd been hours since the fight with the Rex, and her wounds had already been dealt with, but that didn't stop them from hurting if she moved too suddenly.

The doctors had applied some strange balm to her fritz shots before securely wrapping them in bandages. No stitches or anything, which had admittedly worried her at first, before they'd explained their faster healing medications would work similarly on her human body as they did on theirs. Though the process might not be as swift, she was certainly no longer at risk of bleeding out.

Considering that still meant she'd heal faster than she would have on Earth, she wasn't complaining.

"Easy." Ruckus reached out to help steady her, slowly rising from his perch in the chair next to the bed. Aside from checking in on Sanzie once she'd woken up, he hadn't left Delaney's side.

Neither had Trystan, who was currently blocking the doorway, having a heated conversation with someone she couldn't see.

The palace had been in complete chaos, everyone scrambling to deal with the aftermath of both the attack and the revelations about the Rex. Gibus had successfully hacked into all media stations, both in Vakar and Kint, and had broadcast the footage of Trystan's father on a loop. It was still playing, even, but the news stations had regained control over their outlets and were now delivering the story themselves.

Delaney hadn't bothered watching any of it, though she'd been given the option. There was a screen set in the far wall, and the device looked a lot like a regular television back home, only completely clear. She didn't have the energy to relive what had happened just yet, or, if she was being honest, to see the Rex's face again so soon after witnessing him murder Tilda.

Almost kill her . . .

The voices at the door rose higher, and she tapped Ruckus on the arm as she watched the Zane take a threatening step forward, careful not to actually leave the room.

"Tell him to just let them in," she said. Whoever it was, clearly they weren't going to take no for an answer, and really, she was already too exhausted from everything that had happened. There was so much she needed to sort through and deal with; wondering over who was in the hall wasn't another thing she needed on her mind.

"Are you sure?" Ruckus asked, and once she nodded, called, "Zane. It's fine."

"It is not *fine*," Trystan growled, swiveling his head to glare at the Ander. Until he noticed Delaney's look. Though his jaw remained clenched, and he took a second to adjust his uniform, he ended up stepping aside.

Before any of the people standing in the hall could actually enter, however, Trystan flung an arm out against the doorframe, blocking their path a second time.

"If you upset her, you'll have me to deal with." Warning delivered, he moved away, heading over to take up the empty space on the other side of Delaney's bed.

It took her a second to realize she recognized two out of the three who'd entered. She'd never met them in person, but they'd made a lasting impression.

"Ria and Corodonus," she said, trying to keep her voice firm, but friendly. "Right?"

"Hello, Lissa." Ria bowed her head, and then motioned toward the other man. "This is Remus."

"They're members of the Vakar council," Ruckus told her.

"We've met before," Delaney said, shrugging when he frowned questioningly at her. "Projection meeting in Inkwell."

"Apologies for my actions during our first encounter, Lissa." Ria bowed again.

"She doesn't need you sucking up to her," Trystan stated dryly.

"We're actually here because of what the people need." Corodonus took a step closer to the end of the bed, his eyes on Delaney. "What Vakar needs, now that Tilda Ond is no longer with us."

Even though part of her had expected it, Delaney did not want to continue this conversation. Especially not when she was in a hospital bed, only hours after being shot and threatened. To say she was currently in a delicate emotional place would be an understatement. Making life-altering decisions? Not really a good idea.

But aside from letting Trystan toss them out—and she knew he would, despite the fact that he probably wanted this discussion to happen just as badly as they did—there really wasn't anything she could do to stop them from continuing.

It was nice of Ruckus to try, though.

"You can't be serious?" he snapped. "You're going to do this right now?"

"Vakar is on a precipice," Remus replied tightly, "*right now*. We're still counting the numbers lost during the attack, but the civilian death rate is high. Homes and businesses have been destroyed, and our city is flooded with Kint Tellers and Tars who have yet to turn themselves in or be arrested. On top of that, to be told their Basilissa was lost as well?"

"We need a plan," Corodonus said, "something to give to our people."

"The Lissa is not a dish to be served on a silver platter," Trystan told them.

"No," he agreed, "but she is the Lissa, a role she agreed to." He caught her gaze again, held it. "We're here to know if you intend to honor that agreement, Delaney Grace."

"You aren't asking me to be Lissa," she pointed out.

"You'd be made Basilissa as soon as you're well enough to participate in the ceremony," he confirmed. "We need leadership, and tradition dictates the Lissa is next in line for the throne. I'll admit, it's been a long time since death has been the cause of a Passing; however, speeding this process up is not only necessary, but critical to Vakar's survival."

She would have asked what he meant by that, but the side glance he sent to Trystan was answer enough. They believed, with no one standing in his way, the Zane would choose the same path as his father and attempt to take control of the entire planet. Tilda had thought that as well, so Delaney couldn't really blame them for it.

Hell, she couldn't really blame them for it because it was probably true.

"I don't know how to be a Basilissa. Tilda"—she paused, took a shaky breath—"she never got the chance to teach me what I'd need to know."

"The high council will help you," Ria said. "As I'm sure will the Ander and the Zane."

Trystan grunted.

"Apologies. The soon-to-be-named Rex."

Which only brought to light the second part of what they were asking. Delaney would be expected to not only become Basilissa, but also to marry Trystan, which was . . . She didn't know. She didn't know how she felt about any of this anymore, and that was the real problem.

"You want me to answer you now?" she asked, holding out hope that they'd surprise her and say this was just a prequel to a later conversation they wished to have. A much, *much* later conversation.

"We need to deliver reassurances to the people," Remus replied. "As soon as the video released, and the Tars saw that they'd been manipulated, they stopped attacking. They still need to be dealt with, though. They can't be allowed to get away with what they've done, and the streets are rife with anger toward them. It isn't safe for anyone, and won't be until we can restore some semblance of balance."

"The Kints have been helping you round the Tars up," Trystan reminded them. "I'd hardly say you have no aid. Pressuring Delaney—"

"I'll do it." She was honestly almost as shocked as the rest of them were when the words rushed from her mouth. Still, she was sure to remain stoic, not wanting to let on how jumbled up she felt about both the prospect of staying and the idea of leaving them all to their fate. For now, saying she'd do it seemed like the best option, if only to get them to finally leave her alone and calm the city down.

There'd been enough bloodshed; if hearing they had a new Basilissa would help keep people from outright attacking others, then fine. Like her, they probably just needed time to settle, to come down from the emotional high the day's events had created.

"Delaney—" Trystan began, but she cut him off.

"They're right," she said, chucking her chin out toward the council members. "Vakar needs to be told the situation is being handled, and that there's some form of stabilization happening in their government. So, yeah, tell them I'll do it. Tell them I'll be the next Basilissa."

Ruckus remained silent on her other side, and she tried not to give in to the urge to turn and try to figure out what he was thinking.

The Zane watched her for a moment, his eyes slowly narrowing. For a split second she thought he'd seen through her, knew that she wasn't as certain about this as she was letting on, and was going to call her out on it. But then he simply pulled back, straightening to his full height, and nodded at the council members.

"You have your answer," he said, motioning to the door. "Now leave her be. She needs to rest."

The three of them stood their ground, pointedly turning to Delaney, silently awaiting confirmation—which she finally gave with a sigh and a small wave.

Once they were gone, Trystan turned to fully face her. "Delaney—"

"You were right." She couldn't handle talking about this with him, either. "I really should rest."

He clearly wanted to argue but, like so many times before, dropped the issue instead. "Whatever you need, Lissa."

Ruckus continued to say nothing at all.

"ANDER."

Ruckus stood on the far side of the room, near the open door. At the sound of Trystan's voice, he forced his gaze briefly away from Delaney, only long enough to acknowledge the Zane's presence—with a glare.

"She just fell asleep," he said. "She needs to rest."

"I'm not here to disturb her."

"Then why are you here?"

Trystan canted his head. "Presumably for the same reason you are."

Ruckus wanted to disagree, but what would be the point? He wasn't wrong.

The only reason the Zane had even left Delaney's side in the first place had been because she'd asked him to. She'd wanted him to check on the council, make sure they were doing as they'd promised and helping to calm the city.

She'd been worried for the people. Like a real Lissa would be. Her injuries would heal, were already healing, but if Trystan had been even a few seconds later, his father would have killed her. Ruckus closed his eyes, inhaled slowly. All of this could have been avoided if he'd only left her alone in that club. If he'd stood up to the Basileus and Basilissa when they'd suggested putting Delaney through the Uprising ceremony.

The Zane sighed, the sound bordering on annoyed. "Blaming yourself won't do anything to help the situation. Let your guilt go, Ander. It's useless to everyone, especially to her."

"And you'd know about guilt, wouldn't you?" Ruckus scowled. "This is as much your fault as it is mine."

"There's no need to sugarcoat it," Trystan said. "I'm more to blame here than you. I know it. I've accepted that." He held his gaze. "You seemed upset earlier, when she told the council she'd stay and accept the position of Basilissa."

Ruckus crossed his arms and glanced back into the room, not wanting the Zane to see his true feelings before he could get ahold of them.

Sure, it seemed like Delaney had agreed to stay here, but that brief conversation they'd had about leaving was still at the forefront of his mind. He'd told her he would get her off the planet, no matter what the regents wanted. Even with Tilda dead, he intended to keep that promise. If Delaney wanted to go, he'd make sure she had a way to do so.

"I can accept anything, if it's what she wants," he said quietly, settling into that realization himself. He turned back to the Zane. "After everything I've put her through, respecting her choice is the least I can do. Don't you agree?"

Delaney stirred and then slowly eased up in bed, wincing a little. When both he and Trystan immediately stepped farther into the room, she rolled her eyes and waved them off. "I'm fine. What were you guys talking about that required you to stand practically in the hallway?"

Ruckus shook his head and smiled. "Nothing."

"Do you need the doctor?" Trystan asked.

"I told you, I'm fine. Tell me how it went with the council." Delaney shifted into a more comfortable position as the Zane began to speak, moving her legs over when Ruckus came to perch on the edge of the bed.

He watched the two of them as they talked about the council, like it was any other conversation.

Like it was normal.

CHAPTER 28

Delaney."

She groaned and tried to roll over, annoyed when a strong grip on her shoulder prevented her from doing so. It had to have only been a few minutes ago that she'd fallen asleep, and she really wasn't in the mood to deal with anything or anyone in this particular moment.

Three days ago the Basilissa and the Rex had both been murdered and they'd barely gotten people to calm down, the aftereffects being too great. Announcing that they'd soon have a new Basilissa helped ease some of the fear and the tension in Vakar, but the fact that Kints still freely roamed the streets of Varasow didn't.

Both Trystan and Delaney had made it clear the planet was again at peace, that there was no fear of further attack from either side, and that this time, it had nothing to do with the Rex manipulating or blackmailing their leader into it.

Understandably, however, the fact that there'd been a peace treaty before, and yet the old Rex had still created the Tars in order to continue the bloodshed, made everyone wary.

"Delaney, wake up," Ruckus urged. When she realized it was him, her eyes popped open.

"What's wrong?" She sat up, tossing off the blankets and already getting to her feet before he'd even opened his mouth to answer. Horrible possibilities raced through her mind, especially since the last time he'd woken her up in this palace, they'd been under attack.

"We have to move quickly and quietly," he told her, keeping his voice down. Linking their fingers, he began leading her toward the door to the bedroom she'd been given once she'd been well enough to leave the med wing. "I've instructed the Tellers who usually guard your hall to do a general sweep of the area. It'll only buy us so much time."

"For what?" she asked, even as she allowed him to tug her into the corridor, and to the right. Sure enough, they were alone, a rarity these past few days. Typically, there was always someone else around, whether it was a random Teller or the Zane. "Where's Trystan?"

"Being handled."

"What?" She forced him to an abrupt stop, then felt a rush of guilt when he glanced back at her and rolled his eyes.

"He's fine, Delaney. Gibus is just distracting him, that's all." He took them down another turn, peering around the corner before moving them forward. "We were going to do this yesterday, but when Trystan arrived earlier than expected, he threw the whole plan off. I've accounted for him this time."

"Do what?"

Trystan had only been able to put off returning to Kint for a little over a day before his council had insisted he come home at least long enough to undergo his Passing. While the actual attack had happened in Varasow, his people were just as affected by the events that had taken place. Their king had lied to them, after all.

He'd wanted Delaney to go with him, attend the ceremony, but her council had worried if she left, the people's fragile trust in this peace agreement would waver further.

As the future Basilissa, she'd had to do what was best for her people, and he'd had to do what was best for his. Amazingly, it'd only taken an hour or so to convince Trystan to go without her, with the promise that she'd at least watch the ceremony on their version of the television, like the rest of the world was doing.

They hadn't expected him back until sometime today, but he'd returned yesterday evening, surprising them all.

And apparently ruining whatever Ruckus had planned.

"Fawna has the ship ready to go in the hangar," the Ander told her. "By the time anyone notices we're missing, we'll be in the air and it'll be too late to stop us."

Delaney's fingers tightened around his and he shot her another look over his shoulder.

"Don't worry. This will work," he said.

That was why he'd been so quiet lately. He'd been planning this, planning to keep the promise he'd made her. Get her off planet before she had to go through with becoming the Basilissa.

"But what about . . . when we get there?" That was still a problem. "I wasn't overreacting before. You know they'll come after us."

Or maybe only Trystan would, now that Tilda was gone. Delaney's stomach clenched. Now that Tilda had sacrificed herself to protect her. She was still surprised that the Basilissa had done it, and she had tried to convince herself it'd only been one final "screw you" to the Rex.

She knew better, though.

"Let them." The doors to the hangar were visible at the other end of the hall now, and he picked up the pace. "We'll disappear, travel. Once things calm down here and they get used to having Trystan in charge, they'll stop looking."

"You've thought this through."

"It's all I've been thinking about since you told me what Tilda made you agree to," he said. "Obviously, it isn't ironclad; maybe they won't give up and it's just wishful thinking. But if that's the case, I'm fine with staying in motion. Exploring Earth, with you."

Delaney was still stuck on that first part. Because, truthfully, with everything that had been going on, she *hadn't* thought about what they'd do. At least, not to the lengths he clearly had. She'd always just assumed they'd figure it out eventually, and go from there, but she had been too caught up in taking down the Rex, and then dealing with the aftermath. . . . It hadn't even occurred to her that this was Ruckus's plan when he'd gotten her up a few minutes ago.

Their fight had been on her mind, obviously. Their breakup. How horrible she felt about it and her part in it. She should have told him about the agreement with Tilda right away, not kept it from him until the last minute. And she'd been genuinely worried he wouldn't want to risk betraying his people by helping her escape to Earth, a planet that wasn't even his.

Only . . . it didn't really feel like hers now, either.

They'd entered the hangar, and the sight of his ship waiting for them should have given her a sense of urgency and relief. She felt the first, but not the latter.

Which didn't make sense, because this was what she'd always wanted, right? She'd been dragged back to Xenith against her will, had been thrown into terrible situations with horrible people, and through it all the thought of going back home had kept her sane.

But it hadn't been the only thing to do so, had it?

"Wait." Halfway to the ship, Delaney forced them to a stop, unable to meet his gaze as her mind raced to catch up with what she was feeling.

Going home should make her happy.

Yet all she felt was this twisting knot in her gut. All she could picture was the Basilissa's body, bleeding and lifeless in her arms.

Going now didn't just mean leaving Xenith anymore. If they went on the run, it meant they couldn't contact their friends, either, not without putting everyone at risk. They'd never get to talk to Mariana or Gibus or Fawna or Sanzie again.

Trystan wouldn't hurt them, she knew that. But what about the Vakar council? They were trusting her to help restore their kingdom, to help keep Vakar *Vakar*. They wouldn't easily accept a Kint Rex as their ruler, even if Trystan was the only viable option left to them.

"Delaney." Ruckus took her other hand, tried to tug her forward. "We have to go. Now."

Tilda had thrown herself at the Rex without hesitation, just to protect her. She'd sacrificed her life, risked everything she cared about, for Delaney. The only thing she'd had left was Vakar, and she'd entrusted that to a girl she hardly knew, who'd come from another planet.

"I can't," she whispered, the realization hitting her just as hard as it apparently did him, though Ruckus was the only one of them to openly flinch.

"What do you mean?" He tightened his hold, pulled her close so they were only half a foot apart. "If this is because you feel guilty, don't. You don't owe this planet anything, Delaney."

"They're counting on me," she pointed out.

"They created their own problems," he said. "Let them sort it out. We can go—right now. No one can stop us. This was never what you wanted."

"No, it wasn't," she agreed. But before he could feel relief, she forced out, "Before."

He pulled back as if she'd slapped him.

"What do I have to return to?" she asked, trying to make herself understand as much as make him. Having only come to this realization herself moments ago, she was still struggling with it. "I've never known what I wanted to do with my life. My parents are so busy, I see them maybe once or twice a year, and even when I do, they may as well be strangers. Not that it matters, because if I go back, I'll have to leave those things behind anyway. To run. Again."

He opened his mouth, but she didn't let him speak.

"That's all I've ever done, don't you see? I ran from my family to boarding school. And I ran from my future by not even bothering to try to think of what I'd want to do. Did you know, I didn't even look through the majors being offered at my college? Not once. I just clicked on 'Undecided' and let that be that. I didn't think about it again."

"Just because you're good at being a Lissa doesn't mean you have to spend your life being one." He shook her a little. "Delaney, think this through. Tilda is gone. She can't hold you to your promise. You don't have to stay."

"I know that." It hurt, but she forced herself to pull away from him, drop his hands. "But I don't have to leave, either. There's no one left on this planet who's going to take away my choices."

"Are you forgetting about Trystan?" he demanded, a hint of anger slipping through.

"He won't make me do anything I don't want to. I trust that."

"You can't be serious? He's made it pretty clear he fully intends to go through with the bonding ceremony and—" The stricken look that came over him then made her want to wrap her arms around him again, and it took all her strength to refrain from doing so.

"You say you want to be Basilissa because it gives you purpose," he said after a moment, "but that's not it, is it? That might be an added benefit, sure, but that's not why you're choosing to stay. Why you're letting us go."

"Ruckus." She shook her head but he retreated.

"This isn't my home anymore, Delaney. I can't stay here. I don't want to. I know what I want. Come with me."

"I'm sorry." She lifted her arms, then dropped them back at her sides. "I don't know what else to say."

"Tell me you're not in love with him," he demanded. "Even if all those other reasons you just gave are real, look me in the eye and tell me truthfully, you don't actually want to stay because of Trystan."

She stared at him, urging herself to do just that, to confirm that not wanting to abandon Vakar was her sole purpose for not going with him now.

But she couldn't.

Never seeing Gibus or her other friends again would suck. Thinking about it hurt. So did the idea that she'd never get to see stellaperier light up at night, or get to experience something like the Dust Market. All those things made her feel a swell of disappointment the likes of which she'd never felt before.

Never seeing Trystan again, though? She sucked in a sharp breath. She wanted to be able to tell Ruckus what he needed to hear, because he looked gutted and she hated herself for being the cause of his pain.

But she couldn't do that. Because it wouldn't be fair.

"I'm sorry," she repeated, not bothering to stop the tears that came with that confession.

"That you fell in love with someone else," he asked, "or that you only just now realized it?"

"Ruckus—"

"Don't." He held up a hand, took another step back. "I have to go."

"Please, can we just talk about this?"

"There's really nothing more to say, Delaney." He ran a hand through his hair. "Part of me already knew, I think. I've been watching you and him together. The way you both act . . . I was just hoping I was wrong, but I wasn't. I . . . ." He licked his lips. "I want to say I understand, but I don't, not yet. I need time."

"I love you, too," she rushed out, not wanting to hurt him more, but also unable to just let him leave on such horrible terms. Maybe it was selfish, but she didn't want to lose him, either.

"I know you do." He was back in front of her in an instant, one hand cupping the side of her face while the other brushed a strand of hair off to the side. "And I love you. But you won't go because you love him enough to stay, and I can't be here to see that."

She reached up to touch his wrist, wishing there was something she could say. Something she could do to make up for what she was putting him through.

"You have to let me go, Delaney," he told her softly. "Let me go."

She didn't want to. After everything they'd done together, being separated seemed insane. Part of her was thinking the same thing part of him clearly was. How could she be making this choice?

Trystan's words from the cave repeated in her mind. He'd told her she had to decide, and subconsciously that must have been what she'd been doing, because for once she had the option to do what felt right for her, and not just act the way others ordered her to.

And when she thought about the Zane, it felt *right*.

"Tell Mariana hey for me." Her voice cracked at the end, but she swallowed the lump in her throat and forced herself to smile at him.

"I will," he said softly.

"Don't hate me."

His mouth crushed against hers, the kiss rough and over just as suddenly as it'd begun. She didn't try to keep him when he pulled back, when he met her sad gaze with his own tortured one.

"Never," he whispered, almost too low for her to hear. "Until again, Delaney."

Then he was spinning on his heel and practically running toward his ship. He took the stairs so fast, she barely had time to blink before the doors were closing behind him. A few heartbeats later it lifted into the air, easing its way through the opening in the ceiling.

Delaney wasn't sure how long she stood there, staring up at the sky, but it was long after he'd completely disappeared from sight.

"THINKING OF JUMPING?" She tried not to react when Trystan jolted a little at her arrival. She'd never managed to sneak up on him before, so he must have been pretty lost in thought to allow it to happen now. "Yeah, it wasn't really funny that time you said it, either."

"Delaney."

"What are you doing here, anyway?" The past hour had been spent looking for him all over the palace, but she'd been surprised when she'd glanced into Olena's old rooms and found him out on the balcony. She moved up to his side and glanced over the edge to the ground below.

He was silent for such a long time, she actually thought he wasn't going to bother responding. She could feel him watching her, but she didn't turn to meet his gaze, honestly not sure if she could handle that at the moment.

"Reminiscing," he finally said, turning away to stare back over at the Vakar hills. The sun was just beginning to set, resting a golden hue over everything.

"About anything in particular?" She thrummed her fingers against the railing, nervous suddenly.

"About everything, actually."

"Well, I guess congratulations are in order," she said, after an awkward moment of silence. "Is there a specific way I'm supposed to greet a new Rex or . . . ?"

He grunted. "There's no need for formalities."

She blinked at him, making sure the move was more obvious than it needed to be, in a teasing way. "I'm sorry, but the Trystan *I* know is obsessed with being formal. In fact, he probably would have scolded me three times by now for not having bowed or whatever in his presence."

"You are as hilarious as ever, Delaney."

"What's it like?" she asked, trying to decide if that was the reason for his solemn mood. "Being king? Is it everything you hoped for?"

"It was never about hope for me. I was raised knowing that one day I would be Rex. There wasn't a question involved, no doubts or room for me to decide I wanted something else." He chuckled darkly. "I never even considered something else as an option. Don't know what I would choose to do with my life other than lead my people into a better future." He paused, waited for her to look at him again. "I know it's not something you've ever wanted."

This was it: She was just going to tell him and be done with it.

So of course he kept talking before she could.

"Did you come to say good-bye?"

All the words she'd carefully planned out in her head disappeared in a puff, replaced with confusion. "What?"

"This might not be my castle," he told her, not meeting her gaze now, "but the Ander isn't as subtle as he'd like to believe. I know about your plans; in truth, I thought you'd be gone by now."

"You knew about Fawna flying us to Earth?" To say she was shocked would be an understatement.

"I'll admit, sending the Sutter here to distract me was a smart move. But yes, I knew." Finally he straightened, turning to fully face her. "I appreciate you coming to say good-bye, even if you weren't going to actually say the words and risk me figuring it out. Thank you, Delaney."

"We need to go back a step," she said, twirling a finger in the air. "You're saying you knew Ruckus and I were going to run off to Earth."

"We've established that." He frowned. "Are you feeling all right?"

"And you didn't do anything to try to stop us?" Obviously he hadn't; otherwise, she would have seen him racing after them in the hangar. "Why?"

"Why?" This time he was the one surprised. "Hadn't I already taken enough from you? The last time we stood out here on this balcony, all I cared about was myself. Getting out of my father's arrangement. Being freed from a situation I didn't want. You called me a monster once, and you were right, because so was my father, and I was acting exactly like him. I wasn't going to take away your choice again."

She'd said as much to Ruckus, but truthfully, she'd only mostly believed it herself. Hearing him say the words now, confirming . . .

"What about being betrothed?"

"I want that, you do not, and this isn't just about me, so—" He stopped abruptly when she took a deliberate step forward.

Slowly, she brought her hands to either side of his waist to steady herself, then lifted onto her toes so that they were only a breath away from each other.

The whole time he was as still as a statue, as if afraid to move, brow furrowed in confusion. He didn't so much as flinch when she finally pressed her lips to his, tentatively at first, and then more persistently when he still didn't budge.

She was actually starting to get a bit anxious by his complete lack of reaction, was just about to pull back when suddenly his hands were in her hair, cupping the base of her skull to keep her in place. She gasped when he responded to her kiss, lips parting against her own.

The first time they'd done this had been to an audience, because they'd had to, and she'd held back.

She didn't want to do that anymore.

"Delaney." He tore his mouth away suddenly, dropping his forehead against hers. His eyes were tightly closed and he looked like he was in agony.

"I'm not leaving," she said quickly, knowing where his thoughts had taken him. That he believed she was doing this as a parting gift and not for the real reason she was.

He blinked. "But the Ander . . ."

"I let him go without me."

"Why would you do that?"

She took a deep breath in a poor attempt to steady her shaky nerves. "I spent the past hour trying to figure out exactly what I'd say, and I'm still not sure it's right. Honestly, I wasn't expecting this. I wasn't expecting to get kidnapped by aliens or brought to another planet or turned into royalty overnight. I was so focused on getting back home, on regaining control, that I buried what I was really feeling, and convinced myself that Earth was where I belonged. But it isn't."

Really, she shouldn't be surprised that this was so hard. Things had never been easy between them. That sort of made it all a little more worth it.

"You can be so frustrating, and we have a really complicated past that involves some not-so-great decisions on your part, and some less-than-ideal reactions on mine. But you've always been honest with me. And it's time that I be honest with you. You told me I had to decide, remember?"

She'd only ever said the words to one other person before, and she gave herself a split second to really be certain before she said them to someone else now. That feeling from earlier, however, the one screaming inside that this was right, didn't dissipate.

"Trystan," she said, "I'm in love with you."

They'd been forced together twice before, the first time him stuck with her, the second her stuck with him. But neither of them were the same people they'd been at the start of this.

She didn't know exactly how long she'd been carrying this secret, hiding it from even herself, but the truth of it was so clear now that she was amazed she hadn't figured it out sooner. It felt really good getting it out, like a weight had been lifted from her shoulders and she could breathe again.

At least, until it hit her that he'd yet to respond, hadn't even twitched a single muscle.

"Trystan, say something." His feelings for her had been the only part of this she hadn't been anxious about. Now . . . "I know this is a lot, and we have things to sort through—like the fact that I definitely do not want to get married anytime soon, not when there's so much to be done in regard to successfully bridging our people, but—"

"*Our* people." He seemed to snap out of it all at once, his arms banding around her waist to pull her as close as he could. "Tell me this is really happening, Delaney. Tell me I'm not dreaming or unconscious or some other horrible alternative to this being reality. Tell me this is real."

He'd dropped the aloof mask he always wore when he was being Zane, the one that kept everyone at a safe distance from who he truly was inside. From the man she'd gotten to catch glimpses of in Inkwell, and later, here, every time he stepped back and let her make her own decisions, even when he didn't agree.

The tangle of hope and dread making up his expression had her lifting a hand to press against the center of his chest.

"This is real," she said.

He blinked. "Say that you love me again."

She chuckled. "Not if you go back to being bossy and annoying."

"Delaney," he pleaded, cluing her in to just how desperate he actually was. How badly he really needed assurances.

"I love you," she told him. Then she planted another quick kiss to his lips before pulling back to add, "Now say that you love me, too."

He laughed and lifted her into his arms, ignoring her yelp of surprise.

Seeing him happy was a rarity, and it was infectious, washing away any of the lingering nervousness she'd been feeling about staying. Replacing those feelings with ones of confidence and excitement. Because she knew that from here on out, whatever they did, however they decided to handle what came their way, they'd do it together.

"I love nothing on either planet, on *any* planet," he corrected, placing her feet back onto solid ground, "more than I love you."

EPILOGUE

"Relax, Basilissa," Trystan said at her side.

They were standing at the front of the hangar in the Vakar palace, their eyes turned up toward the open ceiling and the clear sky above it. Though they hadn't been waiting long, the fact that their guest was running late made her edgy, and he knew it.

"Don't tell me what to do, Rex." Delaney shifted on her feet when the first telltale signs of an approaching ship came overhead. Instinctually, she reached for his hand, squeezing his palm as a mix of emotions rushed through her all at once.

"Apologies." There was a hint of a smile in his voice, but she didn't bother sparing him a glance as the familiar ship settled over the opening and began lowering.

A pang of old guilt slipped through the excitement and nerves at the sight of Ruckus's ship, even though she knew he wouldn't be on it. Though they hadn't spoken directly in the two months since he'd been gone, Mariana had helped exchange a few messages between them.

Fawna had remained in Earth's atmosphere all this time, making it possible for Delaney and her best friend to talk to each other. With learning her new role as the Basilissa of Vakar, getting the people acquainted with all the changes she and Trystan hoped to enact, this had been the first opportunity they could find for Mariana to visit.

"You're going to like her," Delaney practically screamed at Trystan as the ship came to a stop, the sound of the engines nearly drowning out her voice.

"I'm sure I will," he agreed.

"She might not like you." Finally she tore her gaze off the ship's doors long enough to send him a teasing half grin, taken straight out of his playbook. "Not right away, anyway."

His eyes narrowed in mock offense, and he opened his mouth to retort when the steps to the ship began lowering, abruptly stealing her attention away. He didn't bother trying to stop her when she dropped his hand and stepped forward.

They'd kept the area pretty clear, not wanting to overwhelm Mariana with a welcoming committee of Tellers. Aside from a few guards in the hall, Sanzie was the only other person there with them.

"This place is huge!" Mariana's voice reached them before the sight of her did, her head popping out of the still-opening ship door. When she spotted Delaney, she smiled wide and began waving her hands. The second she was able, she slipped out onto the stairs, rushing down them to meet Delaney halfway.

Behind her, Fawna descended the steps, taking her time to give them space.

Delaney wrapped her arms tightly around Mariana and squeezed, but she didn't get to hold her long before her friend was pulling back to stare at their surroundings.

"Holy crap!" She bounced on her feet and grabbed both of Delaney's hands in a death grip. "Holy crap! I'm on another planet! I am on an *alien* planet! And I was brought here, *by* an alien! And look!"

She thrust a finger at Trystan, who'd remained by the doors. "Real alien royalty!"

"Hey," Delaney said, laughing, "I'm alien royalty, too, remember?"

"Eh." She waved dismissively, her gaze still shooting around, as if she couldn't stay focused on any one thing for fear of missing out on something else. "You don't really count, though."

"Tell that to the entire planet."

"Speaking of . . ." Suddenly Trystan was approaching, his eyes on Mariana. "There's much more to Xenith than this one dusty room. I assume you'd like to see it?"

"An entire galaxy of yes!" She shot forward, grasping his hand and giving it a hard shake. "I am Mariana, and you are very attractive."

He seemed taken aback by that, but when he sent a glance to Delaney over the top of the other girl's head, she merely shrugged. Her best friend had always been blunt; she really shouldn't have expected her to be anything else, even on a foreign world.

"Anyway." Mariana returned to her side, linking their arms. "I really wanted to say something witty like, 'Take me to your leader,' but you kind of made that no fun, considering . . ."

"I am the leader," Delaney filled in.

"Yeah. That." She rolled her eyes dramatically, then winked.

"She's going to be a lot, isn't she?" Trystan sent through their fittings, stepping to the side to allow Mariana to steer Delaney past him toward the open doors leading into the rest of the palace.

Delaney grinned at him over her shoulder. *"Afraid you can't handle having another human around, after all?"*

As soon as they'd reached Sanzie, Mariana had started up an immediate conversation, asking all sorts of questions about the Sworn's position and her uniform, barely giving her a chance to answer anything before asking another.

"*As long as I've got you by my side, I'm sure I can handle anything,*" Trystan replied as they entered the halls, trailing at an easy pace behind them.

"*Well,*" she reached back and took his hand, "*looks like you've got nothing to worry about, then.*"

ACKNOWLEDGMENTS

WOW. I can't believe I'm writing acknowledgments for the third book. In some ways, it feels like this whole process just started last month, and it feels strange that I'm already at the end of the Xenith trilogy. I couldn't have done any of it without the amazing support system I've had, back home and in the Swoon offices.

Like usual, thanks to Holly for helping make this book what it is, and for sticking with me and this series from start to finish. Even though I'm not a fan of the editing process, your notes always made it easier to get through!

I know so many other Swoon staff members had a hand in shaping this trilogy, so instead of listing names, I just want to say thank you to everyone who did! You've all made me feel incredibly welcome among you and in the office whenever I've visited, and I feel honored to be one of your authors.

Thanks to my family—Mom, Dad, Kim, Daniel—for always having my back, and encouraging me to continue following my dream. I love you guys! Thanks to my aunts specifically, Grace and Irene, for continuing with the series and giving me support even from across the country and states away! And to my Uncle Walter for calling me up with congratulations!

Thanks to Josie, Jon, Kat, and Genevieve for dealing with me during the writing process, spacing out and canceling plans last minute! And thanks for all the coffee!

Vicky, thanks for being such a fantastic friend to me, and for always running out to buy copies of my books. You've been a real rock through all the hard times and I feel so blessed to have met you and have you in my life!

Whitney, I definitely would have fallen apart under the stress this year without you, so thanks for always being there and providing great distractions and giving advice!

Mary Ellen and Marissa, you two are amazing! Your support means the world, and I hope you're both satisfied with the way things turned out in this series!

Thanks to Lisa and Matt.

Finally, thanks to all the readers who've read the trilogy to the end! Without readers, a book goes nowhere, and I can't express how much it means to me, knowing you're all out there reading about Delaney and Ruckus and Trystan. I hope you continue picking up any future projects I come out with, and I love interacting with you guys on Goodreads, so thanks to anyone who's sent me a question!

DID YOU KNOW...

readers like you
helped to get this
book published?

Join our book-obsessed community and help us
discover awesome new writing talent.

1

Write it.

Share your original YA manuscript.

2

Read it.

Discover bright new bookish talent.

3

Share it.

Discuss, rate, and share your faves.

4

Love it.

Help us publish the books you love.

Share your own manuscript or dive between the pages
at **swoonreads.com** or by downloading the **Swoon Reads app.**